EBONY MOON

REG GRANT

BRINGING TRUTH TO LIFE
NavPress Publishing Group
P.O. Box 35001, Colorado Springs, Colorado 80935

The Navigators is an international Christian organization. Jesus Christ gave His followers the Great Commission to go and make disciples (Matthew 28:19). The aim of The Navigators is to help fulfill that commission by multiplying laborers for Christ in every nation.

NavPress is the publishing ministry of The Navigators. NavPress publications are tools to help Christians grow. Although publications alone cannot make disciples or change lives, they can help believers learn biblical discipleship, and apply what they learn to their lives and ministries.

Library of Congress Catalog Card Number: 93-27126
ISBN 08910-97457

The stories and characters in this book are fictitious. Any resemblance to people living or dead is coincidental.

Grant, Reg, 1954-
Ebony moon / Reg Grant.
p. cm.
ISBN 0-89109-745-7
1. Americans—Mexico—Fiction. 2. Family—Mexico—Fiction. I. Title.
PS3557.R2679E26 1993
813′.54—dc20 93-27126
CIP

Printed in the United States of America

To Happy and Max—
for all the wonder
(and for the enchiladas too!)

Acknowledgments

Thanks to Steve Webb for asking, to Lauren for listening, to Ros, Gabe, and Nick for encouraging, to Kathy Yanni for making it a book, and to my Lord for blessing.

Characters

(in alphabetical order)

The Alaniz family ....members of the McClendons' house church in Dolores, Mexico
Jennifer Budreau.................secretary to Latigo Jones
José "El Calavera" Cantu ...albino barkeep in Dolores, Mexico
The Carreras family ....members of the McClendons' house church in Dolores, Mexico
(Sam, Juanita, and their children)
Maria Cortez........................a young woman in Dolores, Mexico
Jaime Dominguez ....proprietor of the dry goods store in Dolores, Mexico
Father Escobar ....a Catholic priest in Dolores, Mexico
Armando Estevez................deputy to Jake Skerritt
Carlos Hernandez ....operator of a veterinary clinic in San Luis Potosí, Mexico
Beau Holliman....................rancher and close friend of the King family
Latigo Jones........................sheriff in Rio Bravo, Texas
The King family..................Eli, his wife Hatty, and their sons, Marty and Carl
Miss Irma Light ....long-time friend of the King family
Adolf Mangus ....oil driller
Anita Martinez....................a young woman in Dolores, Mexico

Angus "Doc" McClendon...	missionary doctor in Dolores, Mexico
Estella McClendon	wife of Doc
Rosalinda McClendon	daughter of Doc and Estella
The Montoya family .... (Ray, Renee, and their children)	members of McClendons' house church in Dolores, Mexico
The Morales family .... (Esteban, Danielle, and their children)	a homeless family victimized by drought and greed in Mexico
Mrs. Perez	member of the McClendons' house church in Dolores, Mexico
James "Jim" Pogue	lawyer in Rio Bravo, Texas
Hector Rodriguez................	a troublemaker in Dolores, Mexico
Miguel Sanchez	chief deputy to Latigo Jones
Jake Skerritt	sheriff in Dalton Springs, Texas
Charlie Tilden	ranch foreman for Beau Holliman
Father Enrique Zeuma	Catholic priest in Dolores, Mexico

"If you're gonna throw, throw! Quit foolin' around." The ball whizzed back to pop in Carl's glove. "Let's see you put something on it!"

Carl loved this. He would have pitched to his father all day. His dad's gruffness was all part of it—part of baseball and growing up on a ranch and pitching to your dad at the end of another summer's day. All as comfortably predictable as the cloudless expanse of a Texas sky. Carl looked up absently toward the northern horizon, rubbing the ball with his bare hands.

"C'mon, son!"

"Yessir."

Carl held the ball loosely, trying not to think—trying to let his body take over. Not to aim. Just to do it. To feel the rhythm—like a dance. Down and up and, "unhhh!"

This one sailed high and inside, into the cavernous barn. A chicken squawked and fluttered out of the way just in time. Eli King rose slowly from his catcher's crouch. It had taken him a while to get down there and he didn't like the idea of having to straighten out his stiff knee to chase a wild pitch.

"What was *that*?"

"Sorry, Dad. I'll get it."

Eli was already up, twisting the bailing wire that was supposed to hold the sagging red gate shut but actually did more to hold it up.

He dragged the gate open a couple of feet for Carl, then followed his son into the darkening tin shelter. It had stood for nearly fifty years as a combination hay barn, pig birthing room, implement storage shed, and magic castle. It also served as a sanctuary for lost baseballs. The loose hay granted refuge to any seeking asylum—when there *was* hay.

Carl and his dad had been chasing lost balls ever since Carl had been old enough to throw them back—nearly eighteen years now. But this evening Eli had something else on his mind. He didn't really know how to get at it, so he asked about the mail.

"Mr. Limbley bring you anything today?"

"Nosir," Carl answered, thinking of the college catalogs he'd sent for. "Same old stuff. But we did get the Sears Roebuck. I was sorta thinkin' about a new pair of dress pants. Just in case we get the money in time. . . ."

His voice trailed off as he continued to watch the sunset. The desire his father had planted for a college education had taken root in this youngest King son. But deep down, Carl knew they wouldn't have the money to buy him a new pair of pants, much less send him to college next fall. It had about as much chance of bearing fruit as last year's crop. The drought was in its fifth year with no sign of rain, and they were coming up on another dry harvest. The drought was drying up more than the land.

Eli felt the awkwardness of the moment. He didn't really know how to talk to this "boy-man." How to encourage him without giving him false hope, to help him face the situation without uprooting his dream. And most of all, how to tell him they needed to move. They wouldn't be there for college or anything else. Eli wasn't good with words. He made more enemies by accident than most folks made on purpose. He knew if he said something now—about leaving—that he'd get that old feeling back as if he'd fallen off his horse into a tangle of barbed wire, unable to get out without hurting himself or somebody else. Besides, it was nearly time for supper. The men took their cue from the nip of orange sun dipping below the horizon and turned to go back up the hill to the house. Carl broke the silence.

"Mizz Light says it's gonna rain. I heard her talking to Momma at church."

"Yeah, I think Mizz Light's got clouds in her head."

Carl knew his father didn't take much stock in Miss Irma Light's pronouncements. The two sparred playfully with each other nearly every Sunday after the sermon. She was only four foot eight, but she must have weighed at least a hundred eighty, and most of that was gristle. When she got excited her seventy-year-old voice tuned up to a high-pitched whine, like the wind shinnying through the cracks in the walls of the Lassiter place. She and Eli really thought the world of each other, but they frowned a lot when they met just to keep up appearances.

"Naw Dad, really. I don't think she's said that in a while. Maybe she knows something."

The screen door of the ranch house at the top of the hill creaked open. Hatty King's voice rang out loud in the evening shade.

"Eli! Carl! Y'all come on. It's time to wash up!"

"We're on our way," shouted Eli.

They were only halfway up the hill and they could already smell Hatty's hash and cornbread. It was all the magnet Carl needed. He took off in a gentle lope and leaped the white plank fence at a bound. Eli slowed for a moment and glanced back toward the windmill—not a blade was stirring. "Lord," he said quietly, "I hope Mizz Light is right."

Eli moved slowly up the gentle incline toward the house. He cut across the top of the hill, past the small pumphouse, noticing again that the western wall was peeling, that the door needed a new hinge. He shuffled through the grass, the cuffs of his khaki pants scooping up burrs along the way. Just before he rounded the corner of the garage he glanced down the lane toward number nine, the road that ran north to San Antonio and south to Corpus. Something caught his eye, then his ear. A glint in the setting sun and the scream of a V-8 overhead valve ripped through the evening breeze, leaving swirling coils of dust and old chewing gum wrappers dancing in the corkscrew wind. Then it was just a red streak, heading south. *Fool*, thought Eli. *Fool's gonna kill somebody, or get killed himself.*

From the way Hatty King set her table, nobody would ever have known there was a five-year drought on. Hatty grew, pickled, and canned anything that didn't move, so there was usually a bounty of vegetables. There was a pantry full of jellies and jams to boot. Eli's favorite, and the one that was on the table tonight, was the mustang grape jelly made from the wild grapes that grew down by the Nueces River. This was a particularly good batch.

Tonight's fare was chicken hash and jalepeno cornbread with beans. Carl and his older brother Marty had been known to polish off two deep iron skillets full of Hatty's chicken hash at one sitting. She scolded them for eating so much but took a mother's secret delight in her ravenous boys. Marty had settled down a bit in the last year. He'd just turned twenty, so his appetite equaled that of only two men instead of three. The blue checkered tablecloth was barely visible beneath the skillets, the plates, the jelly, and four towering glasses brimming with iced tea, a ranch staple in south Texas.

Hatty called out to her oldest son, who was back in the cool room working on another ranch improvement project, "Marty, time to eat, son."

Marty King rarely had to be called twice. At six feet two inches and one-hundred-ninety pounds, he could be as late as he wanted. But Marty was the perfect son. It was "yessir" and "nosir," "yes'm," and "no ma'am" from day one. He'd had only one real spanking in his life—and that because he took the rap for peeling the wallpaper off his brother's bedroom wall, when in fact he was trying to find a way to stick it back on so the real culprit wouldn't have to suffer. He took his licking like a man, casting a martyr's glance in Carl's direction just before he entered the bathroom to receive his punishment. Carl had never forgotten his big brother's supreme sacrifice on his behalf. He thought Marty was the closest thing to Jesus he would ever see, and he worshiped him from that day on.

"Let's pray." Eli reached for Hatty's hand on his left and for Carl's on his right. "Father, thank You for this good food. Thank You for the love we share with one another and for our Lord Jesus Christ. Father, we ask again for rain. You know best, Lord, and we know that, but it sure would help us rejoice more if we had rain." Here Eli paused. Hatty and Carl felt his grip tighten slightly. He continued, haltingly. There was that old tangle again, even with the Lord. "Lord, give us the, uh, let me do what's right, what's pleasing to You. Bless my decisions, Father."

Hatty was looking at him now. She knew something was wrong. Eli rarely if ever improvised in prayer. His prayers were short, sincere, and heartfelt. But never spontaneous.

"In Jesus' name, amen."

"Pass the beans, Mom."

Hatty slapped Carl's hand. "Carl, for heaven's sake. Give the Lord a chance to hear the blessing." She handed the bowl to Carl. The family filled the first half of the meal with small talk. Then Hatty said, rather nonchalantly, "I was thinking about, maybe, taking a job waiting tables at the Sunrise."

Eli looked at her as if she had just announced she was going to have twins. Carl stopped eating. Marty frowned. Hatty picked up steam. "Only on Saturdays. It isn't that far and it would help, so why not?"

Carl spoke first. "Mom, you can't work."

Eli broke in, "Carl, hush."

"Dad, you always said—" Carl stopped. He knew his father had said something once about women working at home, but he couldn't remember what and he was starting to feel his face tingle and get tight the way it always did when he got upset. Then he said, defiantly, "If Mom goes to work, I'm not going to college."

"Yeah, right," said Marty. "And what are you going to do around here? Become a rancher all of a sudden? You'd dry up and blow away."

"Both of you hush." Eli glanced down, his eyes darting from object to object, as if he were looking for the right words on the table somewhere. It wasn't like him. The last time he had acted like this was when he was trying to break it to the family that Grandma King had died. Nobody spoke. An unexpected sadness had settled on them all, making them still and a little afraid.

Finally, Eli forced out the words like pieces of a broken bottle that had been filled with some foul-tasting medicine. "We can't stay here any longer. There's no sign of rain. We can't live like this anymore. I'm going to lease the place and use the money for us to go south for a while. It'll only be for a few years. We need to get established, get our feet under us financially, then we'll come back when the drought is over and finished."

"Who wants the lease?" Hatty asked, trying not to sound incredulous.

"Oh, I'll tell you who wants to lease," interjected Carl, angrily. "Jake Skerritt. He's wanted this place ever since Grandpa died. Dad, you're not going to lease it to him, are you?"

"You know better than that, Carl. No, it was Cal."

"*Cal? . . . O'Reagan?*" Carl was more surprised than angry now. It had never occurred to him that his cousin would want to lease their land. Hatty's relative was one of the finest cattle dealers in south Texas. He ran the local auction barn and owned land in five different counties, all due to a combination of hard work and three oil wells on his land so far.

Carl was shocked simply because he hadn't seen much of Cal since he had expanded his operation. Cal had been on the road a lot, running his different businesses. His offer to lease the land from Eli was really more a gift than a legitimate lease, but Cal was a blood kinsman to Hatty, and he wasn't about to see an O'Reagan lose her land or go begging. He knew Eli wouldn't take charity, or even a loan. That would have shamed him. But he would do business. He would take a lease. The offer was generous, and Eli had accepted it gratefully, knowing full well what Cal was doing for him.

Hatty reached out for her husband's hand. "Eli, I know Cal means well. . . ."

Eli stiffened. Hatty had to accept that this was a business deal. He wasn't taking a handout from her relatives.

Hatty responded instinctively. ". . . And I'm sure he needs the land. Cal is a smart businessman—and I know he doesn't throw good money after bad. But Eli, there has to be some other way. Besides, we're making it all right. We have enough food to get us through the winter—we have venison from last fall, and the pantry's still over half full."

Eli continued to stare at the table, silent, his mind made up. They all knew it. "Hatty, we can't wait any longer," he said after a pause. "It'll be another year before we see any crops, if at all. And how long are we going to have to wait to buy more cattle? Three, four years? And that's if we get rain next spring. No, we're done living hand to mouth."

Hatty was worried. "How are we going to get by on a year's lease money? That would barely be enough to get a lease and a few cattle." As soon as she asked the question, she knew the answer. Eli didn't have to say anything. Hatty knew what he was going to say, and it drew her stomach into a tight ball.

Eli could tell that Hatty had guessed what he was about to propose. This was the worst part, the part he hated saying the most. "I'm going to cash in the stocks."

Hatty's face was expressionless. She was trying to remain calm. Her father had given them the old California Company stocks for a wedding present. They had agreed back then to save them for their children. They would divide the stocks and give them as presents when each of them turned twenty-five—the same age as Eli and Hatty when they married. A little nest egg to get them started in life. "I thought we had agreed . . ." she began.

Eli looked her full in the eyes for the first time. "Those stocks are as high as they've ever been. There's no guarantee they'll ever be better. Nothing's set in concrete, Hatty. Nothing was for sure, you know that."

Hatty interrupted, her voice nearly shaking, "Eli, we agreed."

Eli looked at his wife but said nothing. It wasn't out of meanness. He simply knew there was nothing he could say that would convince her. But the way Hatty saw it, Eli had violated a trust. He hadn't even asked her opinion. Her eyes told him that. Just made up his mind and bulled ahead. It was so like him.

Eli turned to his sons. "I want you boys to help pack up starting tomorrow. We'll be pulling out next week—soon's I've tied up some loose ends down at the bank."

"Where'll we go, Dad?" Marty asked. He trusted his father implicitly. If Eli King said move, his oldest son would swallow hard and do it, no questions asked.

Hatty left the table, walking toward the living room.

Carl tried to stop her. "Mom?"

Eli pretended not to notice. "I've been thinking about southern Mexico, not too far from Mexico City. The boys have been telling me the land is still good down there, especially higher up. And it's cheap. We can use the money to buy up a small herd and lease some land of our own. We'll be there four, five years at the outside."

Carl sat impassively, rubbing the baseball he had picked up from the window ledge behind the table. His eyes were fixed on his father. His jaw was set. In four or five years he planned on being in the minors, maybe the majors if he got lucky—not stuck on some Mexican *ranchuelo*. Ranching had never interested him as it had Marty. He had endured it for nearly eighteen years—and now this.

"The drought can't last that long. Then we can move back in pretty good shape." Eli looked toward the living room where Hatty had gone, apparently oblivious to Carl's rising frustration. "Your mother will come around. She just needs some time."

Eli pushed his chair back and rose slowly, taking his plate and glass to the sink. "Can I get you boys to do dishes?"

"Sure, Dad." Marty started to clear away the dishes. Carl glared after his father as he moved toward the living room. Marty was turned toward the sink, away from the table, but he whispered just loud enough for Carl to hear, "Let it rest, Carl."

As he reached the door to the dining room, Eli turned and spoke directly to Carl. "Carl, I imagine this hits you harder than any of the rest of us. I want you to know right now, I realize that, and I wish it could be different. I know it's asking a lot of you, son. But I need your support now. I need your help getting started down there."

Carl sat looking at the ball in his hands, biting the inside of his cheek. He lowered his eyes so his father wouldn't see the tears starting.

Eli was trying his best to say the right thing. "I want you to play ball, son. I want you to go to college. I got bigger dreams for you than you have for yourself. I know it's hard to see that now, but I promise you, some day I'll get you there. Just as soon as I can." Eli didn't wait for Carl to respond. He turned and walked through the dining room to the living room where Hatty sat with a closed Bible in her lap, staring at the RCA radio.

Sounds drifted in through the south window . . . the high moan of the windmill bending its blades into the wind, in the ceaseless work of drawing water . . . the slow "ching-ching" of the sucker rod slapping against the cool steel pipe as it strained to pull water up from far below the parched earth.

"Wind's comin' in from the north," Marty said, absently. "Didn't Mizz Light say somethin' about rain last Sunday?"

Carl couldn't sit still any longer. He bolted out of the kitchen and through the milkroom, knocking his baseball glove off its peg and onto the floor before the screen door slammed behind him.

2

The branches rocked back and forth gently, slowly. Spanish moss hung in long beards, teasing the earth. The big oak groaned in the breeze. Marty lay on the ground staring up at the treehouse he had built with his brother when he was thirteen. They'd built it right: They set the house level on iron rods, roofed it with tarpaper and tin, and sealed it with leadhead nails. A few years ago a windstorm had ripped through and taken the tin right off the big barn. But the boys' house had stood. *This treehouse will be here after I'm gone,* he thought. *It'll outlast me—let the squirrels and the coons have it.*

A fly buzzed close. Gnats were getting bad in this sticky heat. Marty got up and walked to the top of the river bank, half in a daze, pretending again that he would see the cool water. But there wasn't much to see—the bones and skull of an old cow lay scattered across the sandy bottom. They had been there a long time. The river had died, and this dry bed was its long, twisting grave. The cracks in the ground snaked far up the other side. The roots of the tall river trees erupted from the bank, stretching straight out like so many desperate water witches toward the crumbling bed.

A breeze kissed his cheek. *A goodbye kiss for luck*, he thought. But it was nothing more than a brittle wheeze from a dying land. No, you couldn't really call it a river anymore.

A horn sounded in the distance. One long, two short. Marty

wanted to ignore it. Two weeks wasn't long enough to say goodbye forever. He kept looking out at the dry riverbed and the bleached bones, feeling something of himself drain down into that dust. Suddenly, instinctively, he turned and walked away, toward the sound of the horn. He could feel his stomach tightening, his face burning. He started to run. *Don't look back.* The house, still three quarters of a mile off, bounced into view just around the corner of the gravel pit. Quail flushed. A javelina boar grunted and charged back down into the cool sanctuary of the pit. Marty wanted to follow him, to tear through the brush that surrounded the ancient pit and roll down the steep sides into the bottom where he could hide with the old boar.

He was more than halfway to the house now. He could have stopped. Could have taken one last look around. But he kept going.

He was cutting the ties as he went, severing the cords that bound him affectionately to this land. He came to the barbed wire fence that cut the pasture in half and thought he might try jumping it, but he changed his mind at the last minute. *Maybe when I was eighteen,* he thought. *But not now. Not at twenty.* He was too old, he felt, for such childishness. Too old for this place. He'd outgrown it, really. "It's good that I'm leaving," he told himself. He felt a little more confident now, a little farther from the riverbed. A little less attached. He bent the wire down where the staple was missing in the fence post and climbed through for the thousandth and last time. Then off through the brush toward the house.

Marty jogged the last half mile—across the horse pasture and up to the ranch house. He had made the break. He hadn't looked back. He had been strong. Eli was loading the last of the furniture onto the back of the truck. Marty scooped up a handful of dirt and stuffed it in his pocket. He stopped. "Stupid. Stupid kid," he mumbled, as he emptied the dirt, as he left his heart there with the land. They would leave that night.

Just past midnight, the family gathered outside the white yard fence while Eli led them in a short prayer, asking the Lord's safety and His blessing on their odyssey. They crowded onto the front seat, making room, getting settled. The engine growled awake—loud and unnatural at this time of night. Hatty stole one glance in the side-view mirror as the darkened hulk of a house receded quickly and was soon swallowed in the blackness.

As the yellow headlights chiseled through the night, they drove the mile up the gravel road and swung around south onto the road to Dalton Springs, fifteen miles away. Hatty sat next to Eli, then Marty, with Carl by the window. This closeness made them all feel safe—the kind of safe that makes words unnecessary. The only sounds were the creaking of the seat springs, the rumble of the engine, and the ruffle of the night air as it gushed through the windows, dry and warm.

The road between Dalton Springs and Laredo was one hundred empty miles of blistered two-lane asphalt. The Kings lived on the edge of the brush country, only twenty miles from where the desert started. It hadn't always been like this, however. Back in 1891 when Hatty's grandfather had bought the land, the grass was knee-high in most places and waist-high down by the river. There was a drought back then, too; the same year Hatty's family, the O'Reagans, moved from Cuero to the Lassiter homestead to start ranching. That was the drought that killed off the grass and unleashed the brush.

They'd had some good rain years since then, but it was never the same. In fact, most of south Texas never really recovered from the drought of 1891. Now lots of folks were having to sell out. At least the Kings weren't having to sell—at least they could still say they owned the place. The truck bounced along the night road, jostling old memories loose—childhood impressions that sifted and drifted, disconnected as wind-tossed leaves through Hatty's consciousness. The ranch had been in Hatty's family for over sixty years. She wondered if they would ever see it again.

Moonlight slipped through patches in the clouds. Hatty looked up. There, tracing the horizon, was the thin bead of yellow lights that marked Dalton Springs. Another five minutes and they would turn off onto the long road to Laredo. There used to be a clear line of demarcation about three miles outside Dalton Springs where the fertile country ended and the desert began. But that line was blurred now as the sand stretched into the streets of the little town where the King boys had attended school.

They turned onto the last stretch of dirt road between Puentas and Dalton Springs, down past the Mexican shanties and finally over the wooden bridge that spanned the Nueces between the poor side of Dalton Springs and the white side of town. Another turn past Raul's Cafe, across the railroad tracks, and they were on Main Street.

It was about one a.m. The night was clear and gusty. The clouds had peeled back and the moon was bright enough to drive without lights. Dust devils chased each other, swirling grit up the empty street, and Eli thought how glad he was to be leaving this place.

As they passed the courthouse, Eli noticed the dull yellow light leaking from around the edges of the window shade of Sheriff Jake Skerritt's first floor office.

Eli saw that Hatty had noticed the light as well. "Jake must be working for a change," he said offhandedly. "Wonder what he's up to so late?"

"No good, whatever it is," Hatty mumbled.

Eli knew she was no Skerritt fan, but he loved to tease. "Now, Hatty," he interrupted, feigning concern.

"Now, Hatty, my foot. He's crooked as a dog's hind leg and you know it. Jacob Skerritt's the best reason I know for leaving here."

Eli chuckled and Hatty hit him on his arm. She was grinning in spite of herself.

It was easier to laugh now, but the wounds were old and deep. The war between the O'Reagans and the Skerritts stretched back to 1915. Hatty's father, Thaddeus O'Reagan, had been leasing some ranch land for a few years from an elderly widow in San Antonio. When the lease was about to run out, Skerritt paid the widow a personal visit. He concocted a fantastic lie that Thaddeus O'Reagan was abusing the land and was a cheat besides.

The Skerritts boasted a long line of great liars. At the bottom of that line, down in the very sludge of the genetic pool, was Jake. Growing up, Jake had wanted to be a lawyer until he found out that lawyers had to read a lot, so he decided to be a politician instead. The man could sweet-talk a coon out of a tree. He promised the old lady that if she leased the land to him he would take good care of it and pay her half again what Hatty's father was paying. Without even writing, the woman signed over the lease to Jacob Skerritt.

When Thaddeus found out, he went to San Antonio. But it did no good; Skerritt had poisoned the woman against him. Before she died, she sold the land to Skerritt, who had held it ever since. And to make matters worse, they had found oil on it a few years back. Not long after that Jake had been elected to the deacon board at First Baptist of Dalton Springs and then to the sheriff's office—and he had managed to maintain both positions for a number of years at no small personal expense. The Skerritts were among the few people in the county not welcome at the Kings' dinner table.

As they crested a small hill, the few lights of Dalton Springs dipped out of view behind them. The '45 Dodge with its four passengers chugged on into the Texas desert. Hatty stared out on the moonlit landscape and felt inside that now there was no turning back. She shook her head slightly as she thought how crazy this all was. Eli knew she was scared. He knew that she was taking a big risk, trusting him like this. He was scared too, but he had a plan, and he prayed silently that the Lord would let him work it out.

They entered Laredo about two-thirty that morning. After filling up with gas and topping their five-gallon reserve tank, they headed for the Mexican border. The bright yellow lights on the American side cast the other side of the border into ink black. Hatty turned her attention toward her husband, who was talking to the border guard. He looked suspiciously at all the furniture loaded on the back of the truck, but Eli had earmarked a five-dollar bill to help ease any "misunderstandings." The guard waved them on, and they crossed over into the shadows of Mexico.

They had come to the market on the Mexican side many times before. But no matter how many times you came, Hatty thought, you always got the same feeling—as soon as you crossed that line you were an alien. You weren't home anymore. The feeling was inescapable—and this time, more than a little frightening.

The roads changed to gravel as soon as they were outside Laredo. The night turned cooler as they wound their way down into the heart of Mexico. It wasn't an unpleasant ride, but the poor road conditions made it slow going.

They rode for the rest of the night along the bumpy roads, through small villages and farms. Eli had heard there was good ranchland south of Mexico City, so that's where they would establish their new home. Since Hereford cattle were selling for around fifteen cents a pound, he could get a small herd going for a relatively low investment.

Morning crept over the low eastern hills, washing the landscape in a yellow-white haze. Eli had been driving all night on top of working hard the day before. His adrenaline was running on empty as was his gas tank, so when he saw a station off the road ahead he pulled over to stretch and fill up. Hatty broke out some cantaloupe and dried beef and they were off again, quickly, this time with Marty at the wheel. He was to stay on the main road until they got to Santa Maria, at which point he was to bear left. That road would take them to Mexico City. Eli curled up beside the window and soon fell fast asleep.

An hour and a half later, the road began to climb and the air felt cooler. Far off to the south lay a blue line of mountains. And there was another difference in the landscape. The hillsides were covered with grass, and the cultivated fields were filled with corn and grain. Although they were just a few hundred miles into the interior, they had entered a different world, and it seemed to be welcoming them.

Eli was still sleeping as Marty pulled into a small village. There was no sign marking the town, and Marty was tired. He figured he would stop and ask someone once they got to the square. It was only seven-fifteen in the morning, but the inhabitants were busy about their day's work. Most of the men were dressed in jeans and well-worn plaid work shirts. They wore straw hats to keep the sun off, though the climate here seemed delightful compared to the July heat of Texas. The furniture-laden Dodge truck attracted considerable attention as Marty maneuvered between pedestrians and carts.

Just as they were nearing the southern edge of the village, Marty noticed an old Catholic church set off to the left of the road. It was almost hidden back in a bunch of gnarled mesquite and towering salt cedars. Parked beside the church was a bright red Cadillac with a white top.

"Dad would love this. Slow down, Mart," Carl whispered. Neither of the boys had seen a Caddy before except in advertisements, and the thought of a red one parked next to a Catholic church in a poor Mexican village was too much to resist. Even Hatty didn't object to them stopping and waking up their snoring father. Marty pulled over on the right side of the road, opposite the church.

"Let me, Carl," Hatty said as she leaned over to pat Eli's shoulder.

"Eli, wake up, hon, there's something you ought to see. Eli, c'mon now, wake up," she said as she gently shook his shoulder.

It took a moment for the fog to clear from his head, but the elder King finally shook himself awake and stared in the direction of Marty's extended arm.

"Can you believe it, Pop?" Carl was incredulous.

"Look's like the Pope's got his boys set up pretty good down here. Let's go, boys, before we get arrested for breaking the tenth commandment."

Marty pulled out slowly. He watched the car recede in his rear-view mirror as he approached the fork in the road. He had meant to stop and ask someone where they were exactly, but the Cadillac had distracted him. Marty loved cars, and a red Caddy was his dream machine. He glanced in the rear-view mirror and saw someone exit the church and move quickly toward the car.

"How much you figure a car like that's worth, Dad?" asked Carl.

"No tellin'. If it came new, maybe more than five, six thousand dollars. You're lookin' at a small herd of cattle right there, boys, all wrapped up in red paint—look out, Marty!"

Marty had been intent on the man getting into the red Cadillac, not watching the road. He reacted instinctively, swerving to his right, barely missing the vehicle in front of him and sliding to a sideways stop in the ditch. The oncoming truck roared by in a cloud of dust, the driver laughing wildly as he barrelled on through the town.

"Good heavens, Martin, watch what you're doing!" Hatty gasped.

"Man, did you see that guy's face?" Carl exclaimed. He was still staring out the rear window, looking for the truck.

"You saw his face?" Marty was shouting, but he couldn't help it. His heart was beating fast, the adrenaline was racing through his system, and his hands were still clutching the steering wheel in a death grip. "I barely saw the truck. Jeez, that was close. That guy must've been doing eighty."

"Man, I've never seen a face like that in my life." Carl settled back into his seat, shaking his head. The red Cadillac pulled by on their left, heading south.

"Why? What did you see?" asked Eli. His voice was strained, artificial.

"His skin, Dad. That guy was white as snow!"

Eli didn't say anything. He nodded his head slowly, then looked back toward town as if he half expected to see the truck again.

"Let's go, son," he said to Marty, still gazing out the rear window.

"I swear, Dad," Carl insisted. "The guy looked like a ghost."

"Martin." Eli's voice had an edge to it. He wanted to leave. Immediately. He had seen the man, too—just for a split second, but long enough to recognize him. Those dark eyes were like pieces of burned coal sunk deep in alabaster flesh. It was a face you couldn't forget, no matter how hard you tried. Eli had been trying for a long time. And what was worse, the man had seen him. That explained the laugh.

Marty shifted into first and pulled back onto the south fork. They passed a sign nailed to a crooked mesquite post, but they didn't notice it. Their nerves were still settling along with the dust. Had Eli glanced back one last time, everything would have been different. He would have seen that the sign read, "Santa Maria."

The road south was getting progressively worse. For the last half hour Eli and his family had spent more time in the air between bumps than they had on the ground. The "highway" consisted of long stretches of gravelly dirt mixed with a few patches of broken blacktop. They had been climbing slowly, the land to their left falling away so gently and gradually that the change was almost imperceptible. Now, however, the truck was climbing a steep grade. As if waking from a dream, Marty suddenly noticed that the land sliding past his driver's side window had plunged into a valley stretching far away to the southeast, toward the mountains.

Mountains! Where had they come from? He had been so intent on the road, missing chugholes, and thinking how he could have engineered a better grade to this hill that he failed to notice the rugged beauty of the countryside. It reminded him of Colorado, but with the expansiveness of the low mountains just on the other side of the Texas/New Mexico border.

Actually, the "mountains" were only the foothills of a large range that stretched away to the south. The grass was sparse here, but Indian paintbrush speckled the sides of the hills alongside bluebonnets and white thistles. It was a pure, unspoiled land. There wasn't a sign of civilization anywhere.

"Stop the truck," Eli said, just loud enough for Marty to hear.

Marty didn't even bother to pull over to the side of the road.

There wasn't any side to pull onto, and they hadn't passed a car in the last hour anyway. He slowed to a stop and killed the engine right in the middle of the road.

Eli got out and walked around the truck, the gravel crunching under his feet. He looked first to the north and then to the east, searching the skyline for some sign of life. The Dodge was down to a quarter tank of gas, and Eli knew its old tires wouldn't take much more of this kind of road. He'd been watching the temperature gauge, too. It had been inching up as the grade got steeper. They had to find some place with gas and food—fast.

Hatty and the boys stayed in the truck, not saying a word, letting Eli think things through in quiet.

The silence here was magnificent, expansive. There were no bird calls; not even the tall grass was moving. It was like entering a painting. Absolutely nothing stirred. The stillness reminded Hatty of something, but the vague memory was gone as soon as it whispered to her. This wasn't a stillness like back home; there, the wind wouldn't stir because the land had died. There was no movement because there was no life. But here, the calm held a secret, as if something were about to happen. Hatty closed her eyes to try to rest for a moment.

A sudden breeze blew through the windows. Hatty breathed deeply, filling her lungs with the cool highland air, enjoying the quiet of the moment. Then again something familiar whispered to her, this time more insistently. *Where have I felt this before?* she wondered. *What is that smell in the air?*

"Mom, look! LOOK!" Carl was shaking his mother's arm, his eyes fixed on the eastern horizon and the valley that stretched out below them like a wide, dry seabed.

Hatty opened her eyes. The first thing she saw was Eli walking quickly back toward the truck, but that wasn't what Carl and Marty were looking at. Their eyes were fixed on something far beyond their father.

Eli reached the side of the truck where Hatty was sitting. "Hatty! Hat, do you see it? Look, see them there?" He was pointing away to the east.

"Yeah!" Marty had seen them. "Oh, wow, look at 'em run!"

Hatty's eyes were as sharp as a hawk's; she had already seen them. What she saw took her breath away: a black streak in the valley below followed by a thundering mass of brown, black, and roan and a tremendous cloud of dust. In the lead was the most magnificent blue-black stallion she had ever seen, racing full-tilt down the valley, leading a herd of horses in a spontaneous burst of energy. His tail was straight up and unfurled, nostrils flared, ears forward, eyes wild as the impulse that drove him before the wind. The dull rumble of hooves drumming the valley floor rolled up the sides of the foothills, then melted away as it spilled over the top. A hundred or more mustangs in the herd, all racing the wind, followed their majestic leader.

Suddenly the stallion stopped, and all the others halted behind him. He was looking right at Hatty. She felt him see her. He must have been a half-mile off, but she could hear his low nicker. He pranced forward, the wind blowing through his ebony mane, his gaze still fixed on Hatty alone. She couldn't breathe.

Then she noticed, though the herd was still, the soft rumble of thunder. She glanced up to see low, black clouds racing across the sky. Of course—that's what she'd been trying to remember a few minutes ago: the feeling of a coming storm. *Rain!* How long had it been?

A bolt of white-blue lightning ripped the sky at the far end of the valley. Immediately the thunder slapped the air flat in the face. The stallion reared at the same instant, wheeled, and streaked back down the valley, the herd straining to keep him in sight.

Oh, Lord, what an animal, Hatty thought to herself. The wind had picked up and was blowing in rough gusts now, cuffing the foothills. Then came another thunderclap.

"Whooooo—eeeee!" Marty yelled.

"Go, go, go, go!" Carl was pushing his older brother out into the coming storm, eager to feel the cool, wet wind surge around him and through him—to breathe in the rain.

"Quiet!" Eli half shouted.

The boys froze, looking back at their father. He was straining to hear something above the wind and the echo of the thunder.

Carl ventured a whisper. “What, Dad?”

“Shh! Listen—there! Hear it?”

“All I hear is thunder,” Marty whispered.

Eli was growing frustrated trying to describe what he was hearing. “No, no, above the thunder—higher, like . . . ”

“Like bells,” said Hatty. She was looking down the valley, where the mustangs had run. “I can barely make them out. Let’s get out where we can hear better.”

They all stood perfectly still, looking toward the east, trying to squeeze a sound out of the wind. Then they all heard it. The distant sound burst like a bubble all around them—three distinct, clear notes, high and pure, the sweet ring of a bell. Then silence.

“What time is it, Eli?” asked Hatty.

“About noon,” Marty interrupted.

“ ’Bout time to be ringing in the lunch hour, wouldn’t you say, Hat?” asked Eli.

“You mean there’s a house up there somewhere ringing a bell for lunch?” asked Carl.

“More likely a church,” said Eli, starting to move back to the driver’s side of the truck. “And where there’s a church there’s a town. Everybody in. Let’s go before this storm hits.”

They all jumped into the truck, and Eli cranked the engine. “If I figure right, those bells shouldn’t be more than a couple of miles up, but these hills can play tricks on you and we aren’t far from the mountains—maybe fifteen, twenty miles by road; less than ten as the crow flies. That wind can whip sound around and carry it a long way, especially up here. We’ll just have to drive and hope we find it. Y’all keep a sharp eye out.”

The clouds advanced quickly, their wispy edges like the fringe of an enormous black shawl being drawn by an unseen hand over the land. The truck made good progress at first, but they were soon forced to a crawl as the incline steepened and the dropoff to their left became more severe. They inched forward, carefully negotiating the hairpin turns as they headed east up the valley, rapidly gaining altitude.

Gathering darkness forced Eli to turn on his lights. As they rounded a bend, thinking they must be near the source of the bells, Eli stopped, pulled on the emergency brake, and stared. He didn't like what he saw up ahead. The blacktop stopped entirely, yielding to gravel and mud that went up at an angle a goat wouldn't climb. The air outside had turned much cooler, and the clouds threatened to unload any second. The gas tank was down to just above empty and the temperature gauge was reading hot.

"We need to go for it before that rain hits," he said to his family. "Hold on."

With that he released the brake and gunned the engine. They made about two hundred yards before the clouds burst. With an enormous thunderclap, the water rushed down on them in torrents, as if mischievous angels were tipping the pitchers of heaven. They came to a dead halt, unable to see anything through the wall of water.

Eli pulled on the emergency brake and turned the wheels toward the mountain wall on his right so that the truck would veer into the mountain if it started to slide backward. He left the lights on just in case another car came along the road. There was no room to pass without scraping the side of another vehicle. If another car *did* come, they would both just have to sit out the storm, head to head, then flip a coin to see who backed up.

"Everybody just sit real still, and we'll let this thing blow itself out. Hat, now would be a good time for one of those special prayers of yours, if you feel like it."

"I've already said three," she said without laughing.

It rained for a full hour, without letting up.

"If this keeps up much longer we're in for trouble. I'm going to try to find some rocks or logs to put under the tires. Y'all stay put." Eli started to open the door slowly. The handle clicked down and the door opened a crack. The rain gushed in, and the truck shifted.

"Eli, we're moving!" Hatty said, barely stifling a scream.

Eli had one foot on the ground. Instinctively, he tried to stop the backward slide of the truck with his foot, but it was useless. The truck was going and there was nothing he could do about it. He jumped back inside and turned the wheel sharply to the right, hoping to steer into the side of the mountain, but the road was too slippery. They had hit a patch of caliche, calcified deposits in the soil that when wet become as white and slick as ice. The truck spun half a turn and began its downward rush toward the bend in the road. If they didn't stop before they reached that bend, they would go over the edge and straight down almost a thousand feet. They couldn't jump out because the truck was spinning, so they just held on to each other.

"Oh, God, help! Help! Please!" Hatty screamed. She couldn't see for the rain—none of them could—but they all knew the truck must be nearing the edge of the road, which was so narrow it was a miracle they hadn't already gone over. But after one last dizzy spin, the truck came to an abrupt stop as the back tires bumped up against something. Eli reached for the lights slowly. He found it strangely difficult to reach them, as if he were moving in slow motion.

When he turned them on he could just make out through the rain the road climbing up ahead of them at a ridiculous angle. Then he rested back against the seat.

The truck moved, just slightly. He looked in the rear-view mirror and saw the tops of trees. Then it hit him. The front wheels were on the road—just barely. The back wheels were resting on—who knows what, but they were there and that's what counted. The trick now would be to get his family out without sending the truck over the side.

"Everybody okay? All right now, everything's going to be fine. We just need to move real slow and we'll get out of here with no problem. Hatty, you first. Open the door slowly and ease on out. Go ahead now."

"Eli . . ." she didn't know what to say. She couldn't even see his face to see how scared he was. His voice sounded so calm, but she knew better.

"Go on now, Hat. Everything's going to be fine. Open the door and ease on out."

She pushed the handle down slowly until she heard the familiar click. The door swung open more quickly than she had planned. They were tilted back and at such an angle that she almost fell out as soon as the door opened. She slid her right leg out and down onto the ground, then eased her left foot out. The rain was beating down in cold, stinging drops. She held on to the door, waiting for the boys, thinking that she was somehow also helping hold the truck on the side of the mountain.

Now that Hatty was out, she could see just how precariously they were balanced on the edge of the precipice. The front right wheel rested in a huge hole in the side of the road. She couldn't quite see what was holding the left front of the truck in place, but she figured it must have run up on some large rocks and wedged there.

Carl edged out next, smooth as silk. It looked as if the truck was stuck solid. Then Marty slid across the seat and put his right boot down on the ground. Immediately, the truck tipped farther back. Marty slipped and fell out onto the narrow shoulder, nearly rolling over the edge. Carl, who was standing near the front of the truck, grabbed instinctively for the front grill to try to keep the front end down.

"Get back," Eli yelled from inside the truck. They couldn't hear him for the rain. He rolled down the window as quickly yet gently as he could. Without leaning out, he yelled through the rain, "Carl, get back. All of you. Now! This thing isn't going anywhere, but if it does, I don't want you to go with it." Eli knew it was only a matter of time before the truck and all their possessions went crashing down a thousand feet of inhospitable mountainside, but he didn't intend to go down with it. "Carl, you and Marty see if you can find a long branch—something I can grab on to if this thing goes over. I'll try to climb out my side, but I'll need something strong. Hurry, son."

Both Carl and Marty were already halfway up the road scrounging in the twilight for anything they could use to reach their father. Hatty stayed closer to the truck, wanting to be near Eli. She was the first to see the lights far up the road near the top of the gorge.

Some other fool is out in this storm, she thought. *Someone else who might be able to help.* Eli saw the lights, too, but he knew what they really meant.

"Hatty, get out of the way! Move to the other side," he shouted. The lights were coming much too fast to be able to slow down in time to avoid a collision. Once he hit the caliche strip, there would be no way to stop. They would both go over.

"No!" Hatty screamed, as she ran out into the middle of the road waving her arms. The car was only three hundred yards away now. It had disappeared around a bend in the road but was still coming strong. It wouldn't turn again until it was too late. Carl and Marty both heard their mother scream and started running toward her, slipping in the mud, half blinded by the rain.

The car rounded the last turn just as the boys reached their mother. They waved their hands, yelling at the top of their lungs for the car to stop. They were only fifty yards from the truck when the oncoming car caught them in its headlights. It never slowed. Carl shoved his mother out of the way and jumped toward the side of the road, knocking Marty off his feet. Both landed with a thud on the mountain side of the road, a few feet down from Hatty. Hatty slammed up against a sharp-cornered stone and sank into the mud at its base.

Once past the three of them, the car started to slide wildly. Hatty pulled herself up, holding on to something on top of the slick rock where she had fallen. She was bruised, but screaming at the top of her lungs. "Stop, can't you see? Stop!"

Hatty and the boys caught glimpses of the truck as the car's headlights swept the edge of the mountain pass in its slide down to impact. The hood of the truck was pointed nearly straight up now, the back left wheel hanging off the precipice, turning slowly, suspended in the air by invisible wires.

"Jump, Dad!" Marty screamed with Carl, "Juuuump!"

WHAM! The car slammed into the truck going at least fifty miles an hour, caromed off, regained just enough traction to keep it from spinning off the edge, and continued down the mountain road.

Hatty and the boys stared in shock—not at the retreating car, but at the truck. It hadn't moved. Something was holding it in place.

Lightning flashed and thunder pounded the mountainside as the boys and Hatty ran slipping and sliding down to the truck.

"Eli! Eli!" Hatty shouted as she neared the truck.

"Dad, are you all right?" Marty was trying to see inside the cab, but he couldn't get close enough. The rain would drown out any quiet answer. They heard nothing, could do nothing.

"Señora!"

Hatty, Marty, and Carl turned to see, not thirty feet behind them, a man on a horse standing perfectly still. He wore a dark-colored pancho and broad-brimmed hat. His features were indistinguishable in the downpour and leaden light.

"*Señora,* move back. He will be fine, but I must act quickly!" He spoke perfect Spanish, not the Tex-Mex lingo of the border towns. Hatty had grown up within a hundred miles of the border. She knew good Spanish when she heard it. The language of Mexico was almost as natural to her as her native English, and she prided herself in her fluency in it. She moved away from the truck along with the boys to the far side of the road. They watched the man work in short, quick movements with an easy familiarity, as if he had done this, or something like it, before.

He loosened his rope from the side of the saddle and formed a small loop. He edged his horse as close as he could to the edge of the precipice. He swung the rope once, twice, and let it sail on the third turn. The small loop sailed through the rain and the open window, landing neatly inside the cab of the truck. The man wrapped the rope around the horn of his saddle. There was still no sound or movement inside.

"*Señor!* Tie the rope around you. I will pull you free."

No response.

"Do it now, *Señor!*"

Suddenly, the rope drew taut. Eli's hands gripped the rope and started to pull. Slowly, he worked his way out the open window. He was trying to move carefully in order to avoid sending the truck over the edge. He dropped unceremoniously to the rocky ground below. His family moved to his side quickly, slipping the rope off his shoulders, helping him up and away from the truck.

"I'm all right. It's okay. Just a little bump on the noggin," he said quietly as he held Hatty close. She was sobbing. They stood, the four of them in a close embrace, huddled against the storm. Eli broke away to thank the man.

"*¡Muchas gracias! Muchas gracias, Señor!*" Eli's Spanish wasn't as good as Hatty's, but he knew enough to get by. He extended his hand to the man on the horse as the man was coiling the rope and tying it back in place. The man smiled, dismounted, and took Eli's hand in a firm grip.

"*De nada, Señor.* It was nothing. Now you must get to shelter. There is a small cave just up the road. I will go for help. Please, you and your family follow me. We will come for the truck tomorrow."

Eli looked to Hatty for help with the translation. They started up the road toward the cave, talking as they walked, the man in the pancho leading his horse by the reins. Eli wanted to know why the man was out in weather like this.

"I was on my way up from the valley when the storm broke," he said. "I catch horses. The wild ones. The renegades. There is one horse—a black stallion—who runs a large herd. If I catch that one. . . ." His voice trailed off, and he shook his head. "But it is like trying to catch the wind. I have been after him a long time. The crazy man in the car nearly ran me off the road."

"*Señor,*" Hatty said hesitantly, half-shouting against the rain. "We saw the stallion, the black one down in the valley. Not many miles. . . ."

The man in the pancho stopped suddenly and turned to face Hatty. She could see his eyes clearly for the first time, flashing out from under the broad brim. They burned into her, no longer polite, no longer gentle, but intense, strong.

"You saw him? You saw the black one?"

"I suppose it could have been another," Hatty lied. She knew there could be only one horse like that. "I only saw him from a distance. We all did." She looked at Eli and nodded. Eli nodded back, not knowing exactly what he was agreeing to.

"But he looked at you, did he not?" asked the man, still looking hard at Hatty. "Yes, he looked at you. I can see it in your face." He paused and stared back down the road in the direction of the valley, then up to the horizon. "You must be very careful, *Señora*. You are here for a purpose I do not understand. But," he sighed, "we will learn soon enough, I expect. Come—we must get you to the cave."

Another seventy-five yards and they reached the gaping hole in the mountainside. They all entered quickly, glad to be out of the slicing rain.

"Nothing to fear here, *Señora,* and I am afraid no treasure to be found—not here anyway." He smiled, and his voice echoed eerily off the damp walls. "Children play here all the time. Still, I wouldn't go too far back. It gets dark very quickly. The village is only a mile or so from here. I will send help." He shook hands all around, then swung into the saddle and reined his horse back into the liquid air and onto the steep slope.

Hatty called after him, "Please, don't leave yet. At least wait until the storm lets up."

"*Gracias,* but I have already stayed too long. They will come soon," he said, and he was gone up the road, his head bowed into the swirling rain.

Eli moved his family back to a dry spot in the cave. Then he remembered, "Even if we get the truck back on the road I'll need gas. Dummy!" He bolted out the front of the cave and looked up the long narrow road for the man in the pancho. But he was gone.

By nine-forty-five that evening, the rain had let up enough to allow safe passage across the mountain for those who had to make the trip. Doc McClendon had been up the previous eighteen hours delivering a baby to the Garcia family on the other side of the valley. It was time to head home, and a little rain wasn't going to keep him out of his warm bed. He had made the trip in hail, rain, and windstorm, and he had seen some unusual sights over the years—but he had never encountered anything quite like what he was looking at now.

"What in blazes!" Doc eased his truck to a halt on the rain-slick road. His headlights shone through the light sprinkle and up the steep incline on to what looked like a truck standing on its rear end, perched on the lip of the gorge. He got out, leaving the engine running, and walked up the road in the glare of the headlights, taking short, careful steps to avoid falling on the slippery rocks. "Anyone there?" he called. "Hello?"

He saw the passenger-side door open. "Oh, no," Doc whispered to himself, edging closer to the upended truck. He peered out over the rim of the gorge, but it was pointless. A thick blanket of clouds hid the moon and stars. There was virtually no chance that anyone could have survived such a fall. Down below, there was nothing but flat rock and boulders. Doc had been trying to get the town to put up a rail there for years. Now maybe they would do something—now that it was too late for these poor people.

He pulled back, taking short, shallow breaths. The sprinkling of rain had turned to a heavy mist, intensifying the quiet stillness of this high mountain pass. He stood back gazing at the truck, his arms folded over his middle-aged girth, his head cocked slightly to one side, trying to gain a fresh perspective on the puzzle.

"What's this then?" His headlights had revealed something unusual on the rusting undercarriage of the old truck. He was moving forward to get a better look when a call from up the hillside startled him.

"Hello!" It was Carl. He had been cooped up in the cave for hours and had left to explore once the rain had let up a bit. He had just rounded the upper bend when he saw headlights down near their truck.

"Hang on, I'll be right up." Doc jumped into his truck and negotiated the slick road with little effort. Experience and new tires made the difference. By the time Doc reached the upper bend, Marty had joined Carl and Eli was not far behind.

"What's going on—you folks all right?" Doc asked as he pulled up.

"Yessir, thanks for coming. I'm Martin King and this is my brother Carl." Marty reached in the passenger's window to shake hands.

"Doc McClendon. Glad to meet you boys. This your dad?"

Eli made his way down the slithery caliche to the truck. "Eli King, Mr. McClendon. We really appreciate your coming for us. I had a feelin' you'd have to wait the rain out."

"Well, sir," Doc said, "I'm glad I came along and found you folks, but I had no idea you were here. Sounds like you were lookin' for somebody in particular."

"Didn't a fellow send you out from town?" asked Marty.

"A Mexican riding a sorrel—wearing a pancho and a broad-brimmed hat?" Eli continued. "He left here hours ago and was headed into town to get help, he said."

Doc looked hard at Eli before he answered. Then at Carl and Marty. He could tell they were being honest with him. He shook his head and chuckled to himself before he spoke.

"You folks haven't been up here before, have you?" Doc asked. "No, of course you haven't—dumb question." He returned to the point. "Nosir, no one sent me—at least no dark rider. No, I was down on the other side helpin' some good folks fill the earth with babies. Tell you what, though," he continued before Eli could interrupt with another question, "why don't I give you folks a lift into town and we'll see if we can't get someone to come help us with that truck? And call me Doc—most folks do around here."

" 'Preciate it," Eli offered. "My wife's back at the cave—if you wouldn't mind driving up a ways—still asleep, I imagine. She was pretty worn out. Boys, hop in back," he said, as he opened the cab door and slid in. Hatty had fallen asleep in the cave, but she had awakened on hearing the truck approach. As the truck pulled up to the cave entrance, she was there ready to go.

Eli introduced his wife, and Doc graciously welcomed Hatty to the prettiest part of Mexico. "Why, if old Cortez had found this place," he said as they bounced along the rough road, much too fast for Hatty's liking, "he never would have bothered with the land down south. I just wish you could see more of the view on our way in—it's a beautiful sight, I'll tell you. I've been here twenty years now, and I never have tired of it. But from the looks of your truck I'd say you'd have a day or two to do some looking around before you get on your way again. You can stay with us as long as you need."

Hatty started to object, more out of polite habit than anything else.

"No arguments now," Doc continued. "My wife would get me good if she thought I let you get away! Besides, there isn't anywhere else to stay except the church. Father Zeuma's a good man, but he's got his hands full right now with some other things. Besides, my wife's a better cook than he is," he laughed, patting his belly.

Hatty smiled back. She liked this man. Still, she was cautious—that's the word she used to describe her suspicious streak. *A doctor,* she thought. *What on earth is he doin' down here if he's a real doctor? Probably got in trouble up in Texas and came down here to practice.*

"Something wrong, Mizz King?" Doc asked Hatty.

"Oh, heavens, I'm sorry. I didn't mean to stare." Hatty blushed.

"She's got about a hundred questions for you, Doc," Eli said with a smile. "She gets quiet like that, you better watch out—she's just figuring out which one to unload first."

"Well, that makes two of us, then," Doc countered. "Why don't you folks start out, then I'll fill you in on our little piece of the world."

The windshield wipers slapped slowly and rhythmically, sweeping away the highland mist as Eli began to unfold their story. Doc listened intently, his eyes fixed on the winding trail before him. Hatty was noting thankfully that the road began to broaden as Doc's truck rounded still another bend in their upward climb. To their right the mountain still rose sharply up into the impenetrable darkness. To their left she could see nothing but inky blackness stretching out and down who knew how far.

Finally, after climbing what seemed miles, they felt the road leveling out. The trip was taking longer than Eli expected, long enough to finish with the story of the man in the pancho. "He said it was only a mile or so to your town," Eli said.

"Oh, there's a shortcut or two if you're on horseback, but it takes a while longer if you take the road up."

"Would you know him?" Eli asked. "We couldn't get a really good look at his face, but I'd guess him to be in his mid-forties, medium height."

"Oh, it could have been most anyone in town," Doc said. "Most of the men in the village have horses. More horses in Dolores than cars. It's really a step back in time to come here. There's one thing I'm curious about, though. Tell me again about those wild horses. Tell me exactly what you saw."

Hatty retold the story of the beautiful stallion and his herd. Again, Doc was perfectly quiet, listening, trying to absorb every detail.

"He was the most beautiful horse," Hatty recalled. "And I

swear—I know this sounds funny, but I swear—he looked right at me. That's when the lightning hit and he took off back up the valley with his herd."

"Whoever catches that one is going to have his hands full. I wouldn't want to be the one to try to break him," said Eli.

Doc shook his head. Then, after a pause, "No one's going to break that horse. No one's going to catch him," he said, flatly. All the humor was drained from his voice. His response didn't invite further conversation.

They rode on for another couple of minutes, listening to the monotonous squeak of the wiper blades against the almost dry windshield. Doc drove through a small, darkened village without slowing down and continued past it for another mile or so. Finally, the truck pulled off to the right of the road and followed a short drive back into a stand of trees.

There, nestled in a pine grove, was the simple home of Doctor and Mrs. McClendon. Double lanterns hung from each side of the front porch like beacons. Bugs of various feathery descriptions swirled chaotically around the lights, flirting with the flames inside. Doc had barely gotten out of the truck when the front door of the house burst open and out bounded a little girl, pigtails flying.

"Papa!" she squealed as she jumped into the big man's arms. She saw the strangers just as her arms circled his neck. Instinctively, she buried her face in his shoulder.

"Hey, angel, how's my big girl?" he greeted her in Spanish.

She must have been nearly ten years old, but his arms swallowed her.

Hatty climbed out on the passenger's side and got her first real look at the good doctor as he played with his little girl. She hadn't realized just how big a man he was until then. He must have been at least six feet two, with broad shoulders and huge hands.

"Rosa, run inside and get Mama. I want you both to meet some new friends." The girl hopped down and ran into the house, calling for her mother in Spanish.

Doc turned toward his guests. "Please, you folks come on in. Estella will be tickled for the company, believe me."

"Angus?" Estella McClendon crossed the threshold of the door and froze, looking first at her husband and then at the strangers standing around the truck. "Is everything all right?" she asked Doc. She had the most elegant voice Hatty had ever heard. It was smooth and dark and rich-sounding—it fit the night perfectly.

"Everything's fine, sweetheart," Doc answered, as he put his huge arm around the lady on the porch, then turned to Eli and said with obvious pride, "Mr. King, this is my wife, Estella, and my daughter, Rosalinda." He turned to Estella. "Sweetheart, these folks have had a rough time of it over the last twenty-four hours. It's time they rested a bit, wouldn't you say?"

Estella looked up at her husband and smiled. Explanations would come later. They always did. She moved to shake hands with Eli and his sons. Then she embraced Hatty and said, "This is our home—and yours for as long as you care to stay. Please come inside and rest. Rosalinda!" she called to her daughter who had returned to the house and was watching the proceedings through the kitchen window.

Estella entered the house, giving quick, firm instructions to her daughter to prepare food and beds for their guests. Hatty joined her hostess in the small kitchen while Eli and the boys sat at the table with Doc. It didn't take long to get the food ready. The wood-burning stove was still warm from the supper Estella had cooked for herself and Rosa just a few hours before. Rosalinda lit the fire in the belly of the stove and heated up the leftover tortillas and beans with ground beef. The stove served as a kind of second fireplace in the central part of the home, warming the entire kitchen and part of the living room.

Eli and his family made short work of the food—their first hot meal in twenty-four hours. While the Kings ate, the McClendons were busy making extra beds. Their home had two bedrooms—one for Doc and Estella and one for Rosalinda, which also served as Doc's office. The boys would sleep on pallets on the living room floor in front of the fire. Rosalinda would sleep with her parents and give her room to Eli and Hatty.

"I have been trying to get Angus to build on an extra room for years," Estella said, smiling at Hatty. "Now maybe he will listen." She was perfectly at ease, making the Kings feel as though they were family members on a visit rather than total strangers.

"The bathroom is back to your left," she said, indicating a door that stood between two of the bedrooms. "I'm afraid we are still working on getting hot water—we have no electricity, so we must heat everything by making fires. We can have hot bath water in the morning for you. Now, we need to let you sleep. We can talk in the morning. May the Lord give you sweet rest."

"Good night, folks—y'all sleep tight," Doc said, as he took his wife and daughter back to their room.

Eli and Hatty said good night to their sons and retired to the small room where a single oil lamp cast a warm glow. They couldn't make out much detail in the room, but there really wasn't much to see except books. The room was filled with them from floor to ceiling—mostly large, thick volumes that looked well used. A small oak rolltop desk stood against one wall, and the bed was in the very center of the room. Only a portion of one wall—surrounding the door—lacked shelving. That portion was apparently Rosa's special place to display drawings, ribbons, and Hatty noticed in passing, what appeared in the dim light to be hand-lettered Scripture verses.

"This is one for the books, Hat," Eli said as they undressed by the lamplight. He stretched out on the twin bed, his feet just dangling off the end, and put his arm around his wife. She was quiet.

"I love you, Hatty. We'll make it through all this just fine."

"I know we will," she said softly. They closed their eyes and were both asleep before their next breath.

The lamp burned through the night, keeping watch. A chill wind picked up outside, swirling around the house and whining through the crack in the outside wall of the chimney. High up on a ridge overlooking the little village of Dolores, a dark shape squatted on a rock, watching the house with the light inside.

The aroma of fresh coffee woke Marty gently from a sound sleep. He had been dreaming of fishing on the river back on the ranch. He turned over to get out of bed and discovered his strange surroundings. He opened his eyes slowly and looked at his brother, still asleep on his pallet a few feet away. For a moment he was lost. Then the events of the previous night came rushing back. He lay back on his bedroll and put his hands behind his head.

It was still dark, but Marty could see shapes moving about in the kitchen. Muffled whispers and the soft sound of coffee being poured into a cup drifted into his consciousness.

Doc must have to get an early start, he thought to himself. He could hear the pump squeak as someone filled a tin bucket with water. Doc lit an oil lamp and placed it in the center of the kitchen table. He took a book and sat down at the table and began to read. Marty glanced over to his left toward his parents' room and saw the glow from their night light shining from under the door.

Wide awake now, Marty reached over for his jeans and slipped them on under his blanket. He threw back the covers and was immediately aware of how crisp the air was. Only the faintest red glow remained from the fire the night before, and the house was chill.

He sat on the edge of his bedroll and quickly pulled on his cold socks and boots. Doc looked back over his shoulder and whispered, "Mornin', Martin. I hope we didn't wake you."

"Nosir, the smell of that good coffee is what got me goin'," he said with a smile. "If you'd show me where the wood is I'd be glad to chop some for a fire."

"We have plenty of wood ready to go. Out the back door there, you'll see the pile just outside the garden fence to your right. Three or four logs ought to do it, and you'll find some kindlin' in the barrel by the side of the house."

Marty stepped out into the brilliant, thin air and breathed deeply. This reminded him of their trip to Colorado years before. To his immediate right a garden stretched over what looked like nearly a half-acre, framed by a whitewashed picket fence.

It was a private paradise, with the gnarled limbs of large oaks arching high overhead to form a natural arbor. Sunlight strayed through the cracks in the fence to race along the paths. Honeysuckle and roses grew in manicured clusters. Pink and white periwinkle mixed with brilliant splashes of red and yellow daisies. Impatiens overflowed several half-barrels in one of the shadier corners. Ferns grew everywhere, their fronds spilling out into the twisting pathways.

The three paths that Marty could see converged near the center of the garden, where a stone well seemed to grow up out of the earth. Flowering vines curled up one side and across part of the shake roof. A wooden bucket sat on the wall, a lazy coil of rope looping up from its handle to the spindle. A bench swing, suspended on thick rope, hung from one of the lower branches of the largest oak. Round-backed wooden chairs were tucked away in pairs in various nooks. Behind the well, at the end of a short path, a tall white arch of latticework interlaced with pink flowering vines stood at the end of its own little cul-de-sac. Pink granite paving stones circumscribed the clearing and radiated inward in concentric circles toward a large, round, center stone of pure-white marble, perhaps four feet in diameter.

Marty walked quietly along the outside of the fence, letting his fingers follow the contours of the rounded palings, not wanting to violate the sanctity of the place with sound. The land behind the garden dipped away sharply to a mountain-fed creek nearly thirty feet below. Marty had always had a romantic longing to live in the mountains; as he walked back to the house, he wished half-consciously that they would be able to settle down here.

The wood hissed and popped, resisting the heat as it caught fire, but the room was soon filled with light and warmth. Carl was still asleep.

Doc motioned for Marty to join him at the kitchen table. "Your brother must have been pretty worn out last night to sleep through all this racket," he said in a low voice.

"Carl could sleep through a stampede in the middle of a thunderstorm," Marty said as he sat across from Doc. He glanced down and noticed the Bible Doc had in front of him on the table.

"We try to get in a little time of reading each morning and evening," said Doc, noticing Marty's glance. "It makes the day go a whole lot better."

Estella was frying eggs and bacon in a huge black skillet on the stove. "Angus," she said without looking at him, "two eggs or three this morning?"

"Two will be fine, thanks. How about you, Martin? Care for some bacon and eggs?"

"Sure, I'll have a couple and some bacon if you have enough to go around." It was the first time Marty had experienced such natural warmth in a home outside his own—a kind and gentle spirit that made you want to relax and work at the same time. He had grown up in a close family, but there was something different about these people. You could tell it the minute you walked in the door. They were obviously Christians, but not the kind Marty was used to. For one thing, back home a white man would never marry a Mexican girl unless he had to. *Maybe that's what happened*, he thought. *Maybe she got pregnant and they had to come down here to have the baby or something, and they just decided to stay. They sure seem like nice folks, though.*

"Coffee?" Estella asked, smiling at Marty.

"Yes, ma'am, please."

"You speak much Spanish, Martin?" Doc asked.

"Poquito, no mucho," Marty replied. His Spanish was sketchy Tex-Mex at best.

"I thought you and Carl might like to run down to the store after breakfast and pick up some flour for Estella."

"Sure, Doc, just point us in the right direction. Carl's Spanish is better than mine, so—"

"You sure you don't mind? It'll save me a trip in, and I need to get back out to the Garcias' to check on the new baby. You can walk easy enough—it's only three quarters of a mile. We came through it on our way in last night. Rosa!"

Rosalinda had just come bounding into the kitchen from their bedroom. Her pigtails were freshly braided and she was dressed in jeans and a floral print shirt. She gave Doc and Estella good morning hugs and sat at her place at the end of the table.

"We need to get this girl fed, Mama. We have a baby to go see!"

"Good morning, Doc, Estella," Eli said as he closed the bedroom door behind him. He walked over to Carl on his way to the table and patted him on the back. "Let's go, son, time to wake up." Carl stirred and sat up slowly without saying a word. Eli came in and sat at the table.

Doc stood up to get some coffee for Eli. "Hope you folks slept well."

"Like a rock. Thanks." Eli accepted the steaming cup gratefully as Carl slipped into the chair beside Rosa.

"Rosa and I are about to take off for the Garcia place, Mr. King," said Doc. "I thought you might like to come along. Hernando's got a rig we might be able to borrow to get your truck down so we don't break an axle—and I thought while we were down in the valley we might as well see if we couldn't pick up some of the stuff that fell out of the truck."

"Sure, that would be great. And please call me Eli. Let me tell Hatty and we can go as soon as you're ready." He started to get up from the table.

"We've got time for you to eat, Eli," Doc laughed. "Please, sit down—let your wife rest. We can go after you finish breakfast.

Now, we need to thank the Lord for this good food." Doc reached out and took Rosa's hand. She instinctively took Carl's hand to her right. He smiled and bowed his head. Estella came over and stood behind her husband, taking his other hand.

"Father in heaven, thank You for these our new friends. We ask Your guidance and wisdom—help us to love them and serve them as we would our own family. Thank You, Lord, for this good food and for the rain last night."

"And for the Garcia baby," added Rosa.

"And for the Garcia baby," continued Doc. "We pray these things in the name of Jesus Christ and for His glory. Amen."

"Amen," they all chorused.

They passed the meal in lively conversation, mostly concerning the torrential rain of last night. It had been almost two years since they'd had a rain like that, Doc told them, and so the people of the village were going to take the Kings' arrival as a sign that the drought might be over.

Carl laughed when he heard that their coming might be a good omen.

"Us? An omen for rain? I wish!"

"Who knows?" Doc went on smiling. "Maybe the Lord is going to use you to bring blessing to these people, and the rain is sort of, uh—I don't know, a hint, a little taste of that blessing." He laughed good-naturedly, but Eli could tell he was more than half serious. "Martin, if you and Carl are ready," Doc went on, "I can drop you off at the store on my way out."

"Thanks," Marty said. "But I think we'll walk—get to know the place a little bit."

"Fine. I've got a few things I need to get together, then I'll be all set. I'll wait for you out front, Eli."

He rose and kissed Estella goodbye. "C'mon, Rosy, let's go—you can help me with the supplies." Rosa followed her dad out the back door and around the end of the house to a small shed where Doc kept his tools. They gathered the ropes and chain they would need to lower the King's truck and threw them into the back of his own. Eli met them out front just as Doc was cranking the engine.

They pulled out and headed down the short drive to the main road.

Carl and Marty started their walk into the village about a half hour later. They strolled slowly, drinking in the cool air. They were at the end of a wide, cup-shaped valley, a natural cul-de-sac hemmed in by jagged blue mountains on three sides, with one road running its length and disappearing as the valley curved around to the southwest.

The rain from the night before had left large puddles in the road and fields. The young men straddled the road, one walking on either side, picking up an occasional stone and throwing it at nothing in particular. Far up on the mountainside Carl spied a herd of cattle searching for some new growth for food.

"Rain'll do this country a world of good, C," Marty said to his brother. Carl was quiet, his head down, looking straight ahead. "Look," Marty continued, looking at Carl, "let's take a worst case—say we settle around here somewhere, okay? Buy a few head. Shoot, Dad knows a lot more about ranching than these folks. It'll take what—four, five years? I'll bet the drought back home doesn't last anywhere close to that long. We sell the calf crop in Laredo, save the money, and in five years we're back home and you're at UT."

"Twenty-three? Twenty-three years old? That's at least one, maybe two wasted years I could'a been playing in the majors, Marty. Look at this place! These people wouldn't know a baseball from a banana. I'll tell you something, I'm not wasting my time here. I'll find a way out. I'll get a scholarship."

"Carl—"

"You don't know. You don't know, Marty! They might have written and that letter's probably sittin' in Mr. Limbley's office right now."

"Yeah, it may be, but that's not the point, is it?"

"What's not the point?" Carl hurled a rock up the road, hard.

"Dad needs us now. Both of us. I know you've got your heart set on college. I'd like to go, too—oh, don't give me that look, of course I want to go, but I figured you ought to go first. Dad and I talked about it three years ago when your baseball really started taking off. I can go to college anytime, C, but you need to get in while you're young and your arm's still strong. It almost killed Dad to have to ask you to pick up and move down here, and believe me, if he has anything to do about it, it won't be for long."

Marty had gotten through, but his little brother needed some time to let it soak in. Carl stayed on his side of the road, and Marty on his. The town lay just ahead. They walked the rest of the way without saying a word.

"Mrs. King, good morning." Estella greeted Hatty with a cheerful smile and a hot cup of coffee. "May I get you some bacon and eggs? You must be starving." She was already up and moving toward the stove.

"Please, Estella, let me do something to help—I feel awful letting you do all this for us. And it's Hatty, please."

"Oh, no, this is a treat for me. I never have company and I really enjoy cooking—so you just relax and we'll visit while I make your breakfast."

Hatty had trouble believing the kindness of these people. She and her family had done nothing but intrude into their private lives, and they had been met only with smiles and generosity. She leaned back in the cane chair enjoying another cup of the strong coffee, the fragrance of bacon sizzling in the pan, and the company of this remarkable woman. Hatty was usually the one to do the talking, but she found herself asking Estella about their life in the valley, trying to find out what made these folks tick.

Over breakfast, Hatty related in great detail all that had happened. She was reliving the events, experiencing them really for the first time. It had all happened so quickly that she didn't have time to *feel* anything the first time, just to react to it in order to survive. Now her emotions were catching up with her, flooding up into her voice, on the verge of breaking through. She exclaimed to Estella how the truck had performed its miraculous balancing act despite being hit by the car.

"I couldn't believe it was still there!" Hatty said, fighting to hold the emotion in check. "I knew—I knew in my heart that it would go over and I'd never see Eli again. And then, then, there was this—this man. . . ."

Estella reached across the table and took her hand. "I know. Angus told me last night."

"Who was he?"

Estella looked at Hatty for a moment before responding.

"Hatty, may I ask you something personal?"

"Certainly," Hatty sniffed into her napkin.

Another pause. This wasn't easy for either of them.

"Are you a Christian?" Estella asked, looking straight into Hatty's eyes.

Now it was Hatty's turn to pause. The question was so unexpected it took her by surprise. She frowned a bit before replying, "Well, yes—I mean I've gone to church all my life and I know that Christ died for our sins—is that what you mean?" No one had ever asked her that before, at least not in a very long time, and it bothered her that she didn't have a better answer.

Estella seemed relieved. "Yes—I am sorry I had to ask, but I had to know before I could answer your question."

Hatty knew something of the superstition of the Mexican Catholics—these people took their religion very seriously.

"May I ask," Estella continued, "are you Protestant or Catholic?"

"We are Baptist, but I don't see what—"

"Ah, so are we," Estella interrupted. She poured another cup of coffee for herself and took a deep breath before continuing. "I know you only just arrived, Hatty, and you will probably be leaving soon, and you must think all this terribly strange. But your coming here at this time—and what you have seen—is so, how should I say, curious."

Hatty didn't realize it, but she was frowning, trying to figure out where in the world this conversation was going. Estella noticed her expression and continued.

"Let me try to explain. There is an old story here," Estella said. "Many years ago, back in the sixteenth century, when Cortez invaded our country, my forefathers—I am a daughter of an ancient people—"

"Really? The Aztecs?" Hatty interrupted.

"No, the *Aztecas* crushed my people. Hundreds of years ago my ancestors followed a peaceful king named Netzahualcóyotl. They fought the *Aztecas*, but most of them were destroyed. Those who survived slowly became a part of the *Azteca* culture. Who knows where the legend came from, but the *Aztecas* believed in a god named Quetzalcóatl, who had been murdered and was supposed to return one day to reclaim his throne. He was supposed to come from the east.

"When Cortez landed on the eastern shore of Mexico with his *conquistadores*, the *Azteca* king welcomed him as the returning god. The king tried to bribe Cortez with great gifts—to try to keep him from reclaiming his throne, of course. He gave him a sun shield of pure gold as large as a cartwheel, and an immense silver moon shield. But Cortez was no god—he was a devil, and he raped this country. Legend has it that he rode a black horse whenever he made his raids on the people—they call the horse *El Diablo*, the devil—and that horse never left Mexico, they say. Cortez left him behind to torment the people. For four hundred years his spirit has run through the villages bringing death and famine—and once a year he comes to snatch up the souls of the dying, adding them to his herd, and making them follow him wherever he goes. That's the story, anyway."

"And you think what I saw . . ." Hatty began cautiously.

"No, no, Hatty." Estella reassured her. "But you must understand. These people—the people in this town and down in the valley—are very superstitious. They are wonderful and loving and kind—and they are my people, but they live in much fear. The old stories are still around—people still tell the old tales at certain times of the year."

"And our seeing the stallion—that might scare some of the villagers?"

"Some of them, yes. Seeing the stallion *and* the herd *and* the man on the horse. It would be better—much better to say nothing."

Estella knew something she wasn't ready or willing to reveal.

It was clear she didn't want Hatty spreading her fantastic story around the village. Hatty didn't really understand why, but she thought perhaps it didn't matter. Doc and Estella had been so kind, the least she could do would be to keep quiet—at least until she got home. In the meantime she was fascinated with what she had seen and how it seemed to parallel the local legend.

"The man on the horse—how does he figure into the story?"

"They call him the rider. Very few have seen him. No one has spoken to him. But he chases the dark one. Angus does not believe in the rider or the dark one. At least not until you came. Now he doesn't know what to think."

"Well, what I saw was no ghost, I can tell you that. He was real. As real as you are sitting here. And those horses were real. We all saw them, not just me."

"I believe you," Estella said. She paused before going on. "I have seen them, too. When I was a little girl about Rosa's age—when my father died. For years I had nightmares. Later on, I finally convinced myself that it was nothing but a dream—well, that isn't quite true. Angus convinced me. He came here nearly twenty years ago as a Christian missionary. He practices medicine to pay the bills, but he refuses to charge people for sharing the good news of Christ—and half the time he won't charge them for the medicine.

"Five of us put our trust in the Lord that first year he was here," Estella continued. "He taught us from God's Word, and my life began to change. Angus helped me overcome my fears. He helped me find real joy for the first time in my life. And for the first time, peace. He wouldn't tell me last night what you had seen. But there was something in his eyes, and—I think—something in yours. I could tell. In my heart I knew you had seen them. I dreamed of them again last night." She was near tears.

Hatty wanted to help but didn't know what to say. "I'm sorry. I—I'm sure there's a logical explanation for all of this. We both saw real horses. Not the same horses, obviously, but real nonetheless. You were a child—your father had just died. You knew the old stories. You must have associated the horses with his death and the dream just stayed with you, that's all."

"Yes, yes, I know. It all sounds so logical," Estella answered, regaining control. "I have no trouble explaining the rider. He could have come from anywhere. But the horses are different."

"Why?" asked Hatty. "Why couldn't they have been some wild horses from the valley?"

"Because," Estella answered, "there haven't been any mustangs in that valley for a hundred years or more."

Carl and Marty entered the town, passing a dingy wooden cantina on their left. It stood apart from the rest of the buildings that lined that side of the street. Four old men, small and swarthy, leaned against the four-by-fours that supported the porch roof, smoking and talking. They stopped talking and watched the two young white men pass up the street. A friendly nod from Marty got no response.

The brothers turned left at the only corner in town and walked past three unoccupied buildings on their left. The white stucco gleamed a cool, soft white in the early morning light. People were beginning to emerge from the low structures to see these strangely dressed *Yanquis*.

The streets, made of dirt with an occasional sprinkling of gravel, were still muddy from the night's rain. The King boys stayed on the cracked and uneven sidewalks that started at the edge of town and ended where the stores began. There, a boardwalk took over and stretched the length of the tired storefronts—perhaps sixty feet—where it ended unceremoniously. Something lay just around the corner of the last store on the right—two posts supporting a wooden sign with a low fence extending back behind the store.

"Hey, there's something to do at night around here after all," Marty said, nudging Carl.

"What?" Carl was still smoldering over being there at all. He looked up grudgingly in the direction of Marty's gaze. "What is it?"

"What does it look like, C? It's a graveyard," Marty said, smiling.

"This close to town? You gotta be kidding!"

"We're in the stone age, little brother," Marty said, slapping Carl on the back.

Marty glanced behind them as they turned to enter the store. Thirteen, maybe fourteen people, he guessed, were standing along the sidewalk and out in the street looking at them. No one had spoken.

"Marshall Dillon, where are you when we need you?" Carl said under his breath.

A man sporting a snow-white mustache and wearing a blue plaid shirt and straw hat passed them on his way out of the store as they stepped inside and closed the door behind them. A small silver bell over the door announced their arrival. An old woman, bent more by life than by years, swept the floor, slowly mixing dust with dust. Behind the counter, a fiftyish balding man in a white apron was talking to a young woman. He stopped in mid-sentence and stared at the two men.

"*Buenos días, Señor,*" Carl said, speaking in his best Spanish. "We are the guests of Señor McClendon. He asked us to pick up some flour for Estella."

"For Estella? One bag of flour, sure. Right back here. . . ." The clerk smiled, obviously pleased at the young man's proficiency in his language. He excused himself for a minute while he got the flour. Carl started to follow him back, but paused when he noticed that Marty wasn't moving. He was staring at the girl, his mouth slightly open.

"Be back in a minute," Carl said, but Marty barely heard. Carl smiled as he followed the owner to the back of the store. He noticed the girl was staring at Marty, too.

Marty's mind was locked on an image of perfection. Long, coal-black hair, flawless caramel skin, high cheekbones that gave her more of an Indian than a Mexican look. And eyes the color of coffee and cinnamon. Never had there ever been a girl like this.

What is your name? That's what he wanted to say. Not much. Just four words. But he was frozen. And she was frozen. The world had stopped—and there wasn't anything else but them. He would never forget this moment, and he knew it. He had just seen heaven.

Marty advanced slowly, feeling as if he were wading through waist-high grass. Feeling like he was twelve years old again and asking a girl to dance for the first time. He felt a breeze from somewhere, cool, ambrosial. He held out his hand.

"Martin King," he said, almost bowing. His voice sounded funny, like he was outside of himself watching himself. She looked up at him and—blinked. His heart skipped a beat. He thought he saw the hint of a smile at the corner of her perfect mouth.

"What . . . ?"

Oh, man, how do you say it in Spanish? he thought. Then he remembered: "What is your—goat?"

The girl's eyes widened, she put her hand over her mouth and laughed out loud. The crystalline moment was shattered. He had ruined everything. She turned and walked back down one of the aisles as the clerk returned with Carl in tow.

"Oh, Lord, what did I say?" Marty asked himself aloud.

Carl plopped down two bags of flour on the counter along with some sugar and coffee. "I told you, brother, you should have taken that Spanish class seriously," Carl said, grinning broadly.

"What did I say?"

"You don't want to know," Carl said. Then to the clerk in Spanish, "How much, Señor?"

"I thought you were just going to get some flour," Marty said, looking at the pile on the counter.

"Well, I figure they could probably use a little extra—it isn't that much."

The clerk had finished writing up the ticket. "Two dollars and ten cents, American," he said, proud of his conversion from Mexican pesos to American currency.

Carl started to pull out his billfold when he remembered how his mother enjoyed peppermint in her coffee. "I'm sorry," he said. "I forgot something—just a minute." Marty followed his brother back down the aisle to get another look at the girl, who had remained at the far end of the store. They heard the bell ring as the door opened. Someone spoke in a low, guttural whisper. Carl scooped out several peppermints from the jar and walked back to the front, leaving Marty to try to make contact with his mysterious maiden.

As Carl returned to the counter, he saw slouched in a wooden chair beside the door a tall, lean man, dressed in felt hat, jeans, and a solid blue work shirt. He sat motionless, a toothpick jutting from the corner of his mouth, hands folded, eyes unfocused on the floor in front of him.

The man behind the counter was shaking his head, frowning slightly as Carl approached. He wouldn't look Carl in the eye. "I am sorry, Señor, the price I told you was wrong. The total comes to—uh—to ten dollars."

Carl was first stunned, then angry. "Ten dollars?! For what? For this? Ten dollars for flour and sugar and coffee?"

The girl moved quietly behind the scene, crossed in front of the man in the chair, and was out the door, like a shadow in the wind. Marty heard his brother's raised voice and returned to the front only a few seconds behind the girl. Carl had a short fuse that burned fast. Sometimes Marty could calm him down before he exploded.

The clerk glanced nervously at the tall man sitting in the corner. He was still looking at the floor, chewing his toothpick. "*Sí, Señor,* ten dollars—please," he said nervously, looking back to Carl and Marty.

"Give him the money, C." Marty didn't want a fight his first day in town.

Carl was oblivious. "Who is this guy, anyway? Does he set the prices around here?" he demanded, jerking his thumb toward the man in the chair.

At this the tall man rose and spoke. His voice was deep and surprisingly quiet. "As a matter of fact, I do," he answered Carl in Spanish. "The man I work for owns this store and most of the business here in Dolores." He took a step closer to Carl, folded his arms, and tipped his hat back a bit. He was measuring the boy. "You talk good Mexican for a gringo," he said without removing the toothpick. "You run a lot of wets on your big fancy *ranchero*, gringo boy?"

Marty didn't understand all the man said, but he could tell he was getting to Carl. He put his hand on his brother's shoulder. Carl was tense, ready to spring.

The tall man continued, his voice calm, analytical, poking, pinching. "I see. No guts. Typical. The dry goods are ten dollars, gentlemen. But they could go up to fifteen real quick, who knows? If I were you, I'd get them while they're cheap."

Marty took out his billfold and handed a ten-dollar bill to the clerk. He picked up the groceries, handed some to Carl, and pulled him out of the store. Carl jerked free of his brother's grip and started marching toward the corner.

"You want to get killed over a couple of bags of flour?" Marty yelled from behind.

Carl wheeled on his brother. "Killed?! C'mon, Marty, that guy wouldn't have the guts to shoot a snake. Besides, he wasn't even wearing a gun."

"You gotta start lookin', C. Guy with a knife like that doesn't need a gun. I saw it when he stood up—strapped to his belt off his right hip. A hunting knife."

This settled Carl down a little, but his pride had been bruised. "I still bet he wouldn't have used it," he said, without much conviction.

"Yeah, and that's why the clerk was sweatin' bullets, right?" Marty retorted. "Just wasn't worth the risk, Carl. Hey, take a look at this." He reached into his shirt pocket and unfolded a slip of paper. On it were two words, written in Spanish. He handed it to Carl.

"Interpret."

"What's this?" Carl demanded, still angry.

"Never mind, just tell me what it means."

Carl read the note. "What? *She* gave you this?"

"She saw me coming and was writing out something when you started your little fracas. She put it under a bottle of picante and took off before I could say anything. At least I got the note. What's it say?"

Carl shook his head. He could read the words, but he didn't understand what they might mean.

"*Los muertos*. It means 'the dead ones.'"

"Let me make this real easy for you, Mr. Carson. You don't own that land any more—*comprende?* You sold it. Mr. Jones bought it from you fair and square; the papers are signed; the land is ours, Mr. Carson."

Jim Pogue waited until the man on the other end of the line began to respond, then dropped the phone into the cradle, cutting him off. "Try to do business in a businesslike fashion," he muttered to himself. "All it gets you is grief. Nothin' but grief."

James Rockford Pogue had come to Laredo via New York, where he had learned to relish his trade: scavenging land from those too poor to maintain a family trust. It was the fifth year of hard drought, and those who had been able to hang on were being pressured into selling at thirty to forty cents on the dollar. Pogue had always been one to savor the sound of contrition on the other end of the phone. He leaned back in his green leather wingback and lit another Lucky. A sleepy ceiling fan slowly mixed the new smoke with the old in an integrated gray haze.

He shifted his enormous bulk back in the chair as his eyes focused absently on a framed relic from his lawyering days in New York, hung as a daily reminder above his office door: *Beati Possidentes*. It was Pogue's credo. The common translation was, "Possession is nine points of the law," but Pogue knew his Latin. Literally it translated, "Blessed are those who possess." He smiled half-consciously at the thought of his new acquisition—and the bonus that was in store.

A familiar sound and movement caught his eye out the window to his left. Through the half-raised blinds he watched a black-and-white slide into the space marked for the sheriff. Glancing at his watch he muttered a quick curse under his breath for having forgotten the time. He rose quickly and went to a cabinet, where he pulled out a bottle of tequila. He jerked open the door to the small refrigerator under the counter, found a lemon, and sliced it into quarters with his buck knife. Grabbing two of the quarters, he filled two shot glasses to the brim and returned to his desk, placing one of the jiggers with the lemon across from him.

Pogue reached down to his file drawer, figuring he had enough time for one last touch. He leafed through the files quickly until he found the one marked "Jones." The manila folder bulged thick with loose-leaf sheets, court orders, memoranda, title searches, and deeds to various holdings. He spread out a few and tucked the folder away out of sight—just as the doorknob turned.

A dark, muscular man entered the room, dressed in the uniform of a police officer. His black hair was slicked back, perfectly straight, his mustache trimmed tightly, giving the impression of being pasted onto his thick upper lip. Pogue could see his reflection in the officer's sunglasses. He loathed this man, but he was the chosen conduit—the runner for his boss.

The fellow had habits that drove Pogue up the wall. For one thing, he always wore his sunglasses indoors. In fact, in the six months Pogue had known him, he couldn't recall ever seeing him without them. Then there was the ever-present toothpick, never chewed. He concealed it somewhere in his huge mouth when he engaged in conversation—but you could never see it disappear. Pogue had tried for months. He wanted to catch him stashing it somewhere when they began to talk. He simply refused to believe that the man could speak with a toothpick in his mouth. Pogue had attempted it himself and nearly pierced his cheek in the process.

The officer sat down in the chair opposite the attorney without a word, grabbed the shot glass with a grin (the toothpick was gone), downed the tequila in a gulp, and bit hard into the lemon.

"I was just going over the Carson deal," Pogue began. "He called again this morning, moaning, trying to back out, but I handled it. He won't make trouble."

"Forget Carson, he's history," the officer sneered. "The boss has something else in mind over the other side of Dalton Springs—some backwater hole called Puentas. He wants you to check it out, see if you can get your slimy little hands on the title. Look into the wills, too, while you're at it."

"Dalton Springs? That's Jake Skerritt's territory, isn't it?"

"He's on the payroll—you shouldn't have any trouble."

Pogue scratched his chin. "Where's the family?" he asked.

"Pulled out for Mexico. I think Skerritt gave the boss a call—look, I don't know. Just check it out." Sanchez rose and crossed to the door. He was in a surly mood today. Pogue didn't want him running back to the boss and whining.

"Hey, they hassle you down there, Pogue, just sit on 'em." Sanchez grinned as he opened the door. He made a sound back in his throat like a pig grunting. He stared straight at Pogue for a split second, as if he were waiting for him to offer some comeback. He let the air escape from between pursed lips in a slow "psssssss" and shook his head in mock pity. "Pogue, Pogue, Pogue," he said softly. The toothpick emerged from nowhere, and he sauntered out, closing the door softly behind him.

Pogue was ready to break something, but he wasn't willing to give Sanchez the satisfaction of hearing him do it. He took a moment to lick his wounds quietly while he stewed over this putrid brown impurity that had just contaminated his office. He rose heavily from the green chair, took his shot glass still full of tequila, and poured it back into the bottle. Pogue never drank before noon and never in the company of someone he didn't trust. Moving slowly back to his desk, he stumbled in his brooding—what was it Sanchez had said? Some blood connection the boss had . . . Pogue didn't like getting mixed up with family ties. Invariably, it got messy.

The other side of Dalton Springs, he thought to himself. He wheeled around in his chair to look at the Texas map on the wall to his right. *Let's see . . . Live Oak County. Yeah, there we go.* He pressed the black intercom lever. "Darlin', we got a new project cookin'."

Two nights later, Pogue was sitting with two other men at the Cadillac bar in Old Laredo at one a.m. under a single buzzing fluorescent tube. Green and red neon lights hawking *cerveza* spilled their faded colors over the bar, across the room, and onto the three. Pogue perched uncomfortably on the edge of his chair, nursing a Margarita, taking only an occasional cautious sip. He needed his wits about him tonight.

Across the table from Pogue sat a pleasant-looking, middle-aged man in a Panama hat and crumpled linen suit. His right index finger repeatedly traced over the rim of an empty glass that, hours before, had held a whiskey sour. His other hand cupped his chin as he listened to the third man, sitting in the middle.

The large, heavyset man in the middle was Sheriff Latigo Jones, who sat back in his wooden chair picking at his fingernails with a hunting knife while he interrogated Pogue about the new project in Puentas. A wide gap between the sides of his mustache accentuated the space between his two front teeth. A fat, half-chewed cigar poked out the right side of his mouth. A cream-colored felt hat was tilted forward on his brow, nearly covering small, almost black eyes—expressionless, lidless, unchanging. His eyebrows had been burned off in a fire when he was a child, and only the outer few hairs had grown back on each side, giving him a look of constant surprise. Part of the right side of his face was dull pink with the slick, plastic look of a burn victim or a painted mannequin.

"Latigo" had earned his nickname early in life—an exotic Spanish name for scorpion. People didn't cross him unless they wanted to get stung. He had grown up bullying and buying his way to power. He paid good money and expected positive results from his lawyer and "economic advisers." He didn't intend to retire on a sheriff's salary, so he used the power of his office to leverage buyouts of debt-ridden farmers whose land promised to yield better crops and cattle after the drought.

No one knew, or asked, where he got the money to buy the land in the first place. No one at the banks in Old Laredo asked where Miguel Sanchez, Latigo's chief deputy working at near minimum wage, got the thousands of pesos he exchanged every other month for American currency. They wondered, and some thought they knew, but no one asked. People who asked the wrong questions tended to disappear suddenly and never come back.

Mr. Jones was upset. He kept his eyes down and spoke in a low rumble, occasionally punctuated by a half-sucking, half-whistling sound through the gap in his teeth. It was clear as he continued the inquisition that he did not take disappointment well.

"King can't be that clean," Jones growled at Pogue. "He's gotta owe something to somebody on that land."

Pogue repeated what he had said time and again at this meeting. "Mr. Jones, I went all the way back. . . ."

"How far? How far back did you go?" Latigo interrupted.

"Back to the McLellan land grant from the government in 1856. You can't go any further back than that. That's where the records stop. Every transaction was clean, from the state of Texas to the Lassiters to the O'Reagans to the Kings. Legal, tight, no holes, no skeletons."

"Everybody's got skeletons, Mr. Pogue," said the man in the linen suit. "Sometimes you just have to dig a little deeper to find them, that's all."

"I know my business, Mangus." Pogue started out slowly but was losing his temper. "I don't need some hotshot hole shooter comin' in—"

"A petroleum engineer, Mr. Pogue," Mangus interrupted.

"You're a wildcatter in a fancy suit, and you're not tellin' *me* how to set up a deal." Pogue banged the table with the flat of his hand so that the glasses bounced.

"Shut up, Pogue," Latigo said, mildly amused at the quivering lawyer. He turned to the man in the linen suit. "He has a point, Mangus. I spent half the night down here, and so far all I've heard is Pogue making excuses and you making big promises. Now either start talkin' details or stop wastin' my time."

Mangus didn't hurry his answer. He looked Latigo straight in the eye, making up his mind about something. "All right," he said. "I had to make sure, that's all."

"Sure of what?" Pogue asked sardonically.

"That Mr. Jones here could fully appreciate the value of a sound investment opportunity." There was a pause.

"C'mon, Boss. I don't like the smell of this." Pogue started to rise.

"Shut up and sit down, and don't make me tell you again," Latigo said under his breath, not taking his eyes off Mangus. "You got five minutes."

"You're familiar with the Vanacek ranch in Puentas?" Mangus continued, unhurried.

"Yeah. Worthless piece of dirt south of the King place."

"Oh, not so very worthless."

Pogue snorted. "You couldn't grow a shadow at sundown on that land, Mangus—you don't know what you're talking about."

"Once more you fail to dig deep enough, my friend. Read your Bible, Mr. Pogue. There, you'll find it isn't what's on the surface that counts, but what runs deep." He reached for a worn, leather briefcase and pulled out a long, rolled paper. He slid the rubber band off quickly and laid out the map for Latigo's eyes.

"We've already seen that survey," Pogue interrupted. "I got it from the title company in Dalton Springs. There's nothing there. No oil, no uranium, no pot o' gold."

"What you saw," Mangus continued, "was fifteen years old and didn't include the two-hundred-fifty additional acres purchased ten years ago from the Vanacek estate. I did this survey myself just three weeks ago. I've been in this business for thirty years, gentlemen. If there isn't oil under that land, I'll eat my hat."

"Look, even if there *is* oil under the new acreage, we should have picked up some trace of it in the old survey," Pogue insisted. "The formations aren't right."

"You missed them, Mr. Pogue, because you were looking for a swimming pool when you should have been looking for the garden hose that leads to the pool. Look at this line. This is the edge of the King property prior to their purchase of the Vanacek land. It also happens to be the edge of what is known as the Puentas Chalk. It's my guess—and I think it's a good one—that the southern boundary of Eli King's ranch runs parallel to a key section of the Chalk. See this trough?" Here he pointed out a sharp dip in the otherwise smooth contours of the survey map. "This is a rift in the shelf. I believe there is oil running from here to here, north to south, and pooling here on the south side of the fault. Can't be exact, but it's close."

"You sound pretty sure of yourself," Latigo said.

"I was down a few weeks ago with an Austin crew. We were shooting some holes for a doctor over in Bellville. Puentas is on the way and the Vanacek property sits just a few miles off the main road. I gathered from a friend in Bellville that Vanacek's kids had moved up the country years ago—somewhere out of state—and had pretty much abandoned the place since the old man died last year. It didn't really amount to much—only about seven hundred acres after the sale to King. I'd had my eye on it awhile, and thought I'd run a survey, shoot a few holes, see if anything popped."

"So the Vanaceks don't know about this?" Pogue asked.

"What they don't know won't hurt us and it won't help them," Mangus offered. "All it took was one hole. And it's no more than two hundred yards from this rift." He pointed to the depression in the map.

" 'Cept that ain't Vanacek's land no more." Latigo was beginning to catch on.

"Yeah, I guess the boys drifted over onto the King place," Mangus offered with a twisted grin. "I tell those boys to watch the lines, but what can you do?"

"So what do you suggest we do, Mangus?" Pogue was angry. "Just march in and start drilling on Eli King's property? Half that county is related to Hatty King. What do you think they're going to do when they see that rig go up?"

Mangus had anticipated the question. "The nearest highway's more than three miles off, and the hole itself would be in a depressed area—a dry creek bed that runs into the river. Apparently, Mr. King and Mr. Vanacek were on pretty good terms. King didn't even have to put up new fence. He just put a wide gap in the existing fence and used the river as a natural boundary on the east side—here," he said, indicating the river boundary on the map.

"Vanacek already had a fence up on the west side to separate the field from some cattle-grazing land. Since neither of them ran cattle on that piece of land, King just never got around to fencing off the southwest corner. That's where my boys came across. The field's mostly overgrown with weeds and low whitebrush now due to the drought. I doubt many folks even know King bought that property, and Vanacek's people are all gone. There's no family to ask uncomfortable questions. This is only one example, gentlemen. There's more—all good prospects, all widely separated. But this is a good place to start, and it's the cheapest to drill."

"What's your angle, Mangus? What do you get out of all this?" Pogue asked.

"Forty percent off the top of every barrel. If the hole comes up dry or salt, I eat fifty percent of the cost of the well."

The room fell quiet. Latigo's chair creaked as he shifted slightly. "You don't have that kind of money, Mr. Mangus."

"I have several out-of-state investors who have great confidence in my abilities. They agree to protect me on a dry well—I guarantee them half my share."

"Then why come to us?" Pogue asked. "Why not just go in and get the land for yourself? Cut out the middle man?"

"Taxes and overhead, Mr. Pogue. I have no interest, nor do my clients, in acquiring land. And the return on this kind of deal is, as you know, far superior to the average oil lease. You have the contacts, the network, and the investment capital to push the deals through. I have information and experience. And I take most of the risk."

Latigo shook his head and smiled, looking down at the table.

"The numbers don't suit you? Talk to me," Mangus responded.

Latigo tipped his hat back slightly as he leaned forward, propping his elbows on the table. "It ain't the numbers, Mr. Mangus. It's you don't know small towns. People talk, that's all there is to it. That well would be the only oil rig in Live Oak County. There's no way you're going to keep those roughnecks quiet. The Monday morning after the first Saturday night it'll be all over the county. Illegal drilling is too risky."

Latigo managed, in Texas at least, to stay just inside the bounds of the law, if not of decency. He continued picking at his fingernails with the hunting knife, considering Mangus closely. "How many other places you got a bead on?"

"Boss—" Pogue tried to interrupt.

"Enough to make us both very comfortable in our old age," Mangus said, ignoring Pogue.

"I want the names of your backers," Latigo said.

"All of my clients, including you, Mr. Jones, must remain anonymous for obvious reasons. I'm sure, being in law enforcement, you can appreciate the delicate position we all share. All transactions are personal and private. No phone calls between offices. No letters. Nothing traceable."

"How are we supposed to . . . ?"

"Call this number between eight and five, Monday through Friday." Mangus shoved a folded piece of paper toward Pogue with a phone number scrawled on it. "Ask for Gus, then leave a number. I'll call you back at exactly ten o'clock that night."

Latigo stared at him for a brief moment with his unblinking eyes, then looked down and made the whistling sound between his teeth. Suddenly he took the knife by the blade and threw it at one of the wooden pillars supporting the ceiling. It stuck tight in the center of the post, about eye-level. "I don't take dictation, Mr. Mangus." He paused, then looked Mangus in the eyes. "Just a friendly word of advice. No one ever crosses me more than once. Understood?"

Mangus nodded and swallowed hard.

"Then I think we can do some business." Latigo turned to his lawyer. "Pogue, I want you to put in a call to Jake Skerritt. He's got dirt on everybody and his kid in Dalton Springs. See what he can dig up on somebody over at the bank. Lay the heat on. We need some cooperation. I want to see what Eli King's got tucked away in his safety deposit box."

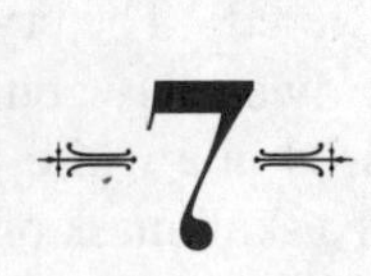

"The bread of the dead?" Carl stood outside the Dolores bread shop with his family and the McClendons. It was November 1, the first day of the two-day Mexican celebration known as the Days of the Dead. Doc had been trying to explain the festival to the Kings ever since they had decided to stay—almost two-and-a-half months ago now.

"Yeah, I guess we forgot to tell you about the bone bread—that's what I like to call it," said Doc. "You remember how I told you they welcome the dead back for two nights out of the year—tonight and tomorrow. Well, the dead relatives get hungry, and these sugar-coated skulls are part of the offering for the dead. Kids'll buy 'em and eat 'em, but they'll always save some to set out at the altar for the spirits of the dead."

"Along with their favorite cigarettes, Coke, wine, maybe a handmade gift or two," added Estella. They continued their walk toward the end of town. "This is how I grew up, believing that the spirits of my dead ancestors came back for a visit once a year. It was our responsibility to welcome them, to make them feel some joy again."

There was a sudden commotion at the end of the street. A crowd had gathered, and music could be heard at the center. Someone was moving, turning in circles. Marty turned to his father and started to ask what was going on when the air was ripped by a scream and then applause.

"El Grito," Doc answered. "The cry of the dead."

As they neared the crowd, they could peer over and through to see a young man dressed in a white T-shirt and jeans. On his head was the upper half of a skull mask of polished porcelain white, complete with trailing white veil. He was dancing in slow, practiced pirouettes, his arms distended, gazing up into the night, whirling to the music for the dead. Suddenly he stopped, threw back his head, grasped the air—and a wail erupted from somewhere just shy of his heart. All of which drew an enthusiastic response from the people.

"If that doesn't raise the dead, nothing will," Carl whispered under his breath to his brother. But Marty was distracted by something beyond the dancer.

"See you folks later. I'm going to look around." Marty walked around the edge of the crowd and out past the end of town. As he passed the last store, he stopped and stared at what lay before him. The Dolores cemetery stretched out into the valley like a separate city of the dead. In the two months they had been in the valley, Marty had visited the cemetery on several occasions, looked at the names and dates on the tombstones, and noted how clean all the grave sites were, but it had been nearly a week since he had been here. It was unlike anything he had seen here—or anywhere before.

The elements before him were familiar, but they didn't go together. It was as if a child had found pretty pictures in different magazines, then ripped them out and pasted them together to create an imaginative if wholly unrealistic scene. Every gravestone was freshly painted. Most were white, trimmed in bright pink and green and yellow. Some had splashes of color, or banded tombstones. A thin haze of copal incense hung suspended in a wispy blanket above the graveyard, establishing an atmosphere of sweetness and an otherworldly calm.

Under a full moon, ridiculously orange in a vast sea of the purest violet, the candle-lighting was still going on. Most of the inhabitants of the valley were there, milling about among the graves, placing and lighting candles. But the most amazing thing was the food. On the top of each grave was at least one and sometimes three or four place-settings of food for the departed spirits, complete with tablecloths, napkins, and silverware. Some of the older people were sitting on the bases of the small stone monuments, speaking softly or simply staring at the graves of their departed relatives. These seemed to Marty to take the event seriously, as if they knew they would be joining their loved ones in that spot before too many more Novembers passed.

Most of the others, however, were standing around talking, joking—even eating! *You don't eat in a graveyard,* Marty thought. And they were laughing out loud. You shouldn't laugh at something serious, like death. These older ones understood. Marty understood.

Unconsciously, Marty reached for something in his shirt pocket. He had gone through exactly the same motion so many times over the last eight weeks that the movement had become automatic when he was in a reflective mood. He pulled out a small sheet of folded paper, traced the creases with his fingernail, then unfolded it slowly and said the words aloud to himself without looking at the paper: *"Los muertos."*

He felt a hand on his shoulder and turned, thinking his mother had found him. Instead he found himself gazing into the eyes of the author of the two words he held in his hand. She smiled shyly and asked in Spanish, "So how is your goat?"

Marty laughed and replied in her language, "I've been working on my Spanish." He held up the piece of paper. "This is what you meant—the Days of the Dead—this time, yes?"

She nodded.

"Good. Marty King." He held out his hand, as he had two months before.

She shook his hand firmly, looking him squarely in the eye. This time she spoke his language. "My name is Maria Cortez. I am working my English." She smiled, pleased with the attempt.

Marty was speechless. "How? How do you know English?"

Maria looked behind her to a small cluster of women and motioned for one of them to join her.

"This is my friend, Anita Martinez. She is like—like—may I speak Spanish?"

"Momento, por favor." Marty saw Carl across the street and motioned for him to join them.

"This is my brother, Carl. Maria Cortez, and Anita—uh . . ."

"Martinez," Anita completed, extending her hand to Carl. She was a year younger, though a shade taller, than Maria and had an infectious smile. Her eyes sparkled in the soft twilight. Carl shook her hand. It was warm and soft.

"Carl King. It's a pleasure to meet you ladies. Has my big brother totally confused you both with his Spanglish?"

"He is doing very well, I think," Maria said, smiling at Marty.

"Why, thank you, Señorita," Marty said, bowing in mock civility.

"Of course, Señor," Maria laughed, with a small curtsey.

"Well, it's obvious they don't need us," Carl grinned. Then, before Maria could object, he turned to Anita and extended his arm, which she took immediately. "Allow me to show you around the town and its lovely cemetery, Señorita Martinez. Are you new to Mexico?" Anita laughed and shot a backward glance at Maria as she walked off arm in arm with Carl.

"I'm sorry," Marty said hesitantly. Maria was still staring after Anita. "I wanted him to interpret for us—for me, that is. You were doing fine."

Maria looked up at him. "Come. We will walk. And we will talk—slowly." She smiled up at Marty and took his arm. He took a deep breath, and wondered what they would name their first son.

Rather than walking back into town after Anita and Carl, Maria and Marty strolled through the graveyard conversing in low voices, occasionally looking at one another, smiling often. The bright colors of the newly painted tombstones were muted now. Evening shadows softened the garishness of the carnival.

They passed among the tombs, where people—mostly younger and middle-aged men—stood in small clusters laughing and talking over the music. Many of the women and a few of the older men puttered among the tombs, wrapped in their shawls, making last-minute improvements on the *ofrendas* for the dead. There was nothing somber or depressing in the faces of these people, or in the music—all of which heightened the mystery of this place for Marty.

Marty stopped. Just to the left in front of him, an ancient woman bent low over a child's grave. The tombstone was old and crumbling, but it boasted a fresh coat of white paint. The old woman's lips were only inches away from the lettering. She whispered over and over to the stone—rocking gently back and forth on her heels. The lower loop in her rosary clicked against the base of the tombstone as she rocked forward.

"This is new for you, yes?" Maria asked.

Marty nodded silently while he watched, transfixed, as the woman prayed, disconnected from the multicolored atmosphere whirling around her. *New,* he thought. *What a strange word for this feeling of being totally alien.* It wasn't that the people of Dolores had made him feel unwelcome. With the rare exception of the local toughs who controlled the town, the citizens of this small village treated the Kings as American novelties at worst and family at best. But for Marty there was an abiding sense of rootlessness, as if he were attending a stranger's family reunion. There was no sense of connection. These feelings seemed embodied here in this shriveled woman, a detached spirit kneeling over a small grave, connecting only with what was ultimately detached.

Maria tugged him back to consciousness, and they continued toward the outer edge of the cemetery. She had been speaking but he hadn't heard. His mind raced to catch up, to try to recall what she had been saying.

"Here it is not like it is in your country," she said. "This is strange to me. You fear death. We make fun of it, talk about it. We dance with death, sleep with death."

"The old woman—"

"She is too close. I do not know her, but I know many like her. She is alone," Maria offered. "Death is her last friend—and, she says, he's the only one who will not disappoint her. She will not laugh at him."

They had come to the edge of the cemetery. Maria stopped beside a simple grave and knelt down. A small white cross adorned a rounded tombstone. A clear jar contained water and other flowers. The inscription on the stone read "*Juan Cortez. Nacer Agosto 1, 1910. Morir Julio 31, 1936. Requiescat in Pace*."

"Your father?" Marty asked.

Maria nodded, saying nothing. Marty knelt beside her and studied the tombstone.

"He was only twenty-six," he said, slipping back into English.

Maria was silent for a time. Then, barely audible, she whispered, "It is only a marker. Our priest, Father Escobar, was kind enough to put it here. They never found his body. He died because of me." She looked up at Marty, blinking back tears. "I am sorry," she said. "I should not tell you this."

Her sudden grief surprised Marty. He felt—what was it—confidence? Love? No—well maybe, but no, not now. . . . He was trying to sort it out, to categorize his feelings even here, even with this magnificent girl—appreciation. That was closer to it. But for what? This pain held up for a stranger to view? *Oh, hang it,* he thought. *You're being too analytical again. Just listen.* Then it hit him with stunning clarity as he lost himself in her eyes: she trusted him. That's what he appreciated. The fact that she would share her tears with him. It was the honor of being entrusted with knowledge of a secret and deeply personal wound.

"No," Marty said, taking her hand. "I want to know. Tell me. Please."

"This is so silly of me," she said, looking away, half laughing, half crying. "This day. It's supposed to be the happiest day of the year. And look at me." She paused and took a deep breath, then continued hesitantly. "I was born on an evil day." She glanced at Marty. There was not even a hint of a smile on his face, and so she decided to go on. "A black Sabbath. A great shadow passed over the sun the day I was born."

"An eclipse," Marty interrupted.

"Ah, eclipse. Yes, the priest told me."

"I have heard his name, the name of your priest, but I forget."

"Father Zeuma is our priest now, but it was a different man then—Father Escobar. He told me about the sign, the eclipse, and the penance I must do."

Marty shook his head. "Father Escobar had you do penance for being born on the day of an eclipse? Why?"

"You do not understand. I was born in the year of the Tochtli. It is a dangerous year of evil omen. The day after I was born Father Escobar came to our home. He told my mother to scrub our house from top to bottom to cleanse it from the curse of the black moon in the year of the Tochtli. That night at midnight she offered food and drink to the spirits of the dead up there."

Maria glanced up at the mountains glowing cold and distant in the wash of moonlight. "The ancient ones used to offer human sacrifice on that mountain. There are times I wish . . ." she didn't complete the thought. "My mother sat there all night praying, watching for the morning, all according to the traditions of my people. Father Escobar had told her what to do. But it made no difference. My father never came home.

"My mother didn't tell me about the curse. But one night—I remember it was on the evening of my twelfth birthday—I went to Mass with Mother. We were the last to leave. I had gone outside ahead of Mother to talk with some of my friends. They had to leave with their parents, and I wandered back into the church looking for Mother. I couldn't see her, but I could hear her voice coming from the prayer room at the back of the sanctuary. She was scared, I could tell. I didn't know what to do. Then I heard something fall, something break, and the door opened quickly. Mother ran out and down the aisle toward me. Just behind her Father Escobar stood in the door wiping the side of his face with the back of his hand. My mother grabbed my hand and pulled me toward the door, but the priest shouted at me.

"'Child!' he said. 'You, child, Maria. Your mother tries to run from me, from God, but you cannot. Come here!' And for some reason, my mother let go of my hand. She sank to the floor, weeping. I wish she had held on to me. I wish she had never let me go."

Marty felt her hand tighten unconsciously in his own.

"I walked up to that man. I was afraid he was going to hit me. He trembled. He had blood on his face and on his hand where he had been wiping it. He looked down at me. I cannot forget his eyes. He said, 'You think your father died in an accident. No. He died because of you. You and your filthy mother. She bore you in the shadow of the black moon. You cursed child. You will die in your sin. No blood of Christ for you, child. No. Only the eternal fires of hell can purge this wickedness. You are excommunicated—both of you. May God have mercy on your souls. Now get out of the Lord's house.'

"I don't remember anything else about that night. Somehow Mother and I made it home. I think I remember going to sleep with her arms around me. But when I woke the next morning she was gone and the front door was open. They found her body at the bottom of the town well."

"What happened to Father Escobar?"

"No one knows. He disappeared the same night. No one has seen him since." She paused, gathering strength. "He didn't kill her," she said with finality. "I killed my mother—just as I killed my father. She lies there." Maria pointed out into the darkness, beyond the fenceless border of the cemetery. "It is a mortal sin to take your own life. She cannot rest in hallowed ground. On this night her spirit will wander from the grave to the old well and back again. It's always the same. I left some of her favorite candies there by her name."

"Where did you go? How did you live?"

"My uncle. The man you saw at the store that first day. I went to live with him and his family. He is a rancher on . . . Martin, look!"

A crowd had gathered quickly back on the main street. Men were running to the edge of the crowd, shouting, trying to force their way in for a better look. Marty picked out the sound of his father's voice at nearly the same time that he heard what he was sure was his mother's scream. He was on his feet quickly, running toward the melee with Maria close behind. He leaped onto the boardwalk for a better view, and there he saw exactly what he knew he would see: his little brother in the middle of a knock-down, drag-out fight—with three men. His father and Doc were on the outer edge of the ring of bystanders, held back by four other men.

Marty shoved his way to the center of the fight. He yanked one of the men's shoulder and plowed his right fist into the surprised fighter's nose, sending him tumbling back into the crowd. Carl added a kick to the belly of a paunchy fellow who had somehow managed to keep his straw hat on during the fray. The third man wheeled on Marty, landing a solid punch to the small of his back. Marty crumpled into the dirt as Carl jumped on the tall man's back and tried to hold him in a hammer lock. Marty looked up from the ground just in time to see the man reach back toward his right hip.

"Hector, stop it!" a woman screamed from the crowd. It was Anita, Maria's friend.

"Carl, he's got a knife!" Marty yelled as he summoned his last ounce of strength to lunge at his brother's attacker. He slammed into the man's legs. There was a loud *snap!* as the man screamed and fell to the street, holding his shattered knee. The other two had melted back into the scenery at the first sign of a fair fight.

Both Carl and Marty were gasping for breath and barely able to stand. Eli and Hatty were at their sides immediately. Marty, leaning on his father's shoulder, aimed a frustrated question at his brother, "What was *that* all about?"

"Jealous boyfriend, I think," Carl wheezed.

"No boyfriend. I hate him," Anita said as she put Carl's arm around her shoulder. "He thinks he is so special just because he can speak English. Ha! My pig can speak better English than he can."

"Okay, miss. We'll take it from here," Eli said, moving his sons away from the crowd. "Let's go, boys. Back to the house, and try to avoid any more fights on the way." Eli and his family walked toward the edge of town. Marty looked back. Maria was nowhere in sight.

"Eli!" Doc called as he trotted to catch up with them. "Sorry, boys. I would have been here sooner, but you left a few broken bones in your wake. You all right?"

"What are you doing helping *them*?" Carl spat out the words, frustrated and angry.

"Medicine doesn't know sides, son. I just help to mend what's broke, that's all."

Carl rolled his eyes.

"Tell you the truth, Carl, you're lucky to be alive," Doc went on. "If Marty here hadn't jumped in that old boy would'a had your hide."

"You know him, Doc?" Eli asked.

"Hector Rodriguez. Comes through about once a month trying to scare folks. Always visits Father Zeuma, then the shops. Never says much, but then he doesn't need to with that pig-sticker he carries around. I saw him use it once in a fight. Kid about your size, Carl, but he didn't have a big brother to help him out. What he did have was a crush on the Martinez girl."

"Hey, I never said—"

"Look, I'm not telling you how to run your life. All I'm saying is be careful. Far as I know Anita Martinez is all right, but she used to run with a rough crowd. Hector's had a little trouble adjusting to the fact that Anita doesn't think he hung the moon anymore."

"I remember him," Marty said. "He was in the store our first day in town. He got Jaime to jack up the price of some groceries. Joe Louis here almost got into it with him then."

"Angus is right. You must not fight them." Estella turned to Eli. "You must not let them." She stood with her arm linked in her husband's. Her voice was calm, but pointed.

Eli wasn't used to being told what to do, especially by a woman. "I can take care of my family, Estella."

"I don't mean to offend you, but you must understand. Rodriguez is not alone. There are more. From the outside."

"Estella, we don't know that—" Doc broke in.

"I know," she said, her voice rising slightly. Then, in a quieter tone, and looking directly at Eli, "Please. To fight like this is not God's way. There is an evil in this, and you cannot fight it with fists and knives." It took great courage to say this. Estella was no mystic. She was a level-headed woman, but she could not deny the suffocating darkness that had been slowly wrapping itself around her heart since they entered town that evening.

"She's right," Doc said, giving her a squeeze around the waist. "Look, Rodriguez's knee is pretty messed up. He'll have to go into Laredo to get patched up. It'll be a few weeks at least before he can get around without crutches—give him some time to cool off. Let's take it one step at a time. You stay clear of him, maybe he'll stay away from you. Fair enough?"

Carl nodded. "As long as he doesn't start anything."

It wasn't the answer Doc was hoping for, but he was willing to live with it for the time being. The Kings started the walk back home, but they hadn't gone fifty steps when Marty turned and started trotting back toward town.

"I'll be right back. Y'all go on, I just need to tell Estella something." Eli and Hatty watched for a moment as he caught up to the McClendons and began speaking to Estella. He pointed back toward the graveyard. They were too far away to hear the conversation. Eli started to go back, but Hatty took his arm.

"He'll be fine," she said. "Let's go home."

With a final glance back, Eli turned and walked with his wife and son down the moonlit road toward home.

"Come in, come in!" Doc stood on the porch of his hacienda, motioning for Eli and his family to join the rest inside.

"Great suspenders, Doc!" Carl said as he snapped one of the cherry-colored straps against Doc's chest.

"Merry Christmas, Doc!" Hatty said, giving him a quick hug. She passed into the kitchen to join Estella and the other women who were preparing the Christmas Eve dinner.

"Merry Christmas! Merry Christmas!" Doc greeted each guest with the same buoyant exclamation and bone-crushing handshake. He had never lost the wonder of the season. "If ever there was a time for men to be boys," Doc always said, "it's Christmas time!"

Rosalinda bounced up and down in the doorway, watching all their friends stream in, wishing them "*Felice Navidad*" in her quiet voice, grinning from ear to ear. The Montoyas were the last to arrive. In all, five families—twenty-six people—crowded into the McClendon home. The air was heavy with the sweet aroma of roast turkey, cranberry sauce, sweet potatoes, and pies.

Christmas wreaths brightened the walls and mantle. Rosalinda's white paper snowflakes, suspended from the rafters by nearly invisible monofilament fishing line, floated just above the heads of the celebrants, each turning in mock pirouette as if conversing first with one, then the other.

Doc was the traditional tree dresser. At his direction, and to Rosalinda's delight, no ornament was left in wrapping. It was his passion to get everything on the tree. This year's project stood erect in the corner nearest the fireplace, a triangular amalgam of glittering color—every chink of green filled with tinsel mail. An engineering marvel to appreciate at a distance. Now, however, because some of the younger elves had been tugging at its popcorn strings and cranberry garland, the diminutive pine, festooned in Christmas finery, tilted uncomfortably toward the center of the room. A bright angel in silver dress and sparkling halo maintained a precarious watch from the top bough, her "o"-shaped mouth signaling mild distress at dipping so near the earth. Only the barricade of presents that had been piling steadily at its base prevented, or at least delayed, total collapse.

A hand-lettered tag dangled from each present—one to a customer. This avoided competition and helped keep the focus where it belonged at Christmas. They had all drawn names from Doc's black hat, and each year for the past three they had added the names of a new family. This year the four Kings and Mrs. Perez joined the others in Doc's hat with Anita and Maria added as special guests.

These weren't just friends and neighbors. Most of these folks shared something much deeper than blood ties. The Montoyas and their three sons, the Carreras with their daughters, Mr. and Mrs. Alaniz and their three children—and for the last two months, Mrs. Perez—all attended Sunday morning worship in the McClendon home. This was Doc's house church.

As soon as Carl crossed the threshold, his mouth dropped open—he hadn't expected to see Anita there. Marty had already discovered Maria and wrapped her in a tender embrace. Estella smiled as she watched the young lovers walk outside where they could talk in softer tones. She had asked Maria and Anita to come as a surprise weeks before. The reunion was even brighter than she had anticipated.

On this once-a-year special occasion Doc brought in the long table from the back yard and joined it to the much shorter kitchen table. One end reached almost to the mouth of the fireplace; the other stopped just short of the kitchen cabinets. Doc stood at the fireplace end of the table and clinked on his glass.

"All right, folks, time to eat!" They all joined hands, bowed their heads, and closed their eyes. The Montoyas sat closest to Doc at the end of the long table. Beside them, Sam Carreras balanced his enormous frame next to his wife, Juanita, who sat beside Hatty and Eli. Across from Ray Montoya was Estella, then Mrs. Perez, then Marty, Maria, Carl, and Anita, and the children deposited around the smaller end table.

As Doc gave thanks for all the Lord's blessings, he remembered to thank God particularly for each family at his table. The prayer was rich and heartfelt. Doc and Estella had stood with these people through extraordinary times—most of them within the last two years. During their first years in Dolores they had prayed consistently for the Lord to soften the people's hearts, but these villagers had inherited the superstition and fear of their forefathers, stretching back hundreds of years. The McClendons needed a chance to show them how much they cared.

It had all started with the Montoyas. Ray and Renee Montoya had lost their little girl to leukemia two years earlier. Doc had done everything he could to save her. He had brought her into the world, nursed her through colds and stomach viruses and measles. He had given her piggyback rides. He had taught her how to read and how to make grass whistle when you stretch it and blow across it just so. He had told her about the love of Jesus and held her hand as she asked Him into her young heart. Doc and Estella had high hopes for little Elisa Montoya, but when she began to fade there was nothing Doc could do.

When it became obvious that Elisa was dying, Doc stayed with her deep into the night, stroking her hair, talking with her about how wonderful heaven was going to be, until she slipped into a coma. Ray wasn't there at the time. It was a Friday night, and as usual, he was down at the cantina, drinking warm beer and trying not to lose his shirt at poker. Renee knelt beside her daughter's bed praying, fingering her rosary in the dying light of a thick yellow candle. There wasn't much to say in a death watch. Doc knew that. He had been in this kind of situation before, but that didn't make it any easier just to sit by and wait for it to happen.

Father Zeuma had been praying too, in his room at the church. He rose slowly from the small altar, feeling a need to walk and pray, to keep watch over this house. He hesitated. One of the neighbors had told him hours before that Elisa Montoya was very sick. His stomach was churning. He wanted to be there. But he had been warned not to visit the homes of these poor—these who could not pay for a blessing. He despised the men who threatened him, but he feared them more. He wasn't the only one—it was the same in the other villages.

Other priests were holed up in their small rooms praying for the poor in their parishes—and for forgiveness, and for deliverance from the greedy, powerful men who demanded money. It would be worse for Zeuma's people if he did go. He didn't doubt for a moment the willingness of these evil men to carry out their threats. Still, to bow to their intimidation ground into his conscience like powdered glass. This night he would go, and pray he would not be seen.

The moon was full as he walked out of his small room, heading for the edge of town. He passed the amber-lit cantina, measuring his steps—they always seemed louder at night—toward the line of shacks that housed dirt farmers like Ray Montoya. One light flickered from a window in the last house. He knocked gently at the door. No answer. He could hear someone weeping softly inside. He opened the door slowly and went in.

The Father knew this little three-room house as well as he knew any in Dolores. He had visited here often before the outsiders had come. He walked quietly through the darkened house to the back room and placed his hand on Mrs. Montoya's shoulder. She grasped it instinctively and kissed it without looking up. A glance at the girl and then to Doc told him Elisa was gone. He had known this would happen. He had known before he left the church, and he was prepared.

Doc left as the priest began to administer the last rites. He walked slowly up the moonlit road toward the cantina. He had not been inside in months; Doc wasn't welcome there. Business tended to drop off when he came around. He walked slowly, trying to control the anger that burned deep in his gut, rehearsing the speech he would utter through clenched teeth to the unrepentant father. Tonight he was a Jeremiah.

Halfway there, he met Ray on his way home, dead drunk. In an instant all the anger drained away. The love of Christ washed over him as he stood motionless on the moonlit road, waiting for the poor wretch to stumble into his arms. He made his way back to the Montoya house half-carrying Ray, asking the Lord's forgiveness for his anger with every other step.

Father Zeuma met them at the door. Mrs. Montoya had fallen into a troubled sleep, exhausted, and Doc had been on his way to see if he could help with Ray. After they maneuvered Ray into bed, they sat down at the kitchen table and lit the oil lamp so they could talk things through. It would be the first time they had really talked at all. To the surprise of both, they spent most of the time praying for Ray and his family.

In the course of their prayers, Father Zeuma felt a growing trust in this man. He wondered if the Lord might have brought Angus McClendon to Dolores for a very unusual purpose. He had to confide in someone. He had to find a way to help his people. If the Lord would not take away the evil men who threatened the church, perhaps He would provide for their needs in another way. A way he couldn't have anticipated. So somewhere in the middle of that night he asked Doc McClendon to take the Montoya family quietly into his care.

Doc agreed, wondering what the Lord might be doing here on this night in this house in this heart. Had he been so spiritually thick that it took the death of a little girl to bridge the chasm, to splice these two unmatched lives?

Father Zeuma's visit hadn't been a decision of the moment. It had actually been a long time coming. It was no secret to Enrique Zeuma that Angus McClendon was a Protestant missionary as well as a medical doctor. In the years since Zeuma had moved in to replace Father Escobar, they had had little contact. Substantive theological differences conspired with racial suspicion and a kind of spiritual provincialism to keep them at opposite ends of town. Gradually, however, the priest began hearing of Doc's sacrificial giving, how he rarely charged the poor for his services, how he gave away much of his medicine and called on his patients simply to check in and say hello. It didn't fit with what he had been told about American Protestants—either in seminary or by Father Escobar. And so he watched and waited until the night Elisa Montoya died.

Doc and Father Zeuma nursed the family through the long nights that followed. It was death as usual: the wave of grief that spreads in widening circles to the edges of life, gradually diminishing until the pain and the memories settle into a murky calm—and the whole thing takes on the cadence of recycled themes from a tired symphony.

Estella worked with one of the other farm wives, Juanita Carreras, to coordinate meals and baby-sitting. Gradually, the three families became friends. In time, even Ray Montoya began to soften and confide in Doc—not so much as a confessor as a compassionate friend. His shame was unbearable. Days passed after the funeral before he could bring himself to face any of his neighbors. The Montoyas started coming to the McClendon home on Sundays for prayer and Bible study three weeks after Elisa's death. Four months later, the Carreras joined them with Father Zeuma's blessing. That was nearly two years ago. Now they were closer than family.

Mrs. Perez had been coming for a little over a month. Her husband had been killed years before in a bar fight in another town. She had moved to Dolores fifteen years ago along with her six-year-old daughter to live with her brother, only to lose both of them to a flu epidemic the next year. She was able to find small jobs around town, but she never married again. These days most of her time was divided between cooking for the bakery, cleaning for the shopkeepers, and visiting her daughter's grave.

Her hope had shriveled until all she lacked on that last night of the festival was the courage to take her own life. That night she had been kneeling in her familiar spot beside her daughter's grave, praying for her soul and asking the Lord to take her to be with her child and husband. She had prayed so often. Why wouldn't He hear this simple request? Why wouldn't He answer her with death when He took so many who had prayed to live? Then out of the corner of her eye she noticed something. In a world that always passed her by, someone had stopped. A young couple stood nearby, watching.

Mrs. Perez pretended not to notice. Most of the people in town had grown accustomed to seeing her there. Over the years she had become a fixture in the graveyard, assuming the same humped shape, the same immobility as the other markers of the dead. Why would these people stop and stare? As if they didn't know. She let the thought carry her back through years of faces until she saw her daughter's lifeless eyes again, and then her own as if in a mirror—and they were the same.

Mrs. Perez knelt alone in the cemetery, the other celebrants having abandoned their posts to watch a fight in the middle of the town's main street. Perhaps a half-hour later, Estella McClendon walked up. She had always been kind—always ready with a smile and a word of greeting. But that night, she was much more direct. Estella knelt there with her in the dust beside her daughter's grave and asked Mrs. Perez to come for a visit the next day. To her own astonishment, Mrs. Perez accepted.

That was the beginning of a friendship such as she had never known before. For the first time in many years, she felt that she was not alone. How many years had she spent crying in the shadows? She had lost count. This Christmas Eve she would cry again, but this time the tears would not come from a sorrowful heart.

The meal was a roaring success, with much laughter and many wonderful stories. The children were excused early to go outside and play in the crisp twilight until dessert was ready. Candles were lit on mantle and table and placed in windows. Though the evening had been building to this, the metamorphosis seemed instantaneous. The home took on a nostalgic softness that was at once real and illusory: real to those who had been given the gift of Christmas sight; illusory to those who were enchanted but not yet transformed by joy.

Estella and Hatty cleared the table, put away the extra food, and started two pots of rich coffee brewing while Renee washed the dishes. Doc and Eli manned the dish towels.

"Here," Marty offered, "let me give you a hand with that." He reached out to help Estella with a large container.

"Shoo!" she said. "You're just in the way in here. Why don't you young folks get some fresh air?"

Doc turned, dish towel and pot in hand. "You better get while the gettin's good, kids. She only makes that offer once a year!" He laughed his big-bellied laugh. Estella winked at Marty and smiled.

"Don't have to kick me in the head. C'mon, Nita." Carl was already halfway out the back door.

"Thanks," Marty said. "We'll be back in a few minutes." He took Maria's hand, and they walked out onto the front porch. Marty closed the door softly behind them.

They walked slowly down the short lane from Doc's house, not saying anything. As they rounded the bend onto the main road, they could see the village laid out before them in a string of twinkling lights. The farmers' shacks, the small homesteads scattered across the floor of the valley, the shops in town, and even the cantina all sported flickering candles. Clouds were lumbering in from the north, pushing a wave of biting air ahead of them. Marty looked toward the west. Resting just above the horizon and glittering brilliantly, Venus defied the clouds to cast a shadow on this night.

Maria moved in under Marty's arm.

"Venus. In the old stories the Greeks called it Hesperus when it set in the west as the evening star and Phosphorus when it appeared in the east as the morning star."

She was quiet for a moment. She looked back into the wind and whispered, "*Ehécatl.*"

"What?" Marty asked.

"Ehécatl. It means 'wind.' There is a very old story Father Escobar used to tell all of us when we were children. It used to scare me so badly I would have bad dreams in the night." She laughed, but Marty could tell the memory was not a pleasant one. "Many years ago, in the days of the Toltecs, there was a legend of a great god named Quetzalcóatl. They say he descended to the hell world of Mictlan on a great quest. He roamed back and forth through the vast chambers of Mictlan, gathering the bones of the ancient dead, the dead not of this world. Those bones he sprinkled with his own blood, and they became our ancestors, the men of earth."

Her eyes were fixed on Venus, her body relaxed and very still. Her voice had changed only subtly, but the effect seemed to suspend ordinary reality. Marty found himself drawn irresistibly into a quiet flow, the words more like a chant than normal speech—a story Maria had heard so many times, repeated so often in her dreams, that it had become a part of her.

She continued. "Quetzalcóatl ruled over the days of ehécatl, the days of the wind. He was a great god and good. He ruled as the priest-king of Tula, the capital of the Toltecs. Many of the gods were vicious. Many, like the Aztec god Huitzilipochtli, demanded the blood and beating hearts of men. Quetzalcóatl never offered human victims, only snakes, birds, and butterflies.

"But there was an enemy, great and powerful in the use of the black charms. Tezcatlipoca, god of the night sky, expelled him from Tula by his dark power. Quetzalcóatl wandered down to the coast of the 'divine water'—the great Atlantic. There, he gathered wood into a pyre and offered himself as sacrifice. Out of that fire he rose as the star we see now. But he will not remain there far away in the heavens. He promised to return"—she turned to the east and pointed to the blue-black horizon—"there. Quetzalcóatl's calendar name was Ce Acatl, One Reed. He will return in a One Reed Year to reclaim his kingdom from the god of the night."

Maria's body had grown stiff. Now she breathed deeply and

relaxed. So did Marty.

"You know the story of Cortez?" she asked. "Why do you think the Aztec Montezuma let him walk in and take his kingdom? Hernan Cortez sailed here from Cuba, to the east in the year 1519—a One Reed year."

"Montezuma thought he was a god—Quetzalcóatl," Marty finished the story for her.

"I know it's a child's story," she said. "But sometimes I ache to believe it." She turned to face Marty. "No, it's more than that. Sometimes something inside me *does* believe it. I know it's foolish. Like a child. That part of me will not grow up." Tears welled in her eyes.

Marty wrapped her in a warm, affectionate embrace, and spoke softly to her of another story in a different land, and another star. One that shone more brightly than any before or since. He told her of another King who yielded to the prince of darkness but rose victorious over death. He told her that this King would come again to reclaim His Kingdom and His people from the god of night.

Then he told her that this story was true, that the desire of her heart to know the true King could be granted. They held each other tightly, then they kissed. The wind shrieked around them in a bone-chilling blast, then settled down to an icy calm. Snowflakes fell like manna, slowly at first, then steadily increasing, blanketing the winter valley, the village of Dolores, and the young lovers. They turned and walked slowly back up the road, through their dream world to Doc's home. They never looked back.

They never saw the slow-moving clouds slip a cold veil over the face of the evening star.

"Will you hold still? How do you expect me to tie this with you wiggling like a schoolboy?" Hatty had been fussing with Eli's string tie for five minutes.

"You know I hate these things. I thought I left this piece of devilment back in Texas."

"You did. I found it when I was cleaning out the drawers. I had a feeling you'd be wanting it down here—there! Done. Now just don't fiddle with it and it'll stay fine all day." Hatty hurried off to the kitchen to add some last-minute touches to the wedding cake.

Eli considered his wife's work in the tarnished mirror and shouted after her, "It's a good thing it's still cool, is all I've got to say, or this father would be tieless!"

"Oh, hush your fussin' and give me a hand with this," she called from the kitchen as she brought out a delicate, white lace tablecloth that her grandmother had made. She unfolded it carefully and handed one corner to Eli as he walked into the kitchen. "Oh, I almost forgot! We got a letter from Beau Holliman yesterday. I think it's in my purse."

"Run get it, we can finish this in a minute."

Hatty found her purse and ripped open the letter from their old friend back home. There was something about the way Hatty read aloud—it could have been letters, books, or a soup-can label—that delighted Eli. More than half the fun of getting letters was hearing Hatty read them.

"All right, let's see . . . oh, it's just a note, really. Oh well:

"Dear E and H,

"Got your letter of the fifteenth. Was going to wait to write a longer letter but know you needed a speedy reply. I can't believe those boys are old enough to get married. Give them all my love. I never realized I'd miss you all so much. Hatty, I know you're reading this to Eli. Tell him that gal from Waco didn't work out. She was ready to get hitched and I wasn't even out of the stall yet.

"What girl from Waco? You never told me about any girl from Waco!" Hatty interrupted herself, giving Eli a look of mock reproach.

Eli's face broke into a mischievous grin that kept Hatty guessing. "He's pulling your leg, Hat. Go on."

Hatty continued reluctantly,

"Wish I could make it, but this drought is taking its toll—I'm afraid I might have to pull up stakes and head north. I don't want to sell, but I've got a firm offer from some fellow out around Laredo. Looks like I'll probably have to if I want to have enough money to buy a few head up in Colorado. Too, I'm looking at some land. You might recall that little piece I bought back in '49 southeast of Alamosa. Turns out my neighbor up there wants to unload about five hundred acres. If I do decide to go I'll be sure to get somebody to check on the place for you. I'll drop you a line when I get settled.

"Speaking of which, I wouldn't mind seeing just where you settled. Where *are* you, anyway? I can't find Dolores on any map. I figure you're probably living in the south of France dancing the hoochy coochy till all hours—you just found some Mexican stamps to throw me off your scent!

Don't worry, your secret's safe with me. You folks be good. God bless!

"Love, Beau

"P.S. Appreciate your prayers for rain. April used to be a wet month, but it's been a long time now. I've never seen this country so bad. Will check in on the place for you in the next week or so."

Hatty held the letter, looking at it. Eli rose from the table and walked up behind her, resting one hand on her shoulder and gently caressing her face with the other.

"Now, don't go clouding up on me, Hat. If Beau needs to move it's not the end of the world. He knows what he's doing."

"Oh, it's not that," she said, pressing his hand to her cheek. "I know Beau will be all right. It's our boys I was thinking about. He's right. Beau's right. They aren't old enough to get married. Lord a'mercy." She took Eli's arm and wrapped it tight around her, cradling her head against his forearm.

"My sons' wedding day." Eli shook his head. He had overcome many of his prejudices against Mexicans during his months in Dolores, and the recent announcement had hardly been a surprise; but the idea of his sons marrying two Mexican girls on the same day—and one of them a Catholic—had stretched his newly evolved impartiality to the breaking point.

"What in the world got into Carl's head anyway, converting to Catholicism just so he could marry this girl?" Eli exclaimed to Hatty. Then, half to himself, "We've never had a Catholic in this family. Never."

"Eli . . ."

"Ever."

Hatty was quiet for a minute. They had been over this ground before, and every time the discussion had escalated into an argument that ended with Eli walking away in a huff, leaving Hatty frustrated and angry. She decided to stop this one before it got started.

"I think we ought to start looking for ways to build bridges," she said. "We have two sons who are getting married today, and that's all there is to it. I don't want us going to either wedding with you upset. I need for this to be a happy day, Eli. I need you with me."

Eli took a deep breath. "Okay, I'm sorry. It's just—well, I think of what my folks would have said."

"Can you see Uncle Josiah?" Hatty said, beginning to smile.

Eli grinned and shook his head. "If that old man hadn't died of meanness, this would have done the trick." They both laughed and hugged again.

"They'll be fine. They will. I'm sure of it. I'm crazy about Maria, and I'm sure we'll grow to love Anita just as much." She said it with a bit of forced confidence as she looked up into her husband's dark brown eyes.

"Oh, the girls are no problem," Eli said quietly.

Hatty could smell a punch line coming.

"It's just, I don't know if I like the idea of being married to a mother-in-law!" He laughed and squeezed Hatty hard so she couldn't hit him.

"Estella! Estella, I can't find the veil—oh, this house!—where is it, do you know?" Anita and her mother were tearing from room to room, looking for the white gauze *velo* for the nuptial mass. The wedding was set for ten; it was nine already, and they were a collective wreck.

Estella answered from the kitchen, "Beside the bed, in the white box on the chair—find it?" There was a knock at the front door.

"Señora McClendon, the door." Anita's mother barked from the back bedroom. Consuella Martinez had the voice of a drill sergeant and the bulk to back it up, though she was only five foot four.

"Yes? Who is it?" Estella was at the door and exercising greater than usual caution.

"Please, Estella, can't I just talk to her? I don't have to come in, I just want to tell her something." It was Carl. He had already been to the house twice that morning, the first time at six and then again at seven. Señora Martinez's eyes flashed, her short supply of patience nearly exhausted. She started to move, but before she took two steps Estella was through the door and had closed it gently but firmly behind her. Carl stood before her looking sheepish and tugging at the tie that almost went with a suit that was on the verge of being too small. Estella suppressed a smile.

"Carl, I don't believe in luck, but if I did, I'd say you're pushing it."

"I just want to talk to her."

"That's a good sign. But you'll have to wait. You two will have a lifetime to talk—and listen. Don't forget to listen. It's often the most important part of talking—"

"Señora McClendon! The shoes!" Señora Martinez bellowed from the bedroom, but her voice pierced the walls.

"Looks like I'm being summoned," Estella said as she turned to duck back inside.

"Señora McClendon!" As the door burst open behind Estella, Carl turned and took off down the lane. "*Men!*" said Señora Martinez as she stormed back into the house. Estella followed, biting her lip slightly and closing the door gently after her.

A pale April sun washed the old church in a soft light. The white stucco walls seemed less harsh; the Spanish tile covering the main roof, cupola, and bell tower more crimson than red. Two massive oak doors, carved to fit the arch of the vestibule, swung on black iron hinges. A bronze-on-black plaque, nailed to the wall just outside the front entrance, heralded the church's name in bas relief: *La Iglesia del Corazón Doloroso*, The Church of the Suffering Heart.

Inside, candlelight radiated off cool walls. The penny candles of the poor had been replaced in recent months by a more elegant variety nestled in red pebbled-glass holders, all lined up in neat rows on the votary table just inside the vestibule. The nave of the

Dolores church was understandably abrupt, given the small population of the community. It would have held no more than 175, but it was rarely half that full. In the chancel above the altar, a beautifully carved eight-foot-tall crucifix hung against the western wall, so that the face of the Lord was turned down and away from the pulpit. Special candles reserved for the nuptial mass cast a silver light from shining candelabra, illuminating the bridal gown with a pure radiance found only in fantasy. The bride fairly sparkled when she moved.

It was as large a wedding as Anita and her mother could muster in the three months they had to prepare. The Martinez money was a matter of common envy in Dolores—they were one of the most affluent families in the church due to some shrewd business dealings in land and cattle by Señora Martinez' father. Anita had three bridesmaids, childhood friends who came up from Mexico City, with Maria serving as maid of honor. Carl asked Ray Montoya, Sam Carreras, and Jaime Dominguez, owner of the dry goods store, to serve as groomsmen, with Marty as best man. Everything bridal about the ceremony, from the pink silk brocade on the bridesmaids' gowns to the tufted velvet pillow that bore the gold wedding rings, was anointed with the perfume of money. The groom and his entourage did the best they could with what they had—they were only a minor annoyance for Señora Martinez, however, since she never saw them.

Father Zeuma's ceremony went flawlessly. Carl had been baptized into the Catholic faith only the week before, and then only at the urging of Father Zeuma and the insistence of Señora Martinez, who viewed spiritually mixed marriages as one step shy of a brothel arrangement and less permanent. Their public union thus received the full blessing of the church, though Carl's conversion was a bit too utilitarian for Father Zeuma's taste. Still, he did demonstrate a willingness to yield to the church's authority, and that was a good sign.

The reception took place at Doc's house and lingered until late in the afternoon, the guests eating and talking, oblivious to the fact that Maria and Marty needed time to prepare for their own wedding at six-thirty. Maria graciously served refreshments and visited up to the last minute. At five, she excused herself, and Eli and Hatty rushed her back to their home to dress.

From the time of his brother's wedding Marty had watched his bride-to-be, marveling at her poise and grace. Anita's family had been able to afford the Cinderella gown, the beautiful church, the fairy-tale wedding. But it was Maria who cast the spell. She was the calm in the eye of the storm. Nothing upset her—not the anxious bride, nor her bellicose mother, nor the gaggle of giggling debutantes who fluttered about waiting to be admired. They all swirled around Maria as a mist curls around a mountain, leaving her as unfazed as the moon in a cloudless sky.

Marty was as captivated by her serenity as by her beauty. He knew it, and he reveled in the enchantment. This was the woman, not the girl—she would never be a girl again in his eyes—this was the woman with whom he would celebrate the rest of life.

Doc's garden provided the natural environment for Martin and Maria's early evening wedding. The sun was still well above the horizon as the small party gathered together. Evening light filtered through leaf and lattice, creating a soft-edged mosaic of shifting patterns. Maria joined Marty and Doc under the white arbor near the well at the center of the garden. Family and a few friends stood on the perimeter of the stone circle. The vines twined in and out, transforming the cross-hatched canopy into a fragrant bower. There the young lovers stood, Maria holding a bright bouquet of garden flowers in one hand, Marty holding her other. The words from Genesis, "what God has joined together . . ." twined around their hearts, elegantly uniting them in an indissoluble bond. In the prayer of consecration, they took an unconscious breath as one, deep and pure, absorbing all the garden had to offer, merging in rhythm with the whispering leaves and the barely discernible pulse of night.

There was no reception, since both couples had some traveling to do that night. The newest Mr. and Mrs. King made their way back to the house to prepare for their honeymoon, while Carl and

Anita put what little remained of their luggage in the back of their new truck, a wedding gift from Anita's parents. With loud goodbyes, many hugs, and a great honking of horns, they drove off for Laredo where they would stay the night and then catch a plane for Saint Croix for a two-week stay, compliments of Anita's uncle Ramon, who lived there.

Marty and Maria had finished most of their packing, but there were a few last-minute items to be tied down. One was the wedding band Maria had given her husband, which had belonged to her maternal grandfather. It was just a bit too big. Marty wrapped a small piece of string around the lower half of the ring and tied it off, then slipped it back on for a perfect fit. Maria was surprised at the scant provisions Marty had packed, but she knew she could trust him to bring what they needed.

They emerged from the house dressed in jeans and woolen shirts and cowboy hats. Eli and Doc already had the horses saddled and the gear tied down. They mounted quickly and trotted off to the north just as the sun slipped below the horizon—off to a surprise location for a week-long honeymoon.

Marty knew that his bride loved camping and the outdoors, so he had spent the better part of five weeks exploring the mountains and valleys around Dolores by horseback, looking for a special place to bring his bride. It had to be somewhere they could be alone, where no one else had ever been, but where everyone would like to go—if they knew. On the way back from one outing to the north, Marty took a wrong turn and found himself in a narrow, twisting ravine that was wholly unfamiliar to him. Since he had plenty of daylight left, he decided to follow the rocky trail as far as time would permit.

After about a quarter mile, the sides of the ravine grew very high, and Marty found himself climbing a fairly steep grade. He urged his horse on around a bend in what now appeared to be a significant canyon. After negotiating a hairpin turn, he swung into a straight stretch nearly half a mile long. Although it was still more than an hour before sunset, it had now grown quite dark. His eyes had been focused down on the rocky bottom of the canyon, watching his horse's footing, but the sudden decrease in light compelled him to look up.

The walls of the canyon crept up almost three hundred feet above him now on both sides, and seemed to grow together at the top. The opening at the rim was so narrow, in fact, that for much of its extended length, the upper branches of large trees on either side formed an arbor, sealing off the canyon rim from all but the most persistent sunlight. The sides, too, had gradually narrowed until now no more than five horses could stand side by side.

There was no wind, no breeze; yet Marty thought he could detect a rushing sound. He looked ahead, straining his eyes to see in the half-light. Fifty yards up the canyon, just in front of a sharp bend, he thought he saw something moving—a small rivulet that ran across the canyon floor and down the other side where it was swallowed by a tumble of rocks and earth. He dismounted and scooped some of the ice-clear water into his mouth. It had the frosty bite of fresh melted snow. He was higher than he thought.

He followed the little stream for a few yards, leading his horse, creating a path, until he rounded the bend. As soon as he passed the corner stone, he looked up and stopped instantly, stunned by what lay before him: a green, sun-drenched meadow filled with what appeared to be daisies and bluebonnets. At the far side of the meadow lay a small lake as blue as liquid sky, fed by an icy crystalline stream that snaked down the mountainside and splashed across large rocks into the lake. Most of the mountains were still capped with snow, the slow spring melt providing the runoff that swelled the stream slightly beyond its normal capacity.

The mountains themselves were an exquisite blend of violet and pine-green set against slate-gray and white. But the most striking effect was their immediacy. They were so close they seemed to be slowly moving inward all the time, and so Marty's gaze returned to the lake and meadow. The whole bowl-shaped valley—though "valley" seemed too grandiose a term for such a diminutive vale—couldn't have totaled more than five acres.

Everything here was so quiet. So magical. Like the river back home, in its way. Marty half expected to see little Mexican leprechauns with tiny sombreros sprouting from the rocks, or Robin Hood's men dropping like pine cones from the trees. At the base of one of the mountains nearest the lake, a large cleft in the rock caught his eye. As he approached the opening, he could tell it was a fair-sized cave that might well reach deep into the heart of the mountain. He dismounted and strode into the cavernous opening. It was just spooky enough, and the light was just low enough, to remind him of the lateness of the hour. He conducted a hasty survey for predators and found only deer sign around the outer edge. It would make a fine shelter, he thought, especially if they kept a fire going.

Over the next few weeks Marty visited the place often, tucking away in a secure spot in the cave camping gear that would make their stay more comfortable. He explored the cave more carefully now until he felt satisfied that no animals of any size inhabited it. He draped a canopy just outside the entrance and made a thick bedding of pine boughs covered with several soft blankets. The night before the wedding he carried food and drink and gathered enough firewood to last a month. The champagne, which his father had brought as a present from Laredo just for the occasion, he left chilling overnight in the lake.

He had marked the trail well, knowing they would probably arrive well after dark, which they did. Marty had not been there himself in the deep night, and so it was a new vision for him, too, as he and his bride rounded the last rock bend to look out on their high Eden. The air was brilliant, so crisp they could snap it if they could catch it in their hands. A silver moon doused the vale in stainless-steel light, so that trees and lake emerged in clear and precise outline. Sounds printed themselves on the darkened landscape, assuming an aural definition more truly their own than the unremarkable version rendered by the full light of day.

Marty tied their horses to two saplings near the stream. Then he took his wife's hand as they walked around the lake to the cave. The low grass grew right up to the lake's edge. Maria knelt there and closed her eyes as she took in a deep breath. Before her, the water lay as a cobalt-blue mirror under the night sky, reflecting not only the moon but the stars as well, accentuating their cerulean luster.

"Oh, Martin, it's wonderful. I've lived here all my life and I never knew this place existed. What should we call it?" Maria asked as she gazed into the lake and then up to the sky.

"Oh, I never was any good at naming things. I wanted to save it for you. This is your place. You get to name it."

"It's our place. From now on what's mine is yours," she said, turning into his arms and looking up to meet his eyes. "Wherever you go I will go. Wherever you live I will live, and I will love you till the end of my life."

Marty drew her close to him. His heart was beating so hard he thought it was going to leap out of his chest. He had never seen any woman so radiantly beautiful in his life. What could he say to the soft wonder in his arms? How could he tell her how exquisite she was? He looked deep into her sparkling eyes—and words from a half-remembered play returned, slowly at first, and then with growing confidence. "What if your eyes were there," he said, glancing up at the stars, "and they in your head?" He looked at her and smiled. "The brightness of your cheek would shame those stars as daylight doth a lamp. And your eyes would through the airy regions stream so bright, that birds would sing and think it were not night."

"That's so beautiful. Did you write it?"

Marty chuckled, and shook his head. "Thank you."

"For what?"

"For thinking that I could. Oh, I love you, Maria," he said, his voice as soft as the night. "I love you with all that I am and all that I will ever be. Thank you for being my bride."

They kissed, then hand in hand they walked up the gentle slope to the cave.

10

"Eli! Time for supper!" Hatty let the screen door slam behind her as she ran back into the kitchen. She grabbed a potholder and tried to move the heavy iron skillet from the wood cookstove. "I swear I will never get used to this thing," she said to herself. "Anita, could you fill up the tea glasses, please?" she called out the window to her daughter-in-law who was making her way up to the house from the cattle pens.

"Be right there!" Anita started to run the remaining fifty yards between the windmill and the house. Her black ponytail bounced from under her straw hat as she came up the hill. She bounded up onto the front porch and was through the door inside of ten seconds.

"Don't forget your boots, dear," Hatty reminded.

"Already off, Mom. Mmm, that chicken smells wonderful. I could smell it halfway to the lot." She moved quickly to the cupboard, pulled down eight large iced tea glasses, and began to fill them at the pump. It was March, time for branding, dehorning, and shots—and for taking the calf crop to auction in Laredo. It was one of the busiest times of year for the ranchers in that part of the country, and especially for Eli, whose herd of crossbred was growing better than he had hoped. The screen door opened.

"Don't forget—"

"Got'm, Mom," Carl answered, closing the door and jamming

his heel into the bootjack Eli had nailed into the porch.

"Hey, babe, let me take that for you." Marty rushed over to help Maria, who was making her way around the end of the house with a load of firewood. Just then Hatty appeared at the door.

"Oh, good, Marty, I was just coming out to see if Maria needed some help." Hatty looked outside the yard and saw Sam Carreras and Ray Montoya leaning against the pump, talking. "Y'all get washed up and come on in," she yelled.

Eli never had trouble finding help with his cattle if Hatty's fried chicken and hot apple pie were part of the deal. After the meal they all moved out onto the back porch to enjoy the sunset and visit for a few minutes over a last cup of coffee before heading home.

"So how are we going to do, do you think?" Hatty asked her husband.

"Well, for our first real year, not bad at all. We'll ship eleven steers and two heifers. I think I'll keep the rest. And I want to get rid of the dun. I don't think she's ever going to calve, do you, Ray?"

Ray shook his head in agreement, then added, "Calf crop was real good, though. That old roan had a good pair, and they're both looking fine."

Sam rocked back in his chair until it bumped against the porch railing. "You know that shorthorn brennel? I know you're thinking about shipping her, but that's going to be a good cow. She's strong and she'll give you some good calves. I'd wait another year or two anyway, see what she does."

Eli shook his head. "I can't afford 'em if they won't calve, Sam. Still, we've more than made up for one or two slow ones just this year alone. Tell you what, I'll think about it. I appreciate the advice."

"What do you see down the road, Dad?" Marty asked.

"I figure at this rate we ought to be built back up in another three years."

"Instead of five?" Hatty asked.

"If the Lord keeps on giving us years like this one, I'd say three to four." He paused and smiled. "Course, we might need a little more time than that if this family gets any bigger," Eli said, winking at Hatty.

Marty sidestepped the hint. "If the market holds we ought to be able to pick up another fifteen head if we're careful, wouldn't you say, Dad?"

"Closer to nine or ten. I'm just not going to get—" Eli broke off in mid-sentence. "Well, looky here."

"Father Zeuma." Hatty rose with Maria and Anita to greet him as he came around the corner of the house.

"Hello. Sorry to interrupt. I—I just thought I would drop by for a little chat. I hope I'm not interrupting your dinner."

"No, no, of course not," Hatty said, reaching for a chair. "Please, sit down."

"Can I get you something to drink, Father?" Maria offered.

"Please, don't bother. I am fine, really. Perhaps I should come another time, when you don't have guests."

"We were just going, Father," Ray said, rising from his chair. "Come on, Sam, your wife's going to think we took off for Laredo if we don't get home."

Everyone was always sure to let Sam have the porch rocker, as he tended to need a bit of extra propulsion to gain a vertical advantage. He tilted back a bit, then rocked forward, pushing off the arms of the chair to help launch his bulk up and out of the creaking rocker. Once he had righted himself, he addressed his hostess. "Thanks for a great meal, Hatty. We'll be seeing you. Father." Sam nodded to the priest as he passed. He had felt uncomfortable around Father Zeuma ever since he left the parish to join Doc and Estella.

"We'd better be going too, Dad. Thanks for a great meal, Mom." Marty kissed his mother goodbye and Maria gave her a hug as they picked up their things.

"What time tomorrow, Dad?" Carl had returned from getting his boots and sat down on the porch step to pull them on.

"No rush. Johnny's going to be here about nine-thirty with the trailor. Plan on takin' off around ten-thirty, eleven."

"Okay then. Y'all sleep tight. Night!"

They all lived within a few miles of each other, so the men

had ridden their horses. Maria climbed into the truck with Anita and the leftover food, and they all pulled out together.

"Really appreciate all the help, boys," Eli shouted to the departing family and friends. "Thanks much, fellas!" He stood on the porch waving goodbye, wondering what in the world might be on the Father's mind that would bring him out here this late. He didn't just "happen by," that much was sure.

Finally, when the truck was out of sight, and the horses had turned off the road and topped the hill—when he couldn't avoid it any longer—Eli turned back to join the conversation Hatty had been carrying on with Zeuma.

"So, Padre, what can we do for you?" Eli refused to address the Father by his clerical title in English, but somehow found it unobjectionable to use the Spanish *Padre,* especially since he and the priest conversed in English. The Spanish form of address was a convenient formality that satisfied all concerned, showing respect for the office of the priest while maintaining the social distance Eli insisted on.

"I'm going to fix more coffee," Hatty said, rising. "Want some?"

Eli didn't want her to leave him alone with the Father, but that was obviously just what she was going to do.

"Sure," he said, shooting her a sidelong glance. "Thanks."

She smiled sweetly and exited to the kitchen.

"Mr. King, I know you find it difficult to talk with me."

Eli was taken completely off guard by Zeuma's sudden and unexpected transparency. He and the Father had never come within miles of a significant conversation. So he said nothing. After an awkward silence the priest continued, obviously uncomfortable.

"I must admit that I have not been the kind of priest that I should to you."

Eli shifted in his chair.

"I realize that I am not your priest. I didn't mean to presume." He cleared his throat and kept his eyes down. "I just—I wanted to, uh. . . ." His hands began trembling slightly. He took a deep breath and went on. "I wanted to ask you . . ." he lifted his eyes to meet Eli's. "I wanted to invite you to attend Mass this Sunday."

Eli sat dumbfounded. He didn't really dislike this man, but he had never had any use for the Catholic religion. He made no bones about it, although he had always tried to be civil and decent on the rare occasions in which he had been forced into a strained conversation with the Father. But this! What could he say?

"Well, uh, Padre . . . I'm really at a loss for words. Uh, you know we are going to church over at Doc McClendon's house. Have been for some time. We are Protestant, you knew that?"

The priest nodded, his head down once again.

"Well, then, I guess that pretty well settles it, wouldn't you say?" Eli offered.

"Please." The priest's voice was choked with emotion that he was fighting hard not to reveal. "Please, you don't understand." He looked at Eli "I know you have no reason to trust me, but I cannot tell you more."

"What's going on here?" Eli's voice was soft but firm. "You're in some kind of trouble, aren't you? Listen, if you need some money, I'm afraid we don't have much to spare this—"

"This isn't about me, you foolish man!" Father Zeuma exploded out of his seat.

"Father!" Hatty had just opened the back door. She came out and sat in the chair between the two men.

"Mrs. King—I'm sorry. Please, Mr. King, forgive me." He sat down again, using the artificial moment to feign a social grace while speaking half to himself. "I had no idea it would be this difficult."

Hatty tried to smooth things over with small talk. "The coffee will be ready in a few minutes. Sounds like you two were having quite a conversation."

"I was just inviting Mr. King and yourself to join us for Mass this Sunday, and I'm afraid I have offended him," the priest said.

Hatty looked at Eli and then back to the priest. Another strained silence.

Father Zeuma continued haltingly. "I have been under much pressure lately. Please consider my invitation a request that has your own best interests at heart. It has been brought to my attention that—how do I say this—my sins are many. I have done many wrong things in the past. I have asked God's forgiveness. Perhaps now I can make up for some of those mistakes. I would like to begin with you."

"How is our coming to your church going to help you make up for some mistake? I don't understand." Eli's stomach started to tighten.

"I should never have sent those families—the Carreras, the Montoyas—I should never have sent them to the McClendons'. No matter what the others said."

"What *who* said?" Eli asked.

There was a long pause. Zeuma was trying to figure out how to broach a sensitive subject. "You know, Mr. King, the church is very dependent on the giving of its parishioners."

Eli got up out of his chair, obviously angry.

"Wait, you don't understand." Father Zeuma stood to face Eli.

"Oh, I understand fine. You don't need folks like Ray and Sam when they're down and out, but let them sell a couple of head of cattle and all of a sudden their souls become precious in the eyes of the church. I understand perfectly well. And now you have the gall to come here and ask me to help line your pockets? Yeah, I'd be ashamed too. You bet I would. You're pathetic, you know that?"

"Eli!" Hatty started to touch his arm but stopped as the priest stepped closer.

"You must listen to me, Mr. King. Sometimes there are interests—sometimes . . ." he started to say something, but changed his mind. He would take a different tack. "God expects His children to support His work. There are some I know in the next parish who did this same foolish thing you are doing, who refused to give when they had enjoyed so many of the blessings of the church. It was very bad for them."

"What are you telling me? That God struck them down with lightning?"

"He judged them, yes."

"How?"

"One man, his cattle began to die from a plague. Another man, his water went bad, went to salt. Another—"

Eli turned and started to walk back into the house.

Father Zeuma yelled after him. "Another man, another man died!"

Eli bent over to pick up his coffee cup.

Zeuma grew desperate. "You know nothing! You know nothing!" he yelled at Eli. "What are you, that you can walk away from the church, that you can trample under foot the blood of Christ?" His voice cracked. He pointed angrily at Eli. "Don't you walk away from me!"

"You get off my porch, mister, and off my land. Now!" Eli turned abruptly to go inside, but Father Zeuma reached out and grabbed his arm. "No! You listen to me!"

Eli exploded. Instinctively he spun and struck, catching the priest hard with the back of his hand—the coffee cup shattering against Zeuma's left cheekbone. The force of the blow knocked him off the porch and onto the ground.

The priest lay still. For a moment no one moved. Eli stood motionless, shocked by his own brutality. Hatty had retreated to the house where she stood just inside the porch door, staring.

Slowly, life began to return to the scene. Father Zeuma moved carefully, pushing himself up to his knees and then to a standing position. He was bleeding from a cut just below the left temple. He dusted off his cassock and looked straight at Eli, who was still standing on the porch, frozen in the ungraceful position one assumes after throwing a punch.

"You pack quite a wallop for a gringo!" he said, and Eli thought he saw the hint of a smile. All the fear was gone, and there wasn't a trace of anger or bitterness in his voice.

Hatty went to get a towel. Eli moved to the edge of the porch and hesitated, looking down at the priest. "I'm sorry, I shouldn't have done that," he said. "I didn't think."

"Well, I shouldn't have come here in the first place." Father Zeuma shook his head and took another swipe at his dusty cassock. Blood was running down the side of his face. "I don't know what's gotten into me lately."

Hatty emerged from the house and handed him a damp towel. He pressed it to his cheek, then folded it and used it to wipe some of the dust off his clothes. Then he straightened and took a deep breath. "Listen, folks, I didn't mean to insult you, and to tell the truth, I didn't really want to come here. But I thought I should at least try. I would just ask you to at least think over what I've said."

"Hatty, go back in the house for a minute." Eli spoke quietly, not taking his eyes off the priest. Father Zeuma returned the cloth, and she walked quickly back through the screen door. Eli stepped off the porch and addressed the priest directly.

"What's this business about other ranchers running into tough luck—and one fellow died, you said?"

"It was not bad luck, Señor King," Father Zeuma replied.

"Who are they? Talk to me."

"No, I cannot."

"Look, I know you're trying to warn me. I want you to know I appreciate that, but I'm not going to run."

"I'm not asking you to run," Father Zeuma said, exasperated that he couldn't seem to get through to Eli.

Eli continued, "If you would tell me who you're afraid of, maybe I could help."

Father Zeuma laughed softly and shook his head. "You Americans. One minute you knock a priest down in the dust, the next you are offering to help him fight someone else. You know who I am afraid of, Mr. King? I am afraid of you. I am afraid you are going to hurt many people in my parish for the sake of your pride. I can deal with the others. I understand them. But you—no, I have said enough. The offer remains. You know where to find me if you change your mind."

He turned and walked around the corner of the house and was gone. Eli sat on the porch and put his chin in his hand. He stared at the setting sun, recalling the sunsets he used to watch with the boys back home on the ranch, wishing he were there now. His eyes drifted down and fixed on the white pieces of bone china lying scattered on the ground. There were darks stains all around where the priest's blood had soaked into the ground. One drop had spattered onto a piece of the cup. Eli felt a hot tear roll down his cheek and fall into the dust.

11

The morning sun broke through the cloud cover and streamed in through Hatty's kitchen window. Eli had just finished breakfast and was looking for his keys. He had to go into Dolores to get shot medicine for his herd from Jaime Dominguez. He came back into the kitchen where Hatty was washing the breakfast dishes and gave her a quick hug and kiss.

"I'll see you in a bit. I'm just going to run into town for a minute. Jaime should have the medicine waiting for me. Then I'm going to run over to Sam's and give him a hand hanging that gate. Be back around noon."

"Love you, hon."

"You too. Bye." Eli walked out to the truck and filled it from the massive gas storage tank behind the house. Ever since his conversation with Father Zeuma a few months before, he had made sure he locked the tank after every fill-up. It was probably a needless precaution, but there was no use in taking unnecessary chances, he told himself.

It took only five minutes to drive up the valley road to Dolores. Eli passed Doc's house on the way and saw him throwing his black medicine bag into the back of his truck. He honked as he drove past. Doc waved and yelled out some greeting that Eli couldn't quite make out.

Jaime's dry goods store was open. The cool October air blew

in behind Eli as he entered the front door. The little bell above the door jingled cheerily, announcing his arrival. Eli looked around but saw no one in the store. He walked to the back of the last aisle. Everything seemed to be in order, but Jaime Dominguez was nowhere to be seen. Eli walked back to the front of the store and looked behind the counter and through the curtained partition that separated the store from the storage room in the back.

"Jaime?" Eli called.

Just then the front door opened suddenly and there stood Jaime, looking dazed and more than a little anxious.

"Oh, Señor King," he sputtered. "You surprised me. I didn't expect you so early." He moved immediately behind the counter, took a feather duster out, and started to clean the shelves under the counter. Eli watched him for a moment in an attitude of mixed fascination and mild frustration. When he took the calendar off the wall and dusted behind it, Eli spoke up.

"Anything wrong, Jaime?" he asked.

"Oh, no, no, no, Señor King. There is nothing wrong. It is just a very busy day, and there is so much to do."

"Like dusting behind a two-year-old calendar? When are you going to get rid of that thing, anyway?"

"It is one of my favorite pictures, Señor."

"All right, fine. I don't have time to argue with you. I just need to pick up the medicine and take off. What do I owe you?"

"The vaccine did not come, I am afraid." He went through the curtain and disappeared back in the storeroom.

"Jaime, come out here."

The little man reappeared sheepishly. "Señor?"

"Quit acting this way. You know you don't have anything to fear from me. Now tell me what happened."

"Nothing happened, Señor. The medicine did not come, that's all."

"Then whose truck was that I saw in here yesterday?"

"It was Carlos Hernandez, but he did not bring your vaccine, Señor."

"Then what was he doing here? The only reason Carlos comes

all the way down from San Luis is to bring the vaccine we order from Laredo."

"He came to pick up specimens for Señor Guitierrez. Laboratory work of some kind, but he said to tell you the vaccine never arrived. Perhaps next month."

"Next month is too late. I guess I'll have to drive up there to get it myself."

"Have you thought about trying Guadalajara? Even Mexico City would be closer than Laredo, Señor."

"No, this vaccine is new. They don't even have it many places in Texas yet. I better get going. See you, Jaime." Eli left, feeling certain that Jaime was lying. He decided to drive to San Luis and check things out for himself with the veterinarian there. He stopped by the house and told Hatty he would be gone until late that night, since the drive to San Luis was eighty miles each way over rough roads.

The trip was uneventful, except for the unexpected pleasantness of being alone for a while and having time to think. Eli's thoughts turned to Jaime. He hadn't seen the shopkeeper that nervous since they first arrived in Dolores. Somehow he was under the thumb of the tall fellow—what did Doc say his name was—Rodriguez? Hector Rodriguez. It could be anything—a debt, an old grudge, something to do with family honor. These Mexican families were very tight, and honor meant a lot since most of them didn't have much else to call their own. Eli wasn't one to meddle in other folks' private affairs, but Jaime's problem with this fellow was starting to hurt his business. He wasn't going to risk losing his cattle to lockjaw or blackleg or brucelosis just to be polite.

Besides, there had to be more to it than a personal vendetta with Jaime. Why would Rodriguez pick a fight with Carl? It wasn't just over Anita, Eli felt sure of that. And what had happened to Rodriguez anyway? He had disappeared after Doc took him to Laredo for knee surgery. No one had seen him in almost a year now. And what could any of that have to do with the medicine from Laredo being late? It didn't make any sense. Probably no connection at all. "Well," he said to himself, "maybe Carlos can help straighten all this out. At least I'll find out what happened with the medicine."

With the bad roads and detours, it took over three hours to travel the eighty miles. Eli had made this trip only once before, but he had an uncanny sense of direction and so had no trouble retracing his route through the busy city of San Luis and on to San Pedro street. The vet's office was about halfway down a long block on the right-hand side. He could see the clean white sign with the black lettering jutting out over the sidewalk. "*Clínica Veterinaria.*" He slowed to a crawl and was just about to pull up to the curb when he noticed something and decided to drive by.

Eli parked at the end of the block and got out of the truck. He stepped up on the sidewalk and went inside a small shop to buy a newspaper, one of the few luxuries he allowed himself when he came to town. He joined an old man on the bench just outside the store. The old fellow had fallen asleep with his head resting back against the glass of the store window, his toothless mouth gaping and sucking in air in a half snore. *I'm blending in pretty well,* Eli thought. *Inconspicuous. A fair number of people out for midday. Now just wait.* He unfolded his paper quietly so as not to rouse the sleeper and casually glanced at the headlines, keeping an eye on the vet's office.

There, parked in front of the clinic, was a bright red Cadillac. The right rear fender was buckled and scraped, but other than that it was in perfect condition. It looked vaguely familiar to Eli, but he couldn't remember where or when he might have seen it. But it didn't matter. It wasn't the red Caddy that concerned him, it was the black Ford coupe with Texas plates and a dent in the right rear fender that was parked alongside. Eli recognized the distinctive X-shaped buckle in the black metal. He had put it there three years ago when the car backed into him.

Five minutes passed, then the door to the clinic opened and two men stepped out into the midday sun. The first man had on sunglasses. He was a muscular young Mexican dressed in jeans and a tight-fitting pullover shirt who looked too American for a local. The second man closed the door behind them and stood with his back to Eli. He was obviously angry, speaking in hushed tones and poking the first man in the chest with his finger. The first man said nothing, showed no emotion. The taller man finished speaking and put his hands on his hips, waiting, it appeared, for the younger one to respond. But the other man simply stared up at him from behind his dark glasses, arms folded defiantly, saying nothing.

The tall man wheeled and marched to the black car. Eli couldn't be absolutely sure until he turned, but now there was no doubt. Jake Skerritt was in San Luis. What on earth could possibly bring him this far into Mexico? Skerritt slammed his car door shut and cranked the engine. It wouldn't start. The young Mexican man stood smiling. Jake never did take care of his car. Finally, on the fourth or fifth try, the engine sputtered to life. Jake threw it into reverse and tried to back out dramatically, but he gave it too much gas and it died halfway into the street.

By this time, people had stopped on the street to stare at the gringo in hot retreat. Even through the windshield Eli could tell Jake was getting red. He cranked the engine again several times until it caught and then lurched the car forward, clattering down the street in a cloud of blue smoke. Several of the younger people applauded.

The young man stepped off the curb and opened the door of the bright red Caddy. Eli noticed his thin mustache and swaggering gait as he swung in behind the wheel. He made a conscious attempt not to judge people on first appearance, but he took an immediate dislike to this man. Something in the way he carried himself reminded him of every bully he had ever known. The engine purred as he backed out into the street and headed out of town in the opposite direction from Skerritt.

Eli rose from the bench, folded his paper, and walked down the block toward the clinic. When he got to the door, he started to open it but noticed that a "closed" sign had been placed in the window. He decided to try the door anyway. It was locked but had been left slightly ajar, and it pushed open at Eli's touch.

"Carlos? Anybody home?"

The clinic was deserted. Not a sound. Eli decided to have a

look around. The small waiting area was further abbreviated by a long counter that ran the width of the room, perhaps fourteen feet. Behind the counter were ledger books, scraps of paper tucked away in cubbyholes, an ancient water cooler in the corner.

A hallway split the building behind the counter with what appeared to be four examining rooms on either side. It was dark except for the last room on the left at the back of the building.

"Carlos, you back there?" Eli called out.

Just as Eli was looking for a way around the counter, something crashed to the floor at the end of the hall. The sound of breaking glass spilled from the lighted room out into the hallway, then silence. Eli jumped over the counter and ran toward the room.

He found Carlos Hernandez lying face down on the floor, blood pooling under his head. Eli bent over the man and tried gently to turn him over. Carlos groaned. The head wound wasn't as bad as it appeared at first glance, but it was obvious that he had been beaten. His eye was swollen and his upper lip was bleeding. Eli helped him to a sitting position and then up onto the examining table. He grabbed a towel from a rack over the sink.

"Carlos, it's Eli King. I know who did this to you—I know one of them anyway. We'll go for the police as soon as you feel up to it." Carlos shook his head slowly.

"No," he mumbled. "No police. I will be fine. I just need a minute to clear my head. Thanks for the towel."

"I know who did this."

"No, you don't. And even if you did, it would not do any good, Señor King. It's best to forget it, believe me. Now, you are here about the medicine, I believe." He tried to get up from the table, but quickly sat back down, holding the towel to his eye.

Eli stood upright. "Forget the medicine and tell me what's going on here. Those men almost killed you and you don't even want to go to the police. Why?"

Carlos evaded the question. "I honestly did not have the vaccine yesterday—not there in Dolores, anyway. But there is some here. Plenty. It is in the refrigerator across the hall."

"I'm not leaving until we talk. I got all day."

Carlos could tell Eli meant it, and he wasn't in any kind of shape to resist. "All right, all right. Help me down and we will get some coffee. There's a thermos in my office." Eli helped the small man off the table.

Hernandez walked stiffly but without assistance up the hall and into the first room on his right. "You say you know who did this," he said to Eli. "Did they see you?"

"I don't think so. No, I'm sure they didn't."

"It really doesn't matter. You were already involved." He handed Eli a hot cup of coffee. "One of the men—the Mexican—has been in here before. His name is Sanchez. The other one I have never seen. He might be the boss man for all I know, but the way he talked I doubt it."

"Yeah, I know him. He's a sheriff, believe it or not, up in Texas. What do you know about Sanchez?"

"Nothing. He's not from around here. I've seen him plenty, though, coming in and out. He doesn't say much, never takes off those sunglasses. He just picks up the money and leaves."

Eli leaned back in his chair. "What kind of business are these guys running?"

"Somebody up north has been twisting arms down here for at least a couple of years. Mostly they hit small businesses like this. We are too little to pay off the police like the big boys—it was cheaper and a lot safer to just pay the protection money."

"Extortion."

"Before long they started leaning on the church—I guess they figured the farmers and ranchers ought to kick in their fair share."

"So they do what—threaten the priests?"

"Whoever the head man is, he never crosses the border. Doesn't have to. He just has one of his boys pay the local priest a friendly visit, sit with the Father over a cup of coffee, and show him the wisdom of contributing to a special charity fund."

"Promises of good things to come, huh?"

Carlos shook his head. "Promises of bad things that won't."

"So these hoods got to Zeuma. When, do you know?"

"I am not sure. I think it was about a year-and-a-half ago. It used to be very low-key. The priests were so scared out there in those little parishes, they would do anything to protect their people. But in the last three or four months it's gotten worse. Maybe the man's overhead is piling up on him. Maybe he just got greedier, who knows? Anyway, I finally decided I'd had enough. I had your medicine here all along. I just didn't have the courage to bring it to you. I told Sanchez and Skerritt today that they wouldn't be getting any more money. It really made Skerritt mad. This was his first time down. He was coming for his first cut. I thought he was going to kill me."

"Are you going to be all right? I'm going to have to get back."

"I'm okay. Don't forget your vaccine."

"What do I owe you?"

"You don't owe me anything, Mr. King. Let's call it even." He shook Eli's hand and rose to get the vaccine for him. Eli followed him back into the supply room. Carlos flipped on the light and stood staring into the room. The cupboards had all been emptied, their contents scattered. The two refrigerators containing all the medicine had been opened and turned over. Broken glass was everywhere, and milky white serum coated much of the floor.

"*¿Por qué?*" Carlos sighed, his voice flat and tired. "Why do this?" He paused; then suddenly, as if waking from a stupor, he turned to Eli.

"Go home," he uttered hoarsely.

"As soon as I help you here. Then I'll go back to Dolores."

"No, Señor King. I mean go home to Texas. Pack up, sell out, and go back where you came from. There are no rules here. There is no law here."

"You need help."

"I have help, Señor King. We will take care of this tomorrow. Now please—*go*."

Eli turned to leave and was halfway out the door when Carlos asked one last question.

"Do you drink, Mr. King?"

The question surprised Eli. "Not really. A beer now and then, I guess. Why?"

"If I were you, I would stay clear of the cantina there in Dolores. They all meet there every so often. Once word gets out that I am not cooperating any more, it will get worse. They will find some other way of pressuring you. Pay attention to what I said about leaving, please." He turned to go back to his office. "Leave the closed sign up, will you? I think today I'll go home early."

It was nearly five o'clock when Eli got home. Anita's horse was tied out front. Eli pulled around behind the house and went in to see Hatty.

"Where's Anita?" he asked coming in through the back door.

"Well, hello to you, too, stranger. You got back earlier than I had hoped. She's out gathering the wash for me." Hatty gave her husband a quick kiss and saw immediately that something was bothering him. "What is it?" she asked.

"Sit down, Hat. We need to talk, and then I'll have to go again." They sat together at the kitchen table, holding hands as they spoke in low tones.

Out in the yard, Anita just finished taking down the laundry. She was coming around the front of the house with a basket full of sheets when she saw Hatty and Eli through the window. She could tell something was wrong. Anita set the load down and leaned back against the wall, thinking it better to wait until they were finished before going inside.

The breeze carried their voices out to her. She caught fragments here and there—enough to piece the story together. Then Eli rose suddenly from the table and went out back to fill up the truck with gas. Hatty went to their bedroom and stuffed some clothes into a bag. Anita could hear her rummaging through the drawers, looking for something. She peeked in the window to see Hatty emerge from the bedroom with a small suitcase and a pouch of some kind in her left hand.

Anita watched Hatty go out the back door. With the back door left open, Anita could see all the way through to the back side of the house, where Eli was checking the oil. Eli took the suitcase from Hatty, threw it on the front seat, and climbed in. Hatty handed him the pouch, kissed him—a long kiss, Anita thought—and waved goodbye as he swung the truck around in a wide arc and headed off toward town.

Anita picked up the basket and went in through the front door, catching it with her heel to let it close softly behind her. She was already putting away the laundry when Hatty came in a few moments later. She didn't look at Anita, but instead sat at the kitchen table and stared out the west window, lost in thought.

Anita continued to fluff and fold the sheets as she casually asked, "Where's Dad off to in such a hurry? I didn't even get to say hello."

Hatty didn't respond. She hadn't heard the question. She was too busy recalling all that Eli had said, trying to understand it all, not wanting to believe they were in any real danger. And wishing she had gone with him.

12

The radiator blew in Monterrey early the next morning, forcing Eli to spend an extra half-day walking the streets to find a reliable repair man who had one in stock. He finally found a man who had a used Chevy radiator that fit and asked him to hurry the job. It was nearly six o'clock by the time the new radiator was installed, so he decided to spend the night there.

The beds at the El Matador hotel were only slightly harder than the bed of Eli's truck and not quite as clean, but at least he had a roof over his head for the night. He rose early the next morning, picked up a taco from a small cafe down the street, filled up the truck, and drove the remaining 120 miles to Laredo.

The sign on the animal clinic said they opened at nine, but it was ten before anyone showed up. They were out of the streptomycin that Eli needed to help fight brucellosis, but the vet said another shipment was due from San Antonio at noon the next day. Eli was uneasy about spending three days away from Hatty, but there wasn't much he could do about it. He walked the streets for an hour, looking in shops, wishing he had brought Hatty with him—then remembering the El Matador and being glad he hadn't.

He decided to visit the market to see if he could find something small for Hatty. The streets of Laredo were alive with the annual decorations for the Days of the Dead, even though it was still two weeks away. As he rounded the last corner, he saw the market, an imposing, barn-like wooden structure, rather splayed at the bottom but still remarkably intact throughout. It was, at its worst, a rickety, rat-infested fire-trap specializing in wrought iron, onyx chess sets, and matching horsehead bookends. He found nothing for Hatty and decided to return to the hotel.

The halls of the La Fiesta Hotel had a fresh coat of lime green paint that, unfortunately, matched the edges of the carpet. Years of traffic had worn a path down the center, leaving the white backing exposed for the length of the hallway. Each room had a window and a small fan to help move the stale air around a bit. As he drew the shade and sat on the edge of the bed with the sound of old Mexico drifting in from the street, Eli thought he had never felt as alone as he did at that moment.

He drifted off to sleep on top of the covers and didn't wake until almost eight that evening. For a minute he had trouble recalling where he was. He went to the sink and washed out his mouth, remembering not to swallow.

The room fan was either broken or the plug had gone bad, but the overhead light still worked. He hadn't flipped a light switch in months. Eli had grown used to living without the luxury of electrical appliances. He enjoyed the simplicity of country life, but he did tire of reading by the light of oil lamps and candles. Now that he had sufficient light to read by, however, he had nothing to read. *Might as well turn in early,* he thought. *Get a fresh start tomorrow.*

He tossed and turned, unable to sleep for what seemed like half the night. He rolled over and groped for the light switch. It took a minute for his eyes to adjust to the glare. He squinted at his watch. One o'clock. Great.

He decided to get up and think things through. He would make some notes—maybe that would help him sort through some of this mess, come up with some sort of a plan. But of course he had brought nothing to write with. He looked in the desk and the night stand. The desk had some cheap hotel stationery but no pen. The drawer of the night stand was stuck, but with a good pull it came free. Nothing but an old Bible. Someone from the states must have left it there—it was in English. Eli thumbed through it quickly, hoping to find a pencil jammed between the pages as a bookmark. Nothing. Only an old scrap of newspaper stuck in between the Psalms.

He fluffed up his pillow and settled back for a short read. The Bible had always been pretty good for helping him fall asleep. He opened to the scrap of paper and began reading Psalm 37.

> Fret not thyself because of evildoers, neither be thou envious against the workers of iniquity. For they shall soon be cut down like the grass, and wither like the green herb.

Eli rested the Bible on his lap and smiled. This had happened once before, when he was a boy. He had gotten into a fix and opened the Bible to some place, he couldn't remember where, but it spoke so exactly to his need he thought there was magic around.

He couldn't recall the mess he was in or even the verse, but he did remember what his mother had to say about it when he told her what had happened. She stopped what she was doing and looked straight at him. "The Lord doesn't usually work that way, son," she said. "But when He does, I'd pay attention. And I'd be sure to thank Him for His grace."

Eli murmured a small "thank You" to the Lord and continued to read.

> Trust in the LORD, and do good; so shalt thou dwell in the land, and verily thou shalt be fed. Delight thyself also in the LORD; and he shall give thee the desires of thine heart. Commit thy way unto the LORD; trust also in him; and he shall bring it to pass. And he shall bring forth thy righteousness as the light, and thy judgment as the noonday. Rest in the LORD and wait patiently for him: fret not thyself because of him who prospereth in his way, because of the man who bringeth wicked devices to pass. Cease from anger, and forsake wrath: fret not thyself in any wise to do evil. For evildoers shall be cut off, but those who wait upon the LORD shall inherit the earth.

This is no accident, Eli thought. *Or at least if it is, the Lord is in it.* "Oh, Lord," he prayed, "let these words of Yours be true in my life. Amen." He put the piece of old newsprint back in the Bible just as he had found it and returned the book to its vault and slid it shut, making sure not to close it too tightly for the benefit of the next pilgrim.

Then Eli enjoyed the best night's sleep he could remember having in a long time. Not because he was tired or had rediscovered some forgotten inner strength, but because he was at peace.

The next day he returned to the veterinarian's office after breakfast and found to his amazement that the shipment had actually arrived early. He bought several bottles of streptomycin along with some clean needles, sulfate, and extra penicillin. By noon he was on the road back to Dolores.

On his way home, Eli kept looking in the rear-view mirror, expecting to see a red Cadillac bearing down on him. He tried to shake off the apprehensive feeling, thinking he was probably making too much of all this. Still, he couldn't explain away the fact that he had all but seen Skerritt and Sanchez beat up Carlos Hernandez, and he did have Zeuma's strange behavior to try to account for. "Well," he shrugged, "just take it one step at a time and see what happens."

He pulled into Dolores just as the sun was setting. The town was quiet. This time of year folks were usually out visiting, getting ready for the Day of the Dead. As he approached the cantina, one of the men standing on the porch hurriedly went inside. The others—the only ones out that night—watched Eli drive by.

Eli turned on his headlights as he rounded the bend toward Doc's house. There was a white piece of paper on a stick beside the lane that led up to the house. There, in large black letters, he read, "Eli, come up to the house."

He pulled up the short drive to the house, not knowing what to expect. He felt unusually calm. He felt he should probably have been more worried than he was. The truck stopped. As he cut the ignition, the door to Doc's house swung open on cue.

Hatty came running out to meet him before he got both feet

on the ground. Doc and his family were right behind her, along with Marty and Carl and their wives. Hatty was the first to speak.

"Oh, Eli. They killed some of the cattle and crippled two of the horses," she said.

"We know who it was, Dad," Carl declared. "It was the albino—the barkeep Calavera and two or three others with him."

"Whoa, slow down, son. I need to hear all this from the beginning," Eli said.

Doc moved up to Eli and put his arm on his shoulder. "Come on inside," he said. "We've got coffee on—we'll fill you in."

Inside, Doc pulled his high-backed armchair nearer the sofa and offered it to Eli. Estella brought coffee as Hatty and Carl started to unfold what had happened over the last two days. They spoke softly to avoid waking Rosalinda.

"After you left, I had a long talk with Anita," Hatty recounted. "She felt like Carl ought to know about the trouble in San Luis right away and I agreed, so she went back to their place to find him and bring him back here."

"We thought you might get back Wednesday," Carl broke in, "but I still didn't want Mom out there by herself, so we got her to come spend the night with us."

"Anyway, I just felt really uneasy for some reason that night," Hatty continued. "When we went back Wednesday morning everything looked all right, so I settled down a little and got some ironing done and cleaned the house. But everything was so still—I kept telling myself it was just you being gone, and how you'd say I was being silly to worry. I really had no cause, I guess. I had the girls with me all day, but I still had a feeling that something was about to happen. So I started worrying about you and thinking about that awful Jake Skerritt and how mad you said he was and what if he saw you—" she started to cry, but held it in. "I stayed last night with Marty and Maria, and things were a little better. But I woke up this morning about one o'clock, and I knew something wasn't right, so I went in to get Marty."

"She was pretty upset," Marty commented, "so I told her I'd go to the house and look things over so she wouldn't worry. I was just about to get into the truck when I heard the first rifle shot. I was still half asleep, and it caught me off guard, so I thought maybe I was just imagining it. But then I heard a second shot from over near the house. I jumped in the truck and hurried over to get Carl up. We got to the house just in time to see Calavera and another couple of guys take off in his truck."

Eli interrupted. "You know it was Calavera? You saw him?"

"We heard him. Nobody laughs like that," Marty replied.

"He was laughing?"

"While they were driving off. Drunk, I imagine, but I don't know. He's crazy."

"How many head did they kill?"

"Five cows, the red bull, a couple of heifers," Carl answered, and then he hesitated.

"Your mother said they crippled two of the horses."

Marty spoke softly. "Medio May and Princess."

"Princess?" Eli asked, the strain evident in his voice.

Marty nodded. "Stray bullets, I think. Medio May had a shoulder wound; I think she'll be okay. But Princess was really bad. I had to put her down."

"Where did he shoot her?" Eli asked.

Marty didn't say anything.

"Where did he shoot her?" Eli insisted.

"The belly."

Eli didn't move. "Lord, son."

"I know, Dad. It would have been a beautiful foal."

"I'm sorry, Eli," Doc intervened. "I know how much you loved that horse. We'll bring these fellows to justice."

"How're we going to do that?" Eli's voice was flat, unemotional. "We don't have positive identification. I don't think a laugh will stand up in court."

"Maybe a laugh won't, but these will." Doc held up three shell casings and three slugs. "I dug these out of the carcasses. Now all we need to do is get our hands on that rifle and find ourselves a ballistics expert and we have a case."

"I don't know," Eli reflected. "Even if we get the rifle, he'll say somebody else fired it. What about the truck—did you see the truck plainly?"

Marty shook his head.

"Dad, it was his truck," Carl asserted.

"You saw it that clearly, Carl?" Eli asked.

Marty jumped in. "It was fifty or sixty yards down the road and moving fast in the middle of the night."

"Under a full moon," Carl continued, building his case. "Besides, who else do you know who drives like that—doing ninety to nothin' across open range, weaving all over the place and howling like an animal? It's Calavera, all right."

"I admit it sounds like something he'd do," Eli agreed. "Carlos warned me about the fellows in the cantina. Said some of them were on the payroll of some honcho up north. And Calavera wouldn't need much of an excuse to do us some harm."

"How's that?" Doc wanted to know.

"A long time ago he used to work for me in the oil fields up in Oklahoma," Eli explained. "He was always a little slow, but it didn't really matter because he had his big brother with him and together they made a pretty good team. He was crazy about his brother. Counted on him for everything. I didn't think much of it one way or another since they got the job done, so I just let things ride.

"Then one night we had a well fire and I had to go out to the field about two in the morning to see what could be done. Usually you just have to let those things burn out or bring in a specialist to try to cap them. They're nothing but trouble. I told the boys to clear out and let her burn, and then up roars Jimmy and Jose—you know, Calavera. Jimmy was always trying to play the hero, always trying to earn points. He doesn't say a word to anyone, just jumps out of the truck, leaves Jose sitting there, and starts running up to the pipe. I don't know what in the world he was thinking. Maybe he was thinking he could turn it off or something, who knows.

"Anyway, I yell at him to get back, but he goes right on ahead, right up to the pipe and grabs a release valve—he must have thought he had the main shutoff—and starts to turn. And that's all it took.

The thing blew up right in his face. He was dead before he hit the ground. And what made it worse was he was surrounded by fire. There was no way to get him out. So I had to leave him."

"Is that where you burned your back, Dad?" Marty asked.

"Yeah. Part of the fireball got me. Anyway, Jose saw the whole thing. He made a run for his brother, but some other guys and I tackled him and held him down. Lord, it was awful. He cried and wailed for the longest time. It took three of us to hold him. Finally, we let him up and asked if he wanted one of us to go home with him. He never answered. He just stared at us. Then he started to laugh, not a regular laugh, but what you heard last night. That high-pitched kind of howl. Almost a scream—like a panther makes at night. Scared the living daylights out of all of us. Then he climbed in the truck—and it struck me I'd never seen him drive before—but he started it and took off. Just left without taking anything. Gone. And that's the last we saw of him. Until we passed him on the road on the way down here."

"You never told us you knew Calavera, Dad."

Eli continued to look away, not focusing on anything. "Didn't have any reason to. He never made any trouble here that I could tell. Pretty much kept to himself there in the cantina. I figured better to let sleeping dogs lie. Trouble is, this one's crazy." He turned to Doc. "I guess half the town knows by now?"

Doc nodded.

"Who do you know, Doc, that we could trust around here?"

Doc looked at Estella and scratched his head. "Felipe?" he asked her. She nodded, and turned to Eli. "Felipe Santiago over in Guanajuato. He's an old friend of my family, and he's in the police force."

"All right," Eli said, "here's what we're going to do. Marty, you and Maria head out for Guanajuato first thing in the morning."

"Why don't we go now, Dad?"

"What good would that do? They've already done what they meant to do. This is as far as they'll go for now. What we need to do now is let Ray and Sam know that they have to watch their animals. They don't have any to lose."

"I went over to see them this afternoon," Doc said. "Ray lost a cow. Sam had a shot fired through his bedroom window. I think they would be willing to fight this if it wasn't for their families. They're real scared, Eli."

"Was anyone hurt?"

"The kids were in the back part of the house. Juanita got a pretty good cut from the flying glass, but she'll be fine."

Maria covered her mouth with her hand and started to cry softly. She had known about the shooting, but the news about Juanita being hurt stunned her. Marty put his arm around her and pulled her close.

"Did anyone see who fired the shots?" Eli asked.

"Ray might have seen something. He was on his way back from the cantina about that time. He remembers hearing the shot, and he thinks he saw Calavera and a couple of others pulling out from around the back of his house and heading over toward your place. When he found Juanita cut up, he ran all the way over to my house and got me."

"You say he was headed back from the cantina?" Eli pressed.

"He's been having a rough time. You know it was this time of year his daughter died—right at the Day of the Dead. He's been going back to the cantina on Friday nights for a couple of weeks now—doing some drinking, but mostly just sitting."

"That changes things. He could at least tell us Calavera wasn't there last night."

"If you can get him to talk," Doc cautioned. "Right now all he wants to do is run, and I can't say I blame him."

"Okay," said Eli, "we'll cross that bridge when we come to it. Right now we need some help, and I think I know who it needs to be. I'm going to ask both you boys to stay here. Don't do anything until I get back with some help. It'll take me a day or two, so I want you to promise me that you won't do anything foolish until I get back. Understood? Carl?"

"I won't do anything foolish, Dad, I promise."

Eli spotted the loophole and closed it. "Don't do anything *at all,* Carl, except take care of your mother and your wife. I'd a lot rather lose some cattle than lose a son. We're gonna let the law handle this."

"We'll wait, Dad," Marty answered for his brother. Carl nodded his assent.

Doc rose to get some more coffee. "Guanajuato's only an hour, hour-and-a-half up the valley at the most. What's going to take so long?"

"I'm not going to Guanajuato."

"Felipe is a good man, Eli. You can trust him," Doc urged.

"I'm sure he is, Doc. But it's been a while since you've seen him. Who knows what kind of pressure they may have put on him? I'd feel more comfortable working with someone I know. And I need to move fast. I want to get my hands on that rifle before it occurs to Calavera to get rid of it. Tomorrow morning I'll go up to San Antonio and talk to some folks who'll be able to help."

"Who, Eli?" Hatty wondered.

"You don't know them. It's been a long time, but one fellow in particular owes me a favor. If he's still around, I'll see if I can call it in."

"Well, if you're going to San Antonio, at least take my truck," Carl offered. "The Ford would never make it."

"I'd offer you mine, but I think it's in worse shape than yours," said Doc.

Eli agreed to think about it, which was his polite way of saying no thanks, and then told them briefly about his trip, explaining his delay in coming back. He didn't mention the incident with the Bible since all the rest seemed more important. Before they left, Doc offered a prayer for the safety and well-being of them all. They all hugged as they departed, each family to their own house.

At home that night, Maria lay in bed staring at the ceiling, unable to sleep. She had been warned. Three days before she had been warned, but she had said nothing. She had been afraid. Afraid to admit that she had seen him again—the one she hoped she had forgotten. Afraid of the dreams. And now this.

She rose quietly so as not to waken her husband and walked down the short hall to the living room. There she knelt in front of a small desk—the only piece of furniture she had brought from her home when she got married. She slid open the smallest drawer in the bottom of the desk—a drawer that had remained closed for a long time—and pulled out the contents. The wooden floor was cold, but she barely noticed as she padded across the kitchen to get a knife.

She sat down at the kitchen table, placing the blade in front of her, clasping tightly the braided cord in both hands under her chin. For the better part of an hour she sat crying, alternately picking up the knife and putting it down. The moon shone clear and bright through the window, illuminating the red checkered tablecloth, the white nightgown, the hands that trembled, and the cold, steel edge of the knife. The dark wind blew, and the thorns on the limbs of an old mesquite scraped against the tin roof. "Fool," the wind sighed. "Witch. Cursed witch. Your fault. Take the knife. Coward. Do it. Do it. Now, witch."

Her hand reached out too quickly, fumbled the blade, grasped the handle. She didn't notice the small wound as she severed the strand and, one by one, pulled off the black and red beads of the rosary. "No one. No one but you," Maria whispered in the dark, as the last bead fell on the table and rolled off onto the floor. She put her head down on her folded arms and slept.

13

The oak door creaked open and closed with the slightest click. A man in dark clothes made his way to the corner of the street and pressed himself against the side of the building, breathing hard. He moved cautiously from shadow to shadow, looking into dark storefront windows, listening for the snap of a twig or the rustle of clothing. He had hunted as a boy. His could still hear his father: "Take ten steps, stop, and look. Always look twice as long as you think you need to, and that'll be half as long as you should." Good advice for hunters. Better advice for the hunted.

He crossed behind the last building and looked out across the valley, bright as day in the moonlight. The road lay like a pale white ribbon dropped carelessly onto the valley floor. There was nowhere to hide if he walked out there. Clustered outside the cantina were three trucks, a car, and some horses; no one stood out front. A murky yellow light leaked through the edges of a shuttered window. He could hear music coming from inside—a guitar slowly played, as if someone was strumming absently while carrying on a conversation. It was Saturday night—actually two the next morning. If the patrons of the bar could still walk by now, they would be moving in the direction of the outhouse, a good thirty yards behind the cantina.

Now. He walked toward the cantina, staying on the opposite side of the street. His fingers tugged at the fold of cloth beneath the too-white collar—trying to cover it, to blend it into the night. An involuntary whisper escaped him: "*Madre de Dios. . . .*" He kept his eyes straight ahead, as if by not looking he would not be seen. He has past now . . . ten yards . . . fifteen . . . twenty. The door to the cantina opened, letting out the sounds of guitar and talk, and then closed. He kept walking, counting the steps, eyes on the road. He didn't hear the slow steps behind him.

Eli sat at his kitchen table, reading his Bible by the light of his oil lamp. It was nearly two-thirty in the morning when he heard the boards creak on his front porch. Quickly, he blew out the lamp and reached for the rifle he had loaded that night. He moved his chair back from the window and sat in the shadow, waiting.

Tap, tap, tap on the front door, like someone with a nickel. *Tap, tap, tap,* this time a little louder. "Señor King," a voice whispered. Eli couldn't tell who it was, but he figured someone who meant to kill him wasn't going to come knocking timidly at his door. Eli crossed the room as the tapping continued and the voice whispered more insistently, "Señor King!"

Eli opened the door to see Father Zeuma leaning against the door frame. He stepped inside without a word of greeting. "Sit down, Padre," Eli said as he stepped out onto the porch, cradling the rifle in his left arm. Eli scanned yard, field, and road but saw nothing. He stepped back inside, satisfied that no one had followed the priest.

Father Zeuma had moved into the living area and was standing near the fireplace, staring down at the blackened hearth as if he were mesmerized by invisible flames. "I must tell you quickly and then go," he said as Eli leaned the rifle against the wall. "There are men here who will kill you if you try to fight them. I honestly did not think they would go this far."

"Keep your voice down—Hatty's asleep. I know what they've been doing down here."

Father Zeuma stared at him. "Of course. Your trip to San Luis. The vet there—what is his name?"

"It doesn't matter," Eli said.

"Hernandez, is it not? Carlos Hernandez. He told you."

Eli said nothing. Father Zeuma sat on the arm of the sofa. All his energy was gone. "When will you be leaving?" There was a note of resignation and some regret in his words.

"I'm not. Not permanently anyway. I'll be going up north to get some help, but I'll be back. I'm not running from this."

Father Zeuma couldn't believe what he was hearing. "What, you will run to the law? What law? The law is behind this, my friend. The law owns this town and the people in it."

"Whoever this guy is, he isn't the law and he doesn't own me."

"You stay and they will kill you."

"I will not run."

Father Zeuma took a deep breath. He was trying to work up the courage to reveal something he had hidden for weeks. "Señor King. I know you love your family very much. Please think of them. These men, these wicked men, they are very strong, and some of them have so much hate—"

"Padre, listen—"

"No, let me finish. I have had not been able to sleep these past weeks. Many nights I have sat at my table, just as you were doing tonight. When I did drift off, horrible dreams came. So real, so awful, I feared sleep, and they are always the same."

"They're just dreams—"

"No. They are always the same. And they are not—they are not like normal dreams. They are meant for a sign."

Eli bit his lip. He hated this kind of talk, this mystical voodoo babble, but he would not interrupt again. Something inside made him listen in spite of himself.

"I know what you think of me. And this only confirms your suspicions of the superstitious priest. I know. I would not—did not—want to admit this to myself. But last night I saw him again."

"You saw nothing. You dreamed."

"*El Diablo*. And it was not a dream. I was praying when, I swear, I felt hands closing around my neck. I stumbled to the door to get some air. When I opened it, he was there. Standing on Eagle

Rock. He did not move. He just stared at me."

"A horse would need wings to get up on Eagle Rock. You were hallucinating or dreaming, but you didn't see any horse up there."

The ticking of the old Regulator clock filled the room. Father Zeuma was sweating and shaking. "The dark one comes as a sign, always a sign." He spoke in a voice so soft, so turned in to himself, that Eli barely heard him.

"Look, Padre, I've got more important things to worry about now than phantom horses. Maybe we can talk about this later. Now let me take you home." Eli started to move toward the door. He picked up his rifle and jacket. Something was bothering him. "How are you going to see anything on Eagle Rock anyway? That's a good mile-and-a-half from the church. Even in a full moon you couldn't possibly make out a horse up there."

"I know. I do not understand it myself." Father Zeuma rose wearily from the couch. He was tired of arguing and emotionally spent but he had one last question. A question for which he already knew the answer. "Señor King, who owns Eagle Rock?"

Eli answered slowly, his back to the priest. "Eagle Rock is a boundary marker," he said, "between Marty and Carl. Marty's land's on one side, Carl's is on the other."

"Don't you see?" the priest whispered. "These men will not start with you, Señor. They will strike where you are the most vulnerable. Calavera is crazy. He intends to avenge the death of his brother."

Eli turned to face Zeuma. "I guess even crazy men go to confession, don't they, Padre?"

"Someone is going to die unless you leave. You and your family. All of you," the priest said.

"Tell you what—just to put your mind at ease—I've already taken a couple of extra precautions for Hatty and the boys. And I'll watch my backside real close on the way up north tomorrow. But right now I'm going to get you home, and we're both going to get at least a couple hours sleep."

"No. They will see the truck. They must not know I have come. I will go back the way I came. Good night, Señor King." He moved through the door and down the steps onto the footpath that led to the road.

"Padre," Eli said. The priest stopped and turned back to face him standing on the front porch. "I appreciate your coming. I owe you."

"Keep your rifle clean, Señor. The wild animals get very bad this time of year." He turned and walked down the dimly lit path toward the road.

Later that morning, Eli walked out to the truck with Hatty and threw in the last of his gear. They didn't say much to each other. It had all been said. There would be one more cry, but Hatty needed to save that for when she was with Maria and Marty. She put her bag in the back of the truck and climbed in the cab, sitting closer than usual as Eli cranked the engine. Part of her hoped the old thing wouldn't start, that Eli would have to stay and work on it; but something deeper wanted him to hurry up and go in order to get this thing over with. She couldn't restrain a sigh. Eli didn't acknowledge it, but continued to turn the key with added determination.

If there was one thing Hatty King wasn't good at, it was living with unresolved conflict. Give her a knock-down, drag-out fight any day, but don't leave her hanging. She liked things settled and routine. This business of having to stay with Marty and Maria for a few days was an alien act, remote and unnatural. It made her feel so dependent on others she wanted to scream. The engine caught on the fifth try, and they swung in the wide arc down the road toward Marty's house.

Eli pulled up to the front porch of the small, wood-framed house. Maria came out to greet them, wiping her hands on her apron before she gave Hatty a hug. "We have the guest room all ready for you, Mom. Can Dad stay for some breakfast?" Eli was just coming back from the house, where he had taken Hatty's bag.

"No, thanks, hon, I need to get on the road. Where's Marty? I thought he'd be here."

"Oh, he's going to be sick he missed you. He had to go get some cattle out of Carl's field. Part of the fence was down over by Eagle Rock."

"How'd that happen?" Eli asked.

"I don't know, Dad. Carl came over this morning—I heard him tell Marty that it looked like maybe a couple of bulls got in a fight. He said it was really a mess. Anyway, they're both out there trying to get the cattle separated. Why don't you come in for some coffee at least? They ought to be back with the truck before long."

"No, thanks. I decided to take the old jalopy here. I wouldn't know how to drive that fancy thing of Carl's anyway. I'm ready to roll—got coffee in the thermos and Hatty packed me a lunch."

"I thought you'd be in a rush, so I put together a little something for you myself. Wait just a second." Maria ran into the house and returned quickly with a brown paper bag. "If you want it hot you'll have to eat it soon," she smiled.

Eli opened the bag and took a long whiff. "Egg-and-sausage burritos—you know I can't resist these things!" He gave her a hug and whispered in her ear so Hatty couldn't hear, "Take good care of your mother-in-law. And remember to pray for me." Maria was surprised by his request. Eli had never shown any sign of weakness for as long as Maria had known him. Now he sounded almost scared. He gave Hatty one last hug and kiss.

"You make it mighty hard to leave, girl," he said. "Guess I've gotten kind of used to you."

"You just come back in one piece, mister," Hatty said, barely able to hold back the tears.

"You betcha. Love you, Hat."

"Love you."

Eli climbed into the truck and started the engine on the first try. "Tell Martin and Carl to keep a sharp eye out, but not to start anything. I'll be back just as soon as I can. And Hat," he said as he backed out, "tell Doc I appreciate it." Hatty smiled and waved.

"Did Dad say to thank Doc for something?" Maria asked.

Hatty pretended not to hear, and Maria pretended not to have asked. They both continued to wave as the truck disappeared around the bend that led through town and on to San Antonio.

It took Marty and Carl most of the morning just to repair the fence. All four strands of barbed wire were broken, and two cedar posts had been snapped off at the ground, leaving splintered stumps jutting up at sharp angles. Carl had first noticed the hole in the fence line as he rode along the base of Eagle Rock that morning to check on his cattle. At first he first suspected that Calavera had run through it with his truck; it didn't seem likely that anything else could have done that kind of damage. But as he drove closer he couldn't see any tire tracks going or coming.

"Stupid bulls," he muttered to himself. It was the only explanation that fit. The ground was torn up on both sides of the fence, suggesting a fight between two hard-headed macho bovines who needed to work off some testosterone. Carl turned the truck around and headed for Marty's place. They had a pact that "shared fence meant shared work." Fixing the fence and separating the few strays would give them an opportunity to talk through some things.

Marty had just finished breakfast when Carl drove up. He hadn't slept well and welcomed the opportunity for some physical work that would take his mind off his worries. They loaded some new wire and a few tools and several cedar posts in case they found more downed fence. They made the short return drive to Eagle Rock, intent on being back as soon as they could. Marty didn't like leaving Maria alone, but he thought she would be safe in broad daylight, and he knew his mother would arrive soon to stay with her.

The white face of Eagle Rock straddled the fence line separating the King properties. Carl passed through a gap at the base of the perpendicular cliff and waited as his brother latched it back. Once they had arrived at the damaged fence, Carl stripped to the waist and went to work with the long-handled posthole diggers, trying to loosen the hard earth.

As Marty pulled out the fence stretchers and started to mend the wire, he noticed something unusual in the way the fence was broken. It was odd enough that all four strands of wire were severed, but stranger still was the fact that each was broken in a different place over a space of nearly twenty feet. "Didn't you say bulls did this?" he asked Carl.

"Near as I can figure."

"Okay, you tell me, C, how two sorry animals could bust four strands of wire, each in a different place?"

"Must'a been some good lookin' heifer up for grabs, huh?" Carl answered, as he jammed the posthole diggers into the rocky soil again.

"Must'a been," Marty chuckled.

They returned to the fence repair and thought nothing more of the small enigma, chalking it up as another in a long line of engaging mysteries of the rancher's life.

"So what do you think about Dad goin' off like that?" Carl asked, as he finished tamping one of the new cedar posts into place.

Marty put down his fence pliers and walked over to his brother. "Here, give me those." He took the posthole diggers and began gouging out the second hole. "He knows what he's doing. I gotta admit I'm worried, though. This whole thing could get nasty real fast."

"You know who he's talking about in San Antonio?"

"Nah, but my guess is it's probably somebody he met back when he was in the oil business. I get the feeling he rubbed shoulders with some pretty powerful people back then. Sometimes I wonder if taking the ranch was a smart thing. I think it was a big step down for him."

Chunk. The posthole diggers finally penetrated the earth. When he was younger and setting posts with his father back on the ranch, Marty liked to pretend he was drilling for oil and that one day a posthole would wind up as a gusher and they would all be rich.

It had always bothered him that his father had left his job as a petroleum engineer to run the ranch Hatty had inherited at her father's death. Marty felt his father's decision was more obligatory than desirable and that, deep down, his dad missed the oil fields. He rarely seemed truly happy—or perhaps it was a matter of not being satisfied. "Not being satisfied" was different from "being dissatisfied," a conscious distinction Marty had developed and maintained over the years of trying to understand his father. He had determined early on that "being dissatisfied" was a negative act of the will—more of a reaction than a settled state. It often emerged as an abrupt, temporary, and controllable passion and was only rarely manifested in Eli King.

Chunk. But "not being satisfied" was a condition of the spirit, an abiding malady of the heart, and far more destructive. Marty imagined it as a gradual whittling down of a man's soul. He had always thought there should be a sense of "rightness" about your place in life, a feeling that you were who you were meant to be, doing what you were meant to do.

Chunk. Somehow, he felt, that confidence had eluded his father's grasp, and Marty felt embarrassed and guilty for having noticed. His father, with his granite constitution, was a permeable man after all and too fragile for a son to think about in this way.

"Well, I think we ought to go in and at least talk to those guys," Carl continued. "Let 'em know we aren't scared."

"Yeah, and what are you going to say when they ask about Dad? 'Oh, he's gone to San Antonio to bring down the FBI to arrest you guys!' We're going to wait for him to get back, C."

Carl didn't say anything. He was embarrassed at his own impetuous response and hurt that Marty was making fun of him. Since he had gotten married he liked to think that he had gained a bit more maturity and discernment than the brief span of a year would actually allow for. Marty wished he had put it differently, but the words were out and the damage was done. The best he could do now was try to patch it up.

"Carl," he said apologetically, and though he didn't intend it, condescendingly, "I just don't think we ought to risk getting the girls hurt, that's all. And when you think about it, Dad might—"

"Look, just shut up, all right?"

The response was totally unexpected and out of proportion to the offense. It stood Marty upright.

"Carl—"

"I said shut up! You aren't always right, you know. I don't need your advice. I'm going into town—if you're scared you can stay here." Carl took off his work gloves and threw them at his brother as he stomped off toward the truck.

Marty stood in stunned silence. Suddenly he felt rage boiling in him, so deep he couldn't control it. He ran at his younger brother and tackled him from the back. The blow knocked the wind out of Carl and he fell, bashing his nose into the ground. Marty rolled him over and started slapping him hard.

"You think you're so tough, huh? You think you're so tough, baseball player, daddy's boy? You'll stay at home like I said, or I'll make you wish you had."

Carl was flat on his back, flailing wildly at Marty, who was sitting on his stomach and trying to grab his arms. One of the wild punches landed, catching Marty squarely on the jaw, and he tumbled off Carl's stomach and banged his head against the side of the truck. Carl was on his feet in an instant, kicking his brother in the back and cursing him. Marty rolled away and grabbed Carl's boot, twisting as he turned. Carl fell hard on to his side with a yelp for his twisted knee. Marty jumped up and reached into the bed of the truck for a shovel. He grabbed the spade by the handle and raised it over his head to strike. Carl raised his arm instinctively to ward off the blow—but Marty stopped.

A long, high whistle froze them both. It was ingrained in Eli's sons: when they heard his whistle, they were to stop whatever they were doing immediately or suffer the consequences. Marty was still staring at his brother lying on the ground in front of him. He shook his head as if coming out of a trance and dropped the shovel behind him. Carl lay back, breathing hard.

"What are we doing?" Marty muttered. He stumbled back to rest against the truck, shaking his head and trying to clear the fog. A darkness had lifted. He reached down and pulled his brother up. "Carl, I'm sorry. I never felt that way in my life. I could have killed you."

"Yeah," Carl said as he got up. He walked slowly to the truck and got his shirt. "Me too. Man, I feel like I've got a hangover," he said, leaning against the tailgate and holding his head in his hands. "Why did you stop?"

"I'm not sure. Something made me pull up short."

"Yeah, it happened to me too. Sort of like coming out of a dream . . . hey, look," he said, pointing toward the gap. "There."

Marty turned and focused his eyes on something at the base of Eagle Rock: a man on horseback riding slowly away from them. "Come on, let's see if we can catch him."

Leaving the tools behind, they both jumped into the truck and roared down the fence line toward the gap below Eagle Rock. "Okay, okay, he's heading into that little box canyon. Did you bring the rifle?" Marty shouted as they raced toward the cliff.

"I thought you said we should wait for Dad!"

"Hey, if you're scared, you can stay in the truck!" Marty grinned at his brother and shifted into fourth for more speed. Carl reached under the seat and pulled out his grandfather's 30-30. He opened the glove compartment, grabbed four shells, and pushed the last one into the breechblock just as Marty ground to a stop at the mouth of the canyon. They got out of the truck slowly. Carl cocked the rifle, sliding a shell into the chamber.

Marty strained his eyes to see down the canyon. He could almost see to the end, but a large outcropping of rock prevented a full view. The two brothers inched their way down the rocky canyon bottom—too rocky to leave any hoofprints. They eased up to the outcropping. They could hear something moving on the other side. They crept around it slowly, moving as quietly as they could. Too late, Marty felt the twig under his foot.

Snap.

There was a tremendous rumbling of hooves as a pack of thirty to forty javelinas coiled past the startled men, grunting and gnashing their teeth.

"Oh, man. Oh, man," Carl whispered as they disappeared up the canyon and he slid his back down the large boulder, slumping to the ground in relief.

"We both saw him ride in here," Marty said, sitting down on

a flat rock.

"Yup."

"And we know he didn't come out."

"Right."

"Jeez, Marie," Marty said, rising from his perch. He picked up a stone and threw it back behind the boulder. It bounced off the rock and fell with a clack among the stones piled at the base of the rear wall. "How does a man on a horse get through solid rock?" He strolled around the giant boulder and inspected the niches in the rear wall for—what? A secret door, an undiscovered passageway—he didn't know. He was just looking for a rational answer for what had happened. Then he turned to come back.

"Nothin' there, right?" Carl asked, leaning back against the rock. Marty didn't respond. "Marty?"

No answer. Carl got up and walked around the boulder. "C'mon Mart, don't play games—" he stopped as soon as he saw his brother. Marty was standing still, staring at the back of the large boulder. Carl moved around to see. There, about three quarters of the way up the side of the rock, were two words written side by side in crimson letters: *Muertos. Suplicad.*

"The Day of the Dead," Carl whispered to himself, then translated the second word, "Pray."

14

That evening Carl and Marty and their wives took Hatty to Doc's for a visit. Rosalinda was in bed asleep, and very sick. Estella sat by her husband and listened as the young men told their story.

"You couldn't tell who he was?" Doc asked Carl.

"Nosir. He was riding easy. Not in any hurry."

"How was he dressed?"

"He was pretty far off when we saw him," Marty said. "But I'm sure he was wearing a hat and a pancho or a riding coat of some kind."

"And both of you saw him go into the canyon?"

"That's right," Marty said.

"I can't explain it any more than you can," Doc shrugged. "Maybe you both saw a shadow passing over the rocks. They can play funny tricks on you. And you both said you were feeling dizzy after all that fighting. It's no wonder you would think you saw something that wasn't there." Doc was beginning to convince himself and sounding more and more confident all the time.

"But the writing, Angus." Estella wasn't easily swayed. She felt sure she knew who the rider was.

Doc was uncomfortable. "Aw, what time of year is it? I mean, think of it. The Day of the Dead is just a few days off. Probably some crazy kid or one of the drunks down at the cantina out to scare folks."

"And Father Zeuma?" she parried.

"What does he have to do with this?" Marty asked.

Estella looked at Doc, waiting for him to respond. "They should know," she said to her husband.

Doc let out an enormous sigh. "Last night Father Zeuma thought he saw a horse up on top of Eagle Rock." He paused, looking for the right words. "He took it as a sign of some sort and went and told your father late last night. Your dad stopped by on his way out of town and asked us to watch out for you folks and to keep an eye on Father Zeuma because he thought he might be dangerous.

"At first I couldn't believe Eli was serious," Doc went on. "I tried to talk to him, tell him Zeuma might be scared but he wouldn't think of hurting anybody. But your dad was set. I told him I'd take care of things and then he took off. Course, I can't tell you boys what to do, but I can offer you some advice as your pastor and your friend. I might not agree with Estella on the nature of this, this vision, or whatever you want to call it. But I learned a long time ago not to take her counsel lightly."

Doc leaned forward in his chair. "Both of us think you ought to lay low for the next few days and stay together until Eli gets back with help. Now listen to me carefully. You need to pray—and I mean pray hard. Take Ephesians six and read it through together. Whatever's going on here, there's more at stake than a few head of cattle. I don't want to scare you. The Lord has won the battle, but the devil's still got a lot of snipers out there."

"So you want us to just sit and pray?" Carl asked impatiently.

Doc measured his words before he spoke. "Believe me, if there was a more effective weapon I'd use it. . . . Now, you have the bigger house, Carl. Can you and Anita manage to take on a few boarders for a couple of days? We'd be glad to have Hatty stay with us, but I'm afraid we're going to have to take Rosa down to Mexico City on the train tomorrow to get her fixed up."

"What's wrong, Doc?" Hatty asked.

"Oh, I don't really think it's anything serious, but it could get that way pretty fast if we don't get this fever down. I have an old friend who's a good pediatrician down there. We'll need to be gone a couple of days at least, but believe me, we'll be back just as soon as we can. We sure would appreciate your prayers. I just wish your dad hadn't gone before I could make my trip, but it can't be helped now."

"You think Dad's in trouble, Doc?" Marty asked.

"I think he may be fighting something bigger than a bunch of local thugs," Doc answered.

"Something bigger than a bunch of thugs—what's that supposed to mean?" Carl muttered only half to himself.

"Take it easy, C."

"No, I want to know," Carl insisted, his voice rising. He had been fuming since Doc began talking about spiritual things. "He's always talking in circles. Come out with it plain, Doc. What is it we're fighting here?"

"The Bible says there are—"

"I don't care what the Bible says!" Carl erupted. "Don't tell me what the Bible says. What do *you* say?"

Doc paused for a moment. "These men, these simple fools with guns, are not our enemies," he said.

"Oh, give me a break," Carl said, rising from his seat.

"Carl," Hatty started, but Doc continued.

"They never have been," he said. "Look, Rosalinda has a physical sickness, and so we know to attack it with physical medicine. But our problem here isn't physical and you can't cure it with a gun. I think you know that, Carl, but you're afraid to admit it. Your anger is blinding you. You're filled with such hatred you have to take it out on something. Calavera's convenient, but he's nothing but a pawn. You're aiming at the wrong target, son."

"What, then?" Carl demanded. "The devil? Evil spirits?" He spat the words out as if the idea were as preposterous as Santa Claus and the Easter bunny.

"It wouldn't be the first time," Estella said quietly.

Carl turned on her sharply. "Estella, you believe this? You seriously expect me to believe the bad guys have wings? Hey, the bad guys get drunk and drive a truck, okay? They go around shooting our cattle and our horses, and then us. And you're not going to pray these guys off the road."

"Carl, settle down. Doc's just trying to help," Marty said.

"Yeah, well, when's the last time you saw a prayer stop a bullet? C'mon, Nita." He took his wife by the hand and marched to the front door. He looked back at his brother and spoke in a quieter tone. "You come if you want, Marty." Then, turning to the McClendons, he spoke firmly and intensely, pointing his finger at Doc. "I'm telling you right now, Doc—two days, that's it. Two days and I'm going looking for Dad. And if they've done anything to him, they're the ones who are going to need the prayers." With that he walked out and slammed the door behind him.

No one said anything until the sound of the truck faded into the night.

Doc looked at Marty and winked. "Good exit line," he said, half smiling.

Marty shook his head. "Doc, I'm sorry. Carl's just blowing off steam. He didn't mean anything by that."

"Oh, I think he meant a great deal," Doc protested. "It's hard for someone who has grown up in the U.S. to come face to face with the reality of spiritual warfare. We'll do anything to put another face on it. Anything rather than come to grips with the fact that by ourselves we are powerless to fight the real enemy."

"So you think this whole thing is satanic?" Marty asked.

"No, not the whole thing. Fallen men lean toward evil without any outside help. But I do believe the devil is real. Heaven knows, we've seen enough here to convince us of that. And the Bible does tell us that he is at war with us. This business with Calavera didn't just happen overnight, you know. It's been building for years, and to tell the truth, I've been trying to ignore it myself. Actually, I owe Carl a debt of thanks tonight. I saw myself in him—flat-out, bull-headed denial in the face of convincing evidence. And that means I owe somebody else an apology." He reached over and pulled Estella closer to him, giving her a one-armed hug. "She's known all along."

"I'm not the only one," Estella said, looking at Maria.

"I know there is an evil in this village," Maria said quietly. "It frightens me."

"We don't have to be afraid," Hatty said from her chair by the fireplace. "Greater is He who is in you than he who is in the world, the Bible says. That's always given me such confidence. I think as long as we depend on Him we'll be all right."

Estella reached over and took her husband's hand. "Angus," she said, "I'm going to stay."

"What?"

"I want you to take Rosalinda tomorrow. It will only be for a day or two, and I need to be here." She spoke with such conviction that Doc knew it was no use arguing. Hatty and Marty protested, but her mind was made up. It was decided that Hatty would stay with Estella, and that if Eli returned first, Estella would be their guest until Doc got back.

They all joined hands as Doc led them in prayer. Marty and Maria returned with Hatty to their house to get her things and to pack a few things for themselves.

Back at Doc's, after Hatty got her things inside, Doc offered Marty and Maria a ride back to their house. On the way back, Doc was unusually quiet.

"Don't worry about Carl, Doc. He'll cool off," Marty said as he closed the door to the truck.

Doc patted Marty's arm. "I'm sure he will, son."

"How are you getting to the train station? Estella doesn't drive, does she?"

"No, but a good doctor's never hurtin' for favors," Doc said.

"Maybe you could get somebody to go with you, Doc."

"You know, that would be a real good idea. I'd like some company and think I know just the fellow who might like to get out of town for a while. Thank you for mentioning it, Marty." The young couple climbed out of the truck and turned to say goodbye. "You folks be careful now," Doc said, "and we'll be praying for you."

"You, too, Doc," Marty said. Maria gave him a last hug through the window before he pulled away and drove back down the darkened lane toward home.

The next two days passed with everyone on edge. Carl and Marty rode out to the pasture morning and night to check on the cattle. They were all accounted for, and no more damage had been done to the fence.

On the third day, when they still hadn't heard from Eli, Carl had had enough. He packed a few clothes and threw the duffel bag into the back of the truck. Marty tried to talk him out of going but soon saw it was useless. He decided to go with his brother as much to keep him out of trouble as to help find their father. They stopped by Estella's on their way out of town to drop the girls off and say goodbye to Hatty.

After kissing their wives goodbye, the two young men climbed into Carl's truck. Estella walked up and put her hand on Carl's arm.

"Thanks for watching our girls, Estella," he said. She hugged him through the window.

"You boys be careful."

Marty kissed his wife one last time out the passenger window. "We'll be back in a couple of days," he said, "unless we find Dad first. If we get in a bind I'll call Carlos Hernandez over in San Luis and he'll get word to you."

It was a cool, bright morning as they drove off toward Dolores. Both young men had a feeling something was wrong. Neither of them wanted to think of what it might be.

The drive was quiet. "Shoot," Marty said, slapping his knee. "I meant to ask Estella if Doc got someone to go to Mexico City with him and Rosalinda. He said he had someone in mind, and I never did ask."

"We'll find out when we get back," Carl said. "You know, these are good folks down here, but it isn't home. Never will be. I'm really looking forward to getting back to Texas, Marty. I really am." Their conversation settled into a relaxed and easy rhythm as they enjoyed talking about things they missed back home. About the ranch and the house—wondering if the place was all right, if it had rained yet, and if their treehouse was still standing down by the riverbed.

They had been on the road nearly six hours, without passing more than a dozen cars the whole time, when Carl noticed something unusual on the horizon—black smoke climbing straight up the sky in a narrow column until it flattened out into a wispy cloud. Carl raced ahead, but it still took them nearly twenty minutes to reach the burning wreck. By the time they got there, most of the fire was out.

Vultures had materialized from nowhere, squatting on the road, waiting for the wreckage to cool. As the honking truck approached, the black-winged obscenities lumbered away, ruffling the air with a feathered darkness. Carl slid to a stop just beyond the charred shell of the old truck, tilted on its side in the ditch. The only part left unscathed by the fire was a section of the undercarriage, where a streak of bright red scored the dented oil pan and rear axle. The buzzards landed in a dead tree with the initials RPW carved in the side a couple hundred feet away, where they sat swollen and indifferent, clacking their gray beaks, waiting with filmed eyes for the poachers to clear out.

Carl jumped out and ran toward the burned-out hulk. But halfway there he stopped and threw his hands over his mouth and nose. Memories of childhood and branding time slammed into his consciousness as he gasped for air. The sickening, sweet smell of burning flesh had always nauseated him. He knelt there in the middle of the road retching violently. Marty held his handkerchief over his nose and mouth and ran to the side of the smoldering truck. The driver's side door was bashed in; it was peppered with bullet holes, and the window had either been broken in the crash or shot out. Marty looked in briefly, then turned away, running to his brother.

"Carl, listen to me. We've got to get back. Come on. Somebody must have found out about Dad going for help. Come on, we've got to get back to the girls and get them out of there."

Carl was lying in the middle of the road moaning, pushing

Marty away. "Leave me alone. Just leave me alone. I'm not leaving him here, I don't care what you say."

"Carl, we can't take him with us."

Suddenly, Carl sprang to his feet, grabbed Marty by his jacket and shook him violently. "Don't you see?" he screamed. "Look! Look over there!" he said, pointing to the vultures. "I'm not leaving him here."

"All right, all right," Marty said, pulling himself free. "We'll cover the window with some cedar posts. The window's busted out, but we can tie them in place with some barbed wire. Come on."

Marty walked to the back of their truck and started to unload the tools. Carl followed reluctantly and they set about the work without a word passing between them. There were no cars. There was no sound—only the occasional flap of wings from the distant tree.

The gruesome job took longer than they expected; they finished just before sundown. The stars were just starting to come out as Marty climbed in behind the wheel of Carl's truck and started the engine. Carl slumped exhausted in the passenger's seat.

"Why don't you try to get some sleep?" Marty suggested. "You can spell me later. It's going to be a long trip back."

Carl stared straight ahead. "Not long enough," he said.

As the red tail lights disappeared over the hill, the first lean bird left the quivering branch.

Later that night gravel crunched under the tires as a red Cadillac glided into the shadows behind the cantina. A "closed" sign swung in the wind outside, but the bar wasn't empty. Clouds ripped past the moon on the edge of an early norther. Sheet lightning flashed across the sky. Grabbing a black valise from the passenger's seat, Miguel Sanchez fingered his revolver instinctively as he looked around, then walked quickly to the back door of the cantina and slipped inside.

Three tables and a stunted bar filled the small room. Fifteen men crowded around the bar and the two remaining tables, their voices rolling in a sustained gutteral wave. Cheap smoke curled from the ash ends of green cigars and hand-rolled cigarettes; dull brown papers, glowing red, dangled from ulcered lips and smoldered in the blackened bowls of cracked terra cotta. Smoke hung suspended above the tables where it spread into a wispy haze that swirled a bit every time someone breathed.

A mesquite cane leaned against the rail behind one of the chairs at the far table. There, three men sat hunched over warm beer, talking quietly.

Latigo had chosen his "posse" carefully. Most of them had no use for one another so the chances of unified opposition to his rule were remote. He chose them with two basic criteria in mind: a love of money, and a fear of the one who made the money possible. Most of them had never grown up. Or perhaps they had been forced to grow up too early, which often has the same dwarfing effect on the personality. Whatever the cause, these grown men retained an adolescent need to control and manipulate to satisfy their greed. Each of them retained the bully's appetite for intimidation and the coward's preference for the weak. Latigo provided in their own hometowns a profitable arena for them to act out their aggression.

The conversation halted briefly as Miguel walked over to the table and pulled out a chair. All eyes were on the valise as the deputy slid it under the table, sat down, and lit a cigarette. A sudden burst of lightning disrobed the night. Through the single northern window Miguel saw, in the frozen brightness of a landscape stripped of shadow, a thin form loping toward them. A second flash gutted the darkness of the cantina for a microsecond, as both thunderclaps struck at the same instant. The front door flew open and the albino stepped inside. A whirl of grit blew in behind him as he closed it and wiped his eyes with his red neckerchief.

"I told you to use the back," one of the men at the table said in a voice that rumbled away with the thunder.

"There's no one in the street," Calavera answered as he moved behind the bar to pour himself a beer. There was no reply.

"Shut up and sit down," Sanchez commanded. He knew his

boss wouldn't take any back-talk from Calavera, and he wanted to avoid a fight. They had too much to do to waste time arguing. Calavera smiled crookedly at Sanchez as he took his time pouring his beer. He sauntered from behind the bar and strolled leisurely over to the table.

Latigo began to chuckle to himself. The others remained quiet at first and then joined him in light laughter. By the time Calavera had pulled up a chair, he was laughing too. As soon as he sat down Latigo reached over and grabbed the glass of beer with his right hand, Calavera with his left. He threw the beer in Calavera's face and smashed the glass against the back wall with such force that he was left holding only the handle and a jagged shard of the mug, which he shoved up under the albino's quivering white chin. Latigo's face was almost touching Calavera's—so close, Latigo's cigar was burning his right cheek.

"We been waitin' for you, son. Old Latigo's been waitin' a long time. I don't like to wait. And I don't like your mouth. You think just because you do one little job, gives you the right to sass me? You been braggin', son? I bet you been braggin' all about it, now ain't you, you snivelin' little lickspit? You got such a loose tongue, maybe we oughta shorten it up a little." He pressed the glass to Calavera's throat. Calavera barely breathed, scared the glass would slip through the soft alabaster shield. Latigo shoved him back into his chair.

"Sit!" he barked, as if he were talking to a curr. "As I was telling the boys before you stumbled in, Calavera, you almost botched the assignment." Latigo sat down slowly.

"He was dead, *Patrón*. I saw him with my own eyes," Calavera whined defensively.

"What was the last thing I said?" Latigo said menacingly. "What was the last thing I told you to do?"

Calavera looked around the table from one face to the other but found no support.

"I told you to burn the body, didn't I?" Latigo said. "Burn it, I said, then get rid of it. I could've asked Hector or even Miguel. But I figured after what King did to your brother, I could count on you to burn the body. So I come along and have to do a hurry-up job and leave him there. That's not what I pay you for, son."

Calavera was breathing hard, looking down at the table top. Latigo's chair squeaked as he leaned back against the wall. Calavera jumped.

"The fire," he said, too loud for the small room. "I could not. He was dead. I thought it was enough."

"Get rid of the gun," Latigo said.

"The police will do nothing, *Patrón,* we have—"

"Federales wouldn't mess with this, but you screwed up, son," Latigo shouted. "You shot an American citizen, then left his body and his truck out in the wide open spaces for every tourista to gawk at. If I were you, I'd pray to the blessed virgin that fire did the job and burned him to ash before the FBI gets involved. Mr. Hoover gets testy about losin' U.S. taxpayers on Mexican soil."

"So what do we do now, Boss?" Miguel asked.

"*We* don't do anything," he said. Then he looked at Calavera. "However, this piece of trash has some driving left to do tonight. There's a dry ravine about a mile east of the truck. Calavera, you're goin' to take some chains and drag that heap over the edge and that'll be the end of it. Now get goin'."

Calavera was up and to the door before before Latigo finished the sentence.

"Calavera," Latigo said, stopping him in mid-stride. "Back door."

The white man mumbled something inaudible and walked out, hat in hand. Latigo didn't notice him reach up and take a bottle of tequila from a shelf just before he reached the door. He tucked it inside his coat and slipped out into the night.

Latigo turned to the man sitting on his left. "Joe, you go with him and make sure it's done right this time." Without a word, the small Mexican pushed his chair back and followed Calavera out to the truck. Miguel watched him until he got out the door.

"Now," Latigo said, "we got a small problem to clear up. I had one of the boys up north follow King to San Antonio. He must've figured out he was being followed, 'cause he didn't go anywhere to meet anyone—checked into a hotel and made calls from his room. The point is we know he must have contacted someone and that means we have to lay low for a while. I told the posse before you got here they were going to have to back off for a month or two. Give the priests some breathing room. No heat, no accidents. It won't kill us to lose two months' worth of revenue, and besides I got a deal workin' over in Puentas that just got a lot sweeter as of this afternoon, and it's going to take most of my time for a while. Deputy, I want you to pay off these boys and get 'em out of here tonight."

"What about Skerritt, Boss?" Miguel asked. "Wasn't he supposed to be here?"

"Jake's taking care of business," he said just loud enough for Miguel to hear. Then, even more quietly, "Now, listen up. Hector here says he saw King's sons head out this morning. That means they'll find their old man before Calavera can get rid of the evidence."

"But—" Miguel started.

"But nothing. If Calavera happens to luck out and get rid of the body before they get there, fine. If they catch him in the act—that youngest King boy's a hothead, and I know for a fact he always carries a gun. Somebody's goin' to get shot, and I don't really care who. Either way, you need to be ready for them in case they come back tonight."

"Why send Joe on a suicide mission?"

Latigo looked hard at his deputy. Miguel was asking too many questions. "Joe's made himself expendable. He's been losing influence for quite a while now. The priest down in Abasolo isn't afraid of him any more—and you don't pay for what you're not afraid of. The King boys kill him, it's no skin off my nose. He's weak and I won't abide weakness in my organization. You don't build a strong herd by coddling the frail. You get rid of them, cull 'em out."

Miguel stared at his boss for a brief moment, blinked, and looked out the window. Miguel had gotten Joe this job. He was an old friend. One of the few Miguel had, but he knew if he said anything to Latigo he would risk losing everything he had worked for.

To question an order was to prove disloyalty.

"You got a problem, deputy?" Latigo demanded.

"I was just thinking, Boss," he lied. "Why not keep the boys around? They could help us take care of the problem."

Hector Rodriguez leaned in. "We don't need no help. I will take them out myself. I owe the big one for this." He reached behind his chair and grabbed his walking cane. He pulled off the silver tip to reveal a needle-sharp point. "If I find him alone, it will take more than a cane to help him walk again."

"Shut up, both of you," Latigo barked. "This has gotta be clean, and I don't want a lot of eyes. You'll get your chance, Rodriguez, when I say so. Those boys will be back. My guess is tonight. Wait 'em out. They won't go anywhere 'til they pick up the women anyway. Once they get on the road they're gonna have a little accident."

"The women . . . ?" Miguel asked.

"Which one you think wouldn't talk? We don't know how much they know. It's too risky. Besides, as long as they're alive, the ranch is locked up."

"How do you want it done?" Hector asked.

"No guns. It's gotta look real. Run 'em off one of the high passes. Just make sure the job's done before you hightail it."

Hector nodded. Miguel took a long drag on his cigarette. Latigo looked over at Hector and winked, then spoke to Sanchez. "What's the matter, deputy, you afraid of gettin' your hands a little dirty?" The skin wrinkled on Latigo's forehead where his eyebrows should have been. He laughed and downed a shot of tequila. "Let me tell you somethin'," he said, "you're already dirty, son. But it don't matter, you know why? 'Cause oil takes out blood real good. Once we get ahold of that land, none of this is going to matter." The smile faded. "Now give these men their bonus and get rid of them like I told you. Tell them I'll be back, and then they'll make more money than they ever dreamed. That ought to keep 'em quiet for a while, anyway."

Latigo rose and pulled on his coat as he started toward the back door.

"You takin' off, Boss?" Hector asked.

"What does it look like, Rodriguez?" Latigo said without looking back.

As the men made way for their *patrón,* Sanchez moved into his place on the far side of the table from the crowd.

Latigo opened the door, then turned to speak. "I'll be waitin' for you, deputy," he said as he looked directly at Miguel and smiled.

No one moved. Rain drummed on the tin roof, ran down the corrugated gutters, and spilled into the muck outside. Latigo turned on his heel and walked slowly out through the rain to his car.

As soon as he was gone, all eyes turned back to Sanchez. He lifted the black valise onto the table and opened it so that the men couldn't see inside. He took out his gun and held it high, for everyone in the room to see, then he cocked it and placed it in the open valise. They were all familiar with the ritual. Hector sat beside him with his cane in his lap. Miguel began to call the names, and one by one they filed past without once looking into the eyes of their benefactor, and without a word passing between them. Miguel wouldn't have to tell them to leave. They never stayed around anyway. But Latigo wouldn't know that. He despised these men, even though he was half Mexican himself. He was always the first one out the door.

15

It was past midnight; the norther had settled in, penetrating the adobe walls and the wood-slatted shacks of Dolores. The rain had stopped nearly an hour before, leaving the traveled roads a slush pit of muck. A low, thick fog wrapped itself sullenly around any stationary object. Along the main street, nothing moved. A loose piece of tin creaked on its own against the eave of the abandoned smithy at the near end of town.

The sound of the truck motor was alien. Its headlights swung past the darkened cantina and shone far down the road. There were no candles left burning in any of the windows—as if the fog had snuffed the life out of the town. It was a night to be inside, safe and warm by a fire.

The truck raced down the muddy road toward Doc's house. Marty almost slid past the turnoff for the short lane leading up to the house. They fish-tailed onto the gravel road and slid sideways for a few feet before slipping into the ditch. Marty pushed it into first and eased out of the mud and back onto the road.

"Stupid!" he muttered to himself. He eased up to the house and turned off the lights. They sat there for a moment listening to their own breathing. "Just like we planned it, okay?" he said to Carl without looking at him.

"Yeah," Carl answered. His voice was thin and weak.

"You okay?" Marty asked.

"Yeah, I'm all right," he said.

He felt sick to his stomach. Marty started to open the door when he felt Carl's hand on his shoulder. "I don't think I can do this. It'll kill Mom."

"I know how you feel. But we've got to tell her sometime. C'mon, let's just go on in and get it over with."

They got out of the truck and walked up to Doc's door. Everything seemed dead. Everything inanimate was dull and weary. The steps leading up to Doc's front porch. The wooden poles holding up the porch roof. Carl had never noticed how badly they needed paint. *This whole town needs paint,* he thought. *This whole world.*

The front door opened and Estella motioned the boys inside. "I thought I heard you drive up," she whispered as she closed the door behind Carl. Neither of them said anything. "Did you find your father?" she asked. The room was dark; she couldn't see their eyes. The young men stood looking down, not speaking. Estella reached out and gave Marty's arm a gentle squeeze. "I'll get your mother," she said quietly.

In less than a minute Hatty was in the room. She stood before her sons, holding on to Estella. "Tell me" was all she said.

Marty found the words and spoke them as gently as he could. They moved into the kitchen and sat around the table. Maria came in, awakened by the soft voices and the crying. When she entered the room, Carl was rising from his place at the table to go wake Anita.

He opened the door quietly and padded to the bedside. He stood there crying. Anita woke and sat up slowly. She took his hand as he sat on the edge of the bed and tried to explain what had happened, though he could barely speak through his tears. Her dark eyes searched Carl's face, trying to strain an explanation from the flood of often incoherent words. As the truth sank in she put her hand over her mouth and said nothing. By the time he had finished, she was staring straight ahead, expressionless.

A cold wind swept across the valley. The limbs on the mesquite beside the house creaked; thorns scraped against the tin roof.

"Ehécatl," Anita said under her breath.

"What?" Carl said between sobs. "What did you say?"

Anita was going to tell him, but something inside made her decide to keep the idea to herself. "Nothing, I was just thinking. Where is Maria?"

"She's in the kitchen with the rest. Why?"

"I was just wondering. I suppose we should—should join . . . Carl?" she said in a dreamy whisper. "What is that?"

"What?"

"That sound. Don't you hear it?"

"It's just the limbs on the roof, sweetheart."

"Listen—there!" she said, and Carl heard it too. A high whinnying, barely discernible from the sound of the thorns scraping against the tin roof. Anita ran from the bedroom, through the living room, and to the front door. She threw it open and stepped out onto the porch. Marty followed her out just behind Carl. They reached her just in time to see a black horse, running against the wind, disappear down the road toward Dolores.

"The dark one," Anita said. Then, before Carl could respond she turned and looked at him. Estella had come out with Hatty and Maria to see what was going on, but Anita ignored them. She spoke directly to her husband. "You must kill it. Before the Days of the Dead. You must kill it or we will all die."

Marty tried to respond. "It's a stray—it broke out of somebody's pen. . . ."

"Go to the priest," Anita insisted, still talking to Carl. "He will tell you what to do. Go now."

Carl stepped off the porch and started walking toward the truck. Marty took Anita by the shoulders. "Call him back. Anita, this isn't going to do any good. Call him back." The truck roared to life, and Carl began to back it around to leave.

"C, wait!" Marty shouted as he ran toward the truck. He jumped into the bed just before Carl gunned the engine. The tires spun on the slick road but soon gained traction and the truck sped out onto the road that would take them into Dolores.

The front of the church was dark. The truck pulled up on the north side, and Carl jumped out with rifle in hand. Marty jumped out of the back and caught up to his brother before he reached the large oak doors.

"What are you taking this for?" he said, grabbing Carl by the shirt sleeve. "You think that stallion ran into the church? Put the gun down, Carl." Carl stopped and looked down at the rifle he held in his hands.

"I didn't even know I had it," he said to himself, and he threw it down on the cement porch in front of the church.

"Father Zeuma's probably asleep in the back anyway. Why not wait until morning, huh? What could happen between now and—"

"Unhhh." The muffled sound came from inside the church. Carl and Marty moved cautiously to the double doors. The right door was ajar. Marty opened it slowly, peering inside, trying to adjust his eyes to the deeper shadows of the church's interior. Votary candles burned quietly; shadows capered on the white walls, along the tops of the pews, and fluttered across the floor. Marty and Carl stepped inside, leaving the door open behind them.

They took two cautious steps toward the votary table. "Father?" Carl whispered.

Something moved in the shadows; a man stood near the altar, took two steps forward, and tumbled to the floor.

"Father!" Carl said as he ran toward the prostrate body. Gently, the young men turned the priest over onto his back. He screamed in pain as they moved him from the aisle into the shadow of one of the pews. Marty rolled up his coat and placed it under his head for a pillow. The single altar candle cast a weak light against the white wall—enough to see blunt forms but not details. The priest was bleeding badly from a cut above one eye. His hair was matted with blood from repeated blows to the head. His nose and jaw had been broken, his eyes were swollen shut, and his face was puffy and badly bruised.

"Take it easy, Father," Marty said softly. "It's going to be all right. Just lie still till we can get some help."

"Can you talk, Father?" Carl leaned into the shadow and asked in a whisper. "Who did this to you?"

The priest's breathing was short and labored. He tried to speak but winced with the exertion. He coughed, and a small stream of frothy blood ran from the corner of his mouth.

"I'm afraid it's his ribs, C. I think he punctured a lung. We need to get him to a doctor fast."

"Doc's still in Mexico City. What are we gonna do?—we can't move him."

A bright light flashed across Marty's back and into Carl's eyes. A truck pulled up outside and two doors opened quickly. There were voices, but they were indistinct.

"Maybe it's Doc . . . " Carl said as he stood.

"Carl, wait."

"Doc, in here!" Carl shouted.

The large oak doors burst open. Two men stood silhouetted against the glare of the headlights. One was short, the other tall and, even in that darkness, pale. He held a rifle in one hand, a half-empty tequila bottle in the other.

"Hey, gringo, you dropped something," said the drunken albino as he lifted the rifle with one hand and fired. The 30-30 slug caught Carl square in the chest and slammed him against the back wall, loosening the enormous crucifix and toppling the altar candle onto the table's cloth runner. He was dead before he hit the floor.

"No! Oh, God, C, no!" Marty lunged toward his brother and knelt beside him, cradling his head in his arms.

The sound of the rifle ejecting the spent cartridge pierced Marty's consciousness. He straightened and whirled toward the two men. The rifle clicked, jammed.

Then three things happened at once. Marty lunged straight ahead in a blind rage. Instinctively, Calavera threw the tequila bottle, missing Marty's head by an inch. Joe leveled both barrels of his shotgun straight ahead. *BLAM! BLAM!*

"Aaaaah!" Anita screamed when the sharp report of the rifle shot crackled the sky all down the valley. All four women rushed out to the porch of Doc's home, just in time to hear the double blast of the shotgun. Anita leaned against one of the corner posts for support. Maria stood beside her with Hatty and Estella, all of them looking toward Dolores, straining to hear. Anita felt as if the blasts had ripped into her own heart, and she cried out, sinking to the porch and weeping. Maria bent down to comfort her, but Anita struck out at her viciously.

"No! This is all your fault!"

Maria pulled back. Hatty stared at Anita in disbelief.

"Anita, that's enough!" Estella snapped. "Get into the house, now."

Anita rose slowly, still clinging to the corner post. "You!" she directed her venom at Estella. "You pretend to be so righteous, so holy, but I know. You've seen the dark one, too. We all have. All because of her—poor little Maria, born under a black moon. It's not the moon, Maria—it's you. *You* are the curse!" she screamed. "You are death!"

The tequila bottle shattered against the back wall, dousing crucifix, altar, and floor. As the overturned candle ignited the liquor, the front end of the church erupted into flame. One of the blasts from the shotgun had splintered the foot of the cross so that it tilted down and to the left, dangling on the one remaining nail and burning furiously; the other shot had ripped through Marty's upper chest and neck. His body lay crumpled and bleeding beside the priest.

Calavera started to walk slowly up the aisle toward the bodies. Joe tugged at his sleeve and motioned for them to go, but Calavera pushed him off. Joe dropped the shotgun and ran out the door and down the street toward the cantina. He passed people on the far end of town running toward the burning church. Calavera heard their cries and turned back to the door. He stumbled in his drunken stupor and knocked over the votary table, spilling the candles out along the carpeted runner; one of the pebbled-glass holders rolled beneath the embroidered tapestry that hung on the rear wall, igniting it immediately.

Sweat poured off Calavera as he staggered forward. He closed and double-bolted the doors from the inside, then ran back to lock the thick door that led to the priest's chambers, tumbling over Marty's body on the way. He slid the heavy bolt shut just as the crowd reached the back entrance. Breathing hard, he leaned against the locked door, listening to the screaming and shouting outside, the loud banging on the doors. But the clamor soon faded into the sounds of the burning—the cracking, spitting, and hissing; the great moaning of the ancient timbers. An eerie peace settled on Calavera's blistered brain—somehow, he felt, this was right. This was home. He rose slowly and walked through the burning church, slivers of burning wood and flaming cloth floating and falling all around him. He held out his hands and threw his head back to catch the fiery flakes on his tongue.

His feet led him to the front of the altar where he stood for a moment, his head tilted to one side, watching the fire consume the crucifix. Then, in one blinding flash of clarity, the confusion receded for a moment—he knew who hung on the cross. And why. It was a desperate act of grace, and it was Calavera's last hope. He understood. Calavera knew. But he was so full of self-loathing he would not accept any offer of love, and he pushed it away—the darkness sealed him up forever. The dark resin in the wood bubbled to the surface and ran down the hot face of Christ like so many black tears to feed the flame and choke the sanctuary with sable fumes. Calavera spoke to the figure on the cross.

"Don't cry. Don't cry, Jimmy. It will all be over soon. Shhhh. There now. You go ahead—I'll be along. Shhh." The great pounding on the doors had stopped. The windows were much too high and narrow for a man to crawl through. The people had given up for lost both the church and those inside and so had turned away to try to save their own homes and businesses from the fire.

Large wooden beams in the ceiling were burning now. Calavera slumped onto the first pew and leaned back. He breathed in the noxious gases and coughed them back out again. He could barely see now, but as he lay back on the pew and looked up, he could still make out the flames racing in sheets along the dry wooden planks that formed the roof. In and out, up and down, between the slats, along the grooves, like yellow fingers caressing the wood. Like his mother's hair, yellow and flowing, reaching down, down until he could touch it, feel it on his milk-white skin. He smiled and coughed and closed his eyes.

There was a great tumble and crash as the center part of the roof fell in. If there was a scream, no one heard it. The oven was vented now; fiery vines curled and twined around the bell tower. The north wind fanned the inferno, transforming the church into a glowing spinneret, whirling silken threads of flame into the night sky—orange and yellow sparks spun out and up, winding in crazy spirals up to the stars and out to the south to land on the rooftops of Dolores.

A bucket brigade had formed. The line stretched from the well at the rear of the church along the south wall, but many of the people were not trying to extinguish the church fire. Men, women, and children, many of them barefoot and dressed in their nightclothes, were dousing the roofs and walls of nearby shops. Already, three of the buildings had caught fire and were burning steadily. More people arrived from farther away; each grabbed whatever would hold water—hats, buckets, or shirts dipped in water to fight the blaze. Two men, however, slipped back into the shadows.

"I told you he was crazy, Sanchez." Rodriguez leaned on his cane, bracing himself against the biting wind, watching the church burn. He shook his head, then said to no one in particular, "This whole business is crazy. I'm getting out." He turned and started to limp away.

"You're getting out of nothing," Miguel snarled, grabbing Hector by the coat and spinning him around. "Here's what you're going to do. You are going back to the cantina to pick up Joe. There are two guns behind the bar—one .45, one shotgun. Then you are going to the doctor's house. We'll take care of the women there. Now go!" He shoved Rodriguez back into the alley and turned and walked back toward the burning church.

Hector yelled after him, "What about you, Sanchez?"

Miguel drew his pistol, turned, and aimed at Rodriguez, who limped away quickly in the direction of the cantina. Miguel holstered his pistol and turned back to the fire. "I got one last piece of business," he said to himself as he walked toward the rear of the church.

16

The wind had blown most of the fog away so that the flames from the burning bell tower were just visible from Doc's house. "Get your things together," Hatty said to the women, her eyes fixed on the orange glow. "If the boys are all right they'll be back soon. If something has happened, we'll need to move fast."

Maria moved immediately from the porch into the house with Estella. Anita dissolved into tears. Hatty crossed to her quickly. "Anita, hush. Hush and listen to me. Now isn't the time for this. They may be all right, but we have to be ready . . . if . . . we have to be ready."

"Ready? Ready for what?" Anita demanded through her tears. "Where are we going to run? And how? On foot? You don't drive; none of us can drive."

"I can drive if I have to," Hatty said. "I just don't have to very often, and I'll admit I don't like it, but I can do it. Now go get ready," Hatty said, putting her arm around her and moving her toward the door.

"What should I take? I don't know what to take," Anita said, whimpering like a frightened schoolgirl.

"Enough clothes to last three days. Now go, go, hurry. We don't have much time."

Anita wiped away her tears and went into the house. Estella passed her on her way back out.

"Hatty, listen," said Estella, walking up to her friend and taking her arm. "I want you to go ahead and leave. Don't wait. If the boys are all right I'll get word to you in San Luis Potosí. You will get there by five if you leave now. You can stay with Carlos Hernandez. Here is his address and phone." She handed Hatty a folded piece of paper.

"You're going with us," Hatty insisted.

"No."

"We aren't leaving without you, Estella."

"No, listen—we don't have time to argue. These men don't care about me. If they come, I can stall them here—tell them you went to Mexico City or something. Right now the most important thing is for you to get to a safe place fast. Doc should be back soon. I'll need to be here for him anyway to fill him in on what has happened so we can do something. Let's get your things together."

"I'm already packed," Hatty replied. "I wanted to be ready to go when Eli came home." Estella put her arms around her friend and the two hugged briefly. Hatty shook with sobs for a few moments, but then drew away quickly, holding Estella at arm's length. "All right. All right. We'll go. How will you contact us?"

"There's a telephone at the railway station in San Carlos."

"Promise you'll call?" Hatty asked weakly.

"Promise," Estella said, smiling. "Everything's going to be fine. Now let's get your things in the truck."

Estella went back to the kitchen and gathered some food for the trip. Thinking of something at the last minute, she grabbed a pencil and paper and started to draw quickly. Maria and Hatty had their bags in the back of Doc's truck ready to go within four minutes. Anita emerged a few minutes later with two bags; she climbed into the cab as Hatty started the engine of the truck. Estella ran out to the driver's window carrying a flashlight, some fruit in a sack, and a piece of paper.

"Stay off the main roads," she said. "Go into San Luis the back way. Here, I've drawn you a little map." She shone the flashlight on the piece of paper.

"What's this?" Hatty asked, pointing to a line on the map that looked like a crooked zipper.

"Train tracks. It's the same line that Doc rode down to Mexico City. It runs all the way to Laredo. The back road to San Luis is on this side, the west side of the tracks, see? You can cross over here."

"Thanks," Hatty said. "Send word fast." Estella patted her arm as Hatty ground the gears.

"The clutch, dear," Estella reminded her, backing away to a safe distance.

"Oh, yeah." She tried again.

"Try not to drive more than sixty miles an hour," Estella shouted. "It starts to shake awfully when you do."

Hatty waved her acknowledgment as she pushed the pedal down and shifted into first, then let it out slowly; the engine was racing when the clutch engaged, and the truck lurched forward and down the lane. Normally, Estella would have stayed to wave goodbye, but tonight she offered a quick prayer as she turned away to walk swiftly back into the house. Hatty made it to the end of the lane, but instead of turning left to go into Dolores, she turned right. She had to get gas at home. Doc kept his tank locked and since Estella didn't drive, he carried the only key on his ring. It would take only ten minutes at most.

Estella walked immediately to her bedroom and pulled out her Bible. She knelt by her bed and began to pray. "Oh, Father," she said, "protect Your children. Set Your holy angels around them and grant them safe passage. We trust You to protect our husbands. Surround Carl and Martin with Your loving care and bring them home safe. Oh, Lord, bring these evil men to justice for what they have done. And Father, bring Angus home soon. Be with our little Rosalinda. Make her well. I'm afraid, Father. I know You tell me not to be anxious, but I am. We are in the valley of the shadow, Lord. Comfort us here. Guide us through—"

WHAM! The front door crashed open. Estella jumped, but then decided to stay by the bed praying and trust in the Lord to deliver her. She tried to concentrate on her prayer, but she could hear the intruders tearing through her home, going from room to room. "Give me strength, Lord, to stand the test. Help me to trust in You."

"McClendon!" a voice screamed from Doc's study. The man sounded out of breath and hoarse from the cold air. The floorboards creaked outside her door. No one spoke, but she could hear the heavy breathing of someone looking in on her. A second set of footsteps—someone with a limping, plunking gait, a man with a cane—came through the door and moved quickly to her side.

"Get up!"

She stayed kneeling, hands clasped in front of her.

"I said, get up!" Hector screamed as he grabbed her hair and jerked her to her feet.

Estella stifled a scream as she tried to gain her balance. Hector grabbed her throat and squeezed hard.

"Where are they?" Hector demanded. His face was close. His breath stank of whiskey and cigars. He eased his grip just enough for Estella to whisper a response.

"Mexico City."

Hector frowned and then laughed slowly. He glanced over at the short man standing in the doorway. Joe showed no emotion—he stared out the bedroom window, refusing to watch. Suddenly, Hector drew back his hand and struck Estella hard on her cheek with the silver handle of his cane. He caught her by the arm as she started to fall.

"One more smart answer and I'll kill you, and then I'll kill your little girl and that pig of a husband. Now where are the King women?"

"We have done nothing to you. My husband took care of you. Why do you hate us? Jose," she said turning to the man in the doorway, "when your wife was sick, who went to San Luis for medicine in the middle of the night?" Joe remained impassive, looking straight ahead.

"Shut up!" Hector yelled, as he tightened his grip and drew her close to him. He was so angry he was shaking. "Woman, I swear on my mother's grave, if you don't tell me where they've gone, I'll go down to that train station, and I'll wait for both of them with that shotgun."

Estella suddenly felt herself relax. The throbbing pain in her cheek didn't matter. His hatred didn't matter. She knew this desperate man could snuff out her life in an instant, but her life wasn't really hers to lose anyway. Estella knew in that moment what she had been afraid of. It wasn't the gun or the threats against her family. What she had been afraid of was lying to protect Hatty. She felt she could justify it to the Lord; but she knew deep inside that there was no real justification even to herself, that there was only rationalization. This was the strength she had prayed for. The strength to do what she knew to be right and trust the Lord for the outcome.

"They are on their way to San Luis," she said.

"How long ago?"

"Not more than ten minutes."

"Hear that, Joe?" Hector said, turning toward the door. "Mrs. McClendon here says our lady friends are headed for San Luis." He looked back at Estella. "You're a liar, ma'am. If they'd been going to San Luis they would've passed through town and I would've seen them. No, I figure if you say they're headed north, they must be headed south—either to the mountains or to the King place. Come on, Joe, let's pay the Kings a visit."

He moved toward the door, but turned back to Estella before he left. "Oh, I wouldn't try to go anywhere if I were you, Mrs. McClendon. Not if you want to see your husband and little girl again. You just stay here and, uh, pray. It's done you a lot of good so far." He laughed as he turned and stalked out of the house, wiping the silver handle of his cane with a white handkerchief.

Estella remained standing until she couldn't hear the men's voices any longer. Then she breathed a prayer of thanks as she calmly went into the kitchen and primed the pump to wash her wounds. *They may be after Hatty,* she thought to herself as she gently daubed the gash in her cheek, *but at least they are headed the wrong way.*

Hatty knew she had the key to the gas tank in her purse somewhere, but she couldn't find it. Finally, she emptied out her purse onto the truck seat and with the help of Anita and Maria found the small Masterlock key. Then she had trouble getting it to turn in the lock. Eli said he always had to jiggle it just right or it would never work. It took a couple of minutes, but she finally felt it turn and the lock sprang free. The silver tank was suspended above the ground so that the flow of fuel was regulated by gravity and the size of the nozzle. Doc's truck was almost empty, so it took a good three to four minutes to fill it. She locked the tank and was ready to pull out when she remembered something she needed from the house.

She ran in quickly, thinking to herself the whole time how frustrated Eli would be for her taking so long, for having to go back into the house for one more thing. For a moment she was strangely disoriented, but as soon as she stepped into the door of their bedroom, a wave of grief swept over her. She knew it was no time to cry; she fought it, but she simply couldn't help herself. Every place in the house was an empty spot where a husband or a son ought to be, and she was haunted by their absence. She wandered from room to room in a daze of grief, touching pieces of furniture, articles of clothing. She picked up Eli's brown leather jacket from the bedpost and held it to her face. This was what she had come in to find. She had given it to Eli for a wedding present; it had his aroma about it—Old Spice, and baby powder, and nearly twenty-five years of a life shared. It was as if he were there, touching her cheek with the back of his hand, telling her it was going to be all right.

She looked up. Maria was sitting beside her on the bed. Her arm was around her and she was speaking to her softly.

"Are you ready, Mom?" she asked softly.

"I'm sorry," Hatty said. "I guess I just got sidetracked." She took a deep breath and wiped away her tears. "All right," she said. "We've got some driving to do."

She walked out through the living room, looking around the house as if she wanted to remember each room just as it was; as if she were leaving for the last time. With Maria waiting for her on the front porch, Hatty locked the door behind her. As she turned to step off the porch, she paused and put her hand on Maria's shoulder.

"Did you hear something?" she asked. "I could have sworn I heard voices, but. . . ." She looked hard out through the darkness and couldn't make anything out. Then, farther up the road toward Dolores she saw the distant headlights of a car moving quickly toward them. The two women ran to the truck.

Hatty jumped into the front seat with Eli's jacket in her hand as Maria ran around to the passenger's side. The engine roared to life on the first try. Hatty jammed the clutch in and spun out around the front of the house. The rain-slick road refused to provide the traction she needed to make the turn from the house into the lane; she bounced hard across the ditch and out into the muddy field before she regained control of the truck.

At the same instant she hit the ditch, a shotgun blast from the far end of the road ripped into the front of the truck, shattering one of the headlights and puncturing the radiator. The jolt from hitting the ditch masked the sound and impact of the shot, so that Hatty wasn't even aware the truck had been hit. Joe, however, was sure his long shot had caused significant damage, and he raced down the road toward the wounded vehicle. Hatty shifted into reverse with Maria's help and looked back to see two shadowy figures—one running down the road, and the other hobbling behind as fast as his cane would go. With the engine racing she changed direction and swung out into the field in a wide curve away from her pursuers, and then doubled back toward the house. Joe ran back to the road and then off for the house. As Hatty made the turn around the east end of the house, she realized that one of the headlights had gone out on her.

"Mom, look out!" Maria shouted.

Hatty spun the wheel left, but not in time to miss the clothesline. Fortunately, the windshield had just enough slant to it to allow the three metal lines to whip over the top. She completed the turn around the back of the house and shifted into third. Mud was flying everywhere. Just as she passed the gasoline tank on the south side of the house, the headlights she had seen earlier pulled into the short road that led to her house.

"Oh, Lord, oh, Lord, help us!" she shouted over the clamor of the engine as she threw it into fourth. The red Cadillac picked up speed at the same time and was closing fast. Hatty saw one shadowy figure leap out of the way of the oncoming car, narrowly missing being run down. With less than twenty yards to go Hatty swerved to the right; her headlight caught the second man aiming a shotgun directly at them. Hatty screamed and threw her hands up instinctively to protect herself, but the truck slammed into the gunman, hurling him up and to the left and through the windshield of the approaching car. The red Cadillac spun out of control and plowed into the field on the south side of the road. The truck spun around in a half circle and back up onto the road so that the front was pointed back toward the house.

"Oh, goodness! Are you girls all right?" Hatty asked.

"I thought you couldn't drive!" Maria said, her eyes as wide as saucers.

"Don't ask me!" Hatty said. She leaned back against the seat and put her hand to her head. "Oh, Lord, I'm too old for this. That fellow had a gun!" she said, sitting up straight again. The adrenaline was still pumping. "Did you see that? He pointed it right at us! If we hadn't hit him he would have shot us! Lord'a mercy!"

"Yeah, him or his partner," Anita said.

"What partner?" Maria asked.

"Didn't you see him at the end of the lane? The other car hit him, I think."

"No," Hatty said, "he jumped out of the way at the last minute. I saw him. That car didn't hit him." They looked at each other for just a second. "So that means. . . . " They all three looked back in time to see Hector just five feet behind them, covered with mud from head to toe. Hatty threw the truck into first and gunned the engine. Mud flew from under the back tires and slowed down their assailant; still, he was able to grab the tailgate and hold on.

"He caught on! He caught on!" Maria shouted.

Hatty picked up as much speed as she could, weaving back and forth on the narrow road that led to the house, but she couldn't shake him off. Hector had managed to climb into the bed of the truck. *WHAM! WHAM! WHAM!* He struck the rear window with the metal handle of his cane, but it refused to break. Hatty had to slow down to make the southeast corner of the house and to avoid sliding down the small hill and into the cattle pens. That enabled Hector to rise onto his good knee, where he could get a better swing at the rear glass. Hatty floored the accelerator and took a straight run for the south end of the house.

WHAM! WHAM! The silver cane would break through any second.

"Mom! Look out!!" Anita screamed. The headlight shone on the clothesline straight ahead, but Hatty knew what she was doing. *Whap!* The line slapped the front windshield, then whipped up and over the top of the cab like a giant metal bowstring tense enough to launch a thousand arrows. The wire caught Hector across both forearms as he was raising his cane for a blow; the forward momentum of the truck combined with the taut line to slam him against the tailgate with such force that it flew open and deposited him on the ground with a thud. He lay unconscious with a broken arm, two severely bruised ribs, and a concussion.

Hatty sped around the west side of the house and on up the lane. Her remaining headlight swept across the red Cadillac stuck out in the field. There was no movement around the car, no sign of life. The windshield was gone. Miguel had been cut badly across the forehead and down his right cheek by the flying glass; he was lying unconscious across the passenger's side seat. Joe lay on top of him, his neck broken. Hatty chugged passed the car. With a small trickle from the radiator trailing behind her, she turned onto the road that would take her back through Dolores and north to safety.

17

Doc's truck bounced uneasily along the dirt road toward Dolores. Hatty's mind was racing furiously. "They must have stopped at Doc's first," she said, thinking out loud. "We must have just missed them by coming here."

"Why did she tell them where we were?" Anita asked, feeling sorry for herself.

"Estella wouldn't do that," Maria said. "She thought we were going straight to San Luis, remember? She must not have seen us turn toward the house when we left her place."

"It doesn't matter," Hatty said firmly. "The main thing now is to pick her up and get out of here before they send someone else."

Anita turned to face Hatty. "But what if Carl. . . ?"

"If Carl and Marty are able, they'll find us," Hatty said. "I'm not leaving Estella to try to handle this bunch. I never should have left her in the first place. It just better not be too late. It better not be."

It took less than two minutes to reach Doc's house. Hatty jumped from the truck before it had come to a complete stop and raced up the steps to the front porch. She ran through the broken door and into the living room.

"Estella!" she called, but no one answered. She searched each room quickly but found nothing.

"Mom!" Maria called from outside. Hatty ran to the front door. Maria was running up toward the house from the dilapidated barn and the log pens.

"Molly's gone!" she said as she ran up, slightly out of breath. "Estella must have gone for help—all of her tack is out of the saddle room. Maybe she rode to one of Doc's patients down in the valley."

"Maybe, but I don't think she would want to put anyone else in danger," Hatty said.

Maria looked up suddenly. "The train station," she said.

"Of course," Hatty agreed. She thought for a moment, then took a deep breath. "All right, let's go," she said.

They all crowded into the front seat and slammed the doors shut. Hatty turned the truck around with some degree of expertise and drove out onto the north road toward Dolores.

"Mom, you think she went to Mexico City for Doc?" Maria asked.

"That's what I think," Hatty said shortly. "She's smart. She wouldn't go running off unless she had a plan. Someone broke in—it looked pretty bad inside. Things were broken in the living room and in the hall. It looks to me like she took off after they left. Right now she's safe, and that's all I care about at the moment."

They rode for some time in silence, not wanting to explore the implication of Estella's leaving. Hatty managed to make it down the narrow mountain road into the valley without incident. A few miles later, they were on the broken blacktop that would lead to San Luis. Hatty pulled to a stop by the side of the road.

"Here, Maria," Hatty said, offering her Estella's hand-drawn map. "You be my navigator. Anita, the flashlight should be over there on the floor somewhere, if we haven't lost it by now. Hold it for Maria, will you?" It had rolled back under the seat, so it took a minute to find it; finally, the round yellow light shone on the small map. "All right, see this line? We need to make it over this way across the railroad tracks. We'll cross over at San Luis and then head on up to Laredo."

"I know this way," Maria said. "Remember, Nita? We used to travel this road with your papa when I came to visit."

"No one uses it much anymore," Anita said. "It should be safe." But as Hatty pulled back onto the road, Anita was formulating her own plan. The road on the map crossed another small dirt road that she knew very well. It led to a highway that would take her to her town and her parents' house. San Luis wasn't far from that turnoff. She had made up her mind that she'd find a way home somehow.

At about five-thirty that morning, the women came to a crossing with a sign pointing eastward to San Luis Potosí. Maria looked over at Anita; she had falled asleep after a few miles on the dirt road. She stirred a bit, turning her face toward the window. Maria adjusted the coat around her shoulders.

"We'll get some breakfast, then check in with Señor Hernandez to see if he's heard from Estella," Hatty whispered. "If there's no word, we'll go on to Laredo. I know someone we can call."

Maria looked over at Anita to make sure she was asleep, then turned to Hatty. "I thought we were staying here until we heard, until Estella called."

"I thought we could," Hatty answered. "But everything changed when she had to leave. I seriously doubt that Estella is in any shape to get to a phone right now. She's probably doing good to be alive. If she hasn't called Señor Hernandez, then I don't think we can afford to wait. We don't know who's in control—who pays Calavera, how many men are involved. . . . "

"I thought Dad told you. I thought you knew."

"No. I'm not sure how much he even knew. He did say that Jake Skerritt was involved, but that was it. Jake is a sheriff back home. I don't know how much to we ought to associate with this Señor Hernandez either."

"He's all right, isn't he? I mean, Dad seemed to think he was trying to get out from under those men."

"Oh, yeah, he wanted out, but that doesn't mean he got out. Those men beat him up once. I doubt they'd hesitate to do it again. He may be so scared he'd do anything to keep his skin."

"Still, Estella might call, don't you think? We don't have any other way of knowing . . . " her voice broke off.

"I know." Hatty paused, not wanting to go on but knowing she must. They rode on in silence for a few more minutes. "Maria," Hatty began, but then she stopped. "Never give up on your dreams, my mother always used to say. Just believe hard enough and they'll come true someday. Well, I still believe that, and you need to believe it too." The words were unconvincing, the tone contrived, and Hatty knew it.

Maria kept her gaze forward on the dimly lit road. Tears welled in her eyes and began to run down her cheeks.

Hatty continued apologetically. "I don't think Marty and Carl are coming back, sweetheart. I pray I'm wrong, but . . ." her voice began to falter and she put her hand to her mouth, unable to keep from crying. Maria reached over and patted her leg. Anita was still turned toward the window, but her eyes were open now, looking out on the black night and the brightly twinkling stars.

Hatty felt as though she were about to burst. She had a sudden, strong urge to shut everything up—to box up time, get out of the truck, and demand some answers from God. She wanted to scream and yell in His face. She wanted to cry uncontrollably. She wanted it to be two days ago. She wanted to wake up. Hatty was struggling to hold on against her need to let everything go—to float in a liquid hush.

There is a balm in silence, a dark peace in denial. But denial only fools you into believing that the world is really quiet, Hatty thought. The real world is noisy. The real world is full of crying babies and guns exploding at midnight. If she wanted to survive, she would have to make it in that world. She couldn't wish the noise away, couldn't pretend it wasn't there.

Her thoughts wandered back to Estella. How did she manage it? Estella heard all the noise, felt the pain, lived in the real world. Hatty knew enough about Estella's background to know she could have had a much easier life if she hadn't married a missionary doctor. And yet she wasn't bitter or resentful about what God had done to her, making her live in little better than a shack without electricity or running water. She didn't hate Him for making Rosalinda so sick she might have died, or for taking her father when she was a little girl, or for making most of her family hate her for leaving the Catholic faith. Hatty had never known a woman with so little give so much. Estella had tried to explain it to her once, but it hadn't made any sense.

Never give up on your dreams, Hatty thought. *What a lie.* She bet her mother never believed it either. But what else can you do?

The lights of San Luis Potosí lit up a small section of the eastern horizon. Within ten minutes they were driving down the center of town. All the store windows, street lamps, and telephone poles were decorated for the Days of the Dead. The day was dawning clear and blustery. The truck made its way slowly down the street as Hatty and Maria looked for a place to eat.

"I used to come here when I was a little girl," Maria said. "My mother would bring me for my birthday to get a special dinner. I haven't been back for years, though."

"Do you remember the name of the street?" Anita asked, stretching and feigning a yawn. "There's the Café San Miguel on Orantes, or El Tambor off San Juan, or there's a wonderful coffee shop called La Dulcería on the north side of town."

"Oh, no, this was some little out-of-the-way place. Probably some greasy spoon where we could get food cheap, but it seemed like a palace to me. I remember it was close to the main street and it had a large orange sign—there! Oh, we just passed it. I saw it down to the right."

"All right," said Hatty, "we can go around the block and take a look. I don't have much money."

"I have a little. I can help," offered Maria.

Hatty pulled up to the curb before making the final turn and stopped. "We'll park here and walk around. No sense leaving the truck parked out front where everyone can see."

The three women walked around the corner and up half a block to the Café del Oro. The orange-and-green neon sign buzzed on and off intermittently.

Hatty peered in the front window past the red checkered curtains. "Well, it looks clean enough. Let's try it, shall we?" Anita sniffed as she went in, but she was so hungry she was willing to try anything.

The early morning sunlight filtered through broken glass and hit Miguel squarely in the eyes. He blinked and tried to focus. He attempted to lift his right arm, but it was pinned between Joe's body and the gear shift. He shoved with his free hand and managed to push the body far enough away for him to slip out.

He looked around. No one was out on the roads. No one had seen his car out in the field, and he was still in one piece. He smiled to himself, but flinched immediately as searing pain shot through his cheek. He glanced quickly in the rear-view mirror and examined the gash across his forehead and down his face. He cursed the women. He would find them. He would kill them.

He dragged Joe's body out of the car and over to a drainage pipe that ran under the road. It was half-filled with mud and standing water, but the body was small enough and Miguel was strong enough to stuff it inside. On his way back to the car he found Joe's shotgun on the ground and threw it in the back seat.

He was about to climb inside when he heard the scream. Over and over—a man's scream coming from the far side of the house. Miguel started to take the shotgun, then thought better of it and reached into the car's glove compartment for his own gun. He had always preferred handguns to rifles or shotguns. This one was particularly nice. A Smith and Wesson .45—exactly the same weight and feel as his service revolver, but he never carried his registered weapon when he came down to Mexico—it would be too easy to trace in the event of an "accident." Privately owned handguns could remain anonymous, especially if they were purchased in Mexico.

He ran the hundred yards to the house and worked his way carefully around the back. There, entangled in a broken clothesline, lay Hector Rodriguez writhing on the ground, one forearm splintered with a compound fracture, the other shoulder dislocated. Somehow he had missed severing a major artery. Bleeding had been minimized due to the fact that he had fallen in a large puddle of water and it had been cold the night before.

Miguel walked over to the screaming man and looked down

at him. He flipped open the chamber of his gun nonchalantly and checked for spent cartridges as he talked. "Hector, Hector, Hector. What a mess you made, man. I give you one simple job, and what do you do? You get Joe killed. You almost get me killed. Hey, look at this, you see this?" Miguel said, pointing to the gashes on his face. "Hey, you look at me when I talk to you!" he yelled and kicked one of his broken arms. Hector passed out immediately. "You did that to me, boy. And you, what am I going to do with you, huh? I'm going to put you out of your misery, son." He snapped the chamber closed, cocked the gun, and brought it up slowly until the top button of Hector's torn shirt was in his sights.

"Hey!" thundered a voice behind Miguel. Immediately, he turned with the gun. It was Doc. In a split second he decided to gamble that Doc didn't recognize him.

"Señor! Please help. I just found this man here. This gun, it was here on the ground beside him. I—I didn't hear you drive up," he said, handing the gun to Doc.

"My horse is out front. Now, what's your name?" Doc asked as he moved past Miguel toward Hector.

"Victor, Señor. Victor Santos. I was on the road over there and I heard him screaming, so—"

"Hector Rodriguez." Doc froze in his tracks, staring at the man on the ground. Estella had met him at the train station less than an hour before and told him everything that had happened. "Oh, Lord, give me strength," he pleaded as he knelt beside him.

"You know this man, Señor?" Miguel asked.

"Yeah, I'm afraid so. But I don't remember seeing you around here before, Victor," Doc said. He laid the gun down on the ground beside him so he could check Hector's vital signs.

Miguel eased up quickly and quietly behind Doc and bent down to pick up the gun.

"And what were you doing out walking the valley road at this time—"

Crack! The butt of the pistol came crashing down on Doc's head. He slumped over unconscious at Miguel's feet.

"So, you must be the good doctor, huh?" he said as he struggled to pull Doc away from Hector. He propped him up against the back porch steps. "Mr. Good Samaritan going to patch up his enemy, huh? Hey, Doc, you're never going to make it in this old world, you keep helping out the bad guys. No, see, when you got a bad guy down you do this—" he wheeled with the gun in his hand and shot Hector twice "—easy as pie. Now here," he said, pulling out his shirt-tail and wiping the gun thoroughly. "We'll just wipe off these old fingerprints and let you hold it."

Sanchez wrapped Doc's hand around the revolver, being careful to place his finger on the trigger. He dragged Hector's body out of the water and away from the tangled clothesline, placing him face down as if he had been running from Doc.

After checking the road once quickly, Miguel ran from behind the house out past Doc's horse and across the field to his car. He climbed inside and cranked the engine. It would barely turn over. He looked at the light switch and cursed as he jammed it in to turn them off. They had been burning several hours. He pumped the gas pedal three times, then turned the key hard. The engine turned once, twice, then caught. Miguel rocked the car forward and back until he got enough momentum to spin out of the field. Back on the road again, he headed north toward San Luis as fast as he could go.

"Well, ladies, we've taken too long as it is. We need to get going," Hatty announced. The breakfast had been hot and filling, and the three women felt physically refreshed as they started to leave the cafe. They paid the cashier and thanked him for the good food. He was a talkative man and in a good humor, though his face turned serious when Maria asked for directions to the vet's office.

"San Pedro street is just three blocks down, Señora," the man said. "But I am sorry to tell you the clinic burned down just two days ago. It was a terrible tragedy—they found the body of Dr. Hernandez in his office. The authorities think he must have fallen asleep on the sofa and then could not get out in time."

"What caused the fire, do they know?" Hatty queried.

The man leaned across the counter and spoke in a low voice so the rest of his patrons couldn't hear. "They are saying it was bad wiring or something—that's what they always say when they do not know what happened. But I will tell you something—Carlos Hernandez was a customer of mine for years and a friend. There are some very bad people in this city, and Carlos had made them angry. I tried to warn him. I tried to tell him, but he was so hard-headed. And now he is dead. So what can you do? Do not make those people angry. Give them a little something to make them happy. Sure, you will be a little poorer, but you will be alive. The only other vet I would trust with a living animal is all the way up in Matehuala, but I imagine you are coming from down south, yes?"

"Thank you, Señor," Hatty said, obviously upset.

"Oh, I am sorry. Were you a friend of Carlos?" the man asked. But the women were already halfway out the door. They walked quickly around the corner to the truck. None of them noticed the dripping under the front bumper as they climbed in. Hatty pulled out and drove to a filling station nearby.

"We have to get gas, then get to Laredo tonight if we can," she said to Maria and Anita.

The attendant came to the window.

"Fill it, please," Hatty said.

"Check your oil and water, ma'am?" the attendant asked.

The request took Hatty a bit by surprise. Usually these attendants were doing well just to fill the tank and clean the windshield. She managed a grateful smile. "Yes," she said, "but please hurry." The man added the necessary oil and filled the near-empty radiator.

"Need to watch your temperature gauge, ma'am. That radiator was near bone dry—probably a small leak. Just keep it filled and you should be all right for your trip."

"Yes, all right, thank you," Hatty said distractedly.

Her fear that they might be followed joined forces with the strong coffee they had at breakfast that morning to keep Hatty awake for most of the day. By the time they reached Monterrey, Hatty had been driving almost eight hours and hadn't slept in the last day-and-a-half. Despite repeated requests from her daughters-in-law to take time out for a nap, she pushed on. They had eaten all the fruit Estella had packed and were running low on cash. They picked up some burritos and more strong coffee outside of Monterrey and headed on.

Hatty had been driving in a near daze for the past hour and had nearly run off the road a dozen times. Now even the black coffee hadn't kept her going. Only the occasional undetected pothole bounced her awake. They hadn't passed a car in ages, and the road stretched out before them like a sleepy gray string winding out to infinity. Suddenly, the engine began to grind awfully. Hatty jerked awake and looked down at the instrument panel. The needle on the heat gauge was pegged over past "H." They could smell something burning as the truck jerked to a clanking halt beside the highway.

Hatty climbed out and, with the help of Maria and Anita, lifted the heavy metal hood. They tried using the flashlight to peer inside, but its batteries had gone dead. It didn't matter, however. Even if they'd had a floodlight they still wouldn't have known what they were looking at. Raising the hood just seemed the thing to do. Everything was too hot to touch anyway, so they slammed down the hood and leaned back against the truck.

"All right," Hatty said, "I'm sure we can fix this. But we can't do it tonight. Help me push it out of sight behind that brush and we'll rest for a bit."

Anita felt like complaining that no one would be traveling the road at that time of night anyway, but she was too tired to fight about it.

The three of them wrestled the old truck across the road and the hard-packed ground, rolling it behind the brush thicket. They settled down—Hatty curled up on the front seat with Maria and Anita making the best of the hard bed in the back, pulling their extra clothes around them for warmth.

Both Hatty and Anita fell asleep immediately, but Maria could not. Despite her exhaustion, her mind was racing. She lay back, gazing up through the spindly mesquite at the black velvet canopy sprinkled with a glittering spray of diamonds—trying to understand why all this had happened, trying to forget Anita's words on the porch. Trying to feel like she wasn't the death of this family.

18

At around three o'clock the next morning, the wind picked up. Maria pulled her wrappings up over her eyes to shield her face from the cold. Finally, she lapsed into a half-sleep, passing in and out of troubled dreams.

Suddenly she saw lights blazing from across the road. The roar of an engine racing and the anxious shouts of men pierced the quiet of the deep night. Doors flew open, and three silhouetted figures ran forward in the glare of the headlights.

The night had grown foggy; the three men stopped short of the truck where the three women lay, the fog swirling around them in a brightening haze. A star streaked across the sky behind them and fell to earth, so close Maria could hear the sizzle and feel the distant thud and rumble of the impact. She couldn't see the men's faces, but she knew who they were. She wanted to run to them and embrace them, but she could only watch as they slowly dissolved first into shadow, then into the fog itself. The fog began to move in a slowly swirling motion, stirred by a roaring wind into a pearl-gray column that ascended to heaven. Then all that was left were the stars.

A lone coyote barked far away, looking for her companion. Soon other howlers joined her, baying to the moon, longing for lost allies. A fire burned on the prairie floor. Maria could see it clearly and from a great height, though it must have been miles away to the south. She could see the coyotes on a bluff on the far side of the fire; they were pacing nervously back and forth, watching the flames grow taller.

The moon, five times its normal size, five times as near, rumbled and cracked. An oily blackness began to seep out through its ruptures and cover the surface until all the light died and Maria stood alone beneath an ebony moon. As the black light spilled in tumbling cataracts down to the earth, the thundering rumble grew. Far away a shining black stallion at the head of a thousand pale gray horses raced toward Maria; and she, dressed in flowing white, now black, floated above the earth waiting for him, singing "*¡Ave, Ave!*" as he circled the pillar of fire.

The flames soared higher and higher, curling into the devil's spine, shooting up through the roof of the bell tower of a small cathedral, and the bells were ringing, crying, and the coyotes were far below fighting, growling, tearing one another to pieces. One of them was speaking, one of them was laughing a crazy laugh, and one of them was screaming the *El Grito*, but not like a real scream—more like a high-pitched squeal, long and sustained.

Maria woke up.

The squealing was coming from across the road—the breaks of a large truck, pulling to a stop. Maria lifted herself cautiously from the bed of Doc's truck and peered out through the tangle of brush. It stopped briefly—just long enough for someone to board—then headed on south. Maria settled back, resting her head on a bundled dress. She reached over to touch the pillow where Anita's head had been. The blanket hadn't grown cold yet. Maria wrapped the blanket around her and sat up again. She looked through the rear window of the cab; Hatty was sleeping, peacefully it seemed.

Moving slowly, Maria climbed out of the back of the truck and made her way out to the road. She looked far away to the south, as far as she could see, and just caught the last flicker of red tail lights before they disappeared over a hill.

Maria walked slowly back toward the trees; she looked up at the moon and was glad to see it bright and round and far away. Deciding to walk a bit to clear her mind, she passed through the small grove to the other side. About fifty feet from the edge of the last tree, the land fell away abruptly into what appeared to be a deep gulley. She strolled out past the cactus and the little bit of whitebrush. Ahead of her a rabbit scampered out of one bush and into another. She watched it and smiled, thinking of how she and Martin loved to go on moonlight walks around Shining Lake—there were more rabbits there than they could count.

Suddenly Maria found herself standing on the precipice of a deep ravine, much longer and wider than it had appeared at first. She sat down, wrapped in the warm woolen blanket, and stared out over the ravine and the empty prairie beyond.

Venus shone bright on the horizon. It seemed like only yesterday that she stood under a moon like this—looking at these same stars with Martin. She thought of the plans they had made, the children they both wanted. *If I could have been a parent,* she thought, *I would have loved my children so. I wouldn't let the other mean children hurt them.* She began to cry. "Lord, I don't understand," she whispered. "Why take them all? Is it for what I've done? Then show me. Oh, please, help me. Help me understand. Help me make some sense out of this life."

She sat rocking back and forth on the edge of the gorge, looking down into the blackness and up to the starry heavens, tears streaming down her cheeks. "Father, what do I call this grief? What name can I give it? Help me know it, Lord; help me kill it and leave it in this grave You have carved in the earth."

She looked down, but there was no reflection of starlight in the abyss, only cold darkness. There was no single name for death. Death owned all names. "I know You hear me, Lord," she said, wiping away her tears. "I know in my mind. But my heart, Father. My heart won't listen."

She felt suddenly drained, tired, and sleepy. She lay down with her back to the ravine, curled like a baby in a mother's arms, and fell into a deep sleep.

Maria felt a touch on her shoulder. She opened her eyes slowly to see Hatty sitting on the ground in front of her. The sun was low and at Maria's back, but the morning was already so bright she had to squint.

Hatty smiled warmly. "I know Doc's truck isn't much, but it has to be better than sleeping out here in the open."

"I didn't mean to fall asleep," Maria said apologetically, raising herself up on her elbow. "At least I didn't fall in."

"Fall into what?" Hatty asked.

Maria frowned and turned around to look at the ravine. The prairie stretched out in every direction, speckled here and there with whitebrush and cactus, flat as the bottom of a skillet.

"Last night—" she started, then hesitated, still looking out at the flatland. "Last night I had a dream. There was a fire, and Martin, and I walked—here, and I could have sworn. . . ." She shook her head, trying to remember. "Oh, Mom, I can't remember which parts were real and which—Anita!" she said suddenly.

Hatty rose from her place and extended her hand to her daughter-in-law. "Let's get going. The truck still won't start. We've got some walking to do—maybe we'll get lucky and catch a ride into Laredo." Maria rose and followed Hatty across the cracked ground toward the truck. "We'll need to travel light. Take everything out of your bag except those things you need for one night. We may wind up walking for a few hours, and these things can get awfully heavy."

They set out walking north at seven-thirty that morning. The air was cold and dry. Hatty lent an extra scarf to Maria to keep her face from getting chapped. There were no cars, no clouds, no animals except for the occasional rabbit and a few stray head of cattle. The women looked back occasionally to see nothing but empty highway.

"Mom, wait," Maria said as she put the suitcase down on the road. "I need to rest, and we need to talk. Now, sit down for a moment."

Hatty laughed softly at the uncharacteristic toughness of her daughter-in-law. She plopped her suitcase down and sat on it, waiting for Maria to ask the inevitable. "You act like you knew about Anita leaving, and what's worse is you act like you don't care. Did she tell you she was going to leave like that?"

"Oh, honey, she didn't have to tell me. I knew it from the time we left that gas station back in San Luis—as a matter of fact, I'm surprised she didn't cut and run while we were still there. I woke up last night when a truck passed, heading south, and I couldn't get back to sleep. Not long after, Nita climbed out of the truck, and I knew right then what she was going to do. When I heard that second truck stop—I didn't look. I guess I didn't want to see her get in and leave. Tell you the truth, she's probably the only one of us three with a lick of sense."

A late afternoon breeze gusted out of the north, catching the two weary travelers by surprise. The scarf in Maria's hand went sailing and she ran back down the road to pick it up.

"Oh, Lord, that's heavenly," Hatty said, stopping in the middle of the road with her head back and eyes closed, enjoying the unexpected coolness. Maria picked up the scarf and started to turn back to Hatty when she noticed a glint far off down the road to the south. She stood erect and shielded her eyes against the westering sun. As the approaching car crested the top of a far hill, Maria caught a flash of red. She turned and started running back to Hatty.

"Mom, run!"

"What? What's the—"

"Come on, we've got to get to the arroyo—he's coming," Maria said, grabbing her suitcase and running across the hard-packed dirt toward the gully seventy-five yards away. Hatty lifted her bag and followed close behind.

They were halfway there when Hatty tripped over a rock and fell hard, twisting her ankle and spilling the contents of her suitcase out onto the desert floor. Maria was at her side immediately, trying to help her up.

"Here, put your arm around me," she said lifting her mother-in-law to a standing position. The wind hoisted one of Hatty's red scarves high into the air and sent it sailing south.

"My things, he'll see them . . ." Hatty protested.

"There isn't time, Mom. Now, hold on," Maria said, clinging to Hatty with one hand and holding her own suitcase in the other. Together they staggered to the edge of the ravine and slid down the rough slope to the bottom. The suitcase lay open for all the world to see, its contents tossed here and there on puffs of desert air like so many rumpled balloons. Hatty stifled a scream as her ankle jammed into the dry gulch floor. Shallow caves, the homes of the animals of the arroyo, dotted the walls of the miniature canyon.

The drought had hastened the erosion of the area, leaving wide fissures in an intricately crazed pattern like so many deepening wrinkles in the face of the earth. The ground along the bed of the arroyo was baked and cracked by a relentless sun and constant wind. The hard-packed surface left little trace of footprints.

Maria and Hatty made their way through the narrow twisting chasm as fast as they could, but Hatty's right ankle had already begun to swell. She leaned on Maria for support, and they hobbled down one of the deeper side gullies. The maze of intersecting ravines and high earth walls served as sound baffles.

The women couldn't tell if the car they had seen had come up to the gully or had continued on north. Maria decided to take a quick look. They stopped near one of the small caves; Hatty sat on the ground opposite the hole, nursing her throbbing ankle, while Maria climbed as gingerly as she could to peek over the top. She had to climb only three or four feet, but the sides were so steep she had trouble getting her footing. Grasping at bits of dried grass and roots she pulled herself up slowly until her eyes just cleared the top of the ravine.

There, not forty yards from her, Miguel was walking slowly toward her, looking down into the gully to his right. She lowered herself quickly before he saw her. Immediately, she picked up a large dirt clod and threw it into the small cave. There was no response—either the cave was abandoned or the animals who inhabited it were out hunting.

"Quick! Into the cave," she ordered as she pushed first her

suitcase and then Hatty into the small opening in front of her. Hatty could barely crawl into the narrow opening, but she managed to get just far enough inside to allow Maria to crawl in behind her. "It's the man in the red car," she whispered to Hatty inside the cave. "Shh—he's coming this way."

Miguel continued to walk along the edge, looking slowly up and down the ravine and its offshoots. He knew this arroyo well. He had hunted wildcats and javelina down here when he was a boy. He knew that all its twists and turns converged at one point and emptied out into the Salado River. If he couldn't find them here, he would catch them on the other end when they came out.

He walked silently, gun drawn as if he were stalking a deer. He hadn't seen them running; he had only seen the suitcase lying open on the ground and decided to investigate. He knew they were in the ravine, but he didn't know how far ahead they might have gotten. The suitcase could have been there for minutes or hours.

Sliding down the bank, he looked first to the east and then to the west. No movement, no sound. The little bit of breeze on the surface was blocked by the eight-foot-high walls of dirt. Both hands gripped his revolver as he turned corners with the practiced precision of an officer who enjoyed his job too much.

Hatty and Maria remained motionless, trying not to breath in the cramped, dark hole. The sun was nearing the horizon now—Miguel didn't have much time left. It would be dark in forty-five minutes. If the women had gotten enough of a head start, they would beat him to the river unless he left soon.

One last corner, he thought, then he would go. He inched down the ravine, barely breathing himself. Coming to a sharp turn, he cautiously looked around it to his left—another dead end. The shadows had grown just long enough to prevent him from noticing the blue corner of a dress trailing out of a javelina den only ten feet from where he stood. He cursed to himself for failing to find them and climbed out of the ravine.

The car bounced along the rough terrain to the road and continued on its journey north. Miguel would hit a cutoff soon that would lead him to the small village of Rodriguez on the Salado river. There he would wait for the women to emerge.

Hatty and Maria remained quiet and still for the next half hour, not knowing what to expect outside their cave. If she twisted her head down and to the right, Maria could just see behind her and out the entrance of the cave.

"He must have gone by now, if he came down at all," she whispered to Hatty.

"Can you see outside? Is it dark yet?" Hatty whispered back.

"Just a little—it looks like the sun is down." Maria backed out of the cave as slowly and quietly as she could. She scanned the surroundings while Hatty crawled out. There was no sign of any other human. Maria climbed up the north bank of the ravine. Hatty handed her the suitcase, then climbed out with her help.

Hatty's ankle was swollen to twice its normal size and was throbbing terribly. She sat on Maria's bag while Maria trotted back to pick up the suitcase Hatty had dropped. She picked up Eli's jacket and folded it carefully before placing it in the battered suitcase.

One of the brass clasps was sprung, but the other metal fitting snapped into place. She brought it back to the edge of the ravine, collecting items of clothing as she went. "I don't know why I didn't think of this before," she said, opening her own bag. She stuffed Hatty's things into her suitcase and had room to spare. She threw the other down into the ravine. "There, that will help us make better time. Come on, Mom, up you go."

Hatty rose stiffly from her sitting position and draped an arm around her daughter-in-law. Maria picked up the rawhide suitcase in her left hand and put her right hand around Hatty's waist. Hatty could barely put any weight on her right foot as she limped along.

"It will be at least an hour before moonrise," said Maria. "We need to move as quickly as we can. We shouldn't be too far from the Salado by now." Then she stopped for a moment, thinking. "Wait, this isn't going to work."

"What? Where are we going?" asked Hatty.

"Rodriguez—it sits right on the south bank of the Salado river, probably no more than three or four miles west of here. But you know, now that I think about it, there is a deep gorge that feeds off the Salado and runs out into the desert. I wouldn't be surprised if it comes out this far. They would expect us to follow this arroyo."

"We can't go back to the highway," Hatty said. "No telling how many of them are looking for us now."

"And the last thing they want is for us to get to the other side . . . " Maria reflected quietly, thinking out loud. "I've got an idea," she said. "We have the advantage here. The man who followed us doesn't know we've seen him. He thinks all he has to do is wait for us to come out the other side of this gully."

"So?"

"So we don't come out the other side. There's another little town called Anahuac not two miles the other side of Rodriguez. We can follow the ravine for a couple of miles, but we will leave it before we reach Rodriguez. If I remember, there's a creek that runs south of the town. We go up the creek to Anahuac."

They pushed on, tracing the jagged line of the trough, Maria helping Hatty along and Hatty trying not to let the pain show. They found that if they stayed about fifteen yards from the edge, they could easily negotiate the numerous side gullies that branched out from the main crevice like capillaries from a black artery. They stayed away from the edge for convenience, but also because they didn't want to know what was down there.

And so they never saw the night eyes that stared out at them from below the rim. They never heard the shuffling, snuffling animal sounds of the deepening hole . . . or the whoosh of an owl's wings ruffling the night as it slipped elegantly from its perch . . . or the frantic clicking of a lizard's claws as it skittered across the black metal door of a burned-out truck lying twisted on its side in the black belly of the ravine. The society of the gorge waited to welcome the two wanderers, as they had welcomed so many before. But the wanderers never even knew they were there. Just as well.

The last of the sunlight faded from the sky, and the stars came out to light their way. The air quickly turned cold, and they stopped to pull on their wraps. Maria's sweater and Hatty's light jacket were barely enough. They were glad for the small blanket Maria had stuffed into the suitcase at the last minute. She wrapped it around their shoulders, holding one corner along with the suitcase while Hatty held the other. A light north wind cut across their path at a right angle. It took them nearly an hour to cover the first mile, and almost twice that long to go the next mile-and-a-half.

It was past eight-thirty when they saw a few lights twinkling in the distance. "That's Rodriguez," Maria said softly. "See that dark spot where the ravine widens out?" She pointed ahead. "That's the Salado river, and this is where—" she paused as she scanned the horizon, looking for a marker. "There, that line of trees off to the left, see? That must be the creek."

"All right," Hatty said, surveying the half-mile of wide-open prairie that separated them from the shelter of the trees. "I'm ready if you are."

Maria didn't hear her. She was gazing up at the night sky. A slow shadow was creeping across the face of the moon.

"Well, look at that," exclaimed Hatty. "An eclipse. It's been a long time since I've seen one of those."

Maria didn't answer for a moment, then whispered, "Me too," keeping her eyes on the shadow, trying to will it to stop, wondering what it might mean.

Hatty knew there was something about the eclipse that haunted Maria, but she didn't fully understand. Although she had heard Anita's accusation on the porch the other night, she wasn't sure what Anita meant by it.

Maria continued to search, trying to find an answer in the fading light, but she could not. A darkening shadow crept over her thoughts as well. Only Martin—only Martin had known about the curse, and they had killed him. She must not tell anyone again, ever.

Hatty put her arm around her daughter-in-law. "Maria," she said gently, "we'd better get going."

Maria lifted the suitcase without a word and put her arm around

Hatty. The wind had picked up slightly, and with it came a soaking, cold drizzle. Deep, black clouds had moved in slowly from the north on the edge of a new front.

"Lord'a mercy, I don't remember the end of October being this cold before," Hatty said, pulling the blanket tighter around her shoulders.

On the far bank of the Salado near Rodriguez, Sanchez sat watching the river, tapping impatiently on the steering wheel of his red Cadillac, wondering if there wasn't some way he could get the department to pay for the damage to his car. He rubbed his eyes and yawned, then sat up straight and refocused on the southern bank. His eyes swept back and forth as they had for the last two-and-a-half hours, trying to detect any movement. They should have been there by now—unless they had made it through before he got there. Either that or they had decided to spend the night out in the desert somewhere.

The moon was nearly half gone now, but the flat landscape was still awash in a silvery light—if anything was moving out on the prairie, he would still be able to see it. He decided to cross over and check things out. He backed up and turned around on the tight road. The wooden bridge was, if anything, narrower than the single-lane road—barely wide enough for one car to cross at a time. But Miguel was experienced here. He had crossed this bridge many times—once with his eyes closed—even though the river was a good twenty feet below. The wood planks rattled underneath his tires.

The streets of Rodriguez were quiet, and only the simplest decorations were up for the Days of the Dead. The white adobe looked cool under the moonlight. Black and white cardboard skeletons hung on nails from the front doors of the small homes, their hinged joints swinging slightly in the evening breeze. Here and there candlelight shone through frosted windows of the houses, and smoke curled from several rock chimneys. Dogs barked at the strange red car and chased it through town to the other side. One old man came out onto his porch to see what was going on, but quickly went back inside when he saw the red car. He had seen it before.

Miguel stopped on the far side of town, his headlights shining out into the night. There was nothing to see except some plowed fields, a far line of trees marking the creek, and the ravine winding away to the southeast. He turned off his lights and watched. He thought he had seen something move over near the tree line. He looked long and hard, but . . . there! Something *was* moving slowly toward the trees.

The engine sprang to life and Miguel took off across the prairie, trying to avoid the cactus and the small, thorny trees as he made a road in the general direction of the creek. He hadn't gone a hundred yards when he caught his prey square in his headlights. Not fifty yards in front of him, a doe and her fawn bolted and made a mad dash for the creek, leaving the red demon behind in a cloud of prairie dust.

Miguel slammed on the brakes and looked hard across the prairie, refusing to believe he had been fooled by deer. Two more ran into the headlights and stopped, looking directly into the shining lamps. Miguel was so angry he forgot about the rough terrain and how much damage one or more full-grown deer can do to a car.

As he took off at full speed for the deer, the first two stepped quickly out of the way of the careening machine. A buck jumped in front of the right fender, then skipped out of the way at the last minute as if it were playing tag with the car. Another large buck leaped in front of the racing car and ran straight ahead. Miguel kept it in his headlights, turning as it turned, gaining on it quickly. The deer made a final wonderful leap, high over a large rock that Miguel failed to see—*crunch!* The right front fender crumpled and the car came to a head-banging halt. The engine rumbled, gurgled, burped out a cloud of blue smoke from the twin silver tailpipes, and died. The deer stood in a group at the edge of the creek, surveying the damage before they turned and disappeared into the wood.

The night was already miserably black with the eclipse, and now the advancing clouds pulled a charcoal blanket over what little starlight remained. The drizzle dripped cold and wet down Miguel's shirt. He pounded the steering wheel and cursed, got out, slammed the door, stomped around the car assessing the damage, got back in, cranked the engine—which started miraculously—backed out, and drove off in a wide circle around the rock, narrowly missing an enormous cactus bush. The car bounced over deep cracks, backfiring at every bump, cactus scraping its side as it struggled back to the road; halfway through Rodriguez the back half of the muffler fell, scraping along the gravel road and across the bridge on the way to Laredo.

From the far side of the large rock two wide-eyed women emerged. "If I hadn't seen it with my own eyes . . ." Hatty began, but then stopped, leaning against the rock. "He must have come within ten feet of us, and he never even slowed down."

"He was coming right for us," Maria said. "We were in his lights. I knew he had seen us—and then those deer! Did you see that? They jumped right in front of him. Where did they come from?"

"The creek, most likely, out to feed. I'll tell you something, girl, you'd better thank the Lord for that evil omen up there." Hatty pushed herself away from the rock and gazed up at a sky that looked like curdled coal.

"What?"

"Without that eclipse and the cloud cover, we would've been sitting ducks. You can't shoot what you can't see. Come one, let's get to that creek before he decides to come back looking for that." Hatty pointed to a large silver hubcap on the prairie floor fifteen yards away.

Maria ran over to it and picked it up; she drew back her arm and sailed it off into the night. Running back to Hatty she picked up the suitcase, then arm in arm they moved toward the line of trees.

The creek bed was dry and sandy. They walked along its bank for the next two miles until they came to the village of Anahuac. The creek ran closer to the village than it did to Rodriguez. From the edge of the woods they could see dogs running back and forth between the houses. The creek sheltered them a bit from the biting wind, but Hatty could barely stand the thought of having to spend the night on cold, wet leaves.

As they neared the railroad tracks, they saw a light flickering through the trees. "What is it?" Hatty whispered.

"A fire, I think. Someone has made a fire by the tracks."

Hatty was thoroughly put out. They had been walking for an entire day, had almost been killed by a crazy man in a red car, and now were about to be displaced by some bum. She'd had enough of bad weather, bad luck, and bad men. "Oh, for heaven's sake!" she said too loudly. "Who in their right mind would be out on a night like this beside a railroad track?" She hobbled off in the direction of the fire.

"Mom, wait!" Maria half shouted, running after her. "We don't know who this might be. Sometimes migrants come through and camp out by the tracks—it wouldn't be smart to surprise them in the middle of the night!"

"I'll surprise them, all right! I'll surprise their socks off! But they're in for a fight if they think they can hog all that fire to themselves!" Hatty was only twenty yards from the clearing now, and there wasn't a sign of a living being.

"Mom, please! I don't like this!" Maria said, stopping beside a large hackberry.

Hatty limped into the middle of the clearing and stood with her face to the fire. There wasn't a soul around. There were no bedrolls, no cooking utensils, no saddles or horses—nothing to suggest the fire had been started by anything other than spontaneous combustion. It took about five seconds for Hatty to quit puzzling over why there was a blazing fire in the middle of the night without a trace of anyone around. The fire penetrated the cold like a warm embrace from an old friend.

Maria edged into the clearing cautiously, looking back and forth in quick, furtive glances. "Fires don't start by themselves, Mom. There's someone here, and they know we're here," she whispered.

The leaves above them rustled slightly. Instinctively, both women looked up at the same time.

"Good evening, ladies!" a voice said from the darkness above.

19

An enormous man swung down from the branch of the large oak tree and dropped to the ground in front of Maria and Hatty. They both screamed and ran to the other side of the fire.

"Who are you?!" Hatty yelled.

"Who am I? Who are you? You are the ones who broke into our camp and scared me half to death." The man's voice matched his size. The words boomed out like cannonballs.

Hatty drew herself up to her full height of five foot five. "There's more of you?" she asked, defiantly.

"What?

"You said *our* camp. How many are there?"

"Listen, Señora—" he said as he started to step forward.

"Just hold it. Now, you just hold it right there." Hatty said, backing up.

"She means it!" Maria said, aiding her mother-in-law.

"All right, all right!" he said, laughing. "You want to know how many of us there are?" He turned his back to the fire and bellowed out into the darkness, "Juan! Belinda! Lisa! Josephina! Danielle!"

From behind the trees, five shadowy figures advanced cautiously toward the fire. They stood on the edge of the clearing behind the man and just out of the firelight.

"Come on, come on!" the man urged them to join him in the firelit ring. "Ladies, allow me to introduce my band of pirates. This is my wife, Danielle," he said, putting his arm around a tiny woman. "A force to be reckoned with, I assure you. And these are our daughters, Josephina, Lisa, Belinda, and Juan."

"Papa, you know I am a boy!" the little fellow shook a playful fist at his mountainous father.

"Ai, me! I am always forgetting! A boy, a boy, a boy! Yes, now I remember! Very well, then—and my *son* Juan!" he said laughing. "And I am Esteban P. Morales, at your service. Girls, the mats please. . . . " He motioned to the girls, who retrieved blankets from the bushes and unrolled them for the women to sit on. "Ladies, do us the honor of joining us at our fire. I am afraid all the food is gone, but we were just about to have some coffee."

"Will you not sit down?" Danielle said, taking Hatty by the hand. "You look like you could use some coffee."

The women were dumbfounded. Hatty tried to sputter out an apology, but Danielle waved it off. She reminded Hatty of a smaller, younger version of Estella.

"Where are you from? Are you some of the bad people? You look kind of like Gran except you are more skinny. Do you know my gran?" Juan was almost five years old and as direct as his sisters shy. He stood eye to eye with Hatty, who had deposited herself squarely in front of the fire with the blanket wrapped around her.

"Juan, give the ladies time to catch their breath. Come on over here now by Mama," Danielle said as she made room for her son.

"Oh, that's all right," Hatty said, smiling. "No, Juan, I'm afraid I don't know your gran. My name is Mrs. King, and this is my daughter-in-law. Her name is Mrs. King, too."

"And what brings you ladies out to the creek on a night like this?" Esteban asked. He busied himself setting up a makeshift grate to hold the coffee pot.

Hatty wasn't sure how much to trust these people, though they certainly seemed friendly. "We, uh . . . we are trying to get to Texas, and uh. . . . "

"And our truck broke down," Maria finished for her.

"Oh, really? Where?"

Maria was evasive. "Oh, way back"—she and Hatty pointed away to the southeast—"there somewhere. We've been walking for hours."

"You know there is a road between here and Rodriguez. It runs along the Salado. Plenty of folks over there to help." Esteban was pressing.

"Yes, well . . ." Hatty's mind was swimming.

"Esteban, quit prying," Danielle said. "I am sorry, Señora King, it is just that we have had some unfortunate things happen recently and we are a little too suspicious sometimes." She shot a reproving glance at her husband.

"I told you she was a force to be reckoned with," he said, laughing. "I hope you ladies take your coffee black, because that's all we have. Come on, Juan. You can help Papa carry the water." He ambled off toward the creek with his son in tow.

"Where is your tent?" Maria asked.

"Right there, see?" Danielle pointed to some bushes beside the large oak tree. Hatty could just see the little face of Josephina inside the front flap of the small tent. "Esteban is very careful—just in case. There have been some bad things happen, and—well, you know, with the Days of the Dead and all, people get crazy, even around here. Esteban is a very good hunter. He showed us all how to hide and be very quiet. And believe me, for Juan to be quiet *and* still for more than a minute is quite an accomplishment." She smiled at the thought of her precocious son, but the smile soon faded.

They sat quietly, staring into the fire, watching the flames leap up. Finally, Danielle spoke again.

"We just lost our farm," she said quietly. "Yesterday. This is our second night out. Esteban is trying to make it a great adventure for the children, but it's hard."

"I'm so sorry," Hatty said. "What happened?"

"The drought. Nothing will grow here. Even the chickens die." She turned to Maria. "You come from the south, do you not?"

Maria nodded.

"I could tell from your accent. I used to teach down near

Aguascalientes. I hear you're still green down that far."

"Yes," Maria said. "It was dry for a while, but nothing like this."

"The mist last night was the closest we've had to rain in years," Danielle explained. "We had a little saved up, but it doesn't take long to run out of money when there is nothing coming in. We aren't the first to leave." She looked away toward Anahuac. "In another year, maybe two, this little town will be gone if it doesn't rain."

"But you could come back someday, when things turn around . . ." Hatty suggested.

Danielle shook her head. "No, I'm afraid not. There's a man in Rodriguez who got some money from somewhere. He waits until the farmers have nothing left to live on, then he offers them one American dollar an acre to buy the land. We all have families. What could we do? So now we have three-hundred-fifty dollars and no farm. It was in our family for seventy-five years. He wouldn't let us stay even one extra night. He brought some law man who said we had to leave—as if he were going to live there. And then of course the train didn't run yesterday, so here we are." She wasn't crying, but her voice had drifted far away. She came back quickly. "But we believe in God. And we know He will take care of us. In the morning we go to Laredo to find work for Esteban. From there we don't know."

"Surely you have some friends there you could have stayed with?" Hatty asked.

"None of them knew. Oh, I imagine some of them suspected, but I don't think any of them knew we had to sell. And I wouldn't ask them, not with four children—no one has that kind of room, not in Anahuac. Anyway, the children are having a great time so far. They think it's all a game. Well, I shouldn't say that—Belinda knows and is having a bit of a time, but the others are fine."

Esteban walked back into the clearing holding his son's hand. In Juan's other hand a speckled tin coffee pot sloshed water with every step. "Well, ladies, we might have slightly less than a full pot," Esteban said, "but what we have will be mighty tasty."

It soon became evident that Esteban enjoyed the role of camp cook. He measured the coffee from a tin using a silver spoon and poured it with just a hint of a flourish. It was, Hatty proclaimed truthfully, the finest cup of java she'd had in months.

"Oh, you should taste it when he has a kitchen," Danielle bragged, patting him on the back.

They talked for another half hour or so. Hatty and Maria kept their secrets, politely avoiding direct answers to concerned questions. Danielle pulled some extra bedding from their tent and Esteban put several more logs on the fire to burn through the night. Hatty and Maria thanked them again for their hospitality, then slipped quickly into a wearied sleep beside the fire. Esteban wrapped himself in a coat and sat with his back against the great oak, sipping the last of the strong coffee and keeping watch over the camp.

The next morning Hatty woke with a terrible empty feeling inside. She had dreamed all night that Eli was sitting by the fire talking to her, giving her advice, and now she couldn't remember any of it. She kept her eyes closed for a few minutes and prayed that God would give her the strength she needed to make it through the day; that He would somehow help her avenge the death of her husband and sons. She had decided not to tell these people what had happened—not because she didn't trust them, but because they had enough troubles of their own. She would keep her pain private. If she cried she would cry where no one could see.

Maria was already up, helping to cook breakfast on the open fire. Hatty squinted and tried to read her. She wondered if she had said anything to Danielle. She sat up slowly and breathed in the aroma of fresh coffee. The Morales clan was bustling.

"Good morning, Señora King!" Esteban greeted her with unabashed enthusiasm, though he had had only an hour's sleep. "I hope you slept well. If you would like to join us for breakfast in a few minutes, we can be finished and ready to catch the train in Anahuac at nine-thirty. As you can see, it's only a short walk into the town, and then perhaps an hour into Laredo, no more. Danielle will show you the ladies' washroom if you would like to freshen up first. Breakfast will be ready when you get back."

Hatty bade everyone a good morning and followed Danielle down to the creek. They returned to a feast of fried eggs, venison, biscuits, and hot coffee. As they were cleaning up, Hatty and Maria spoke together quietly for a moment. Then Hatty took Danielle aside out of Esteban's hearing.

"I'm afraid we can't go with you to Laredo," Hatty said apologetically.

"But we thought you were going to Texas?"

"Well, we are, but—to tell the truth, we were just going to jump in an empty boxcar and ride in."

"Oh, don't be silly, you will be our guests," Danielle insisted.

"We've already imposed on you too much," Hatty said. "And besides, I've never taken a handout in my life. We'll do just fine, but thank you for offering."

Danielle took her arm. "Hatty, you see that big ox of a man over there? Can you see him letting you ride in a filthy boxcar while we ride in a nice clean coach? And besides, who said this was a handout? You can pay us back when you get back on your feet. You give me your address and I will write to you and let you know where we will be staying."

Hatty could only give her a hug and thank her sincerely. "I can't believe we chanced on you last night. And now this—maybe my luck is changing."

Danielle smiled. "There is no such thing as luck, Hatty. God has a reason for everything. The train not running yesterday so we had to stay here an extra night, our having more than enough money at this particular time, you and Maria coming along as you did—it all fits, do you see?"

"I have a good friend you're going to have to meet someday," Hatty said.

Danielle laughed and called to Esteban. He was eager to help and insisted on seeing them safely across the border into Texas. They packed up the rest of their belongings and walked the three-quarters of a mile into Anahuac. The train was due at nine and rolled in right on time. Maria watched nervously for any sign of the red car or the man who drove it, but they boarded the train and pulled away from the stop without incident. Esteban graciously purchased four adult tickets and four for the children.

The children played while the adults sat in the coach opposite one another, talking of future plans. The more they talked, the more Hatty longed for her old home; and the more she longed for it, the more she tried to prepare herself for what it would be like without Eli.

Nuevo Laredo was bustling with late morning traffic. Hatty and Maria took their leave of the Morales family at the train station. They all hugged goodbye, wishing one another the best.

Maria looked down every side street and into every approaching face, trying to recall the man who walked the edge of the ravine. She had gotten only a glimpse, but she remembered the long scar. That would be enough.

They crossed the border from Nuevo Laredo over to the Texas side without incident. Hatty glanced up the street, then turned to Maria. "We're going to get some help, starting right now," she said as she marched across the busy intersection and up to the black-and-white sheriff's car.

Inside, a large man with a thin mustache had been watching them ever since they crossed over. He looked up at the two women through dark sunglasses and a cloud of cigar smoke. "Yes, ma'am?"

"Sir, could you recommend a good lawyer here in Laredo, please?" Hatty requested. "A criminal lawyer."

"Excuse me for asking, ma'am, but are you ladies in some kind of trouble?" The man seemed genuinely concerned.

Hatty was grateful. "I . . ." she started, then resisted the impulse to tell him everything. Hatty often regretted opening her mouth, but she rarely regretted keeping it shut. "I think I should wait to talk to a lawyer, but thank you for asking."

"Tell you what—I'll be glad to recommend a lawyer, but before I forget let me give you my card. If there's anything I can do for you, just give me a call, all right?" He pulled a clean white card from his shirt pocket and handed it to Hatty.

"I'm pleased to meet you, Sheriff Jones," Hatty said, extending her hand. "My name is Hatty King and this is my daughter-in-law, Maria."

"Your daughter-in-law . . ." he said, as if repeating the words to himself would help him comprehend the relationship. He stared just for a moment, then his expression changed slightly but undeniably into one of mixed loathing and pity at this interracial mix. Hatty knew the look. She would have responded the same way not long ago. He greeted both women, but Hatty noticed he subtly wiped his hand on his pants after shaking Maria's hand. She couldn't tell if the insult was intentional or an unconscious display of an ignorant bigot. She hoped Maria hadn't noticed.

The sheriff hooked his thumbs in his belt and looked down at the women. The cigar jutted from the corner of his mouth as he pushed the words out around it. "I guess I don't need to tell you it's not the best idea for two nice-looking ladies like yourselves to be out alone, especially on the other side. If I was you I'd get back with your husbands as soon as you can. Those people will take advantage, if you know what I mean." He smiled briefly, then looked down the street. "Now, there's a fellow I know just down this street about five blocks and take a right. His office is about halfway down on the left side. He's a yankee, but he knows his business. His name is Pogue. I'm sure he'll be glad to help you. He specializes in this sort of thing. Now, how long you plan on staying, miss?" he directed the question at Maria. "You know there's a limit. . . ."

"She's the wife of a United States citizen," Hatty bristled. "She'll stay as long as she wants."

"I see. Well, if you'll excuse me, I'd better get back to work. You be sure and call now if there's anything I can do." He slid behind the wheel and pulled around the corner, in the direction of the lawyer's office.

Pogue leaned forward in his chair and folded his hands on the table in front of him. He had been listening for the last thirty minutes to Hatty and Maria tell their story. He rubbed his face and looked down at the desk as if he were trying to decide on the most prudent course of action. He pressed the intercom button: "Linda, call Jim Tieg and see if he can come over for a few minutes, will you? Thanks." He rose from his chair to pour himself a drink. "Could I offer you ladies something? Scotch? Bourbon?"

"Can you help us, Mr. Pogue?" Hatty asked, ignoring the offer. Pogue sauntered back to his desk slowly, straining to give every impression of concern and sober reflection. He sat down gravely, folded his hands across his stomach, and looked Hatty in the eye.

"The FBI has an office just around the corner; they need to know about this. But I have to tell you right up front that it doesn't look good. And my bet is—I just want to prepare you for this now—the government's going to say the same thing."

Hatty was barely able to control her frustration. "Explain, please."

"Mrs. King, I want you to know I sympathize with you, but there are some hard questions that just don't have the kind of answers we need to proceed with an investigation. For example, if I understand you right, neither your husband's body nor the vehicle he was driving has been found yet, is that correct?"

"Nosir, I told you my sons found the truck and his body inside."

"All right, we've got two problems right there. You told me that neither of your sons actually made a positive identification of the man in the truck."

"It was my husband's truck!" Hatty said loudly.

"And neither of the young men who supposedly—excuse me—who saw the crashed truck are here to corroborate your story."

"I told you, Mr. Pogue, we believe my sons are dead."

"Mrs. King, I know this is terribly difficult for you, but please understand, we have to have hard evidence to go on. How do you know your sons are dead?"

Maria put her hand on Hatty's arm. "My husband would have come back. And there were the gunshots and the fire."

"Could have been some crazy Mexican—'scuse me, miss—could have been some drunk out celebrating the Days of the Dead a few days early. This kind of thing happens all the time. The husband doesn't come home in time, the wife gets worried, starts letting her imagination run away with her. I know you're worried, ladies, but nine times out of ten this kind of thing all works out in the end to be a big misunderstanding. Now your boys may have seen a wreck on the road, Mrs. King, I'm sure they did. And it may, it *may* have been your husband in that truck, but we simply—you simply—do not know that for sure. And without some physical evidence, I'm afraid there isn't a thing we can do. And I'll bet if you both went on back home, you'd find your husbands waiting for you, wondering where in the world you took off to." He belched out a short laugh and leaned far back in his chair, hands behind his head, satisfied that his sage counsel was unassailable.

"Mr. Pogue, Mr. Tieg is here." Linda's voice crackled over the intercom.

"Send him in, please," Pogue said, still smiling. The door opened and a tall young man in a dark suit walked in. He stood ramrod straight. The only crease in his suit was the one in his trousers.

"Ladies, allow me to introduce special agent Jim Tieg of the Federal Bureau of Investigation. Jim specializes in kidnaping cases that involve international flight. Jim, this is Mrs. King and her daughter-in-law Maria."

"Ladies."

Hatty thought she had never seen a colder pair of eyes in her life. Slate gray without a hint of compassion. The man nodded stiffly and turned to Pogue, waiting for a cue.

"The bottom line here, Jim, is that their husbands and Mrs. King's other son are missing down in the middle of Mexico and they are afraid they have been killed."

The man turned to the women. "I take it there are no bodies."

"That's correct," Pogue answered.

"Any witnesses?" the man asked, without taking his eyes off the women.

Again Pogue answered. "None."

"Any physical evidence of wrongdoing?"

Pogue looked at the two women. "Ladies?"

Hatty rose from her seat. "Gentlemen, I'm sorry to have wasted your time." Maria rose, and they crossed to the door quickly.

"Mrs. King," the second man said, stopping her. "Murder is a very serious charge. In the United States, if you have no physical evidence you wouldn't even get an indictment. Please understand, no one here is calling you a liar, but the burden of proof rests with you. Bring me some evidence, bring me something to go on, and I will set the wheels in motion that day. Until then, I'm sorry, but there's nothing I or any other conscientious law enforcement official can do. If I may suggest, I would go back home and see if your husbands don't turn up. It would surprise you how often a simple mistake gets blown out of proportion."

"Just what I told them, Jim. Ladies, if you do find something, please call me. Here's my card. I'll be glad to relay any messages to Jim here."

Special agent Tieg moved to open the door for the women. "I'm afraid you'll have to give them to my replacement. I'm being reassigned as of next week."

"Good day, Mr. Tieg, Mr. Pogue." The women walked out, eyes straight ahead.

Tieg closed the door softly behind them. Pogue put his hands to his lips until he heard the outer door close. He rose from his chair and shook Tieg's hand, then walked around the desk to pour them both a drink.

"Beautiful!" he said in a low voice. "Absolute perfection!"

"Remind you of Elliot Ness, or what?" Tieg slumped in the chair opposite the desk and relaxed into a satisfied grin.

"They didn't even ask for identification. I couldn't believe it," Pogue said, handing a glass of bourbon to his associate.

"You owe me, Pogue," Tieg said as he lit a cigarette.

"Boss?" Linda asked over the intercom.

Pogue leaned forward to depress the brown button. "Yeah?"

"I'm gone for the weekend."

"What? It's only two-thirty!"

"I'm going to see my sister, remember? You said I could. . . ."

"Oh, yeah, yeah," he sighed impatiently. "All right, go, but you're making it up next week."

"Natch. Bye." Linda picked up her purse and hurried out the door. Hatty and Maria were standing on the opposite corner, facing one another. "Mrs. King, Mrs. King, wait!" Linda yelled as she hurried across the street. She noticed Hatty jumped a bit when she called her. The two women were standing arm in arm.

"Mrs. King, I don't mean to intrude, but—by the way, my name is Linda Saliz—I heard you say you were from over near Puentas. I have a sister who lives in Bellville I'm going to see this evening. I noticed you weren't driving a car and I thought maybe you could use a lift."

Hatty stared hard at her, then turned away, crying.

"What? What did I say?" Linda asked.

Maria responded, smiling through her own tears. "I'm sorry. We're not ungrateful. It's just that the last few days have been—difficult. We appreciate your offer very much. In fact, we had just prayed that the Lord would make it clear to us which way we should go—back into Mexico or to Puentas, and then you called out to us. It was so sudden, we both jumped a bit."

"Well, it's the first time I've been the answer to anyone's prayer," Linda smiled. "I packed the car this morning, so I'm ready to go. Have you folks had lunch?"

Neither of the women responded. They were both hungry, but neither had any money to buy food. Linda noticed their embarrassment and charged ahead without missing a beat.

"Well, I'm starved. Come on, let's grab a burger and get on the road—my treat! I just got paid today and this money's burning a hole in my purse."

✥

"Interesting," Pogue mumbled as the blinds snapped back. He turned from the window back to his desk and plopped down in his chair.

"What's up?" Tieg asked.

Pogue leaned back in his chair and stared up at the ceiling, his hands clasped behind his head. A slow, thick smile creased his fat face. He leaned across the desk to pick up his phone.

"Yeah, operator, I need to place a long-distance call to San Antonio. Station to station." Pogue winked at Tieg as he sipped his bourbon. Someone picked up on the other end. "I need to talk to Gus. I'll leave a number for him to call. . . ."

20

"No, she's not a maid!" Miss Light was adamant. The other ladies in the Puentas Quilting Circle had posited various far-flung theories about the identity of the Mexican girl living with Hatty King, but Miss Irma Light would have none of their wild speculations. Miss Light's sister, the main hairdresser in Dalton Springs, had it firsthand: one of the King boys had gotten a Mexican girl in the family way down south, married her, and then was killed by her crazy brother, who was no doubt drunk at the time.

"Why do you think Hatty stays cooped up all day?" Miss Light demanded. "Why, she's hardly shown her face in town, and she's been back what—goin' on a month now? Heaven knows, I'd be ashamed too."

"She hasn't shown her face in town, Irma, because, unlike the rest of us, she doesn't have a car," said Miss Imogene Coker.

"Oh, please!"

"I'm serious. Something happened to it down in Mexico and she had to get a ride back from Laredo with a total stranger." Here, she paused to let the news sink in. Then, quietly, and without making any direct eye contact, she asked, "Has anyone been out to see Hatty? I know I haven't." There was a subdued pause. "We all ought to be ashamed of ourselves, that's what."

"I tried to call," piped up Sweet Smith, ever the voice of contrition in the group. "I guess she just hasn't gotten around to hooking up the phone yet."

Miss Coker put down her sewing and brightened as she addressed the circle. "Why don't we all go over there Sunday afternoon, say around two?" she suggested. "We could take food—a fruit basket, maybe, and some jellies, to say welcome home."

Miss Light ignored the overture. "I just flat didn't like the way she up and left without so much as a howdy-do to any of her friends," Miss Light protested. "And now she comes back and expects us all to trot out there like . . . like . . . "

"Like we're all glad to see her back and sorry for her loss?" Miss Coker asked. "Good lands, Irma, that was over two years ago. I think Hatty's gone through enough without us adding to the pile, don't you? Can you imagine losing your husband and both sons, all at the same time? What an awful thing!"

"Hmph," Miss Light grumped and hunched over her tight stitches with renewed vigor.

"Is this girl actually living with Hatty, or does she have her out in that extra room by the garage?" asked Natty Campbell.

"Right there in the house, I hear," Charlene Wiggins said matter-of-factly without looking up. "And from all accounts she drinks like a fish."

"Oh, now, Charlene, really," Miss Coker said.

"No, just ask Bubba Shanks. If he doesn't know, who would? Says she puts away at least a six-pack a night, not to mention a quart of bourbon each and every week since she moved in. Lord knows where she gets the money. Anyone hear if she's working or just living off Hatty's insurance?"

Miss Coker gave her a sidelong glance. "She's housekeeping for Charlie Tilden," she said shortly.

"You mean for Beau Holliman," Charlene said.

"No, no, I think Beau sold out to Charlie when he took off for Colorado, didn't he?" Natty asked.

"Near as I can tell they have some kind of understanding," Miss Coker said. "Charlie's been the foreman out there for how many years now? I think he's just moved in temporarily until Beau gets back. Heaven knows that big old house could use a woman's touch."

"But Imogene, Beau's been gone for six months at least," Sweet noted.

"Goin' on seven," Charlene chimed in. No one said it, but everyone knew Charlene had been marking off the days since the most eligible bachelor in Live Oak County had been gone. And truth to tell, she wasn't the only widow in the Circle who monitored Beau Holliman's comings and goings.

"Still, we'd know if Beau had sold," Natty said. "You know old Charlie would be crowin' like a rooster if he got hold of that land."

The observation garnered a universal "ummm-hmmm."

"Well," Miss Coker said as she gathered her quilting materials, "let's settle it then. Next Sunday afternoon at two. Everyone bring a little something nice—Sweet, that baked squash of yours is a wonder; and Charlene, don't I remember Hatty going on about your peach preserves at the fair a couple of years ago? You're all such good cooks, let's make it really special for her, all right? Next Sunday at two, then?"

All the women knew when Miss Coker first suggested the idea that they would probably wind up going to see Hatty. That's the way Imogene worked. When it came to doing what was right, she was a consensus of one and everyone else got in line. They all voiced their agreement as though the decision was a foregone conclusion.

The screen door to Hatty's ranch house creaked open quietly. Maria waved goodnight and slipped inside.

Charlie Tilden waited until she was safely in the door before backing out and starting the fifteen-mile drive back home. He had been making the round trip five days a week now for the last three weeks. He had hired Maria at first as a favor to Hatty, knowing his boss would want to help out in any way he could, but also knowing Hatty wouldn't take a handout. But he had been surprised at how hard Maria had worked, how she never complained, how she was always ready and waiting at sunrise when he arrived to pick her up. But there was something else about this girl. A calm. A quiet, deep-running joy that brought out the best in those around her.

Charlie took off his beat-up felt hat and tossed it on the seat beside him. He glanced in the rear-view mirror; the mustache and the ears needed a bit of a trim. He ran his hand through what remained of his silver hair and wished he were forty years younger.

It was almost eight in the evening as Maria walked in past a load of unwashed clothes with a small sack of groceries in hand. She turned on the light in the kitchen and set the sack down on the kitchen table, taking care not to break the eggs. The sound of a radio drifted in from the living room—either a political speech or an advertisement.

In the short time she had been living in Puentas, Maria had come to depend on all the electrical conveniences, but the one she most counted on was the small kitchen radio by the sink. To her it was an exquisite tool for learning English; a well-worn dictionary had displaced one of the older cookbooks in the short book rack on the counter. She turned the volume all the way down before she turned the radio on, then slowly turned it up as she tried to tune to the same channel; but the static was fierce and it crackled loudly.

"Maria? Maria, is that you?" Hatty called from her rocker in the living room.

"Yes, ma'am."

"Goodness, where have you been?" Hatty asked as she walked into the kitchen. "I've been half sick worrying about you." Dressed in her robe and slippers, Hatty had the drowsy look and sluggish gait of someone just awakened from a long sleep.

"I'm okay, Mom. Have you been resting?" Maria began to put away the groceries.

"Yeah. You get the groceries?"

"Um-hm. Eggs, milk. They had hamburger meat on special so I—"

"Did you get my medicine?"

Maria picked up the cereal box and some canned soup and carried them to the pantry.

"Where's my medicine? Didn't you get my medicine?"

"No, ma'am." Maria had been filling Hatty's "prescriptions" for nearly a month now, and she decided it was time to take a stand. She looked her mother-in-law in the eyes and spoke softly but firmly. "I think you're better now and you don't need it anymore. It's only making things worse. It's time to stop, Mom."

"But I need it. I do. You don't know."

"I do know."

"You didn't lose a son," Hatty said, beginning to cry, and putting a heavy hand on Maria's shoulder.

"I lost *your* son. Please, let's not go through all this again." Maria hugged her and helped her sit down. Hatty laid her head on the kitchen table. Maria lifted it gently and placed Hatty's forearm underneath for a cushion.

"All right now, I'm going to fix you the best scrambled eggs you've ever had," she said brightly. "We still have some bacon from last week and I'll brew some fresh coffee. How does that sound?"

"I can't eat anything."

"Oh, you won't be able to resist—besides, we need to get something in your stomach. You know, now that you won't be needing your medicine any longer, we're going to be able to buy better food."

"Tilden isn't paying you enough, is he?" Hatty mumbled.

"Mr. Tilden is being very generous, you know that, Mom. He pays far more than we should expect."

"I need my medicine," Hatty said again before she dropped off to sleep and began to snore.

As Maria prepared the food she reminded herself once again that her life could be much worse, that she was lucky to be alive. She had written three letters to Estella and Doc, and three to Anita, but had received no reply. Her job allowed her to get to the post office only once a week, on Saturdays, and then she had to walk a mile-and-a-half from the ranch house into town. Maybe tomorrow. Maybe tomorrow a letter would come. A sizzling drop of bacon grease popped from the iron skillet and landed on her hand.

"Ai, me, San Antonio!" she said, shaking the burned hand and grabbing a towel. "Such a little speck to cause so much pain. And there's more where you came from, huh, you little devil." She reached over and carefully placed a lid on the skillet. "Now," she mused, "what would Doc say if he were here? He would draw some profound lesson from that spatter." She lowered her voice to approximate Doc's preaching tone. "Why, this old world's full of trouble, Maria girl. And it's a lot like that hot grease there. It's not the bit that pops out that matters, it's the batch that's still in the skillet. Be thankful!"

She smiled as she loaded the plates with food and poured two cups of hot coffee. *Nah,* she thought. *It's the bit that pops out, Doc. That's what hurts.* She brought the plates over to the table and set two places.

"Mom?" she said as she rubbed Hatty's back. "Mom, it's time to eat, okay?"

"Not hungry." Hatty said without opening her eyes or lifting her head.

"I know, but you have to eat. Doctor's orders. Come on, now." Maria lifted Hatty's head and held her in an upright sitting position.

"Oh, I'm going to be sick if you make me eat this."

"Well, that's nothing new. At least now I'll feel like you're getting sick for a good reason." With her left arm around Hatty's waist, Maria took her right hand and thanked God for their food, for a roof over their heads, and for the generosity of Mr. Tilden. Then she picked up a spoonful of scrambled egg and they started to eat.

"Hatty? Hatty King, are you home?" Miss Light stood at the head of a small band of women, all of whom had come, ostensibly, to welcome Hatty home. She knocked again. "Hatty King—are you in there?" She peered in through the screen door to see if she could make out anything inside.

"Well, we know she's here," Miss Light said. "Where's she going to go?" She opened the screen door and tried the inside entry, but it was locked.

"She probably just went out for a walk or something," Sweet said. "I bet she'll be back real quick."

"Well, I don't have all day," Miss Light said. "I'm going to look around a bit, and if we don't find her then that's just too bad."

"Is that so?" Hatty and Maria walked around from the river side of the old garage. Hatty carried a walking stick with an antler handle. The ankle was still bothering her.

"Hatty! It's good to see you again!" Sweet Smith hugged Hatty with her free hand, but it was like embracing a cedar post. "We heard about the awful accident with Eli and the boys and we're so sorry. Imogene wanted so to be here to say hey but she came down with that bug that's goin' around and didn't want to get you infected, so we just wanted to come over and say hey and let you know—"

"Sweet," Miss Light interrupted, shaking her head. "So, Hatty, aren't you going to ask us inside for some coffee?"

"Oh, I don't think so, Irma, not today. I'm just not feeling up to it," Hatty smiled thinly. "I do thank you for coming all the way out here. I know it's a long trip for all of you, and heaven knows, you're all busy as can be with folks comin' in for Thanksgiving and all. I wouldn't dream of holding you here. Now, if you'll excuse me, I need to take a nap."

She started to move through them, but Charlene Wiggins reached out from the back to touch her on the arm. "Hatty," she said, looking at Hatty's forehead—she rarely looked anyone in the eye—"we're sorry."

"You should have come sooner, Charlene." Hatty looked at the other women without saying anything and then turned to go.

Sweet pushed forward. "Hatty, don't be mad. We didn't know what to do or what to say."

Hatty turned on the top step of the porch to face her comforters. "Sweet, you've never in your life been at a loss for words. What in the world were you girls thinking? I mean, I come back here—my husband's dead, my boys are dead—I come back here to nothing. Nothing! Where were you?"

"And where were *you*, Hatty King?" Miss Light demanded, coldly. "You think we haven't all lost husbands? But we were there with them when they died. Where were you when Eli needed you? You don't even know where he is now, do you? Why did you let him die like that?"

The words came quick and sharp and cut deep like a hunting knife slicing a wounded deer's throat. The moment was frozen—women standing in the front yard like old sticks stuck upright in the ground, watching the life drain from Hatty's face. The chilly breeze blew a wisp of gray hair across Miss Light's face of stone. How like a graveyard it felt. How dingy and pointless this gesture.

Maria moved forward to take Hatty by the arm, but Hatty refused to budge. She was still glaring at Irma Light. "I know you and Eli were good friends, Irma. He was good friends with a lot of folks around here. But I was his best friend. I'm the one who lost everything she had in the world, not you. And you're right. I *wasn't* there when he needed me most, but it wasn't because I didn't want to be. I know I've made mistakes in my life, but as God is my witness, I don't deserve this. I didn't deserve to have my husband and my sons murdered, I didn't deserve this godforsaken ranch, and I don't deserve you."

Hatty wheeled away from them and stormed into the house with Maria following close behind.

Miss Irma Light marched back to the cars with the other ladies in tow. She had ridden out with Charlene Wiggins. Charlene got in on the driver's side and slammed the door closed.

"This is all Imogene's fault," Charlene said as she cranked the engine. "We should never have come out here. You were right, Irma. You were right all along."

Miss Light sat hunched against the window pane, looking out at the November-blown afternoon. "What this country needs is some water to bring the life back," she said softly. "It'd be a wonder what just a little rain would do."

21

Charlie Tilden lived out away from most folks beside a twenty-foot Airline trailer. He lived "beside" rather than "in" the trailer, because Charlie was, to put it mildly, an outdoorsman. There wasn't a man or animal that Charlie Tilden couldn't befriend, but there were two things he didn't care for: walls and fences, and so he maintained as few of them as possible. His trailer was nestled between three towering oaks, each thirty to forty feet high, set in the middle of a sprawling pasture of sparse buffalo grass without a fence in sight.

An enormous red hammock swayed in the breeze between two of the oaks. In late spring and summer, if the mosquitoes weren't too bad, Charlie would sleep outside in it. August was his favorite month. "There's more shootin' stars and more animals alive in August than any other time of the year," he would tell Beau. "You can lie there at night and lose track tryin' to count all the sounds."

Charlie was down to twenty Herefords on close to five hundred acres of what used to be outstanding pasture land. A creek cut across the bottom of gentle rolling hill about a hundred yards from the trailer. In a good rain year it would run in the springtime almost like a river, but it was dry and sandy now. He had a cattle trough up on the north end of the place and one windmill that chinged out just enough water to keep the cattle from dying of thirst.

Charlie had bought the land back in the twenties, before they cut the new highway through. Until recently, he couldn't hear a car out there all day unless it was company coming for a visit. Charlie liked it that way.

He kept most of his small herd of Hereford cattle in the same pasture where he had parked his trailer. They would come to his high call, and most would eat cubes right out of his hand. He had names for them all, but one in particular was more a pet than meat on the hoof. His name was Alarm Clock, but Charlie called him A.C. for short. For over a year now A.C. would come up to the trailer every morning between five and five-fifteen, place his head just so against the side, and gently rock back and forth. That was Charlie's wake-up call—it was feeding time and A.C. wanted his breakfast. Beau saw the calf in action early one morning when he had to pick Charlie up for work; before long, the story of Charlie's trained bull calf had spread over half the county so that the old cowboy had more than usual company for a while.

On this particular morning the trailer started rocking a little earlier than usual. Charlie rolled over and pounded on the side to make the animal stop. "Go back to sleep, A.C." The rocking stopped, and Charlie pulled the covers tighter around his neck. The morning was bitterly cold and he didn't want to budge. But after a minute passed the rocking started again, this time more insistently. Charlie again banged on the tin siding and raised his volume: "Go to bed, you crazy animal! I'm not goin' to feed you at this time of night. The moon's still up, for heaven's sake—now settle down!" The rocking stopped. Charlie could hear the animal walking away from the trailer. But then he heard what he thought was a pawing sound. He had never heard of a bull attacking a trailer before, but then . . .

Bam! Something hit the side of the trailer with a terrific blow. Charlie jumped out of bed and jerked his boots on over his bare feet. *Bam!* Almost losing his balance as he reached for his hat, Charlie threw open the door of the trailer and, dressed in nothing but his long underwear and wielding a baseball bat, jumped out yelling like thunder.

"*Mooo, Charlie!*" A big burly man stood leaning against one of the oaks, head thrown back and laughing so hard his knees began to buckle.

"Beau! You rapscallion!" Charlie said as he walked over and shook hands. "I thought A.C. was going to turn that trailer over."

Beau put his arm around his old friend and they laughed again. "Oh, Charlie, what I'd give for a camera. It's good to see you again."

"Same here, Boss."

"Well, come on, I'll feed the cattle while you get dressed. They still cookin' an early breakfast down at the Sunrise?"

"Six o'clock every mornin'."

"All right, then. We've got breakfast to eat, on me, and half a year of catchin' up to do."

Charlie started off at a trot for the trailer, but he stopped halfway there and turned back to Beau, who was on his way to the feed bin. "You haven't been out to the house yet, have you?"

"Nope. Just drove in. It's still there, isn't it?"

"Oh, yeah. Yeah, there's just been a lot of things going on and, uh—good things, good things. I'll tell you all about it at breakfast!" Charlie hurried inside and closed the door quickly behind him, then stuck his head out again almost immediately. "Oh, yeah, and we'll need to swing by Puentas right quick on the way."

"Puentas? Charlie, that's another seven miles. Whatever business you've got there, can't it wait till after breakfast?"

"Tell you what. You go on ahead and order breakfast. It won't take me two shakes to run out there. I'll meet you at the Sunrise quick as a wink." Charlie shut the door again, leaving Beau to wonder what in the blue-eyed world Charlie was up to.

The Sunrise Cafe smelled of bacon and eggs, coffee and tobacco by six-thirty most mornings.

"So where you been, cowboy?" Martha Nell, proprietor of the Sunrise, stood with a coffee pot in her left hand looking down at Beau. She had just poured his second cup.

"Up outside of Denver. Just looking things over, you know."

"Now you're not thinking about leaving us, are you?" She squeezed his arm playfully. "'Cause if you are we'll fence you in. We'll set up a roadblock, won't we, Armando?" she said to the deputy sitting at the next table.

The young man looked up and smiled. "Whatever you say, Martha Nell."

"See, you can tell he's going to be a good man. Beau, you haven't met our new deputy yet. This is Armando Estevez. Jake hired him just before he took off for parts unknown."

The two men shook hands. Beau was struck with how young he was.

"Good to meet you, Armando."

"Same here. I've heard a lot about you. Martha Nell here says—"

"Armando," Martha Nell interrupted, walking over to his table, "don't you need another cup of coffee or somethin' to put in your mouth?" The deputy grinned and winked at Beau as he rose from the table.

"No, no, I've got to get back to Dalton Springs. Thanks, Martha Nell. We'll be seeing you, Beau."

"Look forward to it."

Beau noticed the generous tip Armando left tucked under the plate for Martha Nell as she cleaned away his dishes. A cold gust of wind blew in as the deputy opened the door and stepped out onto the sidewalk. Charlie greeted him on his way in and held the door for an extra beat while Maria entered first. The old cowboy scanned the clientele and quickly spotted Beau at his usual table. He took off his hat and tossed it onto the rack to his right as he closed the door behind him. Maria lifted the shawl from her head as Charlie led her to Beau's table.

"Boss, this here is Maria King. Maria, this is Mr. Holliman."

Suddenly realizing he was still seated, Beau rose awkwardly to greet the young woman.

"Maria—King, you said?"

"Yes, sir, she's—"

"My husband was Martin King, Eli King's son," Maria said, extending her hand.

Beau looked to Charlie, then back to Maria as he shook her hand. "I, well, I'm pleased to meet you, Maria. Sit down, please. Would you like some coffee?"

"Yes, please."

"Martha Nell, two more coffees and—you both want bacon and eggs?—three regular breakfasts please, ma'am. Now, did I understand you to say you *were* Marty's wife?"

"Boss, a lot's happened in the last few weeks. I don't understand the whole story myself, so I thought it would be a good idea to let Maria just tell it to you the way it happened, all right?"

"I'm listening."

Maria spoke softly, unfolding the story of the last two years bit by bit, answering Beau's questions as she went along. But eventually, the questions stopped and she went on without interruption. Beau sat, stunned at the news, amazed at Maria's composure and grace. There was no anger in her voice, only a deep sadness as she told of the disappearance of her husband and his brother. And then of Eli's death.

As she spoke, Beau closed his eyes and rested his head in his hand. It was heavy. Hot. He was tired. And much older than his years. He was sinking into a black hole somewhere deep within himself. Her words echoed, then fell, liquid around him, turning to quicksand and pulling him down into thick darkness. *Surely there is some other explanation,* he thought to himself, but the gravity of her words allowed no light to escape. There was no hope, she said, or Martin would have contacted her by now. She told about Estella and Doc and little Rosalinda as well, about how much they had done and how she loved them and felt helpless to do anything since the law had refused to get involved.

After she finished, Beau remained motionless for a full minute. When he spoke, his voice was low and thick. "Lord, I can't believe all three of them are dead. Not all three. And the law won't do squat." He adjusted his chair a bit to look directly at his foreman. "Remember, Charlie, before I left? We were hearing stories about old what's-his-name. . . ."

"Joe?"

"Joe Diaz came up claiming there was something brewing down in Sabinas with their local boys. But we didn't believe it was anything. Is he still around?"

"Nah, he took off when no one would listen to him; moved back down to try to take care of his family, I think. Nobody's heard from him in months."

"All right," Beau said. "Now I'm just trying to put some of this together. What's this about Jake Skerritt being gone?"

"You know as much as we do on that one, Boss. One day he takes off on a vacation. According to Armando he said he'd be gone a week. That was four—no, nearly six weeks ago now. And here's another thing. He took off right after he took on Armando as deputy. That kid's been a real good surprise."

"What do you think happened to Jake?"

"I imagine somebody got ahold of him," Charlie replied. "Paid him back for some of his back-stabbing. That's what most folks figure."

"I guess everybody's real torn up over that."

"Well, let's just say nobody's tryin' very hard to find out what happened to him. Things have been pretty quiet around here since he disappeared."

"Yeah. Probably doesn't have anything to do with Eli and the boys, but it's sure a coincidence, isn't it—all of this happening at the same time?" Beau sat quietly thinking, trying to unravel the tangled stories, trying to see some connection between seemingly unrelated events that might give him a clue to which path to take. Suddenly he saw Maria again and felt embarrassed for having ignored her feelings in all this.

"Maria," Beau said, leaning forward slightly, "I want you to know how sorry I am for your loss. I don't know if Marty or Eli ever mentioned me to you. Eli and I were pretty close. He and Hatty and those two boys were the only family I had down here." Beau could feel his voice starting to break. He paused, swallowed, and went on. "I'm going to do everything I can to find out what happened. I'll promise you that much."

He sat back while Martha Nell poured another cup of coffee. "I really appreciate your coming out to help keep up my place, but you don't have to anymore—wait, that might have sounded wrong. What I mean is, I've got a little set aside, and I'd be glad to take care of you and Hatty. You need some time to deal with this, to let things settle for a while."

"Mr. Holliman, may I say something?"

"I wish you would. I'm not doing too well here."

"No, you are very kind, and I thank you for your concern. I do grieve over the loss of my husband. Most nights I still cry myself to sleep, thinking of him. I grieve over the loss of my brother-in-law and my father-in-law. I called him Dad—I never had anyone I could call Dad before."

She paused, looking down, searching for the right words. "I don't think a person ever—gets over—something like this; I'm not sure we are even supposed to. I have learned so much about my Lord through all this. About acceptance and forgiveness and . . ." she took a deep breath and drew strength. Tears pooled in her eyes. "And joy. I know. I *know* that He loves me. I used to feel I could never do enough to make Him love me. I was right. What I didn't know was that He loved me already. Martin taught me that. I knew it here." She touched her head. "Now I know it in my heart. Mom needs to know that too, but her pain is so great. . . ."

She sat up straight and spoke with quiet confidence. "God has given me the grace to accept this, Mr. Holliman. And part of His grace is letting me work for you. I think I remember somewhere in the New Testament it says something like, if you don't work you don't eat? God has given me strong hands and a strong back. I want to work. I want to earn my living."

Beau sat back, trying to collect his thoughts, trying to regroup. His mind was whirring, attempting to categorize this woman. Until this moment he thought he had seen and could handle just about anything the world had to throw his way.

For Beau, who was about to turn fifty, life after forty had settled into a comfortable and welcome rhythm, offering variations on tried-and-true themes. Every marriage, every birth, every death, every interested widow—every cow, in fact. They were all basically the same. He had convinced himself that he was grateful there were no surprises left, since every time he thought he'd stumbled upon a legitimate surprise or an authentic discovery it later turned out to be just an old joy or sorrow returned to sucker him again. Like a tramp who comes to the back door twice in the same day, thinking you're too stupid to notice it's him behind the mask.

Over the years Beau had grown proficient at seeing through the fabric of pretense most folks wore. He could spot a fake a mile off and had learned to prepare himself for the encounter by identifying, categorizing, and pigeonholing the pretender before any damage was done. It was, if nothing else, a convenient way to live, affording him a comfortable feeling of "being in control." There was, indeed, nothing new under the sun.

Until today.

It upset the balance, disturbed his mid-life equilibrium, but he had to consider that he might just be looking at the genuine article, an authentic discovery. Maybe. And of what? He wasn't sure. That's the nature of discoveries. It takes some time to figure them out. He got the feeling that if he had met this young woman only a short time before, he would have met quite a different person—one he would have seen before behind a thousand different masks. But here, he thought, was a surprise without a mask.

"Boss?"

"Hang on, Charlie. I'm weighing the options." Beau was silent another few seconds, then asked, "Cal O'Reagan has the place leased, doesn't he?"

"Yes," answered Maria.

"When's the lease up, do you know, Maria?"

"I'm not sure," she responded, "but I think I remember Martin saying it ran through the end of March."

"All right, I'll tell you what. You can work out at my place through the end of March. Then we're going to get you and Hatty set up to run a few head of cattle. Start building the ranch back up again."

Charlie said nothing, but he wondered at the wisdom of Beau's promise. It was true that he had some money saved and that he had a few head of cattle he could sell to Hatty for a modest price, but he had a tendency to be overly generous.

Beau was just like his father in that respect. Charlie had worked for Ben Holliman when he was a young wrangler. Besides his ranch, Ben ran the general store in Dalton Springs for years, but when the Depression hit Ben couldn't bring himself to turn down a request for food. He literally gave away the store and most of what the family had put aside.

At Ben's death, Beau inherited the ranch and seventy-five scrawny cows. He transformed the spread into one of the most profitable ranches south of San Antonio. Beau also helped launch a number of other younger cattlemen in the area, including Hatty's cousin Cal O'Reagan. Charlie was the voice of moderation when it came to Beau's giving habits, but Beau always said the Lord would provide as He saw fit to fill the need.

"Charlie, you still with us, pardner?" Beau asked, slapping his foreman on the back.

"Yeah, sure. I was just thinkin'."

"All right, here's the deal," Beau announced. "Charlie, you and I are going to pay a little visit to the sheriff's office over in Rio Bravo—isn't that where you said that fellow is from, Maria?"

"I believe it said Rio Bravo on his card. Mom has it in her purse."

Beau leaned back in his chair and folded his arms across his chest. "Seem kind of funny to you, Charlie? A sheriff passing out cards and offering help outside his jurisdiction?"

"Could be he's just trying to be helpful," Charlie said slowly. "But then, what would you have done if you were in his boots and you saw a couple of women in need? I'll tell you what you'd do—you'd have driven them a hundred and twenty miles to their front doorstep and then helped them mend their fences, and that's why you'll never be sheriff of this county, by jingo!"

"What did Martha Nell put in your coffee, Charlie? We're just going to check this out, ask a few questions, that's all." Beau pushed his chair back abruptly and stood up. "Come on, let's get rolling. We need to get Maria out to the house, then you and I have some driving to do."

"Just hold on a second," Charlie protested. "When do you plan to sleep? You've been up all night, haven't you?"

"I'll sleep some in the truck. Now, let's go."

"Maria doesn't have a way home."

Beau turned to face the girl. "You don't leave before five, do you, Maria?"

"No, sir, not usually till six."

"We'll be home before four-thirty."

"Yes, sir."

"And one more thing. I'd really appreciate it if you would drop the sir and just call me Beau. I'm old enough as it is, and besides that we're practically related."

"Very well—Beau." She smiled as she said it, half embarrassed.

Her words brought him up short. He was surprised at how hearing her speak his name made him stop and look into her eyes, but he didn't take time to think about it. This day had had enough surprises already.

"Right," he said, turning away quickly and walking to the counter to pay the bill. Charlie opened the door for Maria and ushered her out to his truck. He returned a few seconds later to retrieve his hat, then turned to wait for Beau. As the two men walked out the door, Charlie asked under his breath, "You feeling okay, Boss?"

"Sure, fine—why?" Beau asked as they stepped off the sidewalk into the street.

"Nothin'," Charlie said as he walked on ahead. "You just looked a little flushed back there, that's all." He picked up his pace, chuckling to himself as he walked to the truck.

22

Beau slept most of the way to Rio Bravo. He had decided to wait to go out to Hatty's place until he had some real news. Charlie drove the ten miles to Dalton Springs, where he stopped for gas and a Coke before striking out on the interminable drive to Rio Bravo.

Rio Bravo was a town of close to seven thousand people who prided themselves on maintaining a true frontier image. Unlike her more commercial sister city of Laredo to the southeast, Rio Bravo boasted an economy that was free of the destabilizing influences of the tourist crowd. The chamber of commerce joined hands with one of the older missions to put up a good front, publically denouncing tourism as the canker that leads to corruption (although their town sign seemed to be designed to attract would-be buckaroos with the logo, "Rio Bravo—Where the *Real* West Begins").

It was, however, a conceit that smacked decidedly of sour grapes since, if people wanted to cross over into Mexico, shop, catch a train, or conduct international business, they would do it in Laredo. "Why drive the extra thirty miles?" was the prevailing attitude, and it had remained so for the last hundred and fifty years. Back in the gold rush days, the rowdies always stopped at Laredo on their way to the California gold fields for one last bash before setting out across the trackless wastes of the badlands. A few miles down the trail the cowboys stumbled into Rio Bravo, but by then they had gotten serious and any attempt by the town to draw them into further acts of self-indulgence was looked upon as being indecorous and out of touch with the true pioneer spirit. That and the fact that one all-night blowout was about all a cowboy could stand.

So Rio Bravo was an afterthought in the minds of most folks in south Texas. But the citizens still had their pride. If they couldn't keep up with Laredo, they would go the other way. And that's exactly what they did. With a concerted effort to avoid any semblance of progress, Rio Bravo developed into an authentic throwback to a nineteenth century Texican pueblo. It was a great place to live, if you liked a slow-paced life and had never been anywhere else. Most folks lived in adobe houses, worked in buildings constructed with home-fired bricks, and went to church in the same buildings their great-grandfathers had helped build.

The county courthouse was a decaying fortress three stories high. The entire edifice groaned under the strain of the corrupting influences of sustained drought and neglect. Cracks in the mortar, some more than an inch wide, crept up the sides like slow-moving lightning. The foundation itself was crumbling due to years of neglect, but no one gave it a second thought.

The sheriff's office was the only air-conditioned room in the building. The most obvious piece of furniture in it, other than the extra-long sofa, was an imposing weapons case, standing nearly eight-and-a-half feet tall and covering over half of the eighteen-foot east wall. A small fraction of the sheriff's vast weapons collection filled the lighted case. The artillery section was equally impressive. Double-iron chains secured the weaponry in place, and the case itself was double-padlocked.

Everything about the interior of the office was dark but immaculate, arranged in neat rows, and always dusted the night before even if the sheriff wasn't going to be there. Latigo liked his world ordered and under his authority, especially when he was out of sight, which he was at the moment.

"Won't you have a seat, gentlemen? I'm sure Sheriff Jones will be back in just a few minutes." The secretary was sweet and efficient. She seemed more suited to a corporate office than a backwater hole like Rio Bravo. But she was nervous. When Beau mentioned that their visit concerned some business in Mexico, the young woman looked at him for a few seconds before giving a cautious response.

Beau and Charlie sat quietly, thumbing through magazines. After ten minutes had passed, the secretary took a deep breath, rose, and crossed over to the two men. "I'm sorry you're having to wait," she said. She was having trouble making eye contact. "May I get you gentlemen something to drink? Coffee? Soda?"

Charlie and Beau looked at one another at the same time. Beau stood. "Miss," he said to the young woman, "we don't mean to make you uncomfortable. I'm afraid you've mistaken us for someone else."

"No, no," she said, backing up. "It's just me. I'm being silly, that's all. Sorry." She edged around the desk and sat down. Beau returned to his seat.

"You been with the department long?" Beau asked.

"Sir? Oh, no, not really. Well, six months, if you count that a long time." She smiled, then hastened to correct herself. "But I'm not really *with* the department. I just finished junior college over at LJC this May. This job is to help pay for UT beginning next fall."

Beau was impressed. "Sounds like you've got things pretty well mapped out. You decided on a major yet?"

"Pre-law. I want to be a lawyer, but I don't know."

"Looks like you picked a good place to learn the ropes," Beau said.

"Yeah," she said half-cynically. "That's what I thought when I signed on."

"Not quite what you expected, huh?" Beau asked.

"Let's just say when I go back to college I'll have a better idea of how the system works." She was beginning to let her guard down.

"How's that?" Beau continued.

She paused for a few seconds, looking at the two men, making up her mind about something. She glanced around to make sure no one else was listening, then asked in a quieter voice, "You fellows aren't from around here, are you?"

"No, I run a little place out the other side of Dalton Springs. Why do you ask?"

"Just curious. I'm just a curious person."

"What can you tell me about Sheriff Jones?" Beau asked. "Is he a pretty easy fellow to work with?"

"Oh, sure, he's tops. He's even giving me some extra time off to go home for Thanksgiving. So you haven't ever met him before?"

"First time."

The "exit only" double-glass doors slammed open and shut at the far end of the hall. Heavy boots emphatically marched *heel-toe, heel-toe* up the black-and-white tiled hall toward the waiting area.

"This might not be a good day," the girl said apologetically.

Charlie leaned forward and peered down the corridor. The outside light silhouetted the figure walking toward him. Blue-white puffs of smoke escaped around the head and trailed out behind. The high windows permitted white spindles of light to invade the dimly lit hall. Light of any kind wasn't welcome much here.

Charlie hadn't really been conscious of the light patches until he saw this hulking man emerge from the shadows and pass quickly through them. Each pool of light caught the sheriff in mid-stride, freezing him for a fraction of a second per interval, revealing a little bit more of him with each advancing pool until he stepped out of the last shadow into the waiting area.

Beau and Charlie rose to meet him. "Sheriff Jones? My name is Beau Holliman and this is—"

"Get me Pogue on the line," Latigo growled at the secretary as he walked past them. Within five seconds he had unsnapped his key ring, unbolted his office door, stepped inside, and closed the door firmly behind him.

"Tunnel vision," the girl intoned, shaking her head.

"What?" Beau asked, irritated at the sheriff's rudeness.

"He's got tunnel vision. 'Specially on bad days. He never even saw you."

"Has he got tunnel hearing, too? I spoke to the man plain as day."

"No, no, I mean he's focused, single-minded, you know. Doesn't let things distract him."

"Jennifer!" Jones called from inside his office.

"Yes, sir," she shouted back, picking up the phone. "I'm calling right now."

Beau walked behind the secretary's desk to the door with "Sheriff" painted in gold letters across one of the panels.

"Mr. Holliman, wait, you can't—" the girl said, but it was too late.

Beau tried the door. It wouldn't budge.

"It locks automatically," she whispered, then turned her attention to the phone. "Hello, Mr. Pogue? Sheriff Jones would like to speak to you. Hold, please." She transferred the call to the inner office. Beau and Charlie could hear one ring and then the sheriff's answer.

"He never talks long. If you gentlemen would like to take a seat, I'll let him know you're here just as soon as he's off the line."

Beau and Charlie took their seats again. Charlie was incensed. "The nerve of that guy. How'd a fellow like that ever get elected in the first place? Mr. High-and-Mighty. . . ."

Beau's mind was already on something else. He leaned over and whispered, "Charlie, what was the name of that lawyer that Maria mentioned? The one she and Hatty went to see over in Laredo?"

✥

"Pogue?" Jones growled.

"Yeah, Boss?"

"Talk, and this better be good."

"We're making progress. Mangus got into town a few days ago. He's got a crew out at the King place now shooting holes."

"Shooting holes? Mangus said he *knew* there was oil under that section. He's wasting my money, Pogue."

"I don't think so. He's got the rig out there on the ground. I think he's just looking for the best spot."

"Can you see anything?"

"I didn't even see it and I was standing ten feet from the pipe. Once the rig is up the trees are so thick down there no one will see it. This guy knows what he's doing."

"You better be right. Did anyone see you go in?"

"I went in through the Vanacek property. Not a soul. Puentas is pretty much a ghost town anyway."

"There's always somebody watching, Pogue, you know that. Now what about the lock box?"

"That one's a little harder to crack, Boss. No one in the bank is interested in cooperating."

"Don't give me that. Where there's money there's interest. Up the ante."

"How high?"

Latigo hesitated. "How sure is Mangus?"

"Dead on."

"Fifteen thousand."

"Boss, we don't even know if the deed's in there."

"It ain't just the deed. We need the wills. I doubt those boys had 'em, but just in case—pull it all. We don't want those boys leaving anything to their Mexican tarts. And make sure whoever you get understands this is a one-time offer, one-time payment. They make any noise down the line and they disappear."

Pogue was silent.

"Talk to me, Pogue."

"There's a potential problem here you need to know about."

"Spit it out."

Pogue cleared his throat. Latigo could hear the faint clink of ice in a glass. "You ought to be receiving some visitors today. A couple of cowboys—one about fifty, the other—"

"About sixty-five, seventy?"

"You already talk with them?"

"They're waiting outside. Who are they?"

"One's a cousin of the Kings. Name's Beau Holliman. He's taking a special interest. Seems he and King were college buddies or something, I don't know, but all I'm saying is we need to be careful. The old man's harmless."

Latigo cursed. "None of this would have happened if you'd done your job and taken care of the women."

"I gave the order, Boss. Sanchez screwed it up."

"They shouldn't have been allowed to cross the border! They're *women,* for God's sake. All right, all right, listen. You get into the lock box and keep me up on Mangus. I want to know every move. I'll take care of our two cowboy friends."

"Be careful, Boss. This guy's got connections. He's—"

"Yeah, yeah, later." Latigo hung up the phone and sat for a moment, thinking through his next move.

The door of the office swung open and Latigo started to say something to his secretary. His eye happened on Beau. "Jennifer, are these men here to see me? Why didn't you let me know?" Then, turning to Beau and Charlie, he extended his hand. "I'm Sheriff Jones. How can I help you men?"

Beau was surprised at his reaction to the sheriff's physical deformity. The burn scars were particularly pink in that light.

Latigo noticed his momentary stare. "Burned when I was a kid—Halloween night, of all things. Daddy used to say I was scary enough without a mask! I think he's right, don't you, Mr.—?"

"Holliman. Beau Holliman, and this is my foreman, Charlie Tilden. I apologize. I didn't mean to stare."

"Happens all the time. I'm used to it. Come on in." He motioned them into his office. "Jennifer, get us a round of Cokes, would you?"

Beau and Charlie entered and sat in chairs that were designed to make their occupants look up to the person sitting behind the desk—a small but sometimes significant psychological advantage.

"You're a hunter, sheriff," Beau said, eyeing the weapons case.

"White-tail and birds, that's about it. You?"

"I enjoy hunting deer, but I won't kill unless we can use the meat. I lost any pleasure in hunting birds a number of years ago. Charlie here is a squirrel hunter. One of the finest shots with a .22

you'll ever see."

"That right? You gotta have a good eye for squirrel," Latigo said, with a half-laugh.

"I get by," Charlie said. He hadn't known the man five minutes, but he'd already made up his mind that he was a scalawag.

"Now, you gentlemen didn't drive all the way out here to talk about hunting. What can I do for you?"

"We didn't say we drove a long way. How'd you know?" Charlie was in a challenging mood.

"Well, for one thing you looked worn out. For another, I know most families in this town down to their second cousins. Besides, like they say, anywhere that ain't here is far from here. We're not much of a metropolis here in Rio Bravo, so I figure you're from Laredo at least. Am I right?"

"We're from over the other side of Dalton Springs. I have a little ranch a few miles north of there," Beau replied.

"Dalton Springs? Lord, I haven't been over there in years. What brings you all the way out to Rio Bravo?"

"We have a friend who's in a bind. Actually, she's a relative of mine. Her name is Hatty King. I think you might have met her, in fact. Back about a month ago, she and her daughter-in-law came across the border at Laredo. She asked about a lawyer and you suggested a fellow named Pogue, I believe."

"King . . . King . . . " Latigo said, shaking his head slowly. "You say she had another woman with her?"

"A young Mexican woman in her early twenties."

"Oh. I thought a minute ago you said she was her daughter-in-law." Latigo raised the skin where his eyebrows should have been, puckering his forehead in an expression that made Charlie want to spit.

"That's what I said, sheriff," Beau remarked, coolly.

"I see." Latigo leaned back in his chair for a moment, making a whistling sound between the gap in his front teeth. "Tell you what, gentlemen," he said, abruptly leaning forward and propping his elbows on his desk. "This office doesn't like getting mixed up in domestic disputes, and Mexico is slightly outside my jurisdiction. Now, I'll tell you right up front, if this is about some hot-blooded cowboy getting some little chiquita in trouble down south, I'm afraid there's nothing I can do."

Beau paused for a moment, considered leaving, and then decided against it. His voice was calm and straightforward. "A good friend of mine was killed less than two months ago down in Mexico. His two sons have been missing for more than a month. We have reason to believe they may have been killed as well. There are no bodies and, as far as we know right now, no witnesses. Can you help us?"

"Well, Holliman, I'd say you just answered your own question. You've got no bodies, no witnesses, and no evidence. Not a lot for an old bloodhound to chew on, is it? I'd like to help you, I really would, but what do you want me to do?"

"I think you gave Mrs. King a card and asked her to call if there was anything you could do to help."

"I probably did. It's an election year. I give out lots of cards, and I help whenever I can, but I just don't see what I can do in this situation. Tell you what you might do. Call the Mexican authorities down in San Luis Potosí—see if they can help. That would be about your best bet."

"All right, sheriff. We won't take any more of your time." Beau rose to go. Charlie opened the door and went ahead without a word.

"Your foreman could use some manners."

Beau walked to the door. "I'll be sure to tell him you suggested it."

"If anything does come up," Latigo added, "be sure to give me a holler. I'll be there, you can count on it." Latigo gave a serious wink that made the pink side of his face crinkle up. "Best of luck, now."

"Oh, I don't believe in luck, sheriff," Beau smiled. "And I'll bet you don't either. I'm gonna get to the bottom of this. When I do you'll be the first to know."

"We'll be seein' you, then."

"Look forward to it." Beau closed the door behind them and walked out to the truck with Charlie.

Once outside, he tossed something in the air and caught it again.

"Whatcha got there?" Charlie asked.

"Oh, nothing much. Just a book of matches. Sort of a habit of mine. Helps me keep track of where I've been."

"From Jones's office?"

"He had a bunch sitting out by the ashtray. Ever seen a matchbook cover like this before?"

Charlie looked it over and handed it back as he walked around the truck to climb in the passenger's side. "Fits, don't it?"

"Three black circles and a red bull's eye. Yup," Beau said, tucking the matches in his shirt pocket. "I'd say it fits real good."

23

"Well, I don't believe it for a minute." Hatty was pacing the floor, leaning on her cane for support. Her initial excitement at discovering Beau at her front door had evaporated in the revelation that the sheriff of Rio Bravo couldn't do anything to help. "There's something he can do all right—he's either too lazy or he's hiding something."

"It's not going to happen, Hatty."

"Beau Holliman. You're not going to sit there and tell me that the state and federal governments can't do a blessed thing to investigate the murders of three American citizens on Mexican soil!"

"Not without evidence. All they can do is alert the Mexican officials for missing persons, put up posters, that kind of thing. We aren't going to get any help from the government—not till we get some proof anyway. I'm headin' down there this weekend," Beau said as he stood up from the old blue rocker.

"You're not goin' by yourself, are you?" Hatty asked.

"Hey, somebody's gotta work around here," he said, smiling. "I'll leave Charlie out at the place. He needs to stay around for the cattle and just to keep an eye on things. Say, before I forget—I've got a regular map of Mexico, but I'm going to need you to show me the cutoff for Dolores."

"Beau, I wish you wouldn't."

"Now, Hatty—"

"You don't know what those men are like. At least one of them's a killer—the one they call El Calavera. Tall, skinny, and white as a ghost. An albino. And crazy. His brother got killed years ago in an oil fire and he's blamed Eli ever since. I'm sure Calavera's the one who killed Eli, and he may have killed the boys."

"I'll try to find out something about him. Anything more? Anyone else I ought to be watching for?"

"There's a whole group of men—I don't think any of the really bad ones actually live in Dolores. Sometimes late at night we'd see strange cars and horses down at the cantina, but they were never there during the day. Calavera was working for somebody; I think the cantina may have been a meeting place for other people like him, but who knows? A lot of folks in town were scared. The rest of it—all that about Father Zeuma, Maria already filled you in. . . ."

"Enough for now."

"Beau, please, you've got to find Doc and Estella. I have to know they're all right."

"I'll do my best, Hatty. I promise."

"There are some other families, too—the Carreras, the Montoyas, a widow named Perez, Mr. and Mrs. Alaniz—but Doc will tell you all about them. I'll write down their names so you can ask him, if you wouldn't mind."

"Be glad to," he smiled.

Hatty stood looking at him. "Thanks for going, Beau." She gave him a hug, then moved away to find a pencil for the map.

It was five-thirty that afternoon when Beau walked up to his front door for the first time in nearly seven months. He felt as if his world had changed overnight. Nothing was the same as he had left it—nothing except this house. If there was anything solid in this world, it was the house Beau Holliman built. Seven-foot piers set on a foundation of solid rock. Rock walls and hand-laid oak flooring throughout. A bed nearly as hard as the rock walls and, best of all, a bathtub made to accommodate a six-foot cowboy. No frills.

No extras. The perfect man's house.

And then he opened the door.

A bouquet of freshly cut daisies greeted him from atop a silver pedestal he vaguely remembered inheriting from his aunt Millie, but which to the best of his recollection had been semi-permanently ensconced in the attic. The entire house had been thoroughly cleaned and all the hardwood floors polished to a glossy shine. Everywhere he looked he saw small splashes of color—in throw rugs, pillows, and flowers. The whole house seemed brighter. And softer.

Beau stood in the doorway trying to take it in. His home, his rock castle, had been invaded by a one-woman army. And everything was so, so—clean. Not that he had been a slob, but the house had never looked like this, not even when it was new.

He walked slowly back to the kitchen, then into the dining room. There was a place setting for one, complete with a white cloth napkin and a folded piece of paper on the plate. He picked up the note and examined it gingerly, as if it were tied to a rock that had just been hurled through his window. The handwriting was Charlie's.

Mr. Holliman,

My English speaking is better than my English writing, so I asked Mr. Tilden to write this note for me. I wanted to thank you again for letting me work for you. I made some burritos, beans, and sliced carrots for supper. They are in the oven and should be warm. Green salad is in the refridgerator with iced tea. I hope my little additions around the house are to your liking. I washed all the bedding, so it is fresh. Mr. Tilden will drop me off at 6:45 tomorrow morning, and I will have a breakfast of bacon and eggs, biscuits, and coffee ready for you and Mr. Tilden at 7:15. If you want breakfast later, please leave a note on the plate and I will see it in the morning. Mom still does not have telephone service, so I am afraid we will have to make the best of communicating through notes. I wish you a pleasant night's sleep.

Maria

Beau found a pen on the sideboard and scribbled a hasty note underneath Maria's to confirm: "Sounds fine. Thanks for supper. It was delicious. Beau. P.S. Bacon not too crisp, please. P.P.S. House fine. Good job." He folded the note again and left it on the plate, even though he suspected he would be up well before she arrived. Beau's policy was "be prepared, just in case."

He moved into the kitchen to verify the compliment in his note. He had not eaten anything since breakfast and was ravenous. The meal was indeed delicious. He even ate three of the carrots so he could tell her the whole meal was good. In keeping with a lifetime aversion to dishwater he almost left the dishes in the sink but then thought better of it and left the kitchen as spotless as he had found it.

The fireplace in the living room had logs stacked on the andirons. Kindling was split and standing in a bucket alongside. He glanced into the two guest bedrooms; they were clean and tidy, the furniture left just as he had arranged it. His own bedroom was spotless. The linen closet and back bath had fresh towels, and his porcelain tub was sparkling white. He decided change wasn't such a bad thing after all. The invading gender would be welcomed back in the morning.

As he reached down to turn on the hot water, his phone rang. He unbuttoned his shirt as he picked up the phone on his desk. "Hello?"

"Mr. Hoffman? This is Sheriff Jones over in Rio Bravo. Glad to see you made it back all right."

"Thank you, Sheriff. What can I do for you?"

"Listen, I been thinkin' about your story and feelin' bad about not being able to do anything for you. I was trying to think of someone over in your neck of the woods, but truth is, nobody in law enforcement's going to touch this with a ten-foot pole. So I figured a way I think I might be able to help you out."

"How's that?"

"I got a few vacation days coming and I was planning on going down south of Mexico City by train, do some hunting. If the place where all this happened isn't too far from a depot then I'd be glad to take a day, look it over with you, see what we could find. Now this would all be unofficial, mind you. Strictly tourist."

"Sheriff, I really appreciate the offer, but I couldn't ask you to give up your Thanksgiving holiday."

"This is your best bet, Holliman, and it's no skin off my nose. Matter of fact, I like playing detective. I don't get to do it that much in this job. Now, I've got some business in Dalton Springs on Tuesday, that's tomorrow. I thought maybe we could get together for a few minutes, work out the details. I'd like to ask you a few more questions about the case too, maybe ask Mrs. King a couple of questions if she's up to it. Why don't I meet you for coffee? It'd save me another thirty miles of driving if I didn't have to go all the way out to the King place—by the way, is that drugstore still there on the corner in Dalton Springs?"

"Cantella's—yeah, it's still there."

"Fine. I'll meet you there, say, two o'clock?"

"Two o'clock at Cantella's. I'll bring Mrs. King." Beau was too tired to argue and he thought he might be able to take advantage of the situation once he'd gotten some rest.

He jotted a note to himself on the pad he kept by the phone:

Jones – 2:00
1. San Luis ?
2. 30 miles ?
3. Didn't remember H & M ?

He returned to the bath and turned on the hot water. As the steam filled the bathroom he breathed deeply, feeling the warm moisture slide down his chest and keep going right down to his toes. That bath and that bed, with its crisp, cold sheets, had never felt better than they did that night. He slid under the covers at 6:15 and was asleep before he remembered to turn out the lights.

At four the next morning Beau opened his eyes, fully refreshed. He loved getting up early, and he especially enjoyed the routine ingrained through living nearly thirty years on his own: first brew the coffee, then pull out the Bible. It was good to be home again.

At six-thirty he went out for a quick tour of the ranch. The cattle looked reasonably healthy, but the land was worse than ever. The earth opened its cracked mouth to drink in nothing but sand and wind. Enormous gashes scarred the land as deep gullies crisscrossed each other and emptied into dry creek beds that spilled sand into the windblown cradle of the Nueces.

Half a year before, Beau had looked on this desolation with the same despair as most of his fellow ranchers in south Texas. But things had changed for him in Colorado. Sometimes distance and a little bit of time work together to give a man the perspective he lacks up close. Before long, home becomes the one he left behind to flirt with some new territory up north. He remembers how much he loves the land, how once upon a time he swore he would never leave her, and how he longs to return to live out his days with her, despite all the lines in her face.

It was different now, looking out at this land he loved. The Lord had put him there, and Beau had decided to see it through. If God had called him to this land, this is where God would provide.

He returned to the house to find Charlie opening the door for Maria to go inside. As Maria made breakfast for the two men, Beau asked her how she was doing and if there was anything they needed out at the ranch.

"Oh, we're doing pretty well. Mom's better now than even a week ago. But it's going to take some time. She doesn't really have anyone there in Puentas she can talk to except Mrs. O'Reagan, and she's up in Oklahoma with her sick sister. The other ladies from church, I'm sure they mean well, but they don't really know what to say. I got to meet Miss Light. Dad—Mr. King—he told us so many stories about her and some of the other ladies. I can see he wasn't exaggerating," she laughed.

"Irma Light?" Charlie huffed. "Yeah, she's stiff as a board and twice as splintery."

"Oh, I think she misses Dad. When she lost him she lost the only one who would stand up to her except Mom, and she doesn't know how to fight a woman like Miss Light without both of them getting angry."

"Probably 'cause they're both women," Charlie observed with a wink to Beau over the lip of his coffee cup.

"Probably because they were both in love with the same man," Maria said quietly, and Beau winked at Charlie.

They spoke of things around Hatty's that needed fixing. The windmill needed grease in the gearbox, the rainwater tank needed a bleach shock to kill off all the microbes, and the fence behind the chicken coop needed mending.

Beau told Maria and Charlie about the impending visit of the sheriff of Rio Bravo and of his intended trip down to Dolores. When he mentioned that the sheriff was coming to Dalton Springs, a glass slipped from Maria's hand and crashed to the floor, shattering into a thousand fragments.

"Oh! I'm so sorry!" she said as she leaned against the counter.

"Are you all right?" Beau asked as he opened the broom closet for a dustpan and whisk broom.

"Yes, yes. I just . . . I think I will stay here while you and Mom visit with the sheriff, if you don't mind." She picked up the dustpan as Beau swept the glass into a pile.

Beau looked at Charlie, still seated at the table, for some sign as to why Maria would react so, but he didn't have a clue.

"Is there something you haven't told me, Maria? Something the sheriff said or did that upset you?"

She hesitated, embarrassed by her response. "I told Mom when we were in Laredo that I thought I had seen him before. It's strange. I can't get his face out of my mind, but I can't remember where I've seen him. He makes me very uncomfortable, that's all I know." She looked directly at Beau. "I think you should be very careful around that man."

Beau finished sweeping the glass into the dustpan, and they returned to the breakfast table.

"I didn't like him from the git-go," Charlie said, receiving Maria's intuition as verification of his suspicions. "He's got snake eyes, and—looky here, what's his name?"

"Jones," Beau said patiently. Charlie had been keeping his frustration bottled up and the cork had just popped.

"I heard his name was *Cortez*. And he hates Mexicans—and everybody else to boot, I'd wager. Now you make any sense out of that. The fella was born too big for his britches, now, and that's a fact. I don't trust him, nosir, not a lick, and I think you're loco for even thinkin' about goin' with him. So there now, I said my piece," and he swallowed a gulp of coffee and folded his arms.

Beau wiped his mouth and tossed his napkin on his plate. "You've got a point, Charlie. But it isn't his eyes or his name that bother me. It's a couple of things—here, I jotted them down last night so I'd remember." He reached into his shirt pocket and took out a folded piece of paper. "Oh, yeah, here we go. You remember what he said, Charlie, as we were about to leave?"

"Somethin' about callin' a lawman down in some little town I never heard of."

"Yeah, me neither, but I jotted it down when we got back to the truck, and I looked it up this morning on a map. San Luis Potosí. That's a long way down there, not that far north of Mexico City. Now why would he suggest a specific town that far off? We hadn't said a word about where Hatty had lived or where the fellows wound up missing. Did you say anything to him when you met him in Laredo, Maria?"

"No, I'm sure I remember Mom only asking directions to a lawyer."

"You didn't talk to him at all?"

"I shook hands with him, but I don't remember saying . . . wait." She paused, her eyes fixed on a memory, trying to grasp it and hold it with her mind. "Oh," she said, "I almost had it. I almost remembered where I'd seen him before."

"It'll come, just give it time," Beau said. "So there's one little wrinkle in the sheets. Then, too, there's the fact that he knew exactly how far it was from Dalton Springs out to the King ranch and back. That's why he wanted to meet me in town today, because it would save him an extra thirty miles of driving. How did he know how far it was out here? He told us back in Laredo he hadn't been out to this part of the world in years."

"Could just be a lucky guess," Charlie suggested.

"Not the way he said it, Charlie. There wasn't any doubt in his mind that the King Ranch was exactly fifteen miles from Dalton Springs. Still, I guess he could have asked one of his deputies to do some footwork for him, make a call or two, but why do that when all he has to do is ask me how far it is? It bothers me some, that's all. Oh, and here's something that just dawned on me. What's this sudden business he has over here? Why now? It seems like a pretty big coincidence.

"But the thing that bothers me more than anything is the fact that he says he doesn't remember seeing Hatty and Maria cross the border. That's got a lot of question marks around it for me. First of all, what was the Rio Bravo sheriff doing staked out opposite a border crossing in Laredo? He's got his own store to mind. Second, how many white women with a Mexican daughter-in-law are going to cross the Mexican border, limp up to your squad car on a cane, and ask for a lawyer without telling you why? There's no way that man could have forgotten Hatty and Maria after just a few weeks."

"So why are you thinkin' about goin' with him?" Charlie asked. "You just said yourself you can't trust him."

"Because a liar has the advantage only as long as other folks think he's telling the truth. Once they know he's a liar the jig's up, and the advantage shifts to the other side. I want to watch him. I think he may lead me to something, slip up—who knows? I'll be careful."

Charlie shrugged. He knew there was no use trying to get Beau to change his mind when he had more than one reason for doing something. "When do you leave?"

"I'm not sure. Tomorrow or the next day, I imagine. We're going to work out the details this afternoon."

They finished their breakfast quickly and cleared the table. Beau went back into his bedroom. He heaved his huge traveling suitcase onto the bed and began to unpack those clothes he wouldn't need to take down to Mexico. Charlie stayed and helped Maria wash the dishes

"He's in danger," Maria said, handing Charlie a dripping plate.

"Well, it won't be the first time. He knows how to take care of himself."

"Here, maybe. But the rules change down there. He does not know."

"Yeah, well, he's been up against some pretty tough characters—why, I remember one time over in Sweetwater—"

"We must pray for him, Charlie. For God to protect him."

Charlie took another dish. "Sure," he said uncomfortably, straining for something appropriate to say. "Sure, we'll pray for him."

The meeting that afternoon went smoothly. Hatty reluctantly agreed to attend, insisting the whole time that it was a waste of breath. They met Latigo at exactly two o'clock at Cantella's Drugstore. The sheriff concocted a story about meeting an old friend over in Bellville to help him work through some personal problems. Beau shook his head, ostensibly to express sympathy for the unfortunate man, but in fact to express his disbelief that Jones had managed to tell the story with a straight face.

Latigo asked Hatty to go over the story with him from the beginning. She began haltingly, but it soon poured out of her like old water through a broken cistern. She had to pause often for tissues. The sheriff was endlessly patient. He was particularly interested to know if she or Maria had seen anything suspicious or anyone they might be able to identify as suspects. She recounted all that had happened in Dolores—the sound of gunshots and the fire in the distance the night they ran away; the men coming at them with the gun; the one who chased them in the red car, which Maria alone had seen and reported to Hatty down in the ravine. Perhaps Maria could identify the man in the car, but Hatty certainly could not. They ended their visit by setting a time for departure. The train pulled out at one on Thursday afternoon. Beau would meet Jones at the train station in Nuevo Laredo at noon.

Night took forever coming. After a full day of work at Beau's, Maria dusted and mopped at Hatty's until there wasn't anything left to clean or rearrange. Hatty retired early, exhausted from having to relive the last two years, from remembering things she had been trying to forget.

Maria stayed up late, trying to convince herself that she was tired enough to sleep. She decided to work on her English, so she went into the reading room and took a book at random from the shelf, hoping that the exercise would distract her from the anxiety she felt. But she closed the book after the first two stanzas and decided to read the Bible instead.

She looked for a short book in the Old Testament, thinking she might be able to work her way through an entire story before she got too sleepy. She looked through the contents and discovered Ruth had only four chapters. Since it was about a woman, maybe it would have something special to say to her. Maria had never read the book before and found it a fascinating story of a girl with whom she felt a special kinship. Ruth's love and her unswerving devotion to Naomi touched her deeply. She prayed that God would give her the patience and the godliness of the young Moabite girl.

Maria thought back over her life and how rich God's blessing had been in giving her a wonderful husband like Martin. She thanked Him for all His gifts. Then, in the privacy of that dark house, in whispers that could be heard only by the Spirit of God, she asked the Lord to let Martin know that she was all right and that she still loved him and missed him deeply.

As always, Maria felt a little foolish in asking the Lord to express her love to Martin—she knew in her heart that her husband was beyond anxiety, beyond the pain of separation. And that the Lord God wasn't her errand boy. But somehow talking to Jesus about Martin helped her say goodbye in little ways. Once again, she concluded with a prayer asking forgiveness in case her request was a mistake, in case she had somehow offended her Lord. But deep inside she knew He would understand and that He wanted her to call on Him for help. It was all part of letting go.

Then she prayed God's protecting hand on Beau as he traveled south. She found herself starting to dwell on the sheriff again. Whenever he came to mind, it was as if a dark thundercloud started to roll across her consciousness. She refused to start thinking about him again. She took a hot bath and climbed into bed, drifting off to sleep quickly.

Somewhere in the middle of the night the dark cloud reappeared. Lightning flashed around its edges, and black thunder rolled out to blanket the dark world in a tumbling rumble. Three figures stood on a wide plane beneath the cloud—a tall man with a burned face, a woman, and a little girl. The little girl was holding onto her mother's hand and extending her free hand to the man. He shook it, then wiped it on his shirt. She reached out again. He shook it again, and again wiped his hand on his shirt.

The scene shifted and the little girl was a teenager in the confessional in the church in Dolores, peeking out through the carved fig-leaf design on the small door. A tall man stood with another man talking to the priest beside the altar, where a bright silver cup lay on its side with the wine staining the white linen a deep crimson. The girl in the booth could smell the pine wood of the tight booth, and she could hear the sound of her own breathing. No one knew she was there, not even Father Zeuma.

She could see that the big man was yelling at the Father, although she could hear nothing but her own breathing. The wooden Jesus looked down on the men and did nothing. Her breathing got louder and louder. She was going to start crying, she knew it. She tried to hold her breath, but that just made it worse.

The big man with the burned face poked the priest in the chest. Now she could hear him talking loudly in a voice that sounded like an animal. The priest's mouth opened, but it was the wooden Jesus who spoke quietly. "They have no money," He said. The big man pulled his gun from his holster and shot the wooden Jesus in the heart. He drew back his hand and slapped the priest hard across the mouth, then he wiped his hand on his shirt. He slapped him again, and again, and then again, each time wiping his hand on his shirt.

The girl tried to break through the door of the confessional to stop the men, to tell the tall man she knew who he was, but she was trapped inside. She beat on the thin wood, but it had turned to metal. The shorter man turned toward her with a cigarette in his mouth. He had a long scar down his cheek. He walked over to the booth, took out a match, and struck it on the side of the booth. The wood started to burn, and smoke poured in through the fig-leaf cut-outs.

Maria woke up screaming.

24

Latigo's cigar glowed orange and then faded in the shadowed office. On the desk beside a half-empty bottle of Jim Beam, wax dripped down the sides of a fat yellow candle and pooled in a cracked coffee cup. It was three in the morning, and Latigo was hunched over his favorite rifle—an 1885 Winchester 30-30 with a side-mounted 9X Leupold scope—cleaning it and rubbing boiled lindseed oil into the oak stock and forearm. He had sighted it in the day before; bull's-eye at a hundred yards. Standing. No rest.

There was a knock at the door.

"Come in," he mumbled around the barrel of his cigar.

The door opened slowly. Miguel was not happy about being called down to the office in the middle of the night. But this wasn't the first time.

Latigo didn't look up. "Happy Thanksgiving," he said, grinning to himself. "Pogue ain't gettin' the job done. You're gonna get things moving down in Dalton Springs."

"Today? It's Thanksgiving, Boss. The bank will be closed."

"You catch on real fast, deputy. Now shut up and listen. Clem Fisher is the president of First National Bank of Dalton Springs. He's also a weasel who cheats on his wife. He's got a twelve-year-old daughter named Wanda Jean, who—are you writin' this down? Here." He threw a pencil and piece of scrap paper at Miguel. "He's got a daughter named Wanda Jean who worships the ground he walks on. The other woman's name is Lola, a cashier there at the bank. You get down there, make a friendly call." He took a folded sheet of paper out of his shirt pocket and tossed it across the desk. "Here's the number. That's the address on the bottom.Tell Fisher you know about Lola, but you're willing to keep quiet if he'll do you a favor."

"You sure his wife doesn't know?"

"Of course she knows. Women always know—but Clem figures he's got her hoodwinked."

"You got a lot of information, Boss."

"Pogue's got a nose for this kind'a thing. Get Fisher down to the bank and get into that lock box. Take some tools with you just in case."

"What if he don't cooperate?"

"He'll cooperate," Latigo said as he slammed a cartridge into the chamber. "Just mention his little girl's name. Remind him he's got a lot more to lose than a turkey dinner."

"What about Holliman?"

"I called him last night. He ought'a be here in about six hours, I'd say. Oh, it'll be a lovely trip down south. You know the statistics on hunting accidents are so alarming, though, deputy—makes me wonder if I ought to even *take* a gun." He raised the rifle to his shoulder and tracked an imaginary target through the scope. "I'd sure hate for anything to happen to my traveling companion. Pow!" He put the gun down. "Right through the neck!" he said, smiling.

Sanchez rose uneasily from his chair and started for the door. "I guess this couldn't wait until tomorrow, could it?"

Latigo didn't look up from his gun. "I got a call from Mangus. They hit. They hit good. We got to get that land, and fast. Make sense?"

Miguel grinned. "I'm on my way."

Hatty was the first one up. She had started coughing late the previous afternoon and was now absolutely miserable. The aspirin she had taken the night before had done little to help her relax. She had tossed and turned most of the night trying to sleep. A low-grade fever was climbing slowly and made her skin sore all over.

It was still dark as she wandered from room to room in her robe and slippers, trying to remember where she had left the aspirin. Her ankle was nearly healed now, but she had grown accustomed to the cane and reached for it habitually every morning. The tip of the cane, just bare wood, made a light clicking sound down the hall and then on the kitchen floor as she walked.

It was a cold morning, bitter and dry. Hatty could hear the wind moaning around the eaves of the house as she took a match from the small pewter cup on the stove and scratched it on the iron burner. She lowered the oven door and held the yellow flame to the small gas pipe that would ignite the jets, then left the door standing open.

She put on a pot of coffee and sat at the kitchen table remembering how different this room had been just a few years before. When Marty and Carl were boys they used to come in on winter mornings like this and sit on the old white stools with their stocking feet resting on the open oven door. . . .

It was six o'clock and the coffee was almost done. It dawned on her suddenly that it was Thanksgiving Day. The kitchen door opened quickly and Maria walked in, fully dressed.

"Morning, Mom," she said as she reached for the coffee pot. "I don't have time for breakfast. I'll cook something for myself later." She turned and looked at Hatty. "Mom, are you feeling all right?" she asked, concerned.

"Oh, I've got a little fever, that's all. I imagine I look like something the cat drug in—I haven't even brushed my hair—but I'll be all right."

"Mom, you really don't look good, and I can see you don't feel good. You need to get back in that bed and stay there. I'll give Dr. John a call from Beau's and see if I can't get him to prescribe some medicine for you. I'm surprised Charlie isn't here yet."

"Did you forget?" Hatty asked. "Today's Thanksgiving. Charlie won't be coming for you this morning."

"What?"

"I guess I forgot to tell you. Before he left yesterday he said he would have Thanksgiving with his sister over in Bellville. It looks like we're on our own today. I thought maybe we could—"

"Mom, wasn't Beau leaving for Mexico this morning?"

"What's the matter?"

"Last night I had a dream. I remembered who the sheriff is. I need to tell Beau. Mom, he can't go with him."

"Why not? Who is he?"

"I have to get to a phone. I'm going to the store," she said as she grabbed her coat off the rack inside the hall.

"Honey, the store's closed, and they don't have a phone anyway. Maria, you're not going out in this cold."

"Whose house is closest?" She wrapped an extra scarf around her head and pulled on her gloves.

"Irma Light's house is just down the gravel road where the old telegraph office used to be."

"I'll be back as soon as I can. You get in bed, and I'll fix you something to eat when I get back." Maria hurried out the door and through the gate. The wind was blowing a gale and it was still dark, but her eyes adjusted quickly. She walked the mile-and-a-half to Miss Light's house, barely feeling the cold. She knew that if she didn't get the message to Beau she would never see him again.

Catty-cornered from the Puentas jail, one of the last remnants of the town's nineteenth-century glory days as the county seat, sat Miss Light's house. The shake roof needed work, and the house hadn't seen a new coat of paint in twenty years. The yard was a patchwork of grass burrs and hard-packed dirt. A rusting gutter held up with bailing wire ran along the back side and emptied into the rainwater tank at the southwest corner of the house. The narrow front porch led up to two concrete steps and the front door.

Maria knocked three times and waited, glad for the shelter of the porch. A dim light burned somewhere inside the house, illuminating the windows with the softest possible glow. It looked as though Miss Light might be up and about, but there was no answer. Maria knocked again. No response. She went around to the back of the house where she guessed the bedroom was and tapped on the window. Before she could call out Miss Light's name the window flew up and a double-barreled shotgun popped out.

"Git off my property, you crazy! Git off before I blow you off! This gun's loaded, you better believe it, mister! Now go on!"

Maria jumped back against the wall of the house. "Miss Light, it's me, Maria King, Hatty King's daughter-in-law."

"Who?"

"Maria King. Eli King's daughter-in-law. You were out at the house a few days ago with the other ladies from the church."

"Lands, child, what on earth are you doing out there in the dark? You scared me half to death."

"I knocked at the front door," Maria explained, stepping forward. "You must have been asleep. I'm sorry I frightened you, but there's an emergency and I have to use your phone, please."

"Come in, come in. I'll open the front door."

Maria ran around to the front of the house and waited. She could hear keys jingling on a ring and Miss Light mumbling on the other side as she struggled to find the right key. The door finally swung open and Maria stepped quickly inside.

"It's not Hatty, is it?" Miss Light asked with genuine concern.

Maria was surprised at how old and frail she looked despite her chunkiness. "No, I have to get a message to Beau Holliman quickly. Where is your phone, please?"

"Right over there by that chair. There on the table. Well, I guess it would help if I turned on some lights." She flipped on the overhead in the living room, and Maria was shocked to see it so beautifully decorated. The furniture was antique rosewood; the floor, oak hardwood polished to a soft luster. Pure white lace doilies lay across the backs and arms of chairs and sofa. Pictures of lush landscapes filled with bluebonnets, Indian paintbrush, and amaranth adorned the walls, reminders of younger days and an unselfish land. A nostalgic joy lay hidden in the fabric of this home, a patient desire for something good to return. The outside of Miss Light's house never hinted at the beauty and refinement inside.

"Number, please?" the operator requested.

"Yes, Beau Holliman, please," Maria said.

"One moment, please."

The phone rang and rang, but there was no answer. The operator cut in. "It's about time for Beau to be down at the Sunrise. You might catch him there if it's important."

"Thank you," Maria said as she hung up the phone.

"What's wrong? Is there anything I can do?" Miss Light asked.

"No, no, thank you, Miss Light. I was just hoping to catch him before he left town."

"Must have been pretty important for you to go to all this trouble."

"Yes ma'am, it was. But there is nothing to be done now. We will just have to wait. Thank you for letting me use your telephone. I'm sorry for scaring you like that."

"Oh, it got my old heart going, but that's all right. I haven't had that much excitement in a good bit. I'm sorry I almost blew your head off." She smiled, and Maria was surprised to see her eyes sparkle. In that brief moment Maria felt as though she were looking at an older version of Hatty.

"Are you sure I can't do anything for you, hon? At least let me make you a hot cup of coffee before you go back out in that wind."

"No, I'm fine, really." Maria paused with her hand on the door handle. "But there is something you can do. Mom really needs a friend now. I know you haven't always gotten along with each other, and I know Dad was a good and special friend to you. I would just ask you to give Mom another chance. Sometimes when she's really missing him a lot, she says things she doesn't mean. I guess we all do that. Well, I better get back. She'll be wondering why I took off in such a hurry." She opened the door to leave.

"Maria." Miss Light put her hand on Maria's shoulder and paused, looking for the right words. "Oh, well," she murmured, shaking her head. "I never can get the words out." She paused again, looking down. "I sure miss that old coot," she said, her voice breaking. "He was a special, special man."

Maria turned and embraced her. "I know," she said, wiping away her own tears. "So were his sons."

On the walk back home the temperature continued to drop on the edge of a blue norther, but Maria hardly noticed. She was anxious about catching Beau in time. Still, there was reason to hope. Martin used to say that the Lord always arranges things. Maybe God had orchestrated all this so that Miss Light and Maria could have that talk at the door. She did believe that God was in control. But as she walked through the early-morning shadows, she prayed that He would help her believe it more deeply.

Hatty was waiting at the door as Maria walked in through the yard gate. "Did Irma let you use her phone?" she asked with an edge of bitterness.

"You're supposed to be in bed—and yes, she was very nice. In fact, the last thing she said was to tell you hello and that she would be out to see you before too long."

"I'll believe that when I see it."

"Mom—"

"All right, all right," Hatty said, closing the door behind Maria. "Let's get in out of this cold. I have the fires going and I cooked up a little breakfast for you. Now sit down and tell me all about this dream of yours. What was it you remembered?"

"I'll eat if you promise me you'll get in bed right after."

"Promise."

Maria sat down and started to eat as she told Hatty about the sheriff from Rio Bravo. "He may call himself Jones," she said, "but his name is Latigo. At least that's what we all called him growing up. It means scorpion. He used to show up every now and then to see Father Escobar. No one ever knew why, and no one was brave enough to ask. Then, when he left, Latigo came to see Father Zeuma. I was fifteen, maybe sixteen. I had been to confession and asked if I could stay a little longer to think some things through. Well, the Father went about his business, and I guess I fell asleep.

The Father must have forgotten that I was there or thought I had left.

"Anyway, I woke up hearing people talking, then shouting. I looked out through the little cut-out places in the confessional door and there was Latigo and another man, very young, and Latigo was yelling at Father Zeuma and poking him in the chest. I didn't know what to do. I was scared to death. Latigo was telling him he wanted to see more money coming out of the church and how he was just another lazy, no-good Mexican with a collar, and if he wanted his people to be safe he'd better find some way of making them give more. I'll never forget it." Maria paused.

"Father Zeuma tried to talk," she continued, "but every time he did, Latigo would push him back hard and shout louder. Finally, he turned to go. When he turned and hit Father Zeuma hard across the face, I thought it was all over. Then he wiped his hand on his shirt like he got it dirty or something, and the two of them left. I waited until they were gone before I came out. At first Father Zeuma seemed angry at me, but then he looked worried. He told me to forget what I had seen and tell no one."

Maria paused and then continued. "Last night I dreamed about this again. Only it was more horrible. But that younger one—he was the one who was chasing us."

Hatty was quiet for a moment. "Maria, I know you dreamed all this, but dreams are tricky things. I mean, maybe you read something into it. You only got a glimpse of the young one through a crack in a door—and you weren't much more than a kid. You said so yourself."

"Mom, it was *them*. Somehow the man who was chasing us is hooked up with Latigo, I know it. I'm afraid for Beau. I think Latigo is going to try to hurt him, or maybe worse."

"But see, that's what doesn't make any sense. Why would he want to hurt Beau?"

"Maybe he's afraid of what Beau would find out if he went down to Dolores alone."

Hatty laughed in frustrated disbelief and shook her head. "This all started when we wouldn't cooperate and give money to the church. It didn't have anything to do with that sheriff, or anybody else as far as I could tell. Now I will admit that Father Zeuma tried to warn us about something, but he never would say what exactly."

"You think I'm making too much of this?"

"I just can't believe that a Texas sheriff would have someone killed way down in Mexico over something like that. There's one right way to handle this, and that's through the law. I mean, if we can't trust our own lawmen, who can we trust?"

"Bad men can get into a sheriff's uniform, too."

"Oh, for heaven's sake, Maria. All this over a dream. It could have been *anyone*. It could have been that crazy Calavera, for all we know—you know he had a lot against Eli."

"Mom, Calavera wouldn't have the courage or the brains to do something like that on his own. Think about it. He had two years he could have tried to kill Dad but didn't, at least as far as we know. We barely even saw the man in all that time. If he was going to kill Dad, he wouldn't wait two years unless he was acting on orders. Then I thought, well, maybe he got drunk and went crazy, but that doesn't make sense because he had to drive too far. It *had* to be planned out."

There was a knock at the back door.

"Who on earth?" Hatty asked.

"Mrs. King? Maria? It's Charlie. You ladies up yet?" He had a smile in his voice as he called out.

Maria opened the door for him and gave him a hug. "Oh, Charlie, I'm so glad you decided to come!" she exclaimed.

"Well, Happy Thanksgiving to you too, miss," Charlie said, turing red. "Happy Thanksgiving, Mrs. King."

"You too, Charlie—but I thought you were going to your sister's."

"I did and I am. But I got over to Bellville and started thinkin' how you and Maria probably didn't feel like cookin' anything and how we always had more than we could eat, just Thelma and her kids and me, and so I asked her if it'd be all right if I came to invite you to our Thanksgiving, and she said fine by her, so here I am."

"Charlie, thank you for the invitation, but we can't," Maria said. "As a matter of fact, I need to ask you a big favor."

"Is somethin' wrong? Y'all look worried. Mrs. King, are you feelin' all right? You sure are pale."

"We're afraid Beau might be in danger," Maria said. "I need to ask you to take me down to Dolores."

"What?"

"Maria thinks she remembers the sheriff from Rio Bravo," Hatty said. "She's convinced herself that he means to harm Beau."

"Charlie, I *know* something's wrong. I can explain it on the way down. I know this is a lot to ask, but I think Beau's life depends on us reaching him in time."

Charlie took a deep breath and puffed out his cheeks. "Well, I sure got more than I bargained for on this trip. I'll need to stop by the trailer and grab a couple things, but it's on the way. Then call my sister from Dalton Springs, I guess. All right—what are we standing around here for? Let's go."

"Charlie Tilden, you're crazy as a bedbug," Hatty said. "But if you're going, I'm going too."

"Mom, the only place you're going is straight to bed, like you promised. You shouldn't be traveling, as sick as you are. Besides, you don't want us to catch your bug, do you?"

"She's right, Mrs. King," Charlie added. "You really don't look well. You go on and rest now. We shouldn't be gone too long. I figure we ought to be back tomorrow some time if we can find him."

Charlie's words stunned her. Marty had said the same thing when he and Carl had gone off looking for Eli.

"We'll be careful," Maria said softly. "Now promise me you'll go straight to bed."

"All right," Hatty said. "I can't travel like this, and I don't want you to get sick. But you promise me that you'll come back just as soon as you can."

"Promise." Maria gave Hatty a quick kiss and ran back to pack a few things.

Hatty turned to Charlie. "If you move fast, you might be able to catch the train before it leaves. They aren't pulling out before about two this afternoon, are they?"

"Afraid so. I had to go over last night to talk to Beau. While I was there, the sheriff called and said he wanted to leave on the ten o'clock train if Beau could make it. Said he was anxious to get down there and get some hunting in, so Beau took off real early."

"Don't you let anything happen to that girl, Charlie. Or yourself, either."

"I'll do my best, Mrs. King, and that's a promise."

Maria came running down the hall, bag in hand. She hugged Hatty goodbye and climbed into Charlie's truck. Hatty watched it disappear in a cloud of dust down the lane, praying that she would see them again in a day or two.

25

The cold Thanksgiving morning turned into a colder afternoon. Hatty felt tired and drained but couldn't rest. She looked in the medicine cabinet for some sleeping pills, but there weren't any. After a hot bath, she lay down on top of the bed and covered herself with a blanket. She drifted in and out of a fevered sleep for a couple of hours until she was roused by someone knocking on her door.

"Hatty, you all right?" It was Irma Light.

"Just a minute," Hatty shouted from the bedroom. She put on her robe and went to the front door. "Hello, Irma. Come on in, please. I'm sorry I look such a mess. I didn't even hear you drive up." It was a groggy civility that would have to do.

"Well, if I was feeling as bad as you look I wouldn't have gotten out of bed to answer the door." They both smiled at the same time. "Hatty, I, uh . . . "

"You don't have to."

"Yes, I do. I said some hateful things the other day. I was just hurting so bad, and I wasn't thinking of anybody else. I've been angry a long time, and to tell the truth I'm flat tired of it. It's more trouble than it's worth," she added with a little laugh at herself. "Anyway, I hope you'll forgive me."

"If you'll do the same for me," Hatty said. The two looked at each other and smiled. Miss Light held out her hand.

"Done," she said.

"Done." They shook hands and then gave each other a hug.

"Maria called me from Dalton Springs," Miss Light said. "She told me you might need this." She held out a paper bag from Cantrell's Drugstore.

"What? You went all the way to Dalton Springs to get me some medicine? Oh, Irma, thank you so much."

"From the look of things, I was none too soon. You look like something the cat drug in, old girl. You'd better get back to bed while I fix you some chicken soup."

"Irma, listen, I can't rest and I'm not hungry. I'm worried sick about Maria and Charlie taking off for Mexico like that. I tried to talk them out of it, but it didn't do any good."

"That girl's got a mind of her own. What in the world are they headin' down to Mexico for on Thanksgiving Day?"

"It's a long story. Let's go into town and I'll tell you on the way."

"You just tell me what you need and I'll get it for you. You don't have any business goin' out in this weather."

"Irma, the only thing I need to get is some peace of mind. And the only place I'm going to find it is at the sheriff's office in Dalton Springs."

"You know Jake's been gone for over a month now, Hatty. Can't this wait until tomorrow?"

"I'm afraid not. Please, Irma."

"Lordy mercy, you are one hard-headed woman. Disagreement must set well with you, Hatty. I swear you're lookin' better already. Come on, then. You get dressed and I'll warm up the car."

Irma wasn't much better at driving than Hatty. She kept a large pink pillow on the driver's side of her 1949 Buick Dyna-flow so that she could see over the steering wheel. Her legs were barely long enough to reach the gas pedal if she pointed her toes. She tended to want to look at the person she was speaking with while she was driving, which made for some near misses on the way to Dalton Springs.

After hearing Hatty's abbreviated account of all that had happened, Irma Light fixed her eyes solidly on the road before her and set her jaw. Then she laughed slightly to herself. "Hatty," she said, "did I ever tell you what I wanted to be when I was growin' up? More than anything in this world, I wanted to be a ranger." She laughed when she said it, half embarrassed, half proud for ever having had the courage to dream of such outlandishness.

"A Texas ranger?" Hatty asked, trying not to sound too incredulous.

"When I was six or seven years old my daddy took us all to San Antonio to the ranger's museum there. There was an old man—an old ranger, I think—who sat behind a big oak desk. He had an enormous white mustache and the bluest eyes you've ever seen. For some reason he took a shine to me. He lifted me up on his desk and told me wonderful stories—the kind you don't get in books—while Daddy and Mama looked around the museum. He'd tell me about Black Jack Ketchum, Sam Bass, Blue Duck, Belle Starr—he even said he chased Butch Cassidy down somewhere in Bolivia. Shook hands, so he said, with Bat Masterson and Pat Garrett.

"He used to carry a set of old iron handcuffs on his belt, and he'd let me play with them while he told me stories. Said they'd once been on Bill Bonney himself—imagine that! Well, sir, they had to drag me out of that place. But we came back. Every year on our way up to visit my Aunt Winny for Christmas we would stop by the museum and see Mr. Colton."

"Then one year—I guess I was about fifteen or so—we went by and he wasn't at his desk. Some young fellow was there in a brand-new uniform signing people in who wanted to see the museum. Mr. Colton never used to do that. Well, anyway, when I asked for him, this young fellow says he passed on about two weeks before. When I started to tear up he asked my name. I told him and he said, 'Well, now, I think I just might have something in here for you, Miss Light.' He unlocked the desk drawer and pulled out a sealed package with my name on it.

"I opened it and out fell the old iron handcuffs, a tiny little envelope with a key in it, and a note. It was from Mr. Colton. I memorized that note. It said, 'Howdy, squirt'—that's what he always used to call me—'When you get to be a Texas ranger, maybe you can use these to help catch some badlanders. Love, John Colton. P.S. Don't forget the key.'" Irma laughed again and Hatty joined her. "We never went back," she continued sadly. "It just wouldn't have been the same. I never did catch that badlander. I never had the chance. Till now."

A bright red Cadillac pulled up to a filling station outside Dalton Springs. Miguel Sanchez got out of the car and pulled on his black leather jacket. A cowboy hat and sunglasses completed his cover. He walked into the station and asked to use the phone.

"Sure," answered Farley, the station owner. "It's a local call, ain't it?"

Sanchez switched the toothpick from one side of his mouth to the other.

"Yeah, well, I'm sure you wouldn't be makin' a long-distance call," Farley chuckled nervously. "Go right ahead, back there in the office."

Miguel walked back and shut the door behind him. He took out the slip of paper Latigo had given him and picked up the phone.

"Number, please?"

The phone rang in the house of Clem Fisher, president of First National. Fisher put down his paper and pipe and crossed the living room. His wife, Sharlane, was in the kitchen pulling a turkey out of the oven. She paused and walked to the kitchen door to listen, as she had listened so many nights before at their bedroom door. Clem pushed back his steel-rimmed glasses and answered.

"Fisher?" the voice on the other end said.

"This is Clem Fisher. Who's this?"

"Shut up and listen. I know about Lola. If you want to keep this our little secret, meet me at the bank in half an hour. I don't want money. Just some information. Nobody's going to get hurt. . . ."

"Wait a minute—I don't understand. What do you want?"

"Look, don't be stupid. If you don't want your wife to know about Lola—"

"No, you listen to me," Clem said, taking off his glasses. "You don't call my house, and you don't threaten me. *You don't threaten me!*" he shouted and slammed down the phone.

Sanchez depressed the plunger. "Hello? Fisher?" He placed the handset in the cradle slowly, thinking. He opened the door to the office, walked quickly out to his car, and climbed in. Then he peeled out in the direction of Dalton Springs, shooting gravel out behind.

The Dalton Springs sheriff's office was tucked away in the northwest corner of the first floor of the Live Oak County Courthouse. It was locked, as was the side office adjoining it. Irma tried to peer through a long window that ran beside the second door. The blinds were open, but it looked dark inside.

Hatty knocked on the door by the window. After a few moments it was opened by Deputy Armando Estevez. "Yes, ma'am, what can I do for you ladies?"

Hatty made the introductions, and the deputy invited them in. The office was cluttered with boxes and papers stacked in tilting piles. Two olive-green file cabinets were jammed into one corner, leaving just enough room for two chairs, one in front and one beside the dinged-up desk. "Sorry for the mess in here," he said. "We're still trying to get this space cleaned up. Could I get you ladies a Coke? Some coffee?"

"No, no, Deputy, thank you," responded Hatty. "We're sorry to bother you on Thanksgiving Day like this. Where is everybody?"

"Well, as you know, we put out a missing persons on Sheriff Skerritt almost a week ago now. The department over in Bellville is supposed to send a couple of fellows over to help, but they got tied up on another case. And things are pretty quiet around here. I can always call them if I get in a bind."

"You have family around here, Deputy?" Miss Light asked.

"No, ma'am. They're all back in Laredo. That's where I grew up. I was hoping to get back to see them for Thanksgiving, but things just didn't work out this time around. I did have an old friend come down for a few days for a visit. He's been a deputy out there for quite a while, and he's helping me learn the ropes. Now, your name sounds familiar, Mrs. King. Have we met before?"

"No, I haven't been back that long."

"Wait—I remember now. It was in the Sunrise. Martha Nell was saying you folks had just gotten back from Mexico, isn't that right? And did I hear that you lost your family down there, Mrs. King?"

"My husband and two sons. Just a little over a month ago."

"I'm awful sorry for your loss. How did it happen, if you don't mind my asking?"

"That's part of what we've come to see you about," Hatty said. She took a deep breath and started her story from the beginning.

The sky clouded over quickly that afternoon. Sanchez sat in his car on the poor side of the condemned river bridge outside Dalton Springs. From there he could see across the railroad tracks and up the main street. He had driven past Clem's house and noted the brown Ford station wagon. Fisher would have to come out sometime for milk, eggs, something.

Sanchez had been waiting five hours now. The street was practically abandoned. The last car to rumble into town was an old Buick that looked like it didn't have a driver, almost an hour ago. If Fisher didn't come out soon, Sanchez would have to move up closer to the house. It would be risky, but not as dangerous as going back to Latigo empty-handed.

Another hour passed and the light started to fade. Sanchez started the car and was about to move when he saw a brown station wagon pull onto the main street. He followed it to the grocery store. Fisher was in a hurry—the store was about to close.

Sanchez parked his car on a side street in front of the lumber yard a block away. He took a small black bag out of the car, walked quickly up the block, and got into the wagon, crouching down behind the back seat. Five minutes later, Fisher came out of the store with a small bag of groceries, got into the car, and placed the bag on the seat beside him. He started the engine and backed into the street. When he pulled onto the first side street, Sanchez pulled himself up and put the barrel of his gun behind Fisher's right ear. Fisher jumped, and the car lurched forward.

"Oh, God!" Fisher cried.

"Don't look back. Just drive to the bank."

"Don't kill me. Please don't kill me."

"Shut up and drive. No more talk."

"Right. Yes."

They drove two blocks and took a right turn.

"Park behind the bank. Then get out of the car slowly."

Fisher turned off the engine and slowly got out of the car.

"Keep your back to me at all times. Now walk." They walked up to the back door. "Deactivate the door alarm. As soon as we're inside I'll deactivate the second alarm. I know where it is, so don't try anything."

Fisher inserted the round key in the external door lock just above the regular lock and turned it to the right. They opened the door and stepped inside. Fisher turned on the room light instinctively. Sanchez shoved him away and turned it off.

"One more stunt like that and you're dead," he snarled, jamming the gun into Fisher's back. He pulled a flashlight out of his black bag and pointed it ahead. Sanchez reached over to his left and flipped the switch, deactivating the second alarm. "Now move."

"Where?"

"To the safe, you idiot. Go!" Sanchez pushed him around the corner toward the steel door. "Open the first lock. Hurry up!"

Fisher turned the dial once to the right, two full turns to the left, back a half turn to the right, and then to the left once more. He moved to the second lock and dialed in the combination, then pulled the silver bar down. The door swung back on massive hinges.

"Inside," Sanchez said, pushing Fisher ahead of him. "All right, open the door."

Fisher unlocked the barred door that separated them from the inner recesses of the vault.

"Now, back outside."

Fisher stepped back through the two doors and waited for further instructions.

"I want the master key to the lock boxes. Now!"

"It won't do you any good. Each box has two locks and—"

"Shut up and get me the master!"

They went back to Fisher's office, where Fisher opened a small private safe. He pulled the small key off the top shelf and handed it over his shoulder to Sanchez.

"Strapping tape," Sanchez demanded.

"What?"

"Get me strapping tape, now!"

Fisher went to the closet behind the cashier's desks and pulled out a fresh roll.

"All right, move. Back in the vault." Sanchez pushed Fisher back inside the vault and forced him down on his face. "Hands behind your back, stupid." With his knee in the small of Fisher's back, Sanchez taped the banker's hands and feet, then pulled off his glasses and taped his mouth and his eyes shut. He had succeeded in preventing Fisher from getting any idea of what he looked like or how tall he was.

After finding box 57, Sanchez pulled a drill and a small extension cord from the black bag. Within three minutes, he had bored the personal lock to the King's box. He pulled out the tin box, set it on the table, and opened it. Empty. He cursed silently to himself as he looked again at the piece of paper Latigo had given him. It was the right number, but there was nothing inside.

Sanchez threw the box on the floor and proceeded to drill out several other locks. He rifled through their contents and scattered them on the floor. He took some papers from various boxes, which he would burn later. Finally, he gathered his tools and Fisher's keys, then turned out the light.

"Sweet dreams, Clementine," he said as he shut the vault door behind him and walked calmly out to the car. He drove slowly, trying not to attract attention, across the railroad tracks and out to the abandoned bridge, then down the bank into the riverbed and underneath the bridge. He threw the keys inside one of the supporting pipes and started walking back to his own car, taking the sack of groceries with him. His path took him in front of the courthouse.

A block before he passed by he noticed the Buick he had seen earlier parked out front. He glanced up at Skerritt's corner office and saw a light go off inside. He was still fifty yards from the car when he saw two women emerge through the double-glass doors and slowly descend the courthouse steps. Sanchez started to cross to the other side of the street but decided it might look suspicious. He pulled the collar of his jacket up around his neck and held the grocery bag tight to his chest, tipping his hat at they passed. "Ladies," he said quietly.

The taller one returned the greeting; the shorter one was talking a mile a minute and never saw him. He got into his car and headed back for Rio Bravo.

26

The train rumbled through the day and into the late afternoon, stopping at every village along its journey into the heart of Mexico. Beau had been on this train once before as a boy, traveling to Mexico City with his father. Now, as then, he sat in his favorite spot—the observation car at the back of the train.

Little had changed in nearly four decades. The villages seemed the same. The children still begged for money when the train pulled to a stop. They jostled for position on the tracks behind the caboose, holding up their hands, each one trying to out-shout the others, asking for *dinero*. Then as the train jerked forward the children followed, laughing and running barefoot down the track, stepping expertly on the smooth ties to miss the black cinder bed. The little ones dropped by the wayside first, then the girls.

But here came the little boy who could outrun the rest—shirt tail flying, pants two years too short, lost in the joy of chasing a train. Then, as he began to lose ground, he stopped suddenly, put his hands on his hips, and stood triumphantly in the middle of the tracks breathing hard, as if he had just chased away the black iron monster. He had plundered the gringos' treasure and sent them packing. Beau stood there on the car landing in the late afternoon just as he had forty years earlier, watching the same boy in the same ratty jeans standing astride the same tracks.

A well-dressed lady standing beside Beau waved at the small

figure. But the boy shook his fist, then turned away and ran back to his playmates. "Ungrateful little beggar," she said huffily.

"Not really," Beau said softly.

"I beg your pardon?"

"He's just a kid trying to hold on to a little bit of dignity, that's all."

"Dignity? You call *that* dignified?"

"What's that, ma'am—us throwing a few pennies so we can watch children fight over them, or him taking offense at it?"

The woman opened her mouth, but nothing came out. She shut it quickly and went back inside for a drink.

It was hard for some people to understand what it was like to be so poor you would beg for pennies, and how that eats away at you and turns you sour. Even when you're a kid. The Hollimans hadn't always been well off. Beau remembered going through a drought when he was a boy. Packs of starving coyotes came up from Mexico to raid the cattle herds and kill the smallest calves. There was so little food that the rats were literally eating through the walls, floors, and ceilings of the older wooden buildings. Beau had helped his father pull down a tack room and one hay barn after the rats had destroyed them.

Ben Holliman had been a rancher all his life, and he loved the land. He was a man of great faith, but that early drought had hit him hard—just as he'd gotten his herd up to a decent size. The disaster turned nearly every one of his earthly dreams to dust. Still, Beau couldn't remember ever hearing him complain. The relentless daily pressure of providing for his family forced him to take an additional day job at the refinery for nearly two years—but even then they just barely survived.

Some of the kids at school used to tease Beau about wearing outgrown clothes. They used to call him "hand-me-up Holliman" and then run away laughing. Beau often came home from grade school crying, but not for long—his father had a wonderful ability to make him laugh. Beau liked to pretend that his dad was from a faraway place where there was never any sadness, and people were always nice to you. Where money and clothes didn't matter, but everyone was happy for you if you got some.

Watching his father during those two years, Beau learned a lot about poverty. Maybe the best lesson it taught him was that a family could be poor and happy at the same time. And that even the poor deserve to be treated fairly.

That's why he found Jones's behavior so odd, especially around Mexicans. Jones could speak perfect Spanish—Beau had heard him at the train station—but he rarely conversed in it. He avoided all physical contact with other Mexicans. The entire culture seemed to disgust him, and yet here he was on a train sailing into the heart of old Mexico on a private hunting expedition. There was a lot to figure out about the man.

The train had to stop for two hours in Monterrey for minor repairs. Jones sat across from Beau snoring lightly, hugging his rifle, his hat pulled down over his eyes, oblivious to the mariachi bands serenading along the platform. Most of the musicians were slightly built men who played light and cheerful songs. But at the far end of the platform a movement caught Beau's eye. An enormous man dressed in a white ruffled shirt with silver-lined black vest, pants, and sombrero approached the train and stood directly beneath Beau's window. He carried an equally grandiose guitar, which he strummed as if he were delicately stroking a child's hair. Then he began to sing as if his heart would break. Beau lowered the window and sat back to enjoy the music.

The singer's voice floated on the evening air, timeless and pure. It wasn't particularly loud, but it seemed to cancel out the hiss of the train and the babble of the crowd—as if the song had its source not in a man and his instrument, but in something more permanent that inspired both. Music so true that it unmasked the sounds of the world as false and shadowy. People stopped and listened to his song—the story of a man many years younger than this gray-haired troubadour, and his lost love.

The singer held the final note high and long, and then it was gone. He took off his sombrero and held it out to the crowd. One or two coins dropped in. He turned to the train. Beau dug into his pocket for a dollar.

"Don't do it," Jones said from under his hat. "These beggars'll take your last dime, then stab you in the back for running out."

Beau reached out through the window and put two dollars into the man's hat.

The singer looked up appreciatively. *"¡Que Dios le bendiga, Señor!"* he said quietly.

"Just makin' it harder for the rest of us, Holliman," Jones mumbled indifferently as he repositioned the rifle.

"Well, there's at least two of us who see it differently," Beau said, smiling at the old gentleman. He got up to stretch his legs and wandered two sections forward to the dining car. The whistle sounded and the train jerked just as he entered the car. He hadn't eaten since early that morning and he was hungry.

"Con permiso, Señor," he said to the porter. "How long until dinner is served?"

"Not for another fifteen minutes, Señor, but you may have a seat if you would like, and I will be glad to bring you a drink."

"*Gracias*. I'll have a cup of coffee, please." The coffee was rich and dark but only lukewarm. Beau sat at a small table, enjoying the sunset and watching the prairie sail by.

The first time Beau had ridden the train into Mexico, he had come down with chicken pox. A high fever and general nausea made things fairly miserable for him for the whole trip. His sickness had affected his physical senses. In particular, everything had smelled bad. The odor of the dining car had reminded him of the acrid sweetness of burning cowhide at branding time. Now, forty years later, a trace of that stench still lingered. He wasn't surprised to detect it, although it wasn't as pungent as he had anticipated.

Sheriff Jones was pleasant enough for the rest of the trip, though he rarely moved from his seat. He kept his rifle with him at all times. In the hours after dinner Beau read a Zane Grey novel he'd brought along, when he wasn't dozing uncomfortably in the stiff seat.

It was just past eleven that night when they reached the Dolores stop, a tiny station house with a lone bench outside. Directly behind them the mountains rose quickly into the clouds. The train stopped just long enough for the two men to hop off. Then the cars clanked and the engine pushed on down the slow grade. The sound of the train rolling into the long valley toward Mexico City stretched out into the night and then disappeared.

The men set their luggage down on the platform and stretched the weariness out of their bones. The road ran away from the station north and south. It started the steep ascent into Dolores about a quarter mile back up the tracks.

Latigo had been thinking about when and where to kill Beau ever since they had left Laredo. He considered the Dolores station but decided against it. He would go up and spend a day poking around, putting on a show of concern, then leave ahead of Beau. He needed witnesses to say that he had gone ahead without him.

"Looks like we have some walking ahead of us," Beau said as he picked up his duffel bag.

Jones shouldered his bag and rifle and started walking north.

"Good guess," Beau said.

"Huh?"

"Good guess. You picked the right way. Dolores is up at the end of that road."

"Oh, yeah," Latigo said. "I always was good at finding my way. You got a map or something?"

"Mrs. King drew me one."

"Let's see."

Beau pulled the folded piece of paper from his shirt pocket and handed it to the sheriff. He pulled a flashlight out of his duffel and shined it on the map.

Latigo studied it as if he had never seen the place before. "Hmm, looks like I was right," he said. "Ought to be right up at the end of this road."

Beau looked closely at the map and shook his head in mock wonder. "Well, how about that? Lead on, sheriff. You obviously know where you're going."

Dolores was under two miles as the crow flies, but the walk

was closer to four as the road curved and dipped to follow the contour of the mountains. Neither man was in good condition, and Latigo's rifle was a heavy burden with all the ammunition he had packed. He almost fell a couple of times on the slippery road. Beau offered to carry it for him, but the sheriff pretended not to hear.

After a brief rest at a cave, they climbed for another two hours until they saw the summit and crossed over into the high valley. Beau was struck by the serenity of the place. It looked so peaceful by moonlight, and so permanent, as if nothing had happened there in a hundred years. But he couldn't stop to enjoy it. The wind, cold and thin as a razor, wouldn't allow it.

They neared the edge of town. All of the homes and shops were darkened. The only sound was a loose piece of tin scraping against a roof somewhere in the village. When they reached the center of town, they stood before the cracked and charred walls of the church. The massive doors had been burned off their hinges, only one of which remained. Someone had stacked the fragments of the doors in a neat pile where the votary table had stood.

"Let's take a look inside," Beau said as he stepped onto the short porch.

"I'll wait out here," Jones said, turning away. "I ain't never liked churches, and I sure don't like wanderin' around a burnt-out hulk like this."

"Suit yourself. I'll be out in a minute." Beau walked through the vaulted archway and into the sanctuary. His eyes were immediately drawn upward. There was no roof—only a brilliant array of stars. Beau leaned against a wall and gazed up. It reminded him of one of his favorite pictures, a black-and-white photograph his mother had taken while she was in Wales. It was of a roofless Tintern Abbey. The idea of a house of worship with the true celestial dome for a roof had enchanted him from his childhood. *Well,* he thought to himself, *this is what a church should do. Make you look into heaven as soon as you walk in the door.* Beau was surprised that the feeling emanating from this scarred place was not strange or haunted, but wonderfully peaceful. It felt like a house no one had ever lived in that had been swept clean and made ready for occupancy.

Beau walked among the few remaining pieces of blackened wood, turning them over with the toe of his boot. He still thought of Carl and Marty as boys. He wondered what kind of men they had been and how they had died. He wondered what Jones had to do with it, and how he was linked to Skerritt.

As he turned a piece of wood, something round and small glinted out at him. It froze him for an instant. He walked past it, pushing it out of his mind. He stood at the altar, looking at the place where the crucifix had hung. The smoke and fire had left a frayed outline of the cross on the stucco wall. Stains, darker than the night, were spattered across the altar. Even in the moonlight Beau could see the whiter area around the black splotches where someone had vainly tried to scrub them out.

He made his way back to the left and through the doorway that led to the prayer room. The door was still partly intact, and he pushed it open with some effort. Debris lay in piles against the walls. Sections of large beams—part of the roof, he guessed—were leaning together in one corner. They must have been trying to salvage some of the lumber. Thrown up against a side wall was the iron frame of a slat-board cot and a partially burned chair. Against the south wall was a small table with a kneeling stool tucked underneath, apparently untouched by the fire.

Beau kicked some loose boards out of the way and examined the table and stool more closely. Not a scratch on the table; no sign it had ever been in a fire. As Beau pulled out the small stool, something fell off onto the floor. Beau found it and held it up to his flashlight. A matchbook cover. With a bull's-eye on the flap.

"Holliman!" came a coarse whisper through the front doorway. "Let's go!"

Beau put the matchbook cover in his pocket and walked back down the aisle and out of the church. He pulled out Hatty's map and took a quick look.

"This way," he said to Latigo. They set off in the direction of Eli's house.

It was almost three in the morning when they passed Doc's. Beau recognized it from Hatty's description but said nothing. The walk to Eli's home was short and uneventful, except for one thing they noticed as they crossed over the drainage pipe that connected the fields on either side of the road—a faint odor of something rotting. They glanced down, looking for the carcass of a deer or cow, then moved on, assuming some wounded animal had climbed into the pipe and died there. Whatever it was, the rains would flush it out eventually.

They climbed the steps to the porch and Beau tried the door, but it was locked. He pulled out the key Hatty had given him just in case the McClendons had locked it up for them. The key turned easily, and the door creaked back on its hinges. But for a slight musty smell and cobwebs in the corners, the house seemed to be in passing order. Nothing appeared to have been disturbed in the month it had stood empty.

"I'll take the couch," Beau said, throwing his duffel on the hearth. "The bedroom should be back through that door in the corner."

"Right." Latigo walked back to the bedroom and closed the door behind him without a word.

Beau sat on the couch in the dark for a few minutes, rubbing his legs, getting his wind back and thinking through what he wanted to do later that morning. He didn't want to sleep long; there was too much to do and he didn't know how long the sheriff intended to stay. He looked back toward the bedroom door—no sound from inside.

Beau got down on his knees and prayed, resting his head on the pillows of the couch. First he thanked the Lord for bringing him safely to this place and asked for His continued protection for Hatty and Maria and himself. Then he asked forgiveness for leaving what he was sure was a ring on the church floor. He knew deep inside that it had belonged to Marty. Beau wasn't really sure why he didn't want to pick it up. He only knew it had something to do with not wanting to hurt Maria. But he suspected it might be more than that. He suspected that he didn't want that ring to remind her of her love for Marty. And he felt terribly ashamed.

As he got up, he started to unfold the blanket Hatty had left on the back of the couch when he spied the water pump. There was no water for priming, but he was so thirsty he decided to give it a try anyway. The pump protested, squeaking loudly for a full ten strokes before a trickle of brown liquid gushed out. As it turned clear Beau reached for a glass in the kitchen cupboard, filling it to the brim and draining it three times. The refreshing draught raced all the way down to his toes, ice-cold and well-water sweet.

Hatty had told him there were extra covers in the closet by the bedroom. He tried to walk quietly across the floor, but the boards groaned beneath his boots. Then the closet door creaked as he tried to open it slowly. He closed it quickly after taking the blankets out, then leaned in, placing his ear close to the bedroom door. He heard Latigo snoring. As noiselessly as possible, he made his way back to the couch. Using the armrest of the couch for a pillow, he fell asleep before he could pull his boots off.

In the other room Latigo lay wide awake, running his thumb back and forth along the cutting edge of his knife, waiting for Beau to fall asleep. He had heard the pump and the floorboards creaking. He had heard the closet open. Then there was a silence, and he knew Holliman was listening at the door. So he obliged with a little snoring.

Latigo had decided to kill Beau that night. He was stupid not to have done it before. He didn't need witnesses to see them part separately. All he needed was a good alibi. And the best alibi was not to have been there at all.

He had it all figured out. He would dump the body, then hide in the cave along the road out of Dolores and wait for the return train back to San Luis. He had checked the schedule in Laredo; there was one due in Dolores at five the next afternoon. From San Luis he would get one of his hired men to drive him back to Texas. He could be back in Rio Bravo by early the next morning. Since he had left on Thanksgiving Day while the office was closed, no one there would even know he had been gone. And since he always traveled south under an assumed name, there would be no record of a Mr. Jones on the train manifest.

As soon as he got back, he would call that green deputy over in Dalton Springs and ask whatever happened to Holliman. He would have to sound upset, maybe a little worried. He had waited for Holliman so long he had missed the train. At first he was annoyed, he would say, but then he began to worry when Holliman didn't call with some excuse. He had tried calling Holliman's house, but there was no answer. He was afraid Holliman might be in some kind of trouble and thought he'd better call just to make sure everything was all right.

It was a perfect plan. He lay there rehearsing it over and over in his mind. He started thinking about Mangus' call and the oil on Hatty's land and how close he was to having it all. Who knows, there might even be something on Holliman's land. Something for all this trouble he was going to.

An occasional breeze rattled the windows, but otherwise the house was perfectly still. Suddenly, Beau woke up from a sound sleep. He hadn't heard anything, but something had startled him awake. He had turned on his side so that he was looking out the living room window toward Dolores. Far away, he could see a pair of headlights racing down the road. Within seconds the truck was barreling toward Eli's house.

Beau rose from the couch, trying to see through the window and past the bright lights. He was fully awake as he stepped cautiously out onto the porch and into the full glare of the headlights, closing the door softly behind him.

Just in time. Back in the darkness, just outside the half-closed bedroom door, the moonlight cut across a silent breathing shadow and danced along the edge of a hunting knife.

"Boss! Boss, you all right?"

"Charlie! What in the blue-eyed world are you . . . Maria!" He stepped off the porch and walked over to the truck. "What are you doing here? What's wrong?"

"Aw, Lordy, I'm glad to see you. Maria here remembers seeing Jones before she ran into him in Laredo. She was . . . it was when, uh . . . you tell it, tell him what his real name is," he said, nudging Maria.

"His real name?" Beau asked.

"People here call him Latigo—Scorpion," Maria explained. "He is an evil man. He takes the money my people give to the church. If they don't give enough he kills their cattle or burns their homes."

"Yeah, Boss, and now he's after you right here, sure as shootin'."

"All right, all right, now just calm down and keep your voices low. You're saying Sheriff Jones has been forcing your people to pay protection money through the priests, is that right?"

"Yes."

"You think he might have had something to do with your husband's death?"

"And Carl's and Eli's," Charlie added.

"I know the man with the scar," Maria declared. "The one who tried to kill Mom and me. He is Latigo's man."

"Are you sure?"

"I saw him with Latigo when I was younger. He has been here before many times. He hardly ever came during the day, though. Almost always at night. Anita and I used to sneak over to the cantina when we were older and look in through the cracks in the walls. It was him."

"Why would he kill Eli and the boys?"

"You know how stubborn Dad was. He wouldn't give the money they wanted. He thought he could fight them. So did Martin and Carl."

Beau was quiet for a moment. He rubbed the back of his neck, looking down at the ground. "No," he said. "He wouldn't kill three American citizens over a few hundred dollars, or even over a few thousand. Not a man like Jones. The stakes are too high. It isn't worth the risk."

"Beau, you an' I both know men who'd knife you for the change in your pocket. A few hundred dollars would be—"

"Nothing. Not even a drop in the bucket. If Jones is operating this far south, he's probably working every town big enough to have a church in it from here to Laredo. No, it has to be something else. Something bigger." He paused, then looked at Maria. "You're absolutely sure of this?" he said.

"I'm sure."

Beau smiled at her, then looked to Charlie. "Did you bring your gun?"

"My daddy's forty-five and a thirty-aught-six, which do you want?"

Beau took the revolver from his foreman and loaded it from the box of shells on the front seat. Charlie lifted the rifle out of its mount and slid a cartridge into the chamber.

"We're going to have a little talk with Mr. Jones. He has a rifle, but he should still be asleep. Maria, I want you to wait on the porch until I call you. All right, let's go."

They walked quietly up the steps and across the porch. Beau opened the door without a sound. The two men walked on cat feet across the living room and to the closed bedroom door. The floor squeaked once but then held its peace. Beau put his hand on the knob and turned it slowly. He swung the door open and stepped quickly into the room. Curtains fluttered out from an open window on a gust of wind.

"Beau!" Maria screamed from the porch as Charlie's truck sprang to life. "Stop him! Stop him!" Beau and Charlie ran back through the house and out the front door in time to see the red taillights of Charlie's truck streaking away down the lane.

27

Beau found the matches in the kitchen drawer and lit the lantern on the table. The window was shuttered; the house dark and strangely quiet again. The three of them sat around the table thinking, trying to sort things out. Charlie picked with his pocket knife at a burly knot on the table's corner, trying to smooth it out. Maria twisted and untwisted the fringe on her shawl, staring at the lamp light as if she would find some answer in the yellow flame.

"How much gas is in the truck?" Beau asked.

"I filled it up in San Luis. I'd say about half, three quarters of a tank," Charlie answered. "Where you think he's headed, Boss?"

Beau scratched his head and stretched, leaning back in his chair. "What's a scorpion do when he's backed in a corner, Charlie?"

"He attacks, stings."

"I'd say Latigo is backed in a corner, wouldn't you?"

"You think he's gonna try somethin'?"

"He will be back," Maria said.

Beau thought for a moment. "Has he got men here in Dolores?" he asked Maria.

"A few down in the valley, but none here in town. The people are scared of him. They only do what his men say because they don't want trouble."

"Looks like a lot of folks down here feel that way!" Charlie rarely checked his frustration.

Beau's first response was to defend the weak, but usually he would bite his tongue before jumping in. Tonight he was too tired to hold back. "That's because a lot of folks down here have children to look out for, Charlie—which is something you and I never had to worry about. All right, now, let's think this out. Latigo couldn't possibly get down to the valley, find his men, and get back here inside of two hours. That buys us at least an hour and a half to get over to Doc's and get him and his family loaded up and out of here. Let's go." Beau grabbed his duffel bag and slung it over his shoulder.

Charlie and Maria were still sitting at the table considering the plan by the time Beau was halfway out the front door. They suddenly realized he was on his way with or without them. Once Beau made a decision he was already moving. Maria and Charlie grabbed their things and bolted for the door.

It was five-thirty when they set out on the road to Doc's house. Beau carried his bag in one hand and his pistol in the other; Charlie shouldered his rifle as if he were back in his army days. In fifteen minutes they were walking up the short lane to Doc's front door. A thin trail of smoke curled up and out of the kitchen stovepipe. A soft light was burning inside.

Beau knocked quietly. He heard a chair scraping across the floor, a door closing, and footsteps approaching the front door.

"Yes? Who is it?" a female voice asked.

"Estella? It's me, Maria. I have two friends—"

The door flew open. Estella was already crying. *"¡María! María! Gracias a Dios!"* she exclaimed as she held her friend tightly. "I thought you were dead! Oh, I prayed and prayed! Hatty—is she all right? And Anita?"

"Mom is fine. She's fine," Maria soothed her old friend. "Anita . . . ," she paused, looking for the right words. "Anita decided to go home. I'm sure she went home."

Estella said nothing but nodded slightly. She understood. Maria continued quickly.

"Estella, these two men are friends from Texas: Beau Holliman and Charlie Tilden."

"Mr. Holliman, of course," she said, wiping away her tears and shaking their hands. "Hatty and Eli spoke often of you. How do you do, Mr. Tilden?"

Even in the dim light, Beau noticed the scar on her left cheek.

"Excuse my tears, please. We were afraid we had lost this girl." She hugged Maria again, then opened her door wide. "Please come in out of the cold. I haven't made the living room fire yet, but the stove is going and we ought to have coffee soon." Estella ushered her guests into the kitchen and invited them to sit down. Beau and Charlie removed their hats as they stepped inside the door and hung them on the rack in the corner.

"Oh, I wish Angus was here. He's down in the low valley with some sick families."

"How?" Maria asked. "We had his truck."

Estella smiled. "Antonio Fuentes let Angus borrow his. He and his wife are in Mexico City for a few weeks visiting her family."

"Will your husband be back soon, ma'am?" Beau asked.

"I am a doctor's wife, Mr. Holliman. I learned a long time ago never to 'expect' Angus. It could be ten minutes or ten hours."

"Do you have a horse, Mrs. McClendon?" Charlie asked. "We need to find your husband as quick as we can."

"I did have one, but they killed her. And Angus had more than one family to see. There is a measles epidemic, I'm afraid. There isn't much telling where he would be. Why, does someone need help?"

"It's all right, Charlie. We'll wait," Beau said.

"Boss, we—"

"Charlie—it'll be all right." Beau winked at him and lifted his fingers off the table just a bit to indicate the subject was closed, at least temporarily.

Estella hesitated awkwardly and then turned back to Maria. "We were so afraid that something terrible had happened when we didn't hear from you for so long—"

"You didn't get our letters?" Maria asked.

"No. Nothing. Didn't you receive ours?"

"We never got anything."

Estella paused for a moment. "It's Jaime. It has to be. He takes in the mail at the store, and he's the only one who handles it. I can't blame him, though. I'm sure he's just acting under orders, trying to protect his family." She opened the stove and shoved in another piece of wood. The room was beginning to thaw.

Estella took Maria's hand, grateful for the chance to touch her again. "It's gotten worse," she said. "After you left . . . oh, goodness, I almost forgot! Wait here." She ran back to the corner bedroom, where they could hear her speaking in low tones. As she walked back out, smiling, a few steps behind her was another guest. "Mr. Holliman, Mr. Tilden, this is Father Zeuma. Father, I believe you know Maria," Estella smiled.

"Father!" Maria said as she and the two men rose and shook his hand.

"Father's been our guest for a few days now."

"They've put up with me for a month," he said, smiling.

"Father, I thought . . . well, I . . ." Maria stammered.

"It seems that Latigo made a mistake," Estella said. "He is responsible for all of this."

"How do you know?" Maria asked.

"I told her," a voice came from back in the shadows.

A tall, bony man hobbled into the room, leaning heavily on a crutch, his other arm in a cast and sling.

"Hector, you shouldn't be out of bed yet," Estella said as she reached out to help him. She turned back to face the others. "Gentlemen," she said, "this is our other guest, Mr. Hector Rodriguez."

Charlie drew back from shaking his hand. "Rodriguez? Maria, ain't this the man who—?"

"Mr. Rodriguez is our guest, Mr. Tilden," Estella said, guiding Rodriguez into an extra chair set back away from the table, "and I'm glad to say, a friend."

Maria was in shock. She looked from Hector to Estella for some explanation.

"As I said," Estella continued, "Latigo made a mistake. Father, why don't you and Hector tell them what has happened while I get breakfast ready for Rosa?" Estella got down cups and saucers and served the hot coffee, then prepared toast and juice for her daughter.

"It's amazing what God has done here," Father Zeuma began. "I suppose it all started when Doc asked me to go with him to take Rosalinda to the specialist in Mexico City."

"Is she all right?" Maria asked.

"She's fine," Estella said quickly. "Still in bed, but she'll be up soon. Go on, Father."

"Well, our trip is a story in itself that I must tell you later. It's enough to say that I am not the same man as when I left, and I owe it to Doc."

"What happened?" Maria asked.

Father Zeuma put his coffee down and leaned back in his chair. "When we got back from Mexico City, Estella was waiting for us at the train station. She said there had been some trouble—that Marty and Carl might have been killed and the women were in danger. Doc loaded Estella and Rosalinda on the horse and we walked back to Dolores. We hadn't even reached the top of the pass when I saw the line of smoke.

"I guess everybody in town was at the church. I will never forget seeing it like that, all black and broken. It was still smoldering from the fire the night before. People had been working most of the night trying to save at least some of it, but it was useless. They were all so tired. No one was saying much of anything." He paused and looked out the window toward the town. "It is all like a dream now. I remember hearing women crying. They were just . . . " he paused, searching for the right words. "They had just found the bodies."

"Martin?" Maria whispered.

"Yes. Martin and Carl. And three others."

"Was it the fire?" Maria asked.

"No. There were guns. It was quick."

Maria stared ahead, and everything stopped. Tears flowed suddenly, freely, no longer hindered by a secret hope. There was something about hearing the words that made it real again. Real enough to hear the ripping apart of a life and love and dreams, to feel the piercing of a heart.

Estella stood above her, holding her head against her stomach, gently stroking her hair as if comforting Rosalinda after a fall and a scraped knee. Estella felt infinitely inadequate and yet perfectly placed. It was not the first time. She helped Maria up and they walked back to the bedroom together. The priest followed them with his eyes.

"Who were the others?" Beau asked quietly.

"One was a man named José Cantu. They called him Calavera—the Skull. The other two were Latigo's men as well." Father Zeuma lowered his voice. "One of them was a priest . . . and . . . " his hands were beginning to shake. "He was still alive when we found him."

"What?" Beau whispered.

"He had fallen underneath a pew. I guess that protected him from the fire. His name was Escobar. I knew him. He had done things. To Maria. To her mother and others. He gave me his confession before he died."

"Why would they kill one of their own men? Or did Marty and Carl . . . ?"

"No, no. Martin and Carl had nothing to do with it. There was another man. They found his body back in the prayer room." He looked at Beau. "You are from a ranch in Texas close to Dalton Springs, aren't you, Mr. Holliman?"

"That's right, Father."

"Your sheriff—his name is Skerritt, I believe—has been missing for some time."

Beau looked at him hard as the truth sank in. "You're kidding," he said.

Father Zeuma leaned forward. "He had the badge in his back pocket along with his wallet and identification."

"We had a big meeting that night," Hector said. "Most of the boys from this part of the country were in town to get paid and hear something from Latigo. Father Zeuma here hadn't been cooperating like Latigo wanted, so Latigo told Skerritt to go pay the

Father a visit, rough him up enough to let him know he meant business. Well, Jake was half drunk anyway, and he had never seen the Father. I remember he took his whiskey with him and stumbled out the door of the cantina, and that's the last I saw of him."

Father Zeuma continued. "The way we figured it, Father Escobar was in the church looking for me when Skerritt got there. I'm sure he had been back for some time, you know, pressuring people to give more to the church. Anyway, he was there that night when Skerritt showed up, drunk and mean. Skerritt must have thought Father Escobar was me, and he beat the old man almost to death. His face and body were terribly disfigured when we found him. Apparently Skerritt went back to the prayer room after he had beaten him and fell into a drunken sleep. He never woke up."

"He burned to death?" Charlie asked.

"If it hadn't been for his driving license, no one could have identified him. Two days later, we had the funeral for all five of them. I thought the women might try to come back, but we couldn't wait."

"You performed the service yourself, Father?" Beau asked.

"It is part of a priest's duty, Mr. Holliman. Yes, Doc and I did the funeral together. The people already knew I had not died in the fire. It was only a matter of time before Latigo found out. But I will not run. I will stay here and trust God to deliver me."

"All due respect, Father," Charlie said, "but what about Doc and his family?"

"Believe me, the last thing I want is to put them in any more danger. I am moving back into the parsonage as soon as possible. We should have most of it repaired in another day or two. Hector will be my guest until he fully recuperates and we can get him safely to Laredo to testify. There's nothing in this world I would not do for Doc and his family."

"He's a fine man," Hector added. "If it wasn't for him I'd be dead right now. You see this?" He pointed to his wounded arm and then to his shoulder. "Sanchez did this. I don't remember much except the pain and Sanchez kicking me on my broken arm. Then, while I was unconscious, he shot me here and here. Doc just rode up at the wrong time. Somehow Sanchez got behind him and knocked him out. Doc's lucky he didn't kill him, but I guess Sanchez figured he might be able to make it look like Doc tried to kill me."

"As if anyone in Dolores would believe Angus would kill a man," Estella said, returning with Maria.

Hector shook his head. "He wouldn't have, Señora McClendon," he said softly, gazing at the floor. "But there isn't a man in this town who would have blamed him if he had. Well, after he shot me he put the gun in Doc's hand and took off. Doc must have a hard head, 'cause he woke up before anyone else got there and came over and tended to me. I would have bled to death right there in the mud if he hadn't helped me."

They passed the rest of the day talking over past experiences and wondering what Latigo was doing while they anxiously awaited Doc's return.

The afternoon dragged on endlessly. The men repeatedly walked out onto the porch and stared hard up the road toward Dolores, straining to see the cloud of dust that would herald Doc's return. They considered sending one or two men into town to see if they could get any help from the locals but decided it would be too risky.

As evening neared, Beau called them all together. "Folks, Doc may be home any minute, but we need to plan for a long night. We'll sleep in shifts. Two people need to watch the window through the night. Now we have—what, Mrs. McClendon, a shotgun and a rifle in the house?—plus Charlie's revolver and thirty-aught-six. We probably don't have a thing to worry about. If Latigo's as smart as I think he is, he's long gone. There are too many witnesses piling up here. But you never know with a man like that. Charlie, you and I better get in a couple hours' sleep before we take the late watch. Father, do you think you could handle eight to midnight?"

"Of course. I'm very well rested."

"And I'll keep him company," Hector said. "I may not be able to shoot a gun, but I can still talk, and I've slept enough in the last four weeks to last me a lifetime. Besides, the Father and I have been having some interesting talks."

"It would be a great help, if you're feeling up to it," Beau said.

"Mr. Holliman," Estella said. "Maria and I can take the four a.m. shift. That's only an hour before I normally get up anyway."

"Fine. And let's get on a first-name basis around here, all right?" Beau asked, smiling. "From now on, I'm Beau and this is Charlie. Estella, will your daughter be able to travel if we need to move her quickly?"

"I'm sure she will be fine. She's been begging to get out of bed for a week now anyway."

"Good. If you would just leave a little food out, I'll fire up the stove around midnight and Charlie and I can eat then."

"How does smoked venison sound?" Estella asked.

"Oh, yes, ma'am, that sounds wonderful!" Charlie exclaimed.

"It will be here on the counter waiting for you with a salad and some bread. You can help yourselves to the water. Now let me show you to the beds."

Beau followed her back to the master bedroom while Charlie picked up the duffel beside his chair. The others began to move away to different parts of the home. Father Zeuma went outside for another look down the road.

Hector reached out and touched Charlie's arm as he walked by. "I was just curious," he said in a near whisper. "Why two look-outs? Seems like one man could handle a four-hour shift."

Charlie looked at him for a moment, making up his mind about how or whether to answer. Regardless of what Estella had said, he didn't like Hector. "Because he's the boss, is the first reason," he said. "But there's somethin' else you ought'a know about Beau. For him, the real battle ain't goin' to be fought with guns. Now I know this may be hard for a man like you to understand—it was hard for me for a long time—but he believes in prayer. Believes hard. Harder'n any man I ever known. He says God fights the real battle for us. With two of us watchin' together, one of us can be prayin' or readin' the Bible to the other."

"And you believe in this prayer, too?" Hector asked.

"Not like him, no. Maybe someday, but I doubt it. His father had it too. It's a gift." Charlie feigned a stretch and yawn. "Well, it's going to be a long night, looks like. I better grab a little shuteye. Good night, Rodriguez." He walked away without receiving a response, leaving Hector to sit alone in the chair away from the table, thinking.

The front door opened quickly. Father Zeuma entered and shut it, locking it behind him. "Someone is coming!" he said. "Two men on horses."

Beau came out of the bedroom and crossed over to the kitchen window.

"Both of them have rifles," he said. "You know either of these fellows, Estella?"

She looked out and smiled immediately.

"Estella! Are you all right?" a voice shouted from down the lane.

Estella ran to unlock the front door and rushed outside, arms extended in welcome. "Sam! Ray! Good heavens, what are you doing way out here? Of course I'm fine. Come inside, come, come."

It had been many months since these old friends had been together. They greeted each other with hugs. Then the men stepped inside and put their guns just behind the door before shaking hands all around.

"Beau Holliman and Charlie Tilden, meet two of our oldest and dearest friends, Sam Carreras and Ray Montoya."

"Good to meet you, Señor," Sam said, shaking hands vigorously with Beau.

"And you," Beau said, wincing a bit in the enthusiastic grip of the huge man.

"First things first," Sam announced. "We owe you an apology, Estella."

"No apology needed, Sam."

Ray interrupted. "Yes, yes, there is a need. We have been acting like cowards, hiding away like that."

"You had to watch out for your families. No shame in that."

"That was just an excuse," Sam admitted. "We were scared to death."

"We're still scared," Ray said. "But as of this morning we both decided we couldn't hide anymore."

"Why? What happened this morning?" Father Zeuma asked.

"Well," Ray began, "you know since we started putting money back into the church they pretty much left us alone. We had been trying to help each other out a little bit here and there with the cattle. Believe it or not, we got into a habit of getting together for a little Bible study. You know. Doc better watch out—old Sam here's getting pretty good. I think he might have some preacher in him. Anyway, Mrs. Perez would open up the bakery early on Friday mornings and it would be just us three in there for an hour or so."

"You're the preacher, Montoya," Sam said, slapping his friend on the back. "You got more wind in you than a blue norther. Tell them what happened this morning."

"Okay, okay, I was just getting to that. So there we are minding our own business—Sam leading his horse and I'm walking alongside—right on the other side of old Garcia's house, when all of a sudden this truck comes out of nowhere, spooks Sam's horse so bad it takes off for home, then skids over into the ditch. This fellow jumps out of the truck and starts to cross the road, cussing us up one side and down the other. I knew him right away—Latigo. I've never seen a man so mad in my life—he's ready to kill us.

"But about halfway across the road he finally sees Sam here, and I mean he stops dead in his tracks. I guess he doesn't run into men bigger than old Sam here too often. He stands real still, breathing hard. By this time folks have started to come out—Juan is out on his porch in his nightshirt shouting, and Señora Consuelo behind us is yelling at her husband to get up and come see what's happening. I guess that made Latigo decide it was time to leave, 'cause he starts backing up toward the truck. Then he points his finger at us and says we're dead and he'll be back. Then he says, 'You're all dead, you and your Mexican-loving preacher boy too.' I mean he was crazy. Then he gets in the truck and drives off through Dolores toward the lower valley."

"So that was it," Sam said. "No more running. No more hiding. That's all. No more."

"We would have been here sooner," Ray explained, "but we

had to borrow a horse to get back to Sam's, then get the families situated. It all took more time than it should have. Renee and the kids are over at Sam's now."

"Yeah, they weren't the problem, though. It was Mrs. Perez. It was like pulling teeth to convince her that she needed to stay with us until all this got settled. I thought I was going to have to carry her out the door, but she finally came." Sam rubbed his eyes and laughed. "I told her Doc and Estella would want her to be safe and if she didn't want me to get in big trouble, she needed to come ahead. That's what finally did it—say, where is the old man, anyway? Off being a doctor again?"

Estella smiled. "He's down in the lower valley. He should be back before long."

"Well, you'll have to tell him hello for me," Sam said. "I have to get back to the house. I don't think Latigo even knows where we live, but I wouldn't want to take a chance on it. Ray here is going to hang around and see what kind of trouble he can get into. You're all going to stay here until Doc gets back, right?"

"That's right," Beau answered.

"Good," said Sam. "If plans change, holler. Estella and Maria know where we live. Sure is good to see you ladies again." He gave Maria a special hug goodbye and whispered something to her. Then he turned to Beau and Charlie. "Good to meet you men. I'll check back tomorrow morning if I haven't heard from you."

Estella and Maria walked out onto the porch to see him off. The sight of Sam Carreras trotting away on a horse half his size was enough to make anyone smile, and his two old friends were no exception. It reminded them of better days and happier times.

"He's a good friend," Maria said.

"Yes. He always has been."

Maria looked down for a minute before asking, "Then why did he ever leave?"

Estella put her arm around her young friend. "I guess all of us, at some point, have left when we should have stayed. But it's not the leaving that matters—not in the end. It's the coming home. And Sam has come home to stay."

28

The radio on the night table was spitting out static. The bed was lumpy, the sheets hadn't been washed in a week, and the tissue box was empty. Hatty had come home from Dalton Springs running on empty. It had been only two hours since she had resigned herself to taking the medicine Irma had brought her the day before, and it hadn't had time to start working. She always said she would rather have a cold than swallow a pill. Until she caught cold.

Physically, she was only marginally better than she was emotionally. Everyone she had contacted about the "Mexican situation" (a grand total of two people) had been either impotent or too gung-ho. Armando fell into the first category. He had been kind, but he was green as grass and had no idea of what to do outside of notifying the FBI—and a fat lot of help they had been. As long as he was the only on-duty officer in Dalton Springs, he couldn't very well abandon his post to go off on what would probably amount to nothing more than a wild goose chase with a couple of middle-aged busybodies.

Irma, on the other hand, wanted to go down into Mexico with flags waving and guns blazing, hogtie "the badlanders," and come back national heroes. She had dropped Hatty off at her house and driven off peering over the steering wheel and muttering to herself about the need for some action.

By five in the evening Hatty was going stir-crazy. Her low-grade fever had broken about noon. She had slept so much the night before and most of the morning that she couldn't rest now to save her life. About three that afternoon the medicine had kicked in and she had started to feel remarkably better—so much better, in fact, that she managed to convince herself she'd turned the corner and what she needed most was a good dose of November air. So she decided to go for a walk.

The late afternoon was still and cold. Hatty dressed warmly and put a flashlight in her coat pocket just in case, but she loved walking at night under the stars. The gravel crunched underfoot as she walked down the mesquite lane, following the road that wound around past the big field the Gibraltars used to run their pigs in. By surprise, Hatty found herself in front of the Puentas cemetery. She hadn't been to visit her parents' grave in over three years now. There was the rusting wire fence that twirled into scallops and bordered the front entrance. The iron gate was only half attached. The other half, which had always made her think of heaven's pearly gates, leaned against one of two white wooden columns.

Hatty stood outside looking in. To her left and on the other side of a barbed-wire fence was the Mexican cemetery with its primitive wooden crosses scattered about. Directly in front of her, the much larger Puentas cemetery boasted polished marble and granite headstones arranged in neat rows with family plots outlined in bricks. Hatty entered and stood beneath the flagpole at the center of the yard. It remained amazingly erect, having endured everything from hurricanes to Fatty MacDougle climbing it every Halloween night since Hatty could remember. She remembered standing in this spot as a little girl, hearing the Three Oaks brass band play the "Stars and Stripes" for a World War I pilot who had requested that it be played at his funeral.

As Hatty stared at the naked pole, she remembered all the people she had said goodbye to on this spot. The halyard slapped lightly against the scarred silver staff in a breeze that couldn't be felt at ground level. The hollow metallic clink echoed across the graveyard, disembodied, soulless.

A fat sun squatted just above the horizon as Hatty passed the Wilson family plot and walked over to the three salt cedars. In the shade of those ancient trees rested Eli's father, Benjamin King, his mother, Evie, and a stillborn brother. The plot had been recently tended. *Probably Polly Webb or one of the Wilsons,* Hatty thought to herself. *They always were so nice about keeping the graves presentable.* She stood for a moment wishing Eli was there watching the sunset with her.

Just a few feet beyond, Judge Prescott's headstone rose like a miniature Washington monument—the tallest and whitest marker in the cemetery. She walked over and sat down on its base, leaning back and looking away to the west just in time to see the last trace of orange slip beneath the edge of the world. Down on the creek behind the cemetery an owl hooted and was answered by another, even farther away. *Owls make the loneliest sound in the world,* Hatty thought.

At that moment, Hatty would have given anything to be able to say goodbye to Eli. It occurred to her suddenly that she never had. That there wasn't anything to say goodbye *to*. She started to think about what had happened and where his body might be, but she stopped as quickly as she began—the last thing she needed was more nightmares. Instead, she closed her eyes and pictured Eli's face. She recalled every line until she came to his eyes. What was the color? Blue, yes, but how blue, exactly? It was so frustrating to be unable to get the shade just right. She cursed herself. It hadn't even been two months and already he was beginning to fade. But she could see him smile—she would never forget that. And she could hear him laugh, and almost feel his touch. Instinctively she reached for his hand on her cheek and touched a tear instead.

A car drove up and stopped just outside the cemetery gates. Hatty half heard it but paid no attention until the car door slammed, stirring her from her reflection. She peered around the edge of the headstone to see Irma Light making her way up the gravel walkway, talking to herself. She had three mason jars full of river fern, and she was walking straight for Hatty. Hatty started to rise to greet her but then decided to wait.

Irma stopped short of Prescott Row and turned in toward the King plot. She was wearing gloves and immediately set about clearing the low growth of weeds around the graves of Eli's family. "Now, old son," she said as she continued to work, "I'm running late for the special prayer service up to the church. 'Course you won't be there as usual, being out of town still, but I figured I better get over here and tend to business for you, or I'd catch no end of grief when you get back, you old stinker." She carefully placed the ferns beneath the headstones. "There," she said, taking off her gloves and breathing heavily, "don't you folks fret, now. We'll catch those badlanders, Hatty and me. Soon as she gets feelin' better, and that won't be long, nosir. We'll make 'em say—yes we will. We'll make 'em say. I'll find him, Ben, you can count on that. And bring him home." She turned to go back to the car. "G'night, Ben. Evie. Y'all rest easy."

Hatty sat still until the engine started and the car drove away. There was a sudden rustling to her left and then a burst of raucous laughter. Some boys had been hiding behind the Clark's tombstones and had observed the whole thing. She wondered how long they had been there. They took off at a run out of the graveyard and up the road, yelling back into the cemetery, "Night, Ben! Night, Evie!" Their laughter faded away in the growing dark. Then, when she was sure they wouldn't hear, Hatty cried until she had no tears left.

Hatty decided to take the long way home, up the gravel road past the church where brother Mac Macpherson had called a special meeting to pray for rain. By the time she was halfway up the road she could hear the piano and organ launching into "Be Thou My Vision," a lovely old Irish melody, which had been her father's favorite. She stopped outside to listen. Neither the instruments nor the women's voices did it justice. It called for a lyric tenor—and it needed to be sung, not in a church with a fancy organ, but out in a field riding a horse. To do the hymn justice called for the sweetest voice she had ever heard: her father's, singing it gloriously loud during spring roundup.

Be Thou my vision, O Lord of my heart. That had been her prayer at the dinner table when she was a little girl. She closed her eyes and hummed along, swaying back and forth in the shadows of the old church, feeling more at peace than she had felt in weeks. *Naught be all else to me, save that Thou art. Thou my best thought, by day or by night; waking or sleeping, Thy presence my light.*

"Hatty King!" The hoarse whisper ripped across the churchyard and startled Hatty awake. Irma Light was waddling over, shaking her finger. "What in the world are you doin' out on a night like this? You'll catch your death. You ought to be home in bed."

"Hello, Irma." Hatty grinned as she ignored the challenge.

"Hello, yourself! Now come on inside where it's warm."

The preacher's voice rose above the organ. "The third stanza . . . ."

"You're late," Hatty said, nodding toward the front door.

"Oh, I was out pulling weeds. I had to get cleaned up first."

Riches I heed not, nor man's empty praise.

"I'm surprised at how good it feels just to be back here, listening to the singing—"

"Oh, heavens, I think that fever must have addled your brain."

Thou mine inheritance, now and always.

"Irma, you're a good friend."

Miss Light smiled. "Shoot. I could've told you that a long time ago."

Thou and Thou only, first in my heart.

"It took me a while, Irma, but I feel like I've finally made it back."

"Welcome home."

High King of heaven, my Treasure Thou art.

Miss Light started to go inside, but Hatty stopped her. "Irma, I think you're right. I think I will go on home. I'm starting to feel a little woozy, I'm afraid. Would you mind terribly?"

Miss Light dug the keys out of her cavernous handbag. "C'mon, hop in," she said, turning to her Buick. "But this time you stay put!"

"Yes, ma'am," Hatty said, getting in and slamming the door shut. "You know what, Irma?" They backed out and started on the short drive to Hatty's.

"I'm afraid to ask."

"I'm thinking we ought to take a little trip together. Do a little investigating on our own."

"What did you have in mind?" Miss Light looked over at her and almost ran into the Puentas city limits sign. She swerved back onto the road just in time. "Sorry. Now, where were you wantin' to go?"

"Rio Bravo. I want to ask a few questions of my own. Somebody in that sheriff's office is bound to know something. I can't stand another day of sitting around doing nothing. What do you say?"

Miss Light was quiet for a moment. "Rio Bravo, huh? My stars, I haven't been out to the badlands in over thirty years."

"Come on, it'd be fun. And we sure aren't doing any good around here."

"I'd like to, Hatty, but I don't know," Miss Light said, shaking her head.

"What do you mean? I thought you'd jump at this."

"Well, in the first place, I don't know if you'll be up to it."

"I'll get a good night's rest, I'll take my medicine, and I'll be up to it. What else?"

Miss Light paused, trying to suppress a smile. "I know as much as you say you liked that music back there it'd be a sore disappointment—but our goin' might mean havin' to miss Sweet sing a special this Sunday."

"Oh, heavens," Hatty laughed. "You don't mean it? *Sweet?*"

"On my honor as a DAR. You never heard such caterwaulin' in your born days, and that's the gospel truth."

"Bless her heart. She never could carry a tune in a tin bucket. What happened? Did Brother Mac finally just give in after all these years of her asking to solo?"

"Oh, I guess you haven't heard about what happened to Brother Mac, have you?"

"No, what?" Hatty asked, concerned.

"He lost his hearing aid about a month ago!" The two of them laughed all the way back to the house.

29

A thick layer of dust blanketed the bar and the tables of the cantina. A solitary figure sat brooding at a table where a candle burned low in its holder. Since Calavera's death, the locals had been afraid to come inside. They had heard noises deep in the night—wild laughter, they said, coming from inside the cantina when the moon was full. The row of whiskey bottles stood untouched and gathering dust on the shelf. Only the occasional clink of bottle on glass and the skittering of the rats broke the silence of the room.

The night was perfectly clear and cold. Moon and stars shone down on the tiny village, watching, waiting for something to happen.

Latigo had been busy. He had traveled over three hundred miles that day, making calls in San Luis, rousing his men out of saloons in Matehuala and Guanajuato and Pozos, making sure they understood just how serious he was about joining him the next morning in Dolores. If Mangus was right about the King well, Latigo could afford the bonus he promised these men for an extra day's work—a thousand dollars apiece to be there by six a.m. and do the job. That was more for one day's work than most of them would see in a year. But it was worth it if he could get rid of Holliman and the rest in one hit. He wouldn't catch any flak from the town. They'd all be hiding under their beds or pretending not to see or hear.

That's the way they always responded to intimidation.

Latigo had learned at an early age what fear can do to a man—intimidation had been his father's way—and he was fascinated by it. In the right hands, fear was a transforming tool. It could turn a man's spine to jelly. It could make him crawl and beg and humiliate himself in front of his wife and his son. If concentrated and sustained over a long enough time, fear could disembowel a family by killing love and replacing it with suspicion. Fear could penetrate any armor, paralyze the strongest muscle, arrest any heart.

It wasn't a question of whether or not a man might be fearful; every man was afraid of something. The question was, what would a man fear the most? If you could find that out, you could rule the world. And Latigo had discovered the formula as a youth. The concept was so simple and natural he had almost missed it: the secret to unlocking people's deepest fear was discovering what was dear to them. Identify what they would die for, and you would know what they most wanted to live for. Find out what they held to most tightly, and you would know what they were most afraid of losing.

Latigo knew that the formula didn't necessarily involve material things, although fear of losing personal possessions was easy to incite and usually sufficient. It could be an idea, a dream, a memory. It could be the fear of having a treasured part of your past unearthed. Of having what you privately worshiped exposed and then discarded as rubbish, so that you felt shamefully foolish for ever having treasured it in the first place. Fear of losing the past was money in the bank.

But all those paled in comparison to the fear of losing the irreplaceable—a lover, a husband, a wife, a child. Early on, Latigo had found that people feared losing other people. This was a curious weakness to him. He had never needed—much less feared losing—anyone in his life. He wasn't aware that this was partly because no one had ever feared losing him. All he knew was what worked. Economy and efficiency were the keys to his effectiveness. It didn't take much. To burn a house down, all you needed was one match.

This would be the last night Latigo would have to sleep in a cramped, rat-infested little room. This night marked the end of the old and the beginning of a new life. After tonight, only one obstacle would stand between him and the realization of his dream—and she would be no problem at all. He sat sipping his drink, enjoying the thought of the accident that would take her out of his way. His eyes were heavy. He slumped back in the chair, resting his chin on his chest, and imagined what it would be like. A car wreck, perhaps. A fire.

He looked up and the cantina was filled with men. They were all talking loudly—and none of them to him—but he couldn't understand what they were saying. Some were drinking; others were playing cards. Although he knew these men, he couldn't remember any of their names. He was unable to talk. He could only listen.

A tall man came over to Latigo's table and sat down. He started to speak in a language Latigo didn't understand. And then he said, "Of course you don't. Of course you don't understand, you stupid Mexican. I was the first one." A fire started over in one corner of the cantina and flared up through the cracks in the floorboards. Latigo rushed over to it and smothered it with one of his mother's wicker laundry baskets. Then he sat down on the basket. He was streaming with sweat.

Another man walked up and squatted down to face him. "Hey! You remember me, don't you, partner? I was the first. Yeah, that's right. It's starting to come back now, ain't it?"

Someone tapped him on the shoulder. Latigo remained facing forward. "Yeah, you don't want to look, do you, friend? But you don't have to see. You can smell it. You can feel it, can't you? I'm still smokin', boy. I'm still hot. Open your eyes!"

In front of him stood two forms, white as snow. Fire enveloped them, and they screamed as someone shot them while they turned to ash. In the roof of the cantina, another fire started. Someone else, also white but not as white as the other two, was lying on a table looking up at the tongues of flame licking the rafters. Beads of sweat glistened on his bald head. This one Latigo knew very well. But what was his name? The dull white figure gulped the tequila in his hand and began laughing wildly, staring straight up at the fire above him. He turned suddenly and looked into Latigo's eyes, holding up his index finger just as the roof gave way and burning timbers crashed down on him.

Behind him came a familiar voice. "Son!"

Latigo was crying now.

"Son!"

He looked back to see his father.

"I was the first, Benito," said his father.

Suddenly Latigo found his voice. He was a youth again, sitting there with matches in one hand, a jar full of gasoline in the other, one side of his face wrapped in dirty gauze and tape.

"The first! You were not—"

"Who *was* first, then? Do you remember?"

"No. Leave me!"

"Of course you don't remember. Because there is no first. And no last. All are first. All are last."

"You would not save me. You are no father to me."

"My blood runs through you, Benito. I am in you and you in me."

"You would not save me!"

"But the white man—"

"He would. He would save me. He would risk burning for me."

"The white man hates you, my son. Just as you hate us."

"The white man does not know me."

The spirit threw back its head and laughed so loud the cantina began to shake.

"The world is in flames, Benito. Look."

He felt himself rising to stare out the cantina window. Fire was drifting down from the sky like snow—a sleepy, fluttering cascade of orange and yellow flame, settling silently on the ground and on the buildings of Dolores, burning everything in sight. Far away into the night he could see the firefall. Something black moved along the tops of the mountains and then down the sides, like a wave of black ink sweeping into the high valley and toward Dolores. The heavens glowed a dull, hellish red, but there was no sound.

"No man can save you, Benito."

He spun around. The wooden Christ, who hung suspended on His cross from a burning rafter, was speaking. Blood poured from the wound Latigo had inflicted in His side.

"No man can save you," it repeated.

An approaching thunder grew louder and deeper. It encircled the cantina, pounding the earth with deafening noise. Walls shook. Whiskey bottles clinked together and then crashed to the floor, spilling fuel into the fire.

All the men were gone except one. The wooden man sat at the bar eating a meal, his back to Latigo. "Any time, Benito. Any time," he said without turning around.

Latigo ran back to the window, which exploded inward. The glass rushed through him so fast it failed to cut him. A thousand horses circled the cantina, galloping faster with each passing second until they were flying past, their forms a bright blur. Hooves skimmed the ground, and yet their thunder increased. One black stallion stood inside the circle, perfectly still. Then, although it seemed to be hardly moving, it started to walk, then prance, toward the cantina, its eyes wide and white-rimmed, its ears drawn back, its head high.

The cantina had burned and fallen. It was gone. The wooden man stood, picking his teeth, where the bar had been.

Latigo turned to him and shouted, "Were you the first after all?"

The man smiled. "And the last," he said.

Something behind Latigo nudged his shoulder. He whirled around, screaming.

"Don't shoot! It's me, Sanchez! *Don't shoot!*"

Latigo was standing in the middle of the cantina, pointing the shotgun at his deputy's chest. He shook himself awake and lowered the gun.

"Sanchez?" Latigo blinked the sweat out of his eyes. He stumbled to the table and sat down. "Sanchez?"

"Yeah. Yeah, it's me. What happened, Boss?"

Latigo was quiet for a moment, trying to gather his thoughts. "You had a job to do," he said weakly. "How many did you get?"

"It was short notice, Boss," Sanchez answered.

"How many?"

"Four. Two from Laredo, one from Monterrey. One from Vallecillo."

"They'll be here by six?"

"Yessir."

"Sit down, Sanchez. Have a drink." He pushed a chair across to his deputy and poured drinks for them. As the dream faded, a new anger seized him. He was getting his second wind. "How's that gash in your pretty-boy face healing up?"

Sanchez sat down stiffly, pulling the chair up to the table and keeping his eyes on Latigo's hands. He had learned never to look away or turn his back when the sheriff was talking. And when Latigo was smiling, as he was now, Sanchez had learned not to blink.

"My face is all right," he said.

"You know, Deputy, when I tell you to bring ten men, I expect to see ten men."

"It was late. Everybody's—"

"Not four." He turned the shotgun toward Sanchez. "Now tell me you found those papers."

"I already told you, Boss. The box was empty, I swear. Maybe they're in his home somewhere."

"Don't be stupid. Why have a lock box at all if you ain't goin' to use it? King wasn't the type to stuff his mattress. He'd either keep important papers locked up or . . . that's it. He brought them down here. That's gotta be it. He's got them hidden down here somewhere."

"Why all this trouble over the papers, Boss? They aren't going to do them any good."

"Long as those wills and the title exists, we've got problems. We need to find them and burn them."

"But doesn't the title company have a copy of all the—"

"Pogue took care of the copies already. Now shut up and let

me think."

The back door to the cantina burst open and three men entered. They all stopped at the same time when they saw the shotgun on the table.

"Sit down and shut up!" Latigo barked. The men moved slowly to another table. "Sanchez, take these men with you. Go out to the King place and burn it. Empty all the drawers first. Make sure all the papers are on the floor. There's a gas tank out there. Break the lock off and soak the house. Burn everything. Get it done and get back here fast. Go!"

They made for the back door quickly.

"Sanchez," Latigo said. "Don't disappoint me again."

Latigo sat in silence, waiting for the others. By a quarter to six they had arrived—twelve in all. By six the others returned, stinking of gasoline.

Latigo's instructions were simple and direct. "We finish our business, take the bodies out to the ravine, and dump them there."

"What about the women?" one asked.

"First come, first served," Latigo leered. "Then kill them."

"There is a child," another said.

"I told you what to do. You don't want the money, leave now."

No one moved. By six-thirty they were all walking out the door. Outside, Latigo grabbed his deputy by the arm. "The truck's out of gas. I'm ridin' with you. Where's your car?"

"I just got it fixed, Boss. Wet-sanded and new paint. I don't want to get it banged up again."

Latigo spat and cursed under his breath. "I don't believe this. I refuse to believe that I have surrounded myself with nothing but fools. Now, give me the keys."

"If Doc don't come soon we're goin' to have to move," Charlie said.

"Move where, Charlie?" Beau asked. "Somewhere else in the valley? Some other homestead? Wherever we went he would find us. If we stay here we at least have cover."

Ray turned from his watch at the window. "Maybe Latigo got scared. Maybe he ran."

Maria shook her head. "He would die first," she said.

"Perdónenme," the voice came from the living room. Father Zeuma rose from his resting place on the couch and sat with his head in his hands. "Forgive me," he said again.

Estella spoke softly. "Father?"

Tears were running down his cheeks. "None of this. None of this would have happened if I had . . . if I had resisted. If I had done something—anything," he said, staring straight ahead, speaking as much to himself as to the others. "But I did nothing. Please forgive me."

"Señor Holliman!" Ray shouted.

Beau looked out the window to see a white cloud of dust trailing out behind a truck racing toward them. Estella stood at Beau's shoulder.

"Oh, it's Angus! It's Angus!" she said, running to the front door. Doc pulled the truck around the back of the house and climbed out. Estella ran to him and was in his arms before he had time to catch his breath.

"I'm sorry, baby. I had ten sick kids down there, all of them—"

"Angus, Maria is back!"

"What? Here?!"

"Yes, but there's trouble. Come quickly." She took his hand, and they ran around to the front porch. They hurried inside and, after Doc had greeted Maria, Estella introduced him to Beau and Charlie.

"Doc," Beau said urgently, "I know this is sudden and you must be worn out, but we're sitting here just waiting for trouble to happen. We need to get everybody out of here right away."

Doc looked to his wife. "Estella?"

"He's right, Angus. We can explain later. Right now there isn't time."

"All right, let's go. Estella, get Rosa and I'll bring the truck around front."

"Doc . . . " Ray murmured, looking out the window toward Dolores.

"Hector," Doc continued, ignoring Ray's soft voice, "you come with me and—"

"Doc! Look!" Ray said without turning.

A line of trucks came roaring out of Dolores and down the dirt road toward Doc's house.

Beau picked up his rifle. "Everyone to his post," he said as he moved to the kitchen window. "Doc, why don't you take your bedroom window?"

"Mama, what's all the noise?" Rosalinda stood in the living room in her nightgown, rubbing her eyes.

"Rosa, come. There, put on your slippers." Estella took her daughter by the hand and ran to the back door. She grabbed Doc's coat from the rack and hurried with her daughter out the back door and to the garden behind the house.

"Mama, I'm cold."

"I know, baby. Rosa, listen to me. Go down to the creek and hide."

"Why, Mama? What's—"

"Hush. I don't have time to explain. If you hear shooting, don't move. Do *not* come to the house. Daddy and I will come for you before long. Do you understand?"

Rosa nodded yes.

"Pray, Rosa. Pray for us all. Now go. *¡Ándale!*" She kissed Rosalinda on the forehead and pushed her away. Estella returned to the house and looked back to see her daughter running from the back of the garden down to the creek. She shut the door behind her and locked it, drying her tears before she picked up one of Doc's guns and took her place beside him.

The sun had inched its way just above the horizon, washing the front of Doc's house in a frosty light. Seven trucks and three cars pulled up in a wide arc, all of them facing the house. Their exhaust created a white vapor that dissipated quickly on the early morning breeze.

Doc's front door opened unexpectedly. Beau turned quickly from the window to see Father Zeuma walk out onto the front porch.

"Father, get back inside!" Ray shouted.

Zeuma walked to the edge of the porch and shouted out above the roaring engines. "You men! Why are you doing this? These people have done nothing to you. God can still forgive you—all of you. But you must stop this!"

Latigo raced the cadillac engine to drown out the priest's words. Zeuma crossed himself and stepped forward. "Benito!" he shouted at the top of his lungs. "I know!" Latigo took his foot off the gas and stared at the priest. "I know the truth," Zeuma said. "Let me help you!"

"Shut up!" Latigo shouted, getting out of the car.

"Father Escobar told me before he died—he—"

"I said shut up!" Latigo screamed as he raised the shotgun and fired.

The blast caught Father Zeuma in the right shoulder and spun him back into the wall of the house. Beau was out the door in a flash and dragged Zeuma back inside. Latigo fired a second shot, but it hit above Beau's head. Beau slammed the door shut behind him and lay Zeuma out on the floor.

"Don't fire!" he shouted to the others as he knelt by the wounded man.

Outside, Latigo started to reload. But he stopped as soon as he looked up.

"Señor Holliman! Doc! They aren't firing! Look!" Ray shouted.

Indeed they weren't. They were all leaning out of their trucks staring straight at the house and around the side toward the barn. Sanchez had taken his dark glasses off and was staring along with the rest. He got out of the car and stood with his gun in his hand. Ray noticed it was shaking. Suddenly, as if they were taking an invisible cue, the others started driving away. Fast. Sanchez wheeled around and shouted after them. "Get back here! We can take them!" But they were already halfway down the lane. "Cowards!" he shouted.

"Get in!" Latigo shoved his deputy back to the car and ran around to the passenger side.

"Boss, we can do this!"

Latigo leveled the shotgun at Sanchez. "Shut up and drive!"

They spun around and off down the lane in a cloud of dust.

"They're gone! They're gone!" Ray shouted.

"What happened?" Hector asked. "I couldn't see."

"I need some help here," called Beau. "Doc!"

"I'm right here." Doc moved in beside Beau with his black bag.

"Angus, I'm going for Rosa," Estella said as she wrapped her shawl around her shoulders and headed for the back door.

Beau was bent over the unconscious priest. "He's wounded pretty bad."

"Here, let's get him on the table," said Doc. "Maria, a pillow, please!" They lifted him easily onto the kitchen table, and Doc began to cut away the shredded cassock.

"Here, hold your hand—that's right," Doc instructed, placing Beau's hand on a mass of torn flesh. "That will stem the flow of blood a bit. We won't have to bury our friend yet."

Doc went to the sink and pumped some water over his hands and soaped them quickly. "All right, I've got it. Your turn to wash. Quickly, please. Hector, you and Ray can keep watch. Those fellows might find their courage in a bottle out there and come back."

The two men, who had been hovering over the priest on the table, moved quickly back to their positions. Estella came in the back door with Rosalinda. "Estella! Scrub!" Doc hollered. Without a word she went to the sink and pumped out a bowlful of water.

"Maria, we need towels, please. Rosa, wood for the kitchen fire, quickly," Estella directed. Rosalinda ran out the back and returned soon with an armload of kindling.

"Sterilize the instruments for Papa, sweetheart," Doc told her. "The ones in the top left drawer of my desk."

"All of them, Papa?" she called out from halfway down the hall.

Doc looked at the wound before responding. "No, just the first four on the left should do it, thank you." Rosa and her mother worked fast and efficiently, preparing the "operating room" while Doc and Beau tried to keep Father Zeuma from bleeding to death. It was a serious wound, but Doc's expert responses kept everyone calm.

"You have a real touch, Mr. Holliman. Ever think of going into medicine?" Doc asked, smiling.

Beau smiled back. "What do you think happened out there?" he asked.

"I honestly don't know," Doc said seriously. "They saw something that scared the living daylights out of them and took off. I don't know. Maybe we'll find out someday."

Charlie walked over and looked carefully at the wound. "He don't look too good. How long before we can move him, Doc? We gotta get out of here before they decide to pay us another visit."

"Two hours."

"Two hours?" Charlie blustered. "Can't you work faster than that, Doc? I mean—"

"Oh, he'll be patched up in about forty-five minutes, but I figure it'll take you at least an hour-and-a-half to get over to Sam's and help him get loaded up, then get back here and fill up the truck with gas. We ought to be ready by then."

"Oh, right. Sam's. I'll get over there right now."

"I'll go with you, Charlie," Maria said. "I can help Juanita with the children." She stopped on the way out the door and looked back at Beau. "You saved his life. Thank you."

It was a quick trip to Sam's house. On the way they passed the smoldering ruins of Hatty's home. There was little left standing except the chimney. Parts of it were still burning, but the fire had been so intense nothing of value was left to save.

Sam and his family were all packed and ready to go. They loaded into the back of the truck and were back at Doc's house within forty-five minutes. When they returned, Maria ran ahead of the others to see how the priest was doing. They had moved him to the back bedroom. Doc was talking to Beau and the others.

"It's just not going to work," Doc said. "He's worse than I thought. I think he's going to be all right, but he can't be moved.

Estella, I want you to take Rosalinda along with the rest. You'll be safer in Laredo, and Hatty's going to need help. I'll bring Father Zeuma along just as soon as he can travel safely, believe me."

Estella hugged her husband. "I don't want to leave you," she said.

"It won't be for long, I promise," Doc said gently. "Estella, I honestly don't believe those men will be back, but even if they do come back, who's to say the Lord won't protect us again?"

She poked him lightly on the chest. "Don't be presumptuous, Angus." She looked up at him. "Be careful. We'll be waiting for you—at Hatty's."

"They won't be alone," Beau reassured him. "I'll make sure they're safe."

"She's gassed up and ready to roll, Boss," Charlie announced from outside through the open window. "Let's hit the road!"

30

Two miles outside of Rio Bravo, Hatty began fishing through her purse for a pen and paper. "This time, I'm taking notes," she said.

"What do you think, Hatty?" asked Irma. "Are these people goin' to do us any good or not?"

"Oh, I don't know what to think any more, but I'll tell you what: if this bunch doesn't give me some answers, I'll find them on my own."

"Now you're talkin'," Irma said with a decisive nod. "Sometimes a woman's got to do what a woman's got to do, and that's all there is to it. We'll go right down into their back yard if we have to. Right into their hideout! I'm with you, Hat. Now, where in thunder is that courthouse?"

The double-glass doors closed behind them with a clank. The two women climbed the steps and walked down the cavernous hall without seeing or hearing anyone. At the end of the corridor they entered the reception area for the courthouse offices. The secretary was gone.

Hatty looked around the desk for some sign that she might be returning soon, but found nothing. Miss Light walked surreptitiously behind the desk, glancing with a studied casualness at bits and pieces of paper that lay on the credenza. She saw one promising stack of folders on the end beside the sheriff's office. The top folder was opened to a paper that looked important. As soon as Miss Light touched it the whole stack went tumbling to the floor, spilling papers everywhere.

"Irma!" Hatty whispered, as she ran behind the desk to help her gather the pages. "What are you doing?"

"Investigating. That's what we're here for, isn't it? Now help me get these picked up." They scooped them and stacked them back in place without the slightest idea of which papers went in which folders. As Hatty helped her friend rise with the last of the files, Miss Light bumped the sheriff's office door, and it opened just a bit.

"Well, looky here. Hellooo . . ." she whispered as she peeked inside Latigo's dark office.

"Irma, we ought not—" Hatty began, but Miss Light was already inside. "Irma!" Hatty whispered loudly as she looked around quickly, then tiptoed in. "Good heavens—look at that!" she gasped, gazing at the weapons case.

Miss Light adjusted her glasses and shook her head. "Yup, if you ask me, there's somethin' wrong with a man who can't get by with less than twenty guns and a couple of good spears."

The desk was perfectly clean—no stacked papers, no open files. Irma tried all the desk drawers quickly, but they were all locked. The large map on the wall behind the desk depicted southwest Texas and most of Mexico.

"Lands, doesn't this man believe in light?" Miss Light said, squinting hard, her face two inches from the map. "What was the name of that town you lived in?"

"Dolores. Come on, Irma, someone's going to come back."

"Hush. Come here and show me where."

Hatty leaned over to get a clearer view. "Let's see, it's right about . . . here. Here's Dolores. And see San Luis Potosí?"

"Yeah, I see somethin' else, too," Miss Light said.

"*Ladies!*"

Hatty and Irma both screamed and jumped.

"What are you doing in here? Who are you?" the young woman demanded.

"Lordy mercy, child," Miss Light said, leaning back against the map with her hand over her heart. "You did that on purpose, didn't you?"

"Who *are* you?" she said loudly.

"My name is Hatty King and this is Miss Irma Light. We, uh . . . "

"We needed some help and there wasn't anyone around, so we helped ourselves," Miss Light said firmly.

"I can see that," the girl said. "What did you say your name was?"

"Hatty. Hatty King, and Irma Light."

The girl paused for a moment, apparently taken by surprise, though Hatty couldn't imagine why. Her tone dropped considerably. "All right, Mrs. King, how did you get in here?"

"The door was open," Miss Light said testily. "So we just walked in. We saw the map and thought it might help us. For heaven's sake, why is everybody so jumpy around here?"

The girl uncrossed her arms. "Well, now I'm here and I'd be glad to help you, but we can't do it in Sheriff Jones's office, so if you will follow me."

Hatty and Irma walked out of the office, and the young woman closed the door firmly behind them. Jennifer Budreau sat down and invited the guests to sit in the low chairs opposite the desk. "Now, Miss Light, Mrs. King, why don't you ladies tell me what you were really doing in there before I call the guard?"

"What?" Miss Light asked indignantly.

"Folks don't come to the county courthouse if they're lost. If you wanted a map there are plenty for free down at the filling station."

"I never said we were lost," Miss Light said. "I merely said we wanted to look at the map, that's all."

"Miss, look," said Hatty. "We got off on the wrong foot here. We weren't trying to break in or anything. We just need some help."

"Sheriff Jones isn't here. He's off on a hunting trip for a few days."

"We know," Hatty said.

"So you want to see one of our deputies?" Jennifer asked.

"Well, actually," Hatty said, "we thought you could probably help us more than anyone."

"Me!" Jennifer laughed. "Oh, that's good. You don't understand, ladies. I'm not a law officer. I'm just a college student and a secretary, that's it."

"Jennifer, could I see you a minute, please?" a voice crackled over the intercom.

"Yes, sir, right away," she answered. "Ladies, please don't leave. I'll be right back." She left the reception area and ran up the hall stairs.

"Hatty, the map—did you see it?" Irma whispered as soon as Jennifer was out of earshot.

"Yes, of course I saw it! I was standing right there!" Hatty said.

"Did you notice the red x's beside Dolores and San Luis?" Irma's eyes were so bright with mischief they looked ready to dance out of her head.

"What? No. Are you sure?"

"Sure as I'm sittin' here. And I'll bet you if you draw a line from Dolores to Laredo you'll find little x's all the way."

"What do they mean?"

"Who knows? Maybe they mark banks they want to rob or trains."

"You think she'd let us take another look?" Hatty asked.

"Not likely," Irma said, setting her purse down by the chair. "You stand watch. I'm gonna try to get another peek."

"Irma, no!" But it was too late. Hatty jumped up to watch the stairs while Irma made for the office door.

"Oh, drat!" Irma said loudly.

"What?"

"Little Miss Priss locked it on us."

"Well, thank goodness. Now get over here and behave yourself," Hatty said, as she sat back down again.

"Oh, Hatty, she's not going to be any help at all. None at all."

"She's probably going to see if they can't arrest us for something."

"Big waste of time, if you ask me," Miss Light sniffed.

The two men upstairs were laughing so hard they had to hush each other for fear of being overheard. They had wired the intercom to enable them to monitor office visits without touching the machine. For pure entertainment value, Hatty's and Irma's exchange was the best in weeks. When they heard the knock at the door, they toned down their response.

One of them, a middle-aged man, rose and opened the door. "Come in, Jennifer," he said. "Have a seat. How are you doing?"

"I'm fine, thanks. You heard?"

"Yeah. They're getting too close," he said. He paced the floor, carrying a cigarette in one hand and a small green ashtray in the other. "Find out what they plan on doing. Try to convince them to go home, but if they won't—if they insist on going south—then you'll have to go with them and take care of them down there."

"We'll need clearance," the other man said.

"We don't have time for clearance. I'll take responsibility."

"Chief, please . . ." Jennifer started to resist.

"Hey, little Miss Priss, it's part of the job," he said, starting to laugh again. Jennifer failed to see the humor. He sobered himself quickly. "Jenny, you wanted this assignment, remember?"

"Right," she said as she turned and walked out of the room and down the stairs.

The man turned back to his colleague. "What were the x's for? Banks?"

"And trains," the other said, and they dissolved again into a fit of muffled laughter.

Jennifer was fuming. They always treated women like this. It wasn't that she hadn't been warned. Her female predecessor had told her what the working conditions were like, but that didn't help. Jennifer had put in her time without complaint for over six months without a single day to call her own. *Great,* she thought. *Here I am with my first real break coming up in just two days, and I get Miss Marple and her evil twin.* She rounded the corner into the reception area, determined to talk them into going home, but stopped short. They were gone.

She grabbed her purse and ran out down the hall and out the double-glass doors, searching up and down the street. She spotted Miss Light pulling out of her parking space at the end of the block. Pulling off her high heels, she raced off in her stocking feet, cursing under her breath. "Miss Light! Miss Light! Wait!" she shouted.

Irma jerked on the emergency break and the car sputtered to a stop.

"What on earth, child? That's the second time today you've startled me," Miss Light scolded.

"I'm sorry," Jennifer said. "We couldn't talk in there. I was afraid we were being listened to. Now, I need an answer and I need it fast. It's very important that you tell me the truth, all right?"

"I always tell the truth," Miss Light huffed.

"Are you going to Mexico?"

"Yes."

"Does it have something to do with Sheriff Jones?"

Miss Light looked to Hatty, and then back to Jennifer. 'It might," she hedged.

"I think I know what you're doing. Please don't. Please go home and let the authorities take care of this problem."

"The authorities *are* the problem, honey," Miss Light said as she started to back away.

"All right, all right, wait. Let me go with you."

"What?"

"Let me go with you. I think I know where he is. And besides that, I know *who* he is. I can help. I just need to stop by my house and pick up a few things. Please."

"Why should you want to help?" Miss Light demanded.

Jennifer stood stoically and looked away. "Personal reasons," she said softly.

"Mmm-hmm," Miss Light sniffed. She wasn't impressed.

"Can you drive?" Hatty asked from the passenger's side.

"Of course."

"Move over, Irma," Hatty said, as she got out of the car and climbed into the back seat.

"Well, come on," Irma said, shifting her bulk so that the Dynaflow listed slightly to starboard. "If you're wantin' to go so much, then let's go."

"Don't mind Irma," Hatty said from the back seat as Jennifer opened the door. "She can be surly, but it doesn't last long."

Jennifer climbed behind the massive steering wheel and started feeling the steering column.

"Now, what is your name, hon?" Hatty asked.

"Jennifer. Jennifer Budreau. Where's the ignition on this thing?" she asked. "Oh, here it is. How cute. Does it have a radio?"

Miss Light looked over the seat at Hatty. "Remember, this was your idea," she said, as they pulled into the street and started off in the general direction of Mexico.

31

Eduard Delgado saw it coming a mile off. The red streak slit the face of the sand-brown landscape. Delgado ran from his field back into the house and grabbed his shotgun. "*¡No más! ¡No más!*" he kept repeating under his breath. He walked quickly out his front door without bothering to close it and onto the road that led into La Ventana, one mile away.

Miguel Sanchez was desperate. "No excuses. No turning back. This is it," he muttered. He had been driving since early that morning, stopping at every village along the way, trying where he had failed only two days earlier to muster enough men to satisfy Latigo. He had been without sleep for nearly forty-eight hours, his car was almost out of gas, and he was riding the edge of a breakdown.

Once the group had made it back to the cantina, Latigo had regained his courage and had a change of heart. First he blamed Sanchez for running, then he ordered him to get more men. Get to the King ranch and fill up with gas, he said. He himself would go west looking for men; Sanchez was to go north. Forget the ones who ran, he said. Find others. Drag them there if he had to, by sundown. He wanted an army.

Stupid. Latigo would never find enough men willing to fight that many soldiers. They had walked right into an ambush. Where could so many have come from? Latigo had sorely underestimated the McClendons' influence with higher authorities. Sanchez had replayed the scene at the ranch a hundred times over since that morning. Latigo was to fire first, and then everyone else. At first, everything had gone according to plan.

Until the priest walked out. When he first stepped onto the porch, Sanchez couldn't believe it was Zeuma. Zeuma was inside the church when it burned. Sanchez *knew* he was dead. And yet, somehow, it was Enrique Zeuma standing there. In that instant, in that millisecond of shattering recognition, Miguel Sanchez had known real joy for the first time in his violent life. Some impossible thing had happened. Some impossible hand had intruded, had taken hold of this moment—and he had wanted nothing more than to run to the priest and fall down at his feet and beg his forgiveness.

Then, in the next instant, Latigo fired, and the priest fell. Instead of opening fire as they were supposed to do, Sanchez and the other men had been stunned motionless. Sanchez could still smell the gunpowder and hear the echo of the blast. He had seen men killed before. He had killed men himself. But not like this—an unarmed priest! Sanchez had decided right then to kill Latigo. He got out of the truck, took two steps—exactly two steps, he remembered—and then it happened.

Just as Sanchez had started to raise his gun he saw them—the soldiers. Hundreds of them appeared out of nowhere—on the roofs of the house and barn, in the trees, behind the trees; fifty or more ran out from the garden behind the house and stood shoulder to shoulder, their weapons drawn. When Latigo shot again, they began to move forward.

That's when the rest of the men decided it was time to leave. Why had he turned and shouted? Why had he screamed at them to come back? He didn't want to fight. He didn't want to win any more. He wanted it to be over. None of this made any sense. They couldn't win. In his book, a bunch of street brawlers didn't stand a chance against a trained and well-armed militia. Maybe that's what he wanted—just to surrender.

But not now. Now he would rather face the devil himself than

Latigo. And he was running out of time. He had already been to La Ventana once that day, wasting precious minutes looking for the cowards who had left them to face the soldiers at the McClendon ranch. But word had already spread of what had happened, and the runners had managed to crawl under a rock somewhere. Let them stay there for now. He would pick them up on the way back with the others.

But there were no others. In every village, it was as if Latigo's "posse" had suddenly vanished—and no one else would help. La Ventana was his last stop before returning to Dolores—and his last hope. If he couldn't find men there, he would have to go back to Latigo empty-handed.

His arrival took the town by surprise. It was late afternoon, well past siesta, and the people were going about their daily business when Sanchez roared past the white cliffs escarpment on the outskirts of town and down the main street. He slid to a stop outside the bar and ran inside. The dust hadn't settled back into the street when the saloon door jerked open again and he exited quickly out onto the boardwalk.

"Juan!" he shouted to a man crossing the street. "*¡Ven acá!*" he demanded. "Come here!"

The little man loped over to the side of the street and took his hat off. "*Buenas días, Señor,*" he said with a slight bow to Sanchez. Juan was the town drunk and slightly retarded. He wandered the streets asking for handouts or for work. Often he would spend all night in an alley, sleeping with his back propped against a wall. The night before had been particularly unpleasant—his father, frustrated and embarrassed from years of trying to cope with a retarded son, had finally kicked Juan out for good. This morning he was a little slower than usual.

"Where are Castillo and Melendez?" Sanchez demanded.

"Castillo?"

"René Castillo and George Melendez, you idiot. Where are they?"

Juan stared vacantly down the street and scratched his head. "I do not know, Señor. I am sorry." He looked back to Sanchez and began to smile, and then to giggle.

Sanchez put his head down and muttered something, then drew back his right hand and struck the young man so hard he fell backward into the dust of the street, striking his head on the sharp fin of Sanchez' Caddy. "Where are they? Where are Castillo and Melendez?" he shouted harshly.

Juan was crying, trying to get up, holding his head, but Sanchez cursed him as he lifted him from the ground with one hand. He hit him again hard in the mouth, sending him flying out into the middle of the street. This was no longer the cool street fighter from Laredo. This was an animal. An uncontrollable frenzy took hold of Sanchez as he stomped on and kicked the little man repeatedly in the back, screaming at him to get up and answer him.

But Juan wasn't moving any more. His body lay perfectly still, twisted in tortured arabesque, his eyes staring straight into the setting sun. No one screamed. No one tried to stop it. But when it was all over, the people who had watched from the street and along the sidewalk started to move in toward Sanchez.

Miguel was oblivious to any movement as he spat on the crumpled body and turned to walk away. He found himself facing three young men standing between him and his car. One was holding a two-by-four. Instinctively, Sanchez reached for his gun, but he wasn't in uniform.

"You looking for this, Mr. Big Man?" One of the men held up the pistol, then twirled it on his finger. The circle of people tightened around him.

"Nah, he's looking for these, I'll bet." The keys to the Caddy jingled in another man's hand.

"Yeah, look! Ramone found the keys! Hey, nice car, Ramone!"

"Yeah, I guess. You know, I never did like these gringo cars, though—you drive them too long, you start thinking like a gringo. You start acting like a pig."

"Hey, pig man. Hey, pig," one of the men shouted at Sanchez. "You think you can come into our town and do this? This ain't your town, pig. This is our—"

"What are you?" Sanchez shouted.

The sudden outburst took the crowd by surprise. No one responded. No one moved.

Sanchez took the initiative. "Huh? What are you? I'll tell you—you are *nothing*! You are nothing because you have nothing. You have nothing because you know nothing. Look at yourselves. You look down on me because I have money—because I have a nice car. You call me a pig because I work for a white man. How many of you have been across? You, Ramone, and you, Salinas—you have been. Most of you men have crossed the river at night to go to work the next day for the gringos' money. Why? So you and your families can have it a little bit better here in this hole. So maybe someday you can buy your way out like I did and find out what life is all about. You are not angry with me, my friends. You are ashamed of yourselves."

He continued quickly, walking around the inner circle of men. "Look at me! I do not crawl through a muddy river on my belly. I do not hide in the dark, afraid of the gringo law. I *am* the law," he shouted, pounding his chest. He lowered his voice now, pointing at the crowd. "How did I get so much power? I got power because I know how to get money and use it. Money is power, my friends, but—at least in the beginning—you have to earn it." Sanchez saw one or two grins. "Yeah, you know what I'm talking about." A nod here and there. "Listen, I'm here to help you. You come with me, you men, and I will give you—"

"Juan!" an old man screamed in a cracked voice from the middle of the street. The crowd parted as everyone turned back to see. The smiles vanished; the spell was broken. "*¡Juan, mi hijo!* My son, what have they done to you? *Ay Dios*, I am sorry," he sobbed. "Oh, God, don't take my boy from me."

Eduard Delgado knelt in the dust of the street and held the broken body of his son close to his chest, his own heart breaking, as he rocked back and forth, the shotgun resting by his side.

Sanchez made a sudden grab for the keys and missed. Delgado looked up and saw Sanchez in the grasp of three men.

"You!" he whispered hoarsely. "You killed my boy. You take and you take and you take, and now you kill a poor idiot boy." He reached down for the shotgun. The men holding Sanchez dove out of the way. "*¡No más!*"

The white cliffs of La Ventana rose high and austere as the old Buick chugged down the road leading to Dolores. The village sat high on the edge of an escarpment that ran for several miles and then descended into the level farmland of north-central Mexico. The cliffs forming the northwestern rim of the escarpment rippled in soaring vertical columns that resembled white curtained windows.

"That's why they call the town La Ventana—in Spanish it means the window," Jennifer offered.

"That's nice," Miss Light said. The last three hundred miles had been a running travelogue of Mexican history and culture, courtesy of Miss Budreau. But Irma was not a seasoned listener. She could take ebullience only in measured doses, and then with a stiff snort of maturity to cut the sweetness.

Miss Budreau, on the other hand, was a good talker and a better actress than most of her male colleagues realized or would have been willing to admit.

Hatty had been asleep for the last hundred miles, having suffered another small setback with her fever. She had aspirin in her purse, but they had forgotten to pack enough water. Hatty never had been able to swallow a pill without half a glass of water to wash it down.

"Why don't we see if they have any decent water here?" Miss Light said as they sailed past the lower edge of the escarpment. "I think Hatty really needs some—"

"Wait . . ." Jennifer's voice changed almost immediately.

"What is it?"

"The top of the ridge, see? Isn't that . . . why, that's Miguel's car!" She floorboarded the Dodge. It sputtered, belched, jerked, and died.

"Well, that's just fine," Miss Light intoned, thoroughly disgusted. "Heavens to Betsy, this isn't a hot rod, girl. She's not used to that much gas in one gulp—"

"Irma!" Hatty said from the back seat. She was leaning forward, pointing up the road. "That's the car. The one that was chasing us."

"Mrs. King—" Jennifer began.

"No, that's it, I know," Hatty said, grabbing her cane and getting out of the car. She started up the steep incline at a limping run.

"Mrs. King, wait!"

"Hatty!" Miss Light called.

Jennifer jumped out of the car to follow Hatty. Miss Light started, but returned to find something she had left behind. The red car at the top of the plateau was still moving, now precariously close to the edge of the tallest cliff—which was still a good quarter mile farther up. There was no sign of Sanchez, but Hatty knew that if she found his Caddy, Sanchez wouldn't be far behind.

"Mrs. King," Jennifer said, walking at a quick pace beside Hatty, "please go back and get in the car. We don't know what's going on up there, but it doesn't look good."

"I'm going to find the man who helped kill my husband and my two sons, Miss Budreau. Now, you can come along or you can stay, it makes no nevermind to me, but I'm going to get him. He's not going to get away again." She picked up her pace.

Jennifer stopped. She had tried to work things out, but she had her orders: "Take care of them," her boss had said. Easy to say, but this is where you proved yourself. She reached into her purse and felt the cold metal of the gun; at that moment Hatty stumbled over a rock and fell hard. Jennifer took a deep breath and ran up to her. At the same time the Buick roared to life behind them. Miss Light was back in the driver's seat and headed straight up the road.

"Hop in!" she said from atop her pink pillow, sliding to a halt beside the two women. They all climbed into the front seat and Miss Light patched out, tires squealing. Jennifer looked over at her, her mouth hanging open. "It's all in the clutch," she said, smiling triumphantly.

"Irma, look out!" Hatty had learned to watch the road when Miss Light was talking.

Irma swerved to the right to keep from running off one of the lower cliffs. "Hang on, girls," she said. "The law has come to La Ventana!"

The crowd had moved from the streets out past the edge of town to the tops of the white cliffs with the red car in front of them. Several sat on the hood and trunk, and one of the townsmen was driving slowly forward toward the edge of the cliffs. As they neared the red car, Jennifer could see only men—one of them carried a shotgun and another one carried a pistol. She made her calculations quickly.

The men stopped pushing to see the approaching car. Miss Light pulled on the emergency brake twenty yards from the crowd.

"Stay in the car!" Jennifer shouted as she jumped out the passenger's side. "Put the guns down and back away from the vehicle," she shouted, pointing her revolver at the man with the shotgun. The men in the crowd looked at one another but did nothing.

"Ella dijo que ustedes bajaran las armas," Hatty translated. She was standing behind Jennifer now, alongside Miss Light. The two men laid their guns down, and all of them put their hands in the air.

"I told you to stay in the car!" Jennifer barked at the two women without taking her eyes off the men.

"You also said you were a secretary," Hatty said, holding up a DPS badge. "This fell out of your purse."

"Put that away," Jennifer whispered angrily. "These people can't know that I'm an officer."

"Your name isn't Budreau, either, according to this."

"No, ma'am, it's not. Now, tell them to move away from the car."

"Just hold your horses!" Miss Light exclaimed. "You lied to us, miss, and now you want us to just hop when you say boo."

"Good grief! Look, I'm sorry, all right?! I need your help here. What do you want me to do?"

"Deputize us."

"What?"

"You heard me. Deputize us, or we'll blow your cover all the way back to Laredo!"

"Now? Here? I—I don't know how. I don't even think it's legal."

"Oh, and this *is*?" Miss Light said. "Boy, I bet the papers back home, not to mention the Mexican government, are going to love hearing about this little escapade."

"Raise your right hand," Jennifer whispered back over her shoulder. Miss Light and Hatty both obeyed. "Now do you both faithfully swear to execute the duties of an officer of the state of Texas as best as you understand them in apprehending this suspect, so help you God?"

"Yes," Hatty said.

"We do." Miss Light whispered with eyes closed, savoring the moment.

"All right, you're both deputies. Now tell these people to move."

"Which way?" Hatty asked as she stuffed the badge into a pocket.

"It doesn't matter which way! Back, I don't care, just tell them to move."

"If they move back they'll fall off the cliff," Miss Light said. "Tell them to move to the right, Hatty."

"*¡Muévanse a la derecha!*" Hatty shouted, pointing.

"Hatty," Miss Light said.

"*¡Muévanse!*" Hatty shouted, but the men stood motionless.

"Hatty! You're pointing left!" Miss Light whispered.

Hatty changed hands, and all the men moved to the side.

"Miss Light, pick up the guns," commanded Officer Budreau. "Hatty, you ask them what's going on here."

Following Hatty's question, one man stepped forward and explained what had happened that afternoon. He ended by reaching back into the crowd of men and pulling the slain boy's father out. "Old Delgado here. It was his son," the man said, putting his arm around the old man. "This man with the scar, he always comes to town in his fancy red American car. Bragging, bragging, making the rest of us feel like we are dirt because we do not have money. Delgado almost had him, too, Eduard, did you not? If you had remembered to put shells in your gun you *would* have had him. We thought at least we could destroy this. It is a small thing, but at least he will never see his precious car again. And it helps us to feel that we have done something to fight back."

"So where is he?" Jennifer asked through Hatty.

"When Delgado pulled the trigger and nothing happened, the man with the scar jumped on a horse that was tied up on the other side of his car and took off. We tried, but we could not catch him."

"You let him get away?" Jennifer shouted. "How could you be so . . . " she bit her tongue at the last minute and stomped away.

The man shouted something after her.

"He wants to know if he can go ahead and push the car over," Hatty called.

Jennifer's anger and frustration overcame her better judgment. "I don't care what they do with it," she shouted. "They can make a root beer float out of it for all I care. Let's go!"

The men began to move toward the car again. Hatty started to turn away to go back to Miss Light's car when she heard something. "Wait!" she shouted. "Jennifer, there's somebody in the car."

She and Jennifer ran to the side of the car and looked in while Miss Light held the guns on the crowd.

Sanchez lay bound and gagged in the back seat, only half-conscious. His moaning had saved his life. "Why, hello, Miguel," Jennifer said sweetly. "What a surprise." She turned back to Hatty. "Tell one of these men to pull him out."

As the man came forward one of the others addressed Hatty from the crowd. "Are you the law?" he asked.

Miss Light stepped in front of Hatty. "What'd he say?" she asked.

"He asked if we were the law."

"You tell him yes, we're the law. We're here to take this badlander back to justice and they have the Texas Rangers to thank for it."

Jennifer was about to object, but Hatty caught her eye and winked before translating for Miss Light. "We're here to take this man back to justice. That's all I can say," Hatty announced to the crowd in Spanish. To her surprise they all cheered. Miss Light was beaming.

"Over here." Jennifer motioned for the man to lead Sanchez away from the car and make him lie face down on the ground. The man stood with his foot on Sanchez's neck as Jennifer knelt beside him.

"Oh, great!" she muttered.

"What is it?" Hatty asked.

"Oh, it's not that important," Jennifer said. "I just wish I had my handcuffs—this stuff they have him tied with isn't going to hold. That's all right. I'm sure someone here has some rope we can—"

"Try these," said Miss Light, reaching behind her and lifting something from the belt under her sweater. She handed Jennifer a pair of iron handcuffs. "It's been a while since these were used, miss, but I think you'll find them oiled and ready."

Jennifer shook her head and smiled. "You're an amazing woman, Miss Light," she said. Then she added, "And if the Rangers ever do hire women, you'll get my vote."

Deputy Irma Light was at that moment the happiest woman on earth.

"You do the honors, please. Here, above the wrist. Now just ratchet—not too tight. Good. Congratulations, Deputy," Jennifer said, shaking her hand.

"Thank you," Miss Light said quietly.

"All right," Jennifer said. "Let's get him back in his car. I'll drive it if one of you ladies can take Miss Light's car back. I figure we can get as far as Monterrey tonight, then head on into Rio Bravo tomorrow morning."

"Aren't we going for Latigo?" Miss Light asked.

"Miss Light, Latigo never was in my sights. There's a whole division after him. Your safety and the safe return of this prisoner are my primary responsibilities now."

"How do you plan to get him across the border?"

"Ma'am, the FBI has ways, believe me."

"*Uhhh. Uhhh.*" Sanchez started shaking his shoulders violently and mumbling through his gag.

"Shut up or I'll put you back in your little toy and walk away," Jennifer said. But as she glanced back over her shoulder toward the Cadillac, she saw why Sanchez was so upset. The men had been slowly pushing the car closer and closer to the edge of the cliff as they talked.

"No!" Jennifer shouted.

"Now! Push!" The bright red Caddy rolled the last six feet, picking up speed as it veered away from the men and toward the edge. The right front tire went first, then the front end and side tilted as the chalky road crumbled beneath. Jennifer tried to grab one of the fenders to slow it down, but it was too late.

Silver chrome flashed off the left fin as the car tipped over the edge and began its final journey of six hundred feet straight to the bottom of the escarpment. It didn't strike a single rock on its way down; all four tires spun in perfectly synchronized turns. The shimmering red body arced gracefully as a highboard diver, floating quiet as a feather on the breeze, turning just slightly.

Miguel wanted to cover his ears, but he couldn't help hearing the crash of metal and the shattering of glass on impassive rock. The car crumpled into a heap at the base of the cliff, resting atop a jagged riot of rock for a few seconds before exploding into flame.

Jennifer gazed down and sighed. "So much for corroborating evidence." She turned back to the man on the ground. He lay perfectly still, his eyes cold. "Well, ladies," she sighed, "looks like it's us three up front and Mr. Personality here on the back seat."

Miss Light was already halfway to the car. Hatty stood behind Sanchez and to the left as two of the men lifted him up and carried him to the car. She watched them for a moment, then turned to gaze out over the edge of the white cliffs toward the south. Jennifer stood beside her. "What a waste," Hatty said sadly.

"Yeah," Jennifer agreed. "That was one beautiful automobile."

Hatty looked at her and almost smiled. "I wasn't talking about the car," she said softly. She turned and walked away.

32

The two cars passed each other in Monterrey. Beau had turned off Highway 85 at around two-thirty that afternoon to get some gas just as Miss Light's Buick had rolled into the same town from the north. When Beau's group reached Laredo at five, they decided to stop for an early dinner before trying to cross over into Texas.

"Beau, the only thing to do is try to sneak them over," Charlie said.

"Señor Holliman," Sam began, "me and my family can stay here in Laredo. We don't need to bother you with getting all the way back to your place."

"The same goes for us," Ray chimed in. "We can find a place to stay here until you let us know."

"We have tried before to cross, Señor Holliman," Renee said.

"Yes, and we also," Juanita said. "Sam and I tried to come over for a visit a few years ago. They were very strict."

"All the offices are closed for the weekend," Estella said. "We cannot get visas until Monday anyway."

Beau folded his arms and thought quietly for a moment. "Estella, you told Doc you would meet him at Hatty's."

"I know, but it just can't be helped. You can let Hatty know and she can tell Angus to come back to Laredo for us."

"Do any of you have contacts here in Laredo?" Beau asked.

No one answered him.

"I don't like the idea of these folks stayin' here in Latigo's back yard and him still on the loose," Charlie broke in. "Not to mention spendin' money they don't have on some fleabag hotel with these kids and all. I still say we sneak them over."

"Charlie, you know how I feel about breaking the law," Beau said.

"This is an exception. The law needs to be broke when there's an exception," Charlie argued.

"Charlie, if it weren't for the exceptions we wouldn't need any laws. Now maybe the law doesn't work in our favor this time, maybe it does. But we can't break it just because it's inconvenient. Even if we did manage somehow to get them across, we'd be looking over our shoulders every fifteen minutes for the border patrol. Besides that, the Lord doesn't look kindly on lawbreakers, if I recall. He put the law in place for a reason, and we need to honor it even if it doesn't suit us. *Especially* if it doesn't suit us. What's our faith worth if we can't do that?"

Beau turned his attention to the rest of the people sitting around the long dinner table. "Now look, folks, it seems to me we may be outguessing ourselves here. The prospects for getting across are no better than they are for all of you finding a safe place to stay here in Laredo. Let's give the Lord a chance to work. I say we all go to the gate and see if they let us through. They haven't said no yet. If they do, we deal with it then. What do you say?"

Sam talked it over with Juanita while Ray and Renee did the same. Estella was the first to respond. "It is a good plan," she declared. "We have nothing to lose and much to gain."

"What's so good about it, Estella?" Ray asked. "We waste time and we let the officials see us. What if one of them works for Latigo? Then we're dead. We never get out."

"It's a good plan because it's an act of faith," Beau responded. "It shows God we trust Him more than our own judgment. If we hide or break the law He may still protect us, but we will never know how He might have worked in our behalf if we had trusted Him."

After a short prayer for God's leading, they all piled into the truck and drove the half mile to the border. There were two men in the booth, a border guard and a trainee who remained inside filling out paperwork. The guard asked for Beau's driver's license and visa, examined them, and handed them back. "Your visas, please," he asked the others.

Beau's heart sank, but he decided to ask a favor anyway. "Sir, these people are my friends, and they are in desperate need of help. . . ."

"They must have visas, sir, or they can't enter the United States."

"We have to get help tonight," Beau said. "Their lives may be in danger."

"They can get help in Mexico. If they want to obtain visas on Monday, they can cross over. Not until then. Now please move your vehicle around here and unload."

For a brief moment, Beau considered running the gate and taking his chances with the law on the American side. Then the second man came out of the booth. He stood behind his superior smiling. He tapped the first officer on the shoulder and spoke to him in a whisper. The first man looked back at the people crowded into the bed of the truck and nodded as his trainee continued to talk to him. He gestured with his hand as if to say "carry on," walked back into the booth, and closed the door.

The trainee walked up to the cab of the truck, took off his hat, and introduced himself with a wide grin. "Esteban P. Morales at your service, ladies and gentlemen!"

"Esteban!" Maria shouted.

He leaned back on his heels and laughed a great, barrel-sized laugh.

"What are you doing here?"

"Working! Praise God, Maria, I am working! The Lord has been so good! But I will tell you all about it later. Who are your friends here?"

"Oh, I'm sorry," she said. "This is Mr. Beau Holliman and his foreman, Mr. Charlie Tilden. All these people are dear friends from

Dolores. We are in trouble, Esteban."

"The same men?" he asked.

"Yes," she said. "Can we go through?"

He shook his head. "You may, Maria. You and these gentlemen, but I'm afraid the others cannot—not until they get their visas, anyway. But I have an idea. Why not send them home with me? You know how hospitable Danielle is, and the children would love to have some playmates. They will be safe with us for a day or two until we can obtain their visas and get them across."

"Oh, Esteban, thank you! Yes, that would be wonderful."

"Fine! Fine!" he said. "Just pull around in this circle here, and I will show you the way to my house. I am close to the end of my shift anyway. I was just finishing up my paperwork. This fellow is great in here," he said, indicating the officer in the booth. "I am sure he will not mind my leaving a couple minutes early."

Esteban introduced himself quickly to the other passengers and told them their plans. After hasty thanks, he guided Beau back through the gate and to his house. With introductions made and everyone unloaded, Beau, Maria, and Charlie left their friends in the safekeeping of the Morales clan and headed north to Texas.

Beau's house was dark when they drove up the lane.

"Y'all come on in and get a drink, freshen up a bit," said Beau. "I'm going to see if I can reach the FBI in San Antone, then we'll go out to check on Hatty. Charlie, hand me Latigo's rifle, will you? I want to keep that nice and safe."

Maria and Charlie got out the other side and the three of them started to walk up to the house. The moment all three were inside the front gate, lights flashed on everywhere and someone shouted at them from the darkness.

"Federal agents! Drop your weapons. *Now!*"

Beau dropped Latigo's rifle.

"Step away from the weapon."

As the three moved away from the rifle, six FBI agents ran up to them.

"Wait, wait, Frank, that isn't Cortez."

Another man emerged from behind the lights and walked quickly past the other agents. "Mr. Holliman? James Reed, FBI. This is Special Agent Styles. Sorry to frighten you folks, but we were expecting someone else."

"I believe I've seen you before, Mr. Reed," Beau said, shaking his hand.

"You're very observant, Mr. Holliman. Those eggs are good over at the Sunrise, aren't they?"

"Reading the paper in the corner the other morning."

"Very good."

Agent Styles turned back to his men. "Kill the lights. Back into position. Jim, we need to clear the area. Mr. Holliman, if you would move your truck into the barn, please. Thank you." He turned and walked back to his post without waiting for a response.

"It's his first stakeout with this bunch," Reed said, after he was gone. "He needs to make a good impression. Why don't we go in the house?"

"Actually, Mr. Reed," said Beau, "we wanted to go check on Hatty King."

"Not unless you want to go through this again," he said. "Besides, she isn't home. Let's get that truck in the barn and I'll tell you all about it. Mr. Tilden, you and Mrs. King can go on in the house. Just keep the lights off till we get there. Thanks."

Beau drove the truck into the barn and returned to the house with Reed, who had picked up a legal pad from one of the cars parked behind the house.

"Don't you need to be out with the other officers?" Beau asked.

"We have spotters on every road in and out of here," Reed said. "If they see someone coming I'll know it. Part of my job now is to debrief you."

They passed two other agents as they went into the dining room and closed the doors behind them. "We can turn on the light here in this enclosed area," he said, "but the rest of the house has to be dark."

"You sure it's safe right here in the house? For Maria, here, I mean?" Charlie asked.

"Believe me, Mr. Tilden, Cortez will never set foot in this house. And if he tries, we have two of our best marksmen stationed at the two front windows, plus ten others outside. Until we know exactly where he is, this house is under twenty-four-hour surveillance."

"You keep saying Cortez. You mean Latigo Jones, don't you?" Charlie asked.

"Yes, Mr. Tilden. Let me caution you that a lot of the information you're going to hear tonight is going to sound pretty wild. And some of it, I'm afraid, might sting a bit. Just wanted to warn you before we cut loose. Now, I need to hear your story first, then I'll do my best to answer any questions you might have." He pulled out his pen and pad and began to take notes as the three unfolded the events of the last few days.

Three pages of details and a few interruptions later, he put down the pad and rubbed his eyes. "You don't have any idea why they ran?" he asked.

"Oh, I have an idea," answered Beau. "I think we all do, but you may think it's crazy."

"Try me."

"Mr. Reed, I don't know if you're a religious man or not. I am. Guess I have been most of my life. I believe God delivered us down there. I don't know how, but Latigo's men saw something and hightailed it. It sure wasn't us they were looking at. That's it, plain and simple."

Reed sat impassively, weighing Beau's words. "You two have anything you want to add to that?" he asked the others.

"That's about the best we could come up with, Mr. Reed," Charlie offered.

Maria nodded her agreement.

"Fair enough," Reed said. "Now, if you folks are up to it, I'll be glad to answer any questions I can. Mr. Tilden, I believe you were wondering about—"

"Cortez," Charlie responded. "I'd heard that was Latigo's real name. What's the story?"

"All right," Reed said, leaning forward. "Sheriff Latigo Jones' real name is Benito Cortez. His mother's last name was Jones. As a young girl she ran off to Mexico with one of the nationals. They lived together for over a year in a little town called Las Esperanzas."

"Las Esperanzas?" Maria asked. "Near Sabinas?"

"That's right," Reed said. "That's where Hernan Escobar had his first parish. I'll spare you the details, but suffice it to say that Father Escobar was no saint. He abused his authority to take advantage of young women. Carla Jones was one of many."

"Are you saying that Father Escobar was Latigo's natural father?" Maria asked.

"Yes, ma'am, I'm afraid so. I know he was your priest for a while. I'm sorry."

"Does Cortez know who his father was?"

"Yes, but I can't get into that. We have a deposition by Miss Jones that needs to remain confidential until trial."

"Some things are beginning to make sense," Beau said. "He hated Mexicans because of what Escobar did to his mother—so much he changed his name. He hates the church for the same reason, and the priests."

"He's a very sick man," Reed said. "But he's also cunning. He knows how to exploit any weakness to his own advantage. And he's greedy. He's been buying up land from here to the Valley and over to Laredo at around thirty cents on the dollar from folks who are having to sell out. It's contemptible the way he manipulates people, but you can't arrest someone for being a jerk. Then he gets hooked up with this lawyer named Pogue."

"The man we talked to in Laredo," Maria recalled.

"Same fellow," Reed confirmed. "He left New York before they could nail him for malfeasance. He was tied to the mob for a few years—represented the Gambino syndicate in land grabs, small business buyouts, that kind of thing. We almost had him in a sting when he smelled something and took off for Texas.

"Pogue and Latigo fit hand in glove. Where he tripped up was trying to pull some of his big-city tactics down here. Our office in San Antonio got a couple of letters claiming that original land titles and personal copies of deeds had been stolen. These folks, who happened to be elderly, had been pressured to sell to avoid an expensive court case, which they were told they were sure to lose. So in order to avoid losing the land outright, they decided to settle out of court and sell for a fraction of the land value. I thought that was an interesting coincidence even though these folks lived in different counties and the letters came months apart. No one else in the department had time or interest in it, and I was about to retire, so I thought I'd look into it. Maybe I just wanted to try to help some older folks since I'm getting up there myself, I don't know. Anyway, I stirred up a real hornets' nest."

"How could Latigo do that? I mean, those titles have witnesses. Couldn't they be called to testify?" Charlie asked.

"That's where Pogue was so good. I hadn't been on the case but a couple months when a pattern started to crop up across several counties that pretty well fit the previous two cases. So far, this is what I've been able to piece together. Pogue would ask a few questions around town, then get into the county records office and the title company and find only those relatively small properties where the witnesses had all died and the remaining signatories were limited to two people, usually older folks. Small county offices like that, it doesn't take much to just walk right out with the papers practically under your arm. Then he'd dump the properties into different dummy corporations to get a big tax writeoff. That's how we got him. He's in the Laredo jail right now on tax evasion. He knew how to scam the small guy, but he didn't understand the fine points of the corporate tax code. Plus we've got plenty of evidence for extortion. He'll be gone a long time."

"How do you know he'll get a tough judge?" Beau asked.

"In Laredo," Reed smiled, "they're all tough. Now here's the interesting part. In the last seven months, three of those properties have drilled and struck oil. Cortez was shifting into higher gear. Then—and this is the strangest part—I got a call from Eli King. The last year I was in the oil fields, Eli was my field engineer. He was the best I ever had. That same year, there was a horrible accident. Some fool kid got burned to death in a well fire—a line ruptured or something. My little girl was playing over in a pile of sand, and Eli just happened to be a few feet from her when the fireball shot out. He grabbed her and fell to the ground on top of her. Scorched him pretty good, but saved her life. She grew up to be one fine young lady. Well, anyway, he knew I was going into the FBI. I guess he just took a shot and called the San Antonio office, and I happened to be there. I believe he must have been killed right after that, because that's the last I heard from him."

"Did Eli tip you off about Cortez?" Beau asked.

"No. He didn't know who was behind it, but he felt sure it was somebody in Laredo because he knew Jake Skerritt was connected and Jake wasn't smart enough to run an operation. That's when the front office started to get interested. The upshot is, we hooked up with the Rangers and got two DPS undercovers working down there now: one in Pogue's office, one working for Cortez. I found out about his interest in the King place just before Pogue paid his first visit to the Dalton Springs land and title office. That's when I got into the game.

"Cortez hired me to drill a well on a remote part of the King ranch," Reed continued. "I was posing as Adolph Mangus, a high-stakes player in illegal drilling. We gained access through the Vanacek property, shot a few holes, and put up a short-rig, shallow-hole operation down by the river. If we could make him believe the well came in good, we felt like we might force his hand. I waited until I knew he was getting antsy and then I gave him a call that the well was in and deep. Apparently, that's when he decided to take you down to Mexico with him."

"You were just goin' to let Latigo take Beau down there to kill him?" Charlie asked.

"No, sir, that one caught me off guard," Reed answered. He turned to Beau. "I honestly didn't think you were a significant player. I guess I didn't figure on this much family loyalty even down here," he smiled. "By the time I found out he was planning the trip, you were gone and nobody knew if you took the train or went by car. Cortez didn't normally travel under his own name, and they misspelled your name on the passenger manifest. We didn't know where either of you were until nearly fifteen hours after you had left. By then it was too late. All we could do was gear up here and hope he decided to try to come back across after—"

"You thought he would try to kill me," Beau filled in.

"We thought you were dead. Until we got a call from Angus McClendon a few hours ago."

"You heard from Doc?" Beau asked.

"He said you'd be coming in with a whole truckload. That's why we jumped you when you drove up. We thought you might be Cortez. He's crazy enough he might just come back looking for you."

"Did he say anything about Father Zeuma?" Maria asked.

"No, ma'am, afraid not. He did say, though, that he was planning on coming up tomorrow."

"How? He has no truck. And Father Zeuma—"

"He's taking the train. He ought to be safe. I doubt seriously that Cortez would risk boarding a train now. His picture's in every train station between here and Mexico City. The Federales have been surprisingly helpful on this one. A Ranger will meet Mr. McClendon at the border and escort him up. They should be here around four o'clock tomorrow afternoon, if all goes well."

"One Ranger? When a man like Latigo's out there?" Charlie asked.

Reed looked sideways at Charlie. "I know it's overkill," he said with a grin and a wink, "but if I was to send half a man I'd have to dispatch one of these government boys, and Cortez would eat him alive." The way he said "dispatch" sounded a lot like Special Agent Styles. "There's one more little wrinkle. Mrs. King and a woman named Irma Light are down there now looking for you. One of our undercovers is down with them, but we haven't had contact since they left."

"Couldn't you hold them here?" Beau asked.

"No, sir, not without jeopardizing the operation."

"Are they with an experienced officer?"

"The officer has my complete confidence, Mr. Holliman."

"Would it be possible to get in touch with your man in Laredo?" Beau asked.

"Sure."

"Doc doesn't know that his wife and little girl and the others are staying with friends there. Maybe he could help get them back together and if it wouldn't be too much trouble—"

"These folks are going to be guests of the State of Texas for a while, Mr. Holliman. I'll take care of everything."

"Excuse me, sir." One of the federal officers poked his head in the door. "Agent Styles wants you back out front."

"Oh, he does, does he? Okay, John, thanks. Tell him I'll be right there. Well, folks, duty calls. Now, I suggest you all turn in and get a good night's sleep. We may be in for a long wait."

Charlie rose from the table before Reed was out the front door. "That's it for me," he said. "I'll bunk on the couch. See you two in the morning. If there's any shootin', wake me."

Beau started to leave the room, then stopped and looked at Maria. Her eyes were downcast. Beau relaxed back into his chair. "How are you feeling?" he asked. She hadn't said much since Reed had told her about Father Escobar.

"I'm all right," she said, not lifting her eyes. "I have much to think about. Much to try to understand."

"Much to forgive," Beau said softly.

She nodded, tears running down her cheeks. Beau gave her hand a gentle squeeze. They sat like that for a half hour, saying nothing—she softly crying, he silently praying for her.

"You must know," she said at last.

"What?"

"That last week—the week it all happened—I was alone in the house one night, when I heard someone knocking at the door. I wasn't thinking, I was so upset. But I went to the door and opened it. And there, standing in the darkness . . . was . . . Father Escobar." She wept openly now. "He stepped inside and closed the door and locked it. I couldn't scream. I couldn't run. All I could do was stand there. And then—I saw that he was shaking. Crying. He fell to his knees and held to my skirt weeping, begging my forgiveness. I told him I had forgiven him long ago, but I don't think he heard me. I don't know. Until that moment, I had thought he was mad. He pulled himself up saying, 'You don't understand, you don't understand. You can't forgive me,' he said. 'A bastard child cannot forgive her own father.' Then I saw him for the first time, and I knew."

"That he was your father."

"That he sired me, yes. But more. I asked him, 'Did you do it? Did you kill my mother?' 'You know,' he said. 'You've always known.' 'Never,' I said, 'until this moment.'" Maria sighed deeply. "Finally, I knew. And I thanked him. From the bottom of my heart, I forgave him and I thanked him over and over again. Standing there in the dark crying and crying like a stupid girl, because for the first time in my life I understood. There was no curse. There never had been. He crawled away still weeping himself and ran out the door and into the night. That's the last I saw of him."

"You never told anyone?" Beau asked.

"I had no reason. My Lord had used Father Escobar to bring me the truth. I am free. And that is enough."

"You've been to hell and back."

Maria laughed a small, tired laugh. "No," she said. "Someone beat me to it, thank God. I'm headed the other way." They rose and hugged each other good night.

At five o-clock the next afternoon, three cars turned down the lane toward the Holliman ranchhouse. In front was a green Buick Dynaflow with three passengers. Next in line was a state trooper, followed by a Texas ranger with still more people.

Reed walked quickly out to meet them. Jennifer got out on the driver's side of the Buick. She stood at attention for a moment, looking at Reed, who was standing with his hands on his hips. Then they both walked toward each other and hugged. By that time, Hatty and Miss Light were out, along with Estella, Doc, the Montoyas, the Carreras, and Mrs. Perez. All were embracing and talking at the same time. Even the FBI agents seemed to relax.

Maria ran to greet Estella and her old friends. Doc reassured her that Father Zeuma would be all right. He had developed an infection and other complications that required special care, and Doc had thought it best to bring him to the States for treatment. He was resting and under guard in the hospital in Laredo. Beau and Hatty and Miss Light hugged amid tears and laughter.

Reed waved Beau over to the car. "Gentlemen, allow me to introduce Officer Beth Reed, alias Jennifer Budreau: a decent secretary, a fine undercover operative, and a great daughter."

Beau smiled broadly and looked from father to daughter. "It's our pleasure, Officer Reed," Beau said, shaking her hand. "We've heard quite a bit about you."

She smiled. "I come from a long line of talkers," she said.

"I can testify to that," Miss Light said, laughing.

"What's the word on Sanchez?" Styles broke in abruptly.

Beth turned away to talk to him privately. "Sanchez apprehended and in custody in Dalton Springs jail, sir," Beth reported. "No sign of Cortez."

"We just got word," he said. "The Mexican Federales sighted him down in Veracruz. They haven't caught him yet, but it won't—"

"Oh." Beth put her hand to her mouth.

"What?"

"Excuse me, sir. Miss Light?" Beth turned to find her in the crowd.

"Yes, dear?"

"Miss Light, did you remember the key?"

"Oh, drat that key. It's at home on the piano. We'll have to get it."

"Just a small detail, sir—the keys to Sanchez's cuffs—I'll take care of it right away," Beth said as she and Miss Light hurried away.

"Hold your horses," said Agent Styles. "Another fifteen mintes won't hurt anything. The key can wait that long." He smiled and turned away before it could make a lasting impression.

"Hatty, Hatty, this is for you," Doc said as he turned over a leather pouch tied with a ribbon. "Everything is here—the title, the wills, everything."

"Oh, Doc, I'd forgotten all about this," Hatty said.

"Eli was a very wise man. If he hadn't given these to me before he left for Laredo—well, who knows? The important thing is, you have them now and you can get them back in the bank where they can be safe again."

"That's wonderful, but getting them back in the bank is going to have to wait a day longer," Hatty said. "Heaven knows, I don't need to be driving anywhere the rest of today, except home."

"Well, you better get a move on, girl," Miss Light said.

"Why's that, Irma?"

"Looky yonder. You see what I see blowing in from the north?"

Hatty strained to see, and then her eyes opened wide. "Well, I declare. A rain cloud, about the size of a man's fist, wouldn't you say, Irma?"

"'Bout like," Irma said with a smile.

They all looked, and saw, and wondered at the rapidly gathering clouds. At Beau's invitation the Carreras unloaded their bags and carried them inside to stay with him. The rest went with Hatty. They hugged once more, then got in their cars and drove away through valleys of light until they reached home just ahead of the thunder and the first drops of rain.

Epilogue

In Veracruz, a warm rain lathered the sides of the low adobe jail, pooling in tiny basins where the rusting iron bars had been hammered into the too-solid adobe windowsill a couple or three lifetimes before. Milk-white water seeped down through the cracks in the walls and up through the fractured floor like stone crying. Thunder rumbled away over the Gulf of Mexico, slow and lazy. But there was no lightning, no wind—just a rumpled gray sky that made it feel as if the whole world were under a cloud and in need of a cool wash.

For weeks Latigo had been planning his escape. But it would never happen without a diversion. Not on a night like this. He couldn't even lift himself off the concrete floor. He had collapsed there that morning and hadn't moved since. The heat held him down. It held everything down, even the smells. The stench from the hole in the floor that served as a toilet curled around the board that covered it and hovered in the air, too thick and heavy to rise to the window and escape. Not even the rain offered relief; it was like a steam bath that wouldn't quit.

A tin plate scraped under the metal door, but Latigo made no effort to reach it. Once a day, they fed him a thin brown tortilla on a dirty plate with some beans and water the color of yesterday's tobacco juice. Why bother? He threw up most of it anyway.

Flies and mosquitoes buzzed in and out of the six-by-nine cell, alighting on whatever didn't move, drawing blood and then rising again to pass cleanly through the wire mesh that stretched across most of the cell window. A scorpion slowly and repeatedly traced the inside edge of the sill, unable to fit through the cracks in the mesh and unwilling to drop the six feet to the floor. Latigo stared fixedly at the spineless creature, whose flat thorax scraped across the bleached white stone. One of the guards had cut off his stinger and left him for a toy.

The guard on duty was an old man with a snow-white mustache and small, copper-colored eyes. He was perched uncomfortably on the front edge of a wooden desk chair, an empty bottle on the floor underneath. Thin wisps of white hair lay plastered in uneven rows to his sweat-soaked head. As he leaned forward, cradling his face in his hands, he whispered softly into the air, trying to convince himself that he had fallen asleep, that the events of the last few hours had been a tequila dream. He seemed oblivious to the radio on the file cabinet by the door, which crackled with more static than music.

The jailhouse door opened suddenly and another guard walked in quickly and slammed it with a rattling thud. The old man jumped, then slumped back into his chair with a curse. Deputy Chico Ruiz enjoyed jolting old Martine out of a drunk.

"Wake up, Martine, we got a nasty one blowin' in off the Gulf," he said, trying to tune the radio to a weather report. "Started up real sudden this morning and headed right for us. Shoot!" He gave up, giving the radio a sharp knock. He walked over to the desk and picked up a cup of cold coffee. A folded piece of paper slid off the desk. "So our friend finally had a visitor, huh?" he asked, bending down to pick up the paper.

"What?" the old man looked up slowly.

"The guy on the horse—I figured he was here to see the gringo. Who was he?"

"What'd this man look like?"

"C'mon, Martine, the guy was just in here. I saw him walk out—"

"Tall? Wearing a pancho?"

"Yeah, I spoke to him, but—"

"*¡Madre de Jesús!*" the old man interrupted. He stared straight ahead. "Did he speak to you?"

"No, he just got on his horse, stared out toward the Gulf like he was looking for something, and rode off. No, wait—he did say something. I was about to open the door when I think I heard him say, 'Stay inside.' I turned around, but he was already gone." Ruiz sat on the edge of the desk. "Why? Something happen?"

The old man waited a long time before he answered in a tight voice. "We need to be careful tonight, Chico. We need to watch." He took a deep breath, trying to regain his composure, and pointed to the piece of paper in the young man's hand. "I got the wire this afternoon. They're picking him up tomorrow," he said. "Off to Laredo."

"Yeah?" Chico leaned across the desk, smiling. "How much they get?"

"Two thousand."

"Yeah? Two thousand? So what's that? Three, four—?"

"Five hundred each."

The deputy cursed and laughed. "So the guy on the horse is a runner for—"

"I said it was a wire!" the old man yelled, slamming his hand down on the desk and jumping to his feet. "Now you listen to me! You didn't see nobody on a horse tonight, you get that?"

"Boss, I'm telling you—"

The old man drew back his hand and struck the officer hard across the face. "Shut up! You didn't see nothing! *Nothing*!"

Just then the storm slammed into the side of the old jail like a black fist, rattling windows and doors. Wave after sudden wave of dark water pounded roof and walls. Thunder and wind rolled in a surging wave of deafening sound, roaring like an unchained monster as it knocked out the power and plunged the interior into darkness. Tiles began to fly from the roof. A crack opened in one wall and ran down the floor. Doors and windows imploded, spraying microscopic shards of glass through the air.

For a moment the desk chair hung suspended in midair before whipping around to catch the deputy on the side of the head and knock him out cold. The old man shielded his eyes and staggered over to grope for one of the rifles on the wall, as if he could fight the thing off with something manmade.

Then, above the roar, he could hear it coming: a deep, throbbing rhythm, at first distant and muddled. Out there in the watery darkness, unlit vapors whirled round and down into the Gulf, spinning into an enormous flume that sucked into the belly of the cloud a blackened spirit and gave it form—and now it was coming, *thrummm, thrummm, thrummm*, deeper than the thunder, drumming the earth, shaking the world with wild hooves unshod, to claim a maverick soul.

Something threw the old man hard against the opposite wall. In a blast of lightning he saw a flash of black rush unbridled before his eyes toward the cell door and pass through it. A piercingly high, shrieking wail, half animal and half man, split the air and trailed off into the sky.

Then stillness.

The old man sat for a few minutes trying to catch his breath before struggling to his feet, shaking. He bandaged Chico's head, then took the key from his belt and twisted it slowly in the lock of the prisoner's cell. He drew his pistol and opened the door as he stepped back. "Come out!" he shouted.

No response.

"The prisoner will come out now!"

Nothing.

He walked slowly forward into the darkened cell. Sheet lightning flared, scouring the room with light. It was empty. Martine thought he caught a small movement out of the corner of his eye. But it was nothing—just a cool puff of wind pushing the lifeless form of a scorpion off the windowsill and down through one of the cracks in the floor. The scorpion was gone.

Suddenly, shadows shifted against the walls as if a veil had been withdrawn. The old man started, then realized what was happening. He stepped back and stared up through the jagged hole in the roof. The clouds had parted, the darkness had fled, and the moon was flooding the world with light.